A SPY OF
THE OLD SCHOOL

ALSO BY JULIAN RATHBONE:

Diamonds Bid

Hand Out

With My Knives I Know I'm Good

Trip Trap

Kill Cure

Bloody Marvellous

King Fisher Lives

¡Carnival!

A Raving Monarchist

Joseph

The Euro-Killers

Base Case

A SPY OF
THE OLD SCHOOL

JULIAN RATHBONE

PANTHEON BOOKS
NEW YORK

Library of Congress Cataloging in Publication Data

Rathbone, Julian, 1935–
A spy of the old school.

I. Title.
PR6068.A8S6   1983   823'.914   82-18985
ISBN 0-394-51796-2

For Charlotte,
whose memory is a joy

For, indeed, I am a Communist of the old school —
reddest also of the red...

JOHN RUSKIN, Fors Clavigera, Letter 7
1 July 1871

Prelude

The six-litre Jaguar, bright vermilion, lurched into the rutted track; two observers marked its uneasy progress. One, on the high, long chalk ridge above, pulled his collar about his ears, smacked sheepskin mittens together and tramped away down the combes, through the blackthorns, to the nearest telephone on the far side. The other, more comfortably placed in a rented Cortina parked in the farmyard opposite the junction of the lane with the narrow country road, merely made an entry in a notebook and snapped the band over it. As soon as the Jaguar was out of sight he set his engine going. Thus, by the time Sir Richard Austen reached Briar Rose Cottage a mile away, he was no longer under direct surveillance. It didn't matter. A man who has made a bolt for it, gone to ground in what he hopes may be a safe house, may be expected to stay there for several hours... The point was, he had arrived.

Austen turned off his engine but waited until the last chords of Tchaikovsky's Fourth Symphony had thudded into silence before he turned off the stereo radio too. Cocooned in warm leather and walnut veneer, steel and toughened glass, he took in his surroundings — a quarter of a century lay between this and his last visit: the track had been a pretty lane then, even in winter, but now barbed wire ran along the scars left by hawthorn and hazel. Across what had been hedged meadows his eye was drawn inexorably to the foot of the down by furrows stitched into the chalk as precisely as if they had been machine-knitted. His well-shaped lips grimaced in distaste: not only had centuries-old turf been ploughed in but so too the barely

7

discernible ridges and hollows that had marked an Iron Age field system. He supposed it had been properly recorded first — perhaps it would be worth checking in the county archives... But no. The days when the name of Richard Austen, *Sir* Richard, could command respect in county archaeological departments, or anywhere else for that matter, were probably over.

The thought provoked a wry, self-mocking grin, and briskly he let himself out of the car. The still and frosty air caught his breath. He looked up and around, at the almost immaculate blue sky smirched only with vapour trail, at the down, still unspoilt because it was National Trust — bosky thickets on its flanks, purple shadows cast by the dykes over the fosses that circled its crest; and he supposed there would be things he would miss. With the thought came the kick of apprehension, heavy and cold in his diaphragm, that had become horribly familiar in the last week. If he was to keep his wits about him, it had to be suppressed, pretend it isn't there, it doesn't matter; what is happening doesn't matter.

Round-headed with grizzled, short-cropped hair, small, trim, in a short camel top-coat and red muffler, he lifted the latch on the wooden gate, and his small feet, expensively shod in shoes hand-made on his own last at French's of Southampton, twinkled up the crazy paving to the door. His eyes, pale blue and bright, flickered restlessly over the Sussex flint walls, the small white-painted window frames, the low guttering. One yellow rose, just bursting from bud when the frost had caught it, lorded it over a tiny garden where everything was tidy and dead. George has made a good job of keeping it all up, Austen thought, and he let himself in.

He moved about opening curtains, throwing switches, opening taps, checking the larder. The professional side of his quirky mind quickly took over: it was instructive thus to have entered this capsule sealed off from twenty-five years of change — in its way as rare an experience as opening an unrifled passage grave. The radio — *wireless* — was large, cabineted in wood. He turned the 'on' knob and to his dismay got Jimmy Savile's *Old Record Club*. It took him a moment or two to recall where to find Radio Three on medium wave: on wirelesses there was no VHF, and the place marked 'Third Programme' produced only a babel of

8

French and Russian. Retuning, he found Debussy's String Quartet and November 1980.

The baked beans in the larder took him back again: the label — a far more decorated affair than current ones, indeed almost rococo, belonged to the past and so did the newspaper it stood on. He read, 'Meanwhile the Prime Minister briefly refused Lieutenant Colonel Lipton's demand for the appointment of a select committee... Nor would he be drawn by Lieutenant Colonel Lipton's question about whether he had made up his mind at all costs to cover up the "dubious third man activities" of a former First Secretary at the Washington Embassy.'

It should, he thought, be possible to apply the best principles of stratigraphy and lay bare succeeding occupations. Not that there had been many. That immediately post-dating 26 October 1955 (note the caution — the newspaper gives us a *terminus post quem*, that's all: people line shelves with old paper, still it's a start towards establishing a datum-line) had been baked-bean eaters, and, he was grateful to note, whisky drinkers. The shape of the bottle remained familiar, the label less changed than that on the food can, the stopper though was from earlier times — beneath heavy foil there lay a cork mounted on black Bakelite. The whisky too seemed very good — though perhaps sentimentality prompted and rewarded false expectations; a sure case this for sending a sample to the archaeological laboratory before we pass judgement. Or could it be that it had mellowed in the bottle? Anyway jolly nice. And, as always, the very act of archaeological investigation, the sifting, evaluation and recording of evidence, also inevitably destroyed the evidence, or much of it. He took another mouthful. I think we'll call these people the White Horse Folk, but while we trust their whisky I think baked beans so old should be left for the museum.

The telephone was recent, the sort in current use. Austen recalled that he had been asked ten or twelve years ago to authorise the replacement of the earlier handset when the little country exchange at last joined the STD system. Putting down his glass, fingering out from an inside pocket a little book bound in soft black leather, he dialled a number.

9

'George? George Partridge?'

'Speaking. Who's there?' A voice with a marked western throb to it, west of the Itchen if not the Test.

'Richard Austen here, George.'

'Sir Richard. Well, I'm blessed. You'll be coming down to the cottage then ... well, I am blessed, after all these years.'

'No, George. Not coming. I'm here already ... '

Yes, everything was fine. Just as it should be. No, the garden was quite all right. Yes, he had checked there was coal in the coalshed, no one had stolen it and the taps were running. '... but George, there is one thing. I know it's Sunday, and that is the problem. I mean, I've nothing fresh to eat ... No. No I wouldn't hear of barging in on your Sunday lunch.'

George would be around, after he had finished his dinner, and he'd find something to bring, of course he would.

Austen picked up his glass and climbed the narrow wooden stairs to the bedroom. Roses on the curtains and on the wallpaper, a large down bed beneath a heavy cotton counterpane. Twice a year George's wife came in and gave everything an airing and a wash, thus it would need the keenest archaeologist's eye to detect ... well, it was easier if you knew what to look for.

Russet stains on the wallpaper, now so faded that they only showed on the off-white ground, not on the sprays of cabbage roses themselves. One large blob, several smaller ones. 'What do you make of that, Sir Mortimer?' 'Difficult to say, Sir Richard, without a lab test, but it looks jolly like vital fluid.' 'Predates the White Horse Folk, would you say?' 'Can't be sure ... very different culture though ... '

Yes. I'd say so. Decidedly. Blood sacrifices, the Goddess, the Bitch. Austen ran his finger along the line of his jaw, feeling the ridge of a scar. He shuddered. She was a weak link, one of many. He was lucky to have had such a long run. And, if she found out he had bolted, she would know where. The Bitch. Still he would need a day at the most, probably less; there was a chance he'd get away with it. Meanwhile, if he was going to sleep up here, he'd have to light a fire in the small cast-iron grate as well as in the bigger one downstairs — he'd better get a move on.

On a shelf at the back of the coalshed six empty bottles of

Beaujolais 1950. That's quite good evidence for a fairly narrow timespan. A good Beaujolais is drunk within the year. So — November 1950 to November 1951 would seem to be the outer limits of the Six Bottle Folk. Not folk, I was the only one, thought Austen. The other two got out on the Southampton ferry after all, though it had been a near-run thing by all accounts. Anyway Briar Rose remained unused and I drank the wine.

That Shapiro woman did keep on about them.

He carried in coals, fooled around inexpertly with *The Times* of 1955, and coughed on smoke. But he was now preoccupied with the events that had brought him here, particularly with what he still could not understand about them. That man — *Catkin?* From MI5? — had asked Mother about Guy. Why had he done that? MI5 were supposed to have been choked off. What was he then? A journalist? A blackmailer? Probably I'll never know, thought Austen, and I'm sure Mother got the name wrong. Catkin! He stood up, and the unaccustomed weight and bulk in his jacket pocket swung with a heavy clunk against the wooden arm of the small cottage chair.

He took out the pistol, hefted it in his hands, and shuddered again — he hated the things. He had no idea how it worked, supposed he ought to try to fathom it out: no; if the finale turns out to be that sort of business, I shall lie on the floor and wait until it's over. I've had enough of being shot at.

He sniffed the barrel. What do you make of that, Watson? Why, Holmes, it's been fired, quite recently. He put it on the small round table in front of the window and his grin broadened into an audible chuckle as he thought of the tall American blundering about the Forest shooting the thing off in all directions. Well, Newman would be all right for up to three weeks, or so the brochure of Vival Shelters claimed, and if no one killed Austen before then, he would see Newman was let out. But not in a hurry. No. Not after the fright he'd suffered, being shot at at his age.

Meanwhile, there was nothing to do but sit and wait and see who turned up first.

He poured more Scotch, and sat back in front of his fire — the opening prelude of Rheingold began to swell out of the large old

wireless and he turned it off again — Wagner was the composer
he could not stomach. He felt warm, cosy, even protected, in his
tiny living room, though he knew he was more exposed than he
had ever been — not *more* exposed. Just plain exposed.

   Odd about that Catkin chap though. Catkin *can't* have been
his name, too absurd. Nevertheless, where did he fit in?

PART ONE

1

The Housemaster was a tall thin man who always wore loose-fitting, good-quality tweeds. He kept his lank hair short, brushed sideways across his scalp; he was fairly clean-shaven, though invariably his skin was razor-scraped somewhere, usually just below the jawline; he had small eyes, thin lips, bony wrists and long fingers. When he talked to you he put his head on one side, and he smiled often — but it was a cold smile inwardly directed. He had been an actual housemaster once for a short spell after the war, before being recruited when the Service expanded again — a housemaster at the College, naturally. There he had had the reputation of being able to lay a malacca cane so accurately across a drum-tight pyjama bottom that six of the best would later look like only two of the very best. At only two years off retirement, he still affected the style of a house-master sitting behind an old-fashioned desk, with silver cups in a glass case behind him, and the complete works of Trollope, leather bound. The cups were for pistol shooting. And in effect he was a housemaster — head of one branch of the Service; one of its four deputies; answerable only to the Director, the chief. And the Service itself is much like a public school, much like the College. It is an uncomfortable thing to be part of — the pay is poor, one's colleagues bitch and backbite, and are usually discontented: but there is also that unconsidering loyalty which states of siege always promote. My country, my school, the Service — right or wrong.

William Cargill hated the Housemaster, was on the point, though he hardly knew it, of hating the Service.

15

'William. Good of you to come by so promptly. Park yourself, won't you?' The Housemaster smiled his inward smile. Cargill, he thought, is like a *dog*. He looks like a dog with his big brown eyes, his heavy jaw, his large short-fingered hands like paws on his knees in front of him. And like the old dog he is, he is beginning to smell, in his case of pipe and old clothes. The moustache, heavy, thick, which no doubt looked manly, even threatening, in the sixties when he had been such a good interrogator, is now a mess. 'Not too busy just now, are we?' he asked.

Cargill knew the tone and inside him the acid of humiliation corroded another micron of life out of the spring that kept him going. 'No. Not too busy.' He would not Christian-name the Housemaster back, and knew he would be rebuked if he Mr-ed or Sir-ed him.

'Closing in on that signalman at Windscale, are we?'

'Yes. Gave him a marked fiver, usual stuff.' Cargill rammed his pipe-bowl in his soft leather pouch whose flap was embroidered in one corner with the arms of one of the smaller, later Oxford colleges. He thumbed coarse, dark tobacco into the bowl. 'There's not much quality about these days. Not like there used to be.'

The Housemaster forbore from correcting the grammar — but only just.

'Routine from here on in then?'

'Just about.'

'Good show. Right.'

He paused, waited while Cargill sucked flame of blow-lamp force into his pipe and puffed out clouds of yellowish smoke. At one point he even had to dab the carpet with his heavily shod toe — extinguishing flying cinders.

'Right. Fosdike will tidy up, you can leave it to him?'

'Oh, yes.'

'Right then. Well, William. Something's cropped up, something that might just have about it the sort of quality whose disappearance you seem to be regretting. Something from the old days. A big one. One that got away.'

He was gratified to see that he had Cargill's attention. The dog had stopped puffing, and if his ears had been just a shade

16

floppier than they were they would no doubt now be pricked. The Housemaster stood up, went to the narrow but high sash window and looked down. 'And this one may still be alive and active, definitely not one of Blunt's cell... You know about PSIKE?'

Cargill assented. An American computer made by United Special Steels on lease to the CIA.

'Well, she's at the Golf Club and Chess Society just now, has been for some time, and she's come up with something. Am I interesting you?'

'Of course.'

'I thought I might be.' He turned back. 'Hut Three. There were getting on for about a hundred thousand signals between September 1939 and May 1945, and the silly bitch has been going through them chronologically, matching each one against, I am told, something over a million other inputs she has in her maw. Well... perhaps I am telling this the wrong way round. Do you recall when Zamyatmin came over in 1968...'

'February '69.'

'Yes, you're right. Do you recall one of the files he brought showed that the KGB, or whatever it was called in 1945...'

'NKGB.'

'Don't you mean NKVD?'

'No. NKGB from '43 to '46. Under Merkulov.'

'Oh, really? Right then. NKGB in 1945 had actually got wind of where Gehlen was holed up, Misery Meadow, and all that, and damn near moved in on him.'

'Yes. I remember that.'

'And we've never found the source of that leak. Well. PSIKE has. The signals the NKGB had in May 1945 are transcripts of three pieces of ULTRA. And they were passed on. Are you with me now?'

In spite of his hatred of the Housemaster, Cargill was beginning to smile. He shook his head slowly, in mock disbelief, and slapped the side pocket of his jacket where he kept his tobacco pouch. 'Well, I'm *damned*,' he said. '*Well*, I'm damned.'

'I thought you'd be interested. So. I want you to look into it if you would. Do it your way. Try not to draw attention, at least in the early stages. If the bastard's still around we don't want him

17

to get wind of anything. Kill your granny and go to her funeral. Put the shutters up. When you have a name, then we'll get together a team, with you as Case Officer of course, and move to phase two. Right, William? Any questions?'

'PSIKE? She's working for...?'

'Just the Cousins. But we're getting her product while she's working on ULTRA. They had to agree to that.'

'So. They've had the same information.'

'Yes. If they bothered to check it. But it's our backyard, and they're not going to butt in for as long as they think we've got someone out there with a broom and a shovel. Someone they respect. That's why...'

He left the flattery unsaid and hoped thereby to make it more telling.

'So. Run along. Check back to me when you're on to the bastard, or near him. Right? Fine.'

Cargill's office was a hutch, but he was lucky to have one to himself at all. He sat in it for an hour after his interview with the Housemaster, leaning back in the crotchety chair to within a millimetre of the point at which its once-self-adjusting mechanism would slip and pitch his head against the filing cabinet behind him, and he smoked, and he watched the air-extractor spin in the windowpane six feet in front of him: November, frosty, the air outside cold, the air in his hutch warming up nicely. He smoked, and thought about it.

Taking it through in chronological order, this is what it added up to. The Golf Club and Chess Society was the Government Codes and Ciphers School. At a country house, Bletchley Park, during the war, it had swiftly developed into the receiving house for all military signals monitored from the German wavelengths. There the ENIGMA decoding device was cracked by some of the cleverest minds in Britain at the time, and the product thus generated, known as ULTRA, was assessed, interpreted and dispatched to where it would do most good. In fact ULTRA did a great deal of good, perhaps more than all other sources of intelligence put together, was an achievement of which every Britisher could be justly proud.

Up to a point. Until, in fact, in late 1947, when a protégé of the by then disgraced and later to be executed Merkulov defected to save his skin and brought news to the British, and of course to the Americans, that the Russians knew just about everything there was to know about Bletchley Park: how it had been organised; how its functionaries had been recruited; who, indeed, many of them were; how they had cracked ENIGMA; how the processing of ULTRA was carried out, and so on. In short there had been a leak. Or rather, a bloody great hole.

Now all this Cargill knew, and knew very well, although it had all happened well before his time; that is, well before he had reached his present eminence as a sort of House Prefect to the Housemaster. The subsequent enquiry had quite quickly fastened on one prime suspect, who, perhaps fortunately since he was a peer of the realm, was already dead. Too quick was the judgement of the man who was later Cargill's immediate superior and mentor, but very convenient, since Edward Bridge Lord Riversdale had been declared missing, believed dead, in one of the last V2 explosions of 1944. But the evidence that had come to light in 1947 and '48 had been good and no one had been prepared to dispute it.

And now, thirty-two years later, a third-generation computer had turned up irrefutable evidence that information post-dating the death of Lord Riversdale by five months had also found its way from Bletchley Park to the NKGB.

Where to begin on a trail as cold as this? There were many possibilities: the most likely was that Riversdale had not been the only leak. Bletchley Park had been staffed with several hundred of the cleverest men and women in Britain, recruited for their ability in Maths or German but also if in their particular lines they had shown any great flair for what is now known as lateral thinking: the ability to create and marshal endless possibilities out of inadequate data far beyond what mere step by step, cause and effect logic would indicate; men and women also with extraordinary memories and retrieval systems; with intimate knowledge of German procedures and command structures, industrial, financial, military; experts in German transport systems and methods of requisition and supply — all so that out of a mass of minutiae, of tiny scraps of incomplete information, a train rerouted here, petrol moved a hundred miles there, a requisition for a ton of first-aid dressings in another place, a picture could be built up of a division en route for a different front or pulled back to train with a new weapon.

Oxford and Cambridge had been the principal recruiting ground for this small army of intellectual wizards. Young dons, research fellows, even undergraduates already showing remarkable promise, had all been pulled in: but also there were refugees from fascism, and men and women whose intelligence had attracted attention even though they had grown up outside that magic circle of public school and Oxbridge that was the common background of most of the recruits. All this and more indicated that there must have been a very high proportion of leftists, fellow-travellers, even a sprinkling of party members, and, with the refugee element, some even who had actually worked actively for the Communist International, the Comintern, based first in Berlin, then in Paris. That is, people employed directly by the Soviet government.

Ironical, that's the word people use nowadays, Cargill thought, as he reached forward and tapped out his pipe in a tin ashtray, ironical that the one man pinpointed as the Bletchley Park leak should have been a raving fascist.

If Riversdale had been the leak, but not the only leak, then it would be like looking for a needle in a haystack. However, another possibility was that he was not the leak, that the already dead man had been framed: in which case he had probably been framed by someone who knew of the real leak, or by the real leak himself. A first line of enquiry then indicated itself: to look again, from the outside, with the benefit of hindsight, but very closely indeed, at just how Lord Riversdale had been implicated.

Cargill reached for his phone and ordered clearance for himself at Registry Three, to be operative in just half an hour.

In high-crowned, wide-brimmed grey trilby with a black band, in the sort of coat that can't make up its mind whether or not it's a raincoat or a winter coat, with a grey muffler round his neck, his pipe in his mouth, and his gloved hands swinging lightly at his side, Cargill walked briskly across the park. No doubt he believed he was inconspicuous — but his total lack of smartness on one side and meticulous neatness on the other, coupled with the fact that all his clothes were, however clean and well pressed, at least twenty years old, rendered him really quite remarkable.

He was, he realised, in rather a good mood. The air was still sharp with the night's frost, a weak sun penetrated the pale lemon haze above Westminster, a flight of mallard whirred overhead towards the Serpentine. For a moment the meaningless roar of the city receded, and he paused to watch two fur-hatted black ladies with similarly dressed toddlers throwing Mother's Pride into the lake for the mandarins. Two mandarins of a different breed — sleek in camel hair, with black and chrome document cases, their voices braying at each other in mindless insensitivity to everything else, trotted by on their way to Whitehall. Cargill set off again, reflecting with grim amusement that one thing was virtually certain: if there was another Bletchley Park leak to be found, and if he was still alive, the chances were that he would be *someone*. There would be more to it — not more fun, for fun was something Cargill did without — more *zest* than there had been in hounding out the technician who had revealed to the press details of the latest emergency at Windscale.

Registry Three is in a complex of cellars beneath blocks of Edwardian flats behind Victoria Street. If one enters the lift in Beaufort Mansions, and presses the emergency button twice, the lift goes down not to the basement but to a floor below; and here one needs to have the right sort of ID, *and* know the day's password before a well-armed Special Branch policeman will let you in. But if you satisfy him he'll pass you through two steel fire doors and into what looks like, and indeed is, a spacious well-lit and modern reading room: modern, because there are no books — just two long tables, beech with blue leather tops, each supporting ten VDUs, that is, microfiche readers. There were only two whose screens were lit: Cargill vaguely remembered one user from a context now forgotten and raised a finger; the other was a stranger, an American — he had that unmistakeable look that junior CIA operatives share with Mormon

21

evangelists, the ones who cycle round our suburbs with personal introductions from God. Like the Mormons the CIA are usually in pairs and Cargill wondered where this one's partner was; he guessed in the café opposite Beaufort Mansions, providing cover in case World War Three broke out.

A glass door swung back and the Librarian came in — a small, fussy little man, with spectacles, bald head, and finger-nails bitten short.

'Bill,' he said. 'Long time no see. How's tricks? What can I get you?'

Cargill gave two file numbers.

The Librarian put his head down, clenched the top of his broad nose between thumb and forefinger for five seconds, then lifted his face again, looking up into Cargill's.

'Oooh,' he said, the inflection mock-camp. 'Well. I see the connection. How exciting. Won't be a jiffy,' and he turned to go.

'I'd like the originals,' said Cargill, 'not this celluloid stuff.'

'No can do, old chap. That would take two months normally, ten days with a ministerial say-so. They're boxed and at the end of a Kent coal-mine gallery. If you want it now, old son, it's on microfiche or nothing.' He waited, head chirpily on one side. Cargill shrugged, and said he'd settle for microfiche now.

'Take five and I'll be back.'

Cargill recollected that the Librarian went in for amateur dramatics in Cheam. His production of J. B. Priestley's *An Inspector Calls* had been praised by the Housemaster himself.

He looked bothered when he returned. After glancing round at the other two VDU users, he fussed Cargill through the glass door and, after a brief glimpse of a well-lit corridor lined from floor to ceiling with numbered drawers, into his own office. This was comfortable, by Cargill's standards luxurious. It contained a desk, two chairs, a white filing cabinet, a small aquarium with fantails and angel fish, and an avocado plant grown four feet from its stone. Above the filing cabinet was an original oil painting of Dame Peggy Ashcroft as, Cargill rather thought, Hermione in the Gielgud production a quarter of a century ago.

'Let's have a thimbleful of sherry, shall we? While we wait.

It's only manzanilla so it won't do a thing.' The bottom drawer of the filing cabinet slid open noiselessly.

'Wait?'

'For the . . . well, the Bletchley Park file, actually. We turned up the Riversdale straightaway. But B-P seems to have gone astray. Sally's looking for it, she's a good girl, I'm sure she won't be more than a jiffy.'

Cargill sipped the sherry and could not forbear wrinkling his nose. It was very dry and rather thin. He preferred his sherry robust. 'So it's all on celluloid now,' he said.

'Every scrap.'

'That must have left a lot of room free.'

'My dear, *acres*.'

For a moment they listened to the bubbling in the fish tank.

'And now you're going to ask me what it's being used for, and I'm not allowed to tell.'

'No need to ask,' said Cargill. 'I can guess. Fall-out shelters for those of us not senior enough to get out to Berkshire or take to the air.'

'Well, you said it, not me. But now you know where to come when the balloon goes up. And I can tell you there are some quite reasonable preserves amongst all the Heinz — I made sure of *that*. Ah, Sally.'

Sally was indeed a good girl. Besides being quite tolerably pretty she had in her hand the missing cardboard wallet containing fifteen blue celluloid rectangles each about the size of a large postcard, and each carrying a good sixty thousand words of print.

The Librarian put it on his desk, and another like it.

'Fascinating,' he said. 'Absolutely fascinating. I'll confess — I treat myself to a little read every now and then and one of my favourites is the Riversdale file. Not, I hasten to add because of the naughty pictures, which don't amount to much in negative, but he was *such* a fascinating person. And really rather a good poet, you know?'

2

Always there must be more than one point of view
Where control of syphilis is called into question.
Certainly Heine died of it, and others too. But
Look at the whole of society, take a cross section,
Think of the bad wood that needs to be cut out,
The jews, those that put money out, and lovers of
   niggers.

These are the friggers that go with the whores
That went with the sailors, who stopped off at Naples
And had a good time. Nice lads don't do it,
Just moral cripples, the greedy, disabled, and physical
   failures,
And she'll poison their bones and turn them to lime.

The worm that I speak of can crumble the shins
Of jobbers who fancy themselves on the back of a hack
And as for the jew whose sins are not kosher
She softens the bones in his nose and his back
And as for the masher who made bombs in the
   wartime
His phiz is pitted not with shrapnel, but clap.

Cargill's nose wrinkled in distaste. He shifted the tray in which
he had laid the celluloid fiche and the writing projected on the
screen in front of his face swam into a blur until what was
obviously a column of pictures caught his attention. He swung
the images back and found he was looking at a sequence which

24

portrayed a black male nude with white hair, bleeding white from wounded buttocks. They're in negative of course. The poor lad is white not black. The sequence closed in on the buttocks, became sexually specific as well as sadistic, and Cargill, his neck suddenly hot, cheeks reddening, reduced them to a blur again. Suppose someone had looked over his shoulder...? He glanced round. The American had gone; the other user of Registry Three, who had raised a finger acknowledging acquaintance, was quietly absorbed in what looked like pages and pages of scientific formulae. Cargill recalled that the man was a biologist whose first job for the Service had been in connection with the Lonsdale case two decades ago. Did his presence here, now, mean there had been yet another leak from Porton?

Not my business, thought Cargill, and returned to the microfiche. Really, there was no point in wading through all this unpleasant stuff... reams and reams of poetry, some Riversdale's own, some copied out, nearly all of it distasteful; diaries in verse recording 'thoughts' like the one about syphilis rather than events; events done in abbreviated form and relating to sexual activity of one sort or another — by now Cargill was not too bothered to look into it that closely. He replaced the celluloid strip and went back to the first in the series which was not Riversdale's own stuff, but the report of the posthumous investigation. Cargill had already glanced at it — now he went through it very carefully, trying to commit to memory anything he felt might be important — for note-taking in the Registry is carefully vetted by the Librarian's staff, and that can be a tedious business at the end of the day, just when you think you can go home.

Edward Fitzgerald George Bridge: born 1911 at Scales, Co. Wicklow, first child and only son of the eighth Earl of Riversdale and of Mary Eliot Slaker, only child of Sir William Slaker of Slaker House, Bloomsbury, and Castle Slaker, Warwick. Edward succeeded in 1922 when his father was assassinated by the IRA. Educated at The Meads School, Old Biggin, Co. Durham, 1919-24; Beaufort College (the College, thought Cargill), Wintoncester, 1924-29; Balliol, Oxford, 1929-32; recruited for Government Codes and Cyphers School, Bletchley Park, June 1941;

25

reported missing December 1944; declared presumed and officially dead in July 1946 as a result of a V2 explosion. His cousin, the present Lord Riversdale, succeeded. Publications: Blood-Tide (*poems*) *printed privately, 1931;* The Field's Chief Flower — Studies in Renaissance Representations of Adonis, *1935;* The Steel Phalanx — A Poet Argues the Case for Fascism, *1936. Prosecutions...*

There had been several and in every case he had been acquitted or the charge had been reduced to something innocuous. Thus, when charged with a barman for attempting to procure two young soldiers for acts of grossest indecency, he was acquitted for lack of evidence and the barman got four years; a charge of Grievous Bodily Harm and wilful damage to property in Whitechapel had been reduced to one of making an affray for which he received a conditional discharge; driving under the influence of drugs and failing to report an accident was reduced to lack of due care and consideration with a fine of thirty shillings... and so on.

Cargill referred forward to an appendix and discovered that the drug in question had probably been cocaine.

His distaste grew. He was mildly irritated that the photograph at the head of the dossier was again, like the obscene pictures, in negative. Riversdale had had the usual mop of probably fair hair, falling Rupert Brooke-like across his forehead; his face was thin, with large eyes and pursy lips ... but this was deduced rather than seen. In the celluloid he looked like a night animal startled by a flash light, or a species of troglodyte, grey-fleshed, white-eyed, white-mouthed. Cargill shuddered — this was uncharacteristically fanciful. He touched the tray and returned to the text.

Recruitment to Bletchley Park had been through his Oxford tutor. His knowledge of German was excellent and he had stayed there with family friends and cousins on five occasions between 1927 and 1937. Cargill looked in vain for any suggestion that his clearance before going to Bletchley might have been held up while his pro-German, indeed pro-fascist, past had been examined (to Cargill he looked more like a candidate for internment than a position in an organisation as sensitive as the GCCS), but there was none. He was not surprised: if that sort of security risk had been allowed to become a consideration, most of Burke and Debrett would have been excluded for years from the war effort while one half of the British upper classes looked into the pasts of the other half.

And so to Riversdale as the Bletchley Park leak. There were two main factors. First the assumption, unproved but strongly indicated, that he had been blackmailed. The photographs involving him in sadistic sexual activity with young boys had, an expert asserted, been taken in Guy Burgess's Bentinck Street flat. The second and conclusive factor was that minute examination of the large file of personalia Cargill had been looking through indicated that Riversdale had been in contact with Soviet agents through dead letterboxes, and on two occasions had visited what were later known to have been safe houses. Lists of numbers typed on Riversdale's machine had been convincingly shown to be mnemonics for finding dead letterboxes with times at which product should be left in them; the addresses of the safe houses were actually written out in his own hand; sheets of bank typing paper that now had long-hand first drafts of poems on them were shown to have been previously used as backing paper in the same typewriter when a detailed account of the organisation and personnel of Hut Three had been typed on the top sheets. Hut Three was the section at Bletchley Park that dealt with all Wehrmacht and Luftwaffe signals after they had been deciphered in Hut Six. In Hut Three they were translated, interpreted, assessed and passed on to whatever branch of the allied war machine could make best use of them. It was as a translator and because of his knowledge of German institutions that Riversdale had been engaged.

Cargill switched off the visual display unit and leant back against blue leather. Part of the strip lighting in the cornices of the reading room had developed a flicker, and he was beginning to feel the irritability that comes with working for too long in a de-ionised atmosphere — a slight lassitude, a prickliness of the skin, a dryness of the eyes.

Virtually all the evidence against Riversdale came from this very large file of personal material. If he had been framed, then he had been framed by whoever was ultimately responsible for

27

discovering the material's existence and directing the Service to it. Presumably the same person doctored it — to have done that so well, he or she must have been an intimate.

Clearly also the suspicion that Riversdale was the leak had not been initiated with this file; it had existed before the file came into the investigating team's hands. So somewhere there should be a record of just why they had gone to Riversdale in the first place.

He turned to the second wallet, slid out the first microfiche, put it in the VDU and switched on again.

Bletchley Park – First Stage Screenings; Elimination; Second Stage Screenings. With a growing sense of weariness Cargill discovered that the original list of suspects had numbered three hundred and fifty-eight people out of the total known to have been employed at B-P of more than fifteen hundred. The suspects broke down into known members of the CP, British or foreign (26); members of affiliated organisations, peace groups and so on (the net had been cast wide — a further 187); unaffiliated lefties, mavericks, fellow-travellers (63); the remainder (82) included those who had been vulnerable to blackmail or bribery: here were adulterers, perverts, those who had cheated at cards, and those who had passed rubber cheques. There was a viscount who had shot his wife's lover in a duel, and a vicar's son who had sold the church plate. There were several who could not pay their tailors, their wine merchants, their bookmakers. Most pathetic of all was a lad called Evelyn Smith who had gone through Oxford claiming that his father was an Argentinian landowner and that he had been privately educated. In fact he was an orphan, and had achieved his first in PPE on the savings of a devoted aunt who had sold her sweet and tobacco shop to support him.

Riversdale duly appeared: a brief note explained that he was a known homosexual with sadomasochistic tendencies — again his various brushes with the law were listed, together with references to one incident at his prep school which had led to the death of a fellow pupil and to another on his Irish estate when a private prosecution for the corruption of minors had apparently been bought off.

The original list had been reduced to ninety-six: back-

28

tracking from the information the Russians had been known to have in 1947 had cut out those who did not have access to it; some had been thoroughly vetted at the end of the war before returning to or taking up sensitive posts in the Civil Service; some, for all Cargill could tell, simply because the investigators had not been able to believe them capable of treachery; and some whose membership in the CP turned out to be spurious — they were, after all, *agents provocateurs*, paid infiltrators.

Riversdale had of course been carried over into this second list but there was still no indication as to why and when the focus had narrowed down to him and him only. At this point the resources of the whole Service had been brought into play. Even in cases where the suspect was living abroad, Heads of Station had been briefed to make initial enquiries and even interrogate. Much of this had had side-effects — a Labour member of Parliament and junior minister was asked to resign, but for supplying information to the Americans rather than the Russians; a promising barrister on the point of taking silk shot himself; a handful more of the files were closed on instructions from above for no good reason that Cargill could see. Nor, still, could he see why Riversdale remained in the net when other fish swam clear.

He turned back to the Riversdale file, or rather the cardboard wallet of microfiches. There was a sort of index and, guessing to some extent for certainly he did not at this stage want to go through the lot, he selected a fiche from towards the back which contained reports of those separately engaged on the investigation. And still there was a gap: an operative had gone to a Lady Kitti Bridge at her address in Fennimore Gardens, and obtained the large folder of private papers, photographs and so on that now made up the Riversdale personalia and contained the main body of evidence against him. But still there was no piece of paper recording why this had been done, no indication of how the team had known that Lady Kitti Bridge had these papers.

The file had been tampered with, it must have been. Cargill, interest now quickening again, checked that Lady Kitti Bridge was Riversdale's sister, and checked again that the instruction to the operative had not been minuted. Or if it had it had been removed. Moving quickly now, efficiently, he fed fiche after fiche into the tray, scanning each, checking as rapidly as possible that the missing instruction had not been photographed in the wrong context. This was not as difficult as it sounds — the minute would have been on government paper so he could reject instantly anything that was not stamped with the Royal Arms or Cipher, and those that were could usually be dismissed after a cursory glance at reference numbers. Of course later, if a case were brought against person or persons unknown and it rested to any extent on the fact that this piece of paper was missing, then the whole file, the actual file, would have to be taken from its hole in the Kent coalfield and gone through by an independent assessor: but for the time being Cargill was satisfied that he had found a trail, a scent, a hint of something wrong, and at this stage that was all he needed.

There had been no need to take notes before he left. The address of Lady Kitti Bridge in 1948 was all he needed to remember.

3

He intended to return to St James's to order a trace on her but it occurred to him that nothing would be lost by simply consulting the telephone book. And not only was she in it — she was still, after over thirty years, at the same address. Taking more of a chance, he rang her up straightaway — a chance, because under normal procedures the Housemaster would pave the way, at least with a phone call, probably with a letter, where someone with possibly influential connections was concerned.

The pips, his 5p piece chunked in and a voice repeated the number he had dialled and added, 'Lady Kitti Bridge.' It was husky, even faintly seductive — and very definitely out of the very topmost drawer. Cargill briefly explained that he wanted to ask her some questions about her brother.

'Are you a journalist?'

'No.'

'A writer then, I suppose.'

'No.'

There was a pause.

'Tell me with what authority, under whose auspices, you are making this enquiry.'

'I am with the Home Office.'

'And you have a document that says so?'

'Of course.'

'Then I shall see you.'

There was a most musical cadence to this which gave it a weight of finality and decision.

'When, Lady Bridge?'

31

'Now. Why not?' It was just past five o'clock.

Fennimore Gardens are in South Kensington — a square of drab lawn with plane trees clutching about them a few heavy umber leaves like dirty rags. These are shut off by a rusty chain-link fence from the large houses, each with its Corinthian portico, the stucco so overpainted that the acanthus has lost its edges and looks like over-boiled grey cabbage.

The street door to number thirty-five was unlocked and opened on to a drab, linoed hall, painted cream and brown and furnished only with a table, a mirror and a pay phone. Cargill climbed brass-edged stairs to a first floor which, since the conversion, now had one landing window and one modern front door with spy-hole and Chubb locks — what other doors there had been were now bricked up, plastered over, and painted in the same cream and brown. Clearly Lady Kitti occupied the whole floor — which meant a not insubstantial apartment for one person in these tight-fisted times.

He explained into the small microphone by the bell-push, raising his voice above the frenzied yapping of a small dog on the other side, that he was the Cargill who had telephoned twenty minutes earlier. Then he posted his Home Office ID through the letterbox. A chain rattled against the door-post, and at last he was in.

Lady Kitti Bridge was already moving away from him into the large front room that overlooked the gardens and so his first view of her was of her back. She was thin, small, stood very straight, had a lot of silver-blond hair backcombed above cashmere and a perfectly styled tweed skirt. For a second he thought there had been some mistake — this woman, he would have sworn, was not more than forty-five, and if she was as old as that then she had taken a great deal of care of herself: from behind she could even have been as little as twenty-five — then she turned.

Her face, though small, was large for her body and the skin on it looked like tissue paper that has been heavily crumpled and only partially flattened; round her eyes and beneath her chin it had the oddly puckered yet dead look of cosmetic surgery done many years ago, and the bright lipstick went far beyond the

32

shrunken edges of her lips. Yet in the middle of this desolation, which recalled imperfectly embalmed corpses from ancient tombs, her pale eyes were alive — but cold, hard, like chips of amethyst.

In her arms she held a tiny border terrier. This she now dropped into a basket in a window embrasure where it whined then whimpered. Meanwhile, a thin, claw-like hand with long nails immaculately painted red waved him to a chintz-covered chair. This was of a quality that gave the conventional pattern of tea-roses and so on a freshness, even a significance, that no imitation could match. Cargill looked around and was aware that everything in the room had the same feel of paid-for uniqueness that is a surer sign of real wealth than polished marble, silver gilt and cut crystal. For historical reasons the rich have lost what true sense of the beautiful they ever had: loveliness has been reduced to the irreplaceable.

She offered whisky, he offered to get it; but she poured the drinks herself at the sideboard. He realised why she had quashed him when he saw that her glass — which *was* cut crystal — contained at least half a gill, whereas his held barely more than a conventional pub measure. The water was Malvern and he accepted it.

'You want to ask me about my brother. I am sure you know that he has been dead for thirty-six years. You must also know that some three years after he died your people questioned me very closely about him. I do not think that you can imagine that I shall say anything new now.'

'Do you know why you were questioned?'

'I do now. At the time I did not. When I discovered, I was, you may imagine, extremely discomfited. I felt that I had been a victim of deceit.'

'Let me be sure I understand, Lady Bridge,' Cargill leaned forward with his elbows on his knees, his glass held between them, 'you now know that three years after his death Lord Riversdale came to be thought of as a Russian spy. But you did not know that at the time?'

'That is correct.'

'What *did* you think at the time?'

She had been sitting very straight on the edge of her chair.

Now she stood and moved to a glass-fronted cabinet by the large window. She seemed for a moment to be lost in admiration for the carved detail of a jade horse.

'Am I to understand that this business is to be re-opened, re-considered?'

'Yes. There may have been a mistake.'

She gave a short hard laugh and drank about a third of what was in her glass.

'I was deceived before. How can I be sure that I am not to be deceived again?'

He gave the slightest of shrugs and said nothing. The rumble of London's rush hour, muted by double glazing, was a thing felt rather than heard. Lady Kitti came back to her chair, stood behind it for a moment, then with a toss of her head (a gesture that had inflamed young hearts in 1934) sat down again.

'Well, ask away and we'll see where it leads.'

Cargill drank, put his glass on the table at his elbow, and sat back, large hands now together making a church just below his chin. 'I was nothing to do with the first enquiry. I was an under-graduate at the time. Could you tell me first just what you were told, what the deceit was?'

'The man who came said that a junior minister at the Home Office, a socialist of course, had instigated, at the insistence of their backbenchers, an enquiry into people who had had pro-German . . . fascist leanings in the period before the war. He said that the whole matter was very embarrassing and would, he was sure, very quickly die down and be forgotten, but that then it was necessary to bustle, to make a show of doing something. I accepted this. Teddy had been an active member of the Anglo-German Fellowship and had travelled in Germany several times in the thirties. Through family connections — my mother was a Slaker and her mother was a connection of the Krupps — he had in fact met, and indeed was friendly with, some of their highest people. We were of course questioned about all this in late 1938 and again in 1940. By then we had dropped all that, it had become clear that patriotism demanded a narrower view of the issues. And that, we thought, was that. However, when your predecessor called in 1948 I accepted what he said: there was a

34

quite unpleasant streak of vindictiveness in that post-war government which made it credible. Something incidentally which many of us have not readily forgotten or easily forgiven.'

'What sort of things did he ask you?'

'Oh, very harmless stuff, as far as I remember. But then he wanted to know if I had any private papers of Teddy's, things which could perhaps be used to show that his attitude was properly patriotic and anti-German during the last years of his life, during the war.'

'And you had just such a collection.'

'I did.'

'And you gave it to him.'

'Yes. And not a single sheet of it has been returned, although I have made representations to very high levels. I was, and still am, very angry about it. Quite apart from the personal value these papers have for me they contain drafts, some of them final drafts, of unpublished poems. You know Teddy was a poet?'

'Yes.'

'Well. Yes. And rather highly thought of. Tom spoke very well of his work.'

'Tom?'

'Tom Eliot. So I think they should be returned to me, don't you? The least I can do for Teddy is get out a collection.'

Cargill was impressed — by 'Tom' Eliot, that is. But he brought her back to the real matter of his questions. 'And then later, perhaps because you were making representations, you were told that the enquiry into Lord Riversdale was nothing to do with his supposed pro-fascism.'

'*Not* through my representations, no. In the fifties I was acquainted with — well, knew rather well — a man whose name I will not bother you with who happened to be a barrister employed by your people to interrogate spies, possible defectors, suspected *moles*. He was rather good at it. Anyway, in the course of his work he came upon the fact that Teddy had been pin-pointed as the source of information to the Russians of every-thing they knew about Bletchley Park, and that his personal papers, which I had handed over, contained the irrefutable evidence that this was so.'

'Did you believe this?'

'Not at first, no. But my friend, the barrister, did — and he pointed out to me that sympathy for the Bolshevik cause need have had nothing to do with it. In short, that Teddy was, for various reasons, a remarkably apt person to be blackmailed. You know what I am talking about.'

'Oh quite.'

'Oh *quite*.' She mimicked, and again the hard laugh came. She threw back her head and emptied her glass, then fixed him with the unblinking amethyst eyes as if challenging him to react.

She went to the sideboard and as she lifted the stopper from the decanter he asked, 'Lady Bridge, how did those papers, your brother's papers, come into your possession?'

Again the silence settled across the room like a presence breathed out of the Aubusson carpet. Only the dog snuffled and its basket creaked. The crystal chimed, and Lady Kitti breathed out a slow sigh.

'Almost I was afraid you would not ask,' she said, and her voice was now deeper than ever, yet scarcely more than a whisper. 'They were brought to me, three months after Teddy's death, by a very dear friend of us both. A friend who had shared digs with Teddy in Bletchley itself.'

'This friend worked at Bletchley Park too?'

'Oh yes.'

Whisky flowed as if from a burn into her glass.

'His name was, is, Richard Austen.'

She looked up, again with the imperious little shake of her head. 'He is quite eminent. *Sir* Richard Austen. The archaeologist. You know?'

Cargill knew, knew as much as any of us: Sir Richard Austen FBA, FSA — distinguished Bronze Age expert; discoverer of the Sidon Treasure; author of popularising books on the development of primitive metallurgy examined from an avowedly Marxist viewpoint; director of the Gold Museum in Bloomsbury; television personality; one of Harold's knights. He was not, Cargill thought, a likely friend of the Bridge family — Anglo-Irish aristocrats with extreme right-wing views.

He put this to Lady Kitti.

'Well, they were at school together, and friends. Both schools.

36

A rather nasty kids' school in the north-east which my mother insisted on for Teddy — apparently all Slaker boys went to it — and then of course the College. Incidentally, Austen has Slaker blood — we are third or fourth cousins, something of that sort. I expect that's why he went to ... The Meads, yes, I think that's what it was called.'

Cargill asked, 'How did their ages compare?' Which was an odd way of putting the question but, having seen, one way or another, too much of too many who had been through the same educational system, he knew it was significant.

Lady Kitti took the point: 'Teddy was the older by two years,' she said dryly.

'So probably the attachment was, at some point or other, well, forgive me, *romantic*. Would you say that was the case?'

'Oh, very probably. I should think they buggered each other whenever they had the chance — once they were capable of it. One refreshing thing about the present is that one can now say such things.' Again the hard laugh.

Cargill, however, remained a creature both of the past and of his methodist upbringing and knew that he was blushing again — as he had when he came across the obscene photographs in the Riversdale file.

'Did they remain, er, close friends after they left the College?'

'Not as far as I know. There was a gap of five years. Teddy was at Balliol; Austen, I think, at St John's, Cambridge. I don't think they saw each other during that time.'

'They met again at Bletchley Park?'

'No. There was an interlude before then.'

She explained that she had taken up archaeology in the early thirties (' — very much the thing then, you know?'), had met Austen at the Maiden Castle Dig, where she had been one of Wheeler's small-finds recorders and Austen had fallen in love with her without knowing that she was Riversdale's sister. She had been there because she and her mother had wanted to set up an excavation on the Riversdale estates in the Wicklow Mountains, which were a Bronze Age source of both gold and copper; and she was to learn the rudiments under Wheeler. There she had also met Fernando González García, a Spanish archaeologist who was especially interested in establishing

37

Bronze Age links between Ireland and north Spain. The upshot was that, together, she, González and Austen had planned and, the following season, 1935, put into effect the excavation of a Bronze Age settlement and discovered a small hoard of axes, celts, dagger hilts and so on in the hills behind Scales, the Riversdale country house. Riversdale himself had taken an interest and the old friendship between him and Austen had been renewed.

While she recounted all this she drank a further gill of whisky, and her speech became thicker, her manner truculent. The dog too began to complain, leaving its basket and snuffling around a door which Cargill imagined led to a food supply or possibly a litter tray. He judged it was time to leave, but there were still questions to ask.

'Sir Richard and Lord Riversdale were close again at Bletchley?'

A faint touch of pink was now present in the middle of her forehead and on her lined cheeks. In contrast her eyes seemed brighter and harder than ever.

'I doubt if they were buggering, if that's what you mean. Austen's tastes had become quite boringly conventional and exclusively heterosexual by then. But they were certainly friendly. I believe they worked very closely together too. Herman, for God's sake shut up.' She stopped and quite viciously slapped the little dog's rump — the whine died again into a whimper.

'And when it was decided that Lord Riversdale might have been a V2 casualty, three months or so after he disappeared, Austen brought you his personal effects including his private papers?'

She brusquely assented. They were both standing and she was effortlessly signalling his departure much as if he were a higher grade hireling — a bailiff or a solicitor.

'So, in the interim, three months, Austen had unrestricted access to them?'

'Of course he bloody did.'

They were now in the small hall and her hand was on the chain.

With something not far off desperation, Cargill took a card

from his wallet: 'Lady Bridge, I must go. But if you want to get in touch with me at all, if you think of anything you haven't told me which might materially assist in clearing your brother's name, and restore his papers to you, do please contact me at either of these phone numbers...'

The door closed behind him and in spite of Herman's piercing yap — suddenly the small dog was in full voice again — he could hear the multiple locks re-engaging. He wondered why she had been so desperate to get rid of him.

4

The next morning at ten o'clock Cargill was back at Registry Three. He asked for the same two files again and this time both were immediately forthcoming. It did not take long to find out that Austen had been one of those who had been considered possible Bletchley Park leaks; then again that his name had been carried forward to the second list of ninety-six names. That meant that he must have been investigated and that therefore there should be a file on him.

He found Sally in a cubicle just inside the glass door and asked her to get it; as he returned to his VDU, he realised that the Porton biologist was back at his seat and the Mormon-like American too. The latter was sitting with his legs crossed in front of his unlit machine, silently drumming idle fingers on the blue leather table top: Cargill vaguely wondered why, sat down and began to run through parts of the Riversdale file he had looked over only casually the day before. If he had anything in mind at all, it was Kitti Bridge — since his interview with her she had been almost continually in his mind. At home, in his bachelor's flat in Knightsbridge, he had rung up a journalist friend and been told what he should have remembered himself. Like Unity Mitford a would-be acolyte of Hitler before the war, then scandals in the fifties — the decade of Onassis, Callas and Garbo; the Dockers and their feud with Rainier. Lady Kitti had bravely jetted about the Mediterranean in suspect Comets, was twice cited in divorce proceedings, and to less effect for contravening currency regulations. Of course the latter charge did not stick and she won a libel action against a socialist review which suggested that it should. For a time she was thought to be addicted to heroin. Cargill's friend had concluded that she must now be well over sixty so it wasn't surprising that she led a quieter life: it was also probable that she had run through her own money and now lived on interest from tied capital — presumably Slaker Group stock.

'Mr Cargill — would you mind awfully. The Librarian would like to see you again.' Sally — empty-handed at his elbow.

The little man was standing over his aquarium, his back to the door. With one hand he waved Cargill in, with the other he manipulated a plastic fly-swat to recover a dead fantail from the bubbling water. Almost reverently, he let the small carcass flop onto a sheet of blotting paper he had laid ready.

'I really don't know what to make of this.'

'Of what?'

'This is the second in a week.' He folded the paper round the body, drawing the long sides together, turning down the ends. The package patchily darkened.

'Perhaps it's your water.'

'Well, *quite*. Perhaps it is. And it's from the emergency tank, not from the mains. Do you think Dr Baldwin would do an autopsy for me?'

Baldwin was the biologist in the reading room.

'You could ask. But why not change the water? I mean, use the mains.'

The Librarian faced him. 'William, it may surprise you but I am not a fish fancier. I am, however, concerned to establish that the water in the emergency tank is capable of supporting life. That file on Richard Austen is lost. Missing. Mislaid rather... can't be found.'

Cargill felt a sudden surge of excitement which he knew he must control.

'Perhaps it's the air,' he heard himself say.

'What *do* you mean?'

'I mean the air you're bubbling through the water. Perhaps that's killing your fish.'

'Oh, my Lord. Do you think so? Why that's terrible. I mean,

41

it's what we are breathing. Actually I'm not at all sure there was a file on Austen. It's not catalogued. It's not cross-referenced. Anyway, it's not *here*.'

'But it must be. There must have been a file here. He was investigated. Oh, for heaven's sake, you know the procedure.'

'Yes, of course I do.' The Librarian retreated to his desk, sidled behind it. 'Sit down, won't you? Of course I know the procedures. I also know very well what you know too and that is that files can be moved from here and kept in the Director's Registry; that they *can* go missing; that they can even be lost by accident. The system's not foolproof.'

'All right.' Cargill uncrossed his legs and leaned forward. 'I want to know what happened to that file. A good starting point for finding that out would be to check the other ninety-five files — see just how many of them are missing, and, if any are, just which ones, and for what reasons. I'm not going to make a fuss yet . . . not until I know to what extent the fact that Austen's file is not here is exceptional. How long will it take you to give me that sort of breakdown on the other ninety-five?'

'Well. I only have five girls here at the moment, and they're quite busy, if not actually rushed off their feet . . . Oh, all right, all right. Give us until tomorrow.'

As Cargill reached the door, the little man added, 'Of course it might be the food.'

Cargill looked at the now quite soggy package on the bookcase. 'That should ease your mind,' he said. 'Or are you planning to eat fish food as well as drink their water and breathe their air, once the bomb has dropped?'

He called back at head office and asked Research for a Who's Who on Austen to be prepared for him; then, half an hour later, again in his high-crowned trilby, muffler and unclassifiable coat, he stood on the top step of the portico of what had once been the neo-classical church of All Saints, Regent Square, and read the plaque set into the west wall to the left of the large bronze doors.

The Gold Museum – Incorporating the Institute of Primitive Metallurgy. Trustees: The Slaker Foundation. Director: Sir Richard Austen, FBA, FSA. This, also in bronze, was grand — beneath it, framed

like the notices outside West End theatres, was a placard: —
*A magic palace of entrancing delights (The Observer); No child up from
the country for the day should miss it (The Times); Put it on your list
below – no, above, The Tower (The Guardian).*

Ten years after its opening the interior had a dated feel to it,
or rather, like Snowdon's Aviary, a feel that was datable. There
was for a start a lot of light: although it had been built in the
year when energy conservation first became dinner-talk, the
designers had remained immune. There was also a lot of glass
framed in matte-finished stainless steel with solid contrasted
colour as backgrounds to the exhibits. There was movement —
hardly a case left its contents at rest, all shimmered, revolved or
spiralled in a ceaseless ballet that put the receptive viewer in
mind of the magic space-shuttle-to-the-moon sequence in *2001 :
A Space Odyssey* — at least it was intended to.

There were five principal areas, on split levels of course,
reached by cantilevered staircases and seemingly unsupported
galleries: one for each of the main periods dealt with — Late
Neolithic, Early Bronze, Middle Bronze, Late Bronze and Early
Iron; each with round, oval, even serpentine (but almost never
simply square), cases in which copper, bronze, silver and above
all gold worked out their soundless, ceaseless revolutions; each
with dioramas depicting processes of extraction, smelting,
moulding, hammering, beating, finishing and decorating.

Cargill took his time: it was his first visit. His wife and two
daughters had left him ten years before the Gold Museum was
opened and his daughters were now grown up — normally it
would not occur to him to visit such a place without the excuse
of children to educate. But it was not only the impressiveness,
even, he soon had to admit, the delightfulness, of it that slowed
him down. It was too the captions on the cases, which seemed to
him to be contentious . . . in fact, he decided at about the middle
of the Early Bronze Age, tendentious:

'Possession of copper and tin turned the British Isles into
manufacturing countries producing for a world market when
bronze was the principal metal . . . the Late Bronze Age is
ushered in by a technological revolution and drastic reorganis-
ation of the distributive side of the industry . . . the cemeteries
tell us even less of the prehistoric smiths and miners than those of

43

the workers who toiled in the nineteenth century...the armament industry is generally international...the revolution was in the economy of a de-tribalised industrial group producing for an international market...new techniques of production, large-scale if not mass production, meant inevitably that the means of production were wrested from the workers and in time ownership of labour became institutionalised as slavery...' and so on.

But finally it was the gold that enraptured the eye, filled the imagination and (Cargill looked round...at midday in a working November week what had been the nave of the neo-classical church was already busy) brought in the crowds. Some of it was spurious in the sense that where a representative item could not be borrowed or bought the museum had employed modern smiths to recreate what was wanted; and much of it was Middle Eastern though placed in a British context — but all of it gold, real gold, refined, burnished, cut into ribbons, incised, soldered, annealed, twisted, hammered to an airy thinness, stretched into wire and coiled — studs, buttons, brooches, rings and fibulae; bracelets, armlets, amulets and chains; torques, masks, dagger hilts, bosses for bucklers and sun discs; wreaths, head-bands, coronets and crowns.

One could digress, wander off, cut corners or explore byways, but inevitably, for so the place was laid out, one came — not at last for there was still the walk down the centre of the old nave to the west end where there was a book and card stall — one came eventually to the semi-circular apse. Here, in a cave or cyst of stone slabs, but raised from the ground on a plinth, was an unadorned skeleton of brown bones crouched with a simple pottery beaker between its feet. The caption to this was exceptional. It read:

> Dear dead women, with such hair too — what's become of all the gold
> Used to hang and brush their bosoms? I feel chilly and grown old.

A staircase — a cantilevered three-quarter spiral — wound round and up from this in front of the bay of leaded but plain glass windows to galleries that ran back the length of the church

44

to the old organ loft. This area was now offices. Along one of these galleries crisp footsteps rang — the noise amplified to Cargill below by the ceiling. He glanced up and inevitably recognised, just as he came to the top of the stairs, the small trim figure of Sir Richard Austen. Instinctively Cargill looked away — searched for something to fix his eyes on, and found the plainest case of all in a small niche to the side of the mock tomb. In it was a small pottery beaker like the one in the mock tomb and three gold discs, each about the size of an old halfpenny, each with a simple repoussé cruciform pattern. For once the caption was utterly conventional:

> Late Neolithic or Early Bronze, 'B' Beaker, recovered
> from a barrow with ditch, South Meon, Hampshire,
> 1929. Kindly lent by George Partridge, Esq.

Sir Richard — neat in a suit a shade or two paler than is usually worn by senior academics, and certainly better pressed, grey hair trimmed and feathered stylishly close to his round skull, silk tie in blue and scarlet diamonds, leaving just a hint of very good cologne in the air behind him, glossily shod feet twinkling on the marble beneath him — tripped on past Cargill with his eyes fixed expectantly on the big doors at the west end, where the area round the circular kiosk had filled with a gaggle of schoolboys: black blazers, ties loosened from unbuttoned collars, down at heel shoes.

Austen welcomed the dowdy-looking teacher, shook hands, waved the thirty or forty adolescents into an uneven semi-circle around him. Cargill came up within earshot.

'Welcome to the Geold Museum. We are always heppy to see leds from William Collins Comp here and eh think eh'm right'n sayin' most of your chaps hev enjoyed bein' heah. Eh certainly hope so.

'Well then. First things first. One is awfen asked how the Geold Museum cem into bein'. End it does mek a fescinatin' story...'

('He sounds like Prince Charles,' whispered a boy at the back.)

'We-ell, bek in 1952, before eny of you cheps were boarn, eh deh seh, eh heppened to be on a dig in the south of Lebanon.

45

Thet's the little chep on the mep just above Pelestine, or Israel, es of course it neow is...'

Cargill edged behind the group to the kiosk. There were reproductions of some of the more startling exhibits, postcards, guides, but, prominent amongst it all, the centre of the display, a stand filled with copies of a brand-new, glossily dust-jacketed hardback. Printed on the cover was a coloured photograph of the crouched skeleton from the apse but surrounded now with gold flame. *The Burning Matrix* by Richard Austen. He took down a copy, opened it at the blurb: '*The Burning Matrix* is the long-awaited autobiography of one of the most colourful personalities of our times... £7.95. Michael Joseph.'

'I'd like a receipt please. A full one. Not just the till slip.'

'Neow Lord Slaker's ideah was thet it should be a museum entirely devoted to geold, but eh prevailed on him to widen our horizons and include the hoal complex of metal industries and he saw this would indeed provide a setting, context as it were. Incorporated with the museum is the Institute of Primitive...'

The bright confident voice chatted on. Cargill, with his wrapped book under his arm, moved back behind one of the big doric pillars that supported the old organ loft — he imagined he had become inconspicuous if not invisible: in fact only by turning up the collar of his nondescript coat could he have drawn more attention to himself.

Half an hour later he was still around and, as Austen almost scampered down the steps of his museum into Regent Square, he fell in behind. Austen now had on a short camel-hair coat cut like a British Warm, a red silk scarf, no hat or umbrella. He looked like the brighter, healthier sort of army officer — a colonel or brigadier with a desk at the Horseguards, who had won his spurs at Alamein or Palermo, and now keeps fit with a spot of otter-hunting or fly-fishing according to season in the more private parts of Hampshire or Dorset...

He had gone, disappeared. For a moment Cargill looked up and down Hunter Street, at the ziggurat-like development of the Brunswick Centre, at the taxis bustling up to St Pancras, or speeding south to Charing Cross or Victoria, at the milk floats purring and rattling back to the Express Dairy depot in the side street behind him. For a moment the trivial busy-ness of the city, the mechanised crowd, filled his consciousness with a vertiginous sense of being a speck amongst millions; then, hurrying to a corner, he caught sight of the camel coat passing beneath a red and white striped pole set in a high fence of blockboard.

The barrier descended, the security guard who had operated it saluted and Austen passed on in. Now, from the roar of the city, Cargill could distinguish the throaty clanking of a Ready-Mix Concrete transporter, the throb of heavy plant, while a huge derrick a hundred feet above their heads swung a hopper of conglomerate in a slow parabola whose weight dragged the cable slightly but sickeningly out of the vertical. Below, the ground was trenched, mined, churned into an abstraction of intercut squares and rectangles, their corners marked by square pillars of concrete out of which twisted-steel fingers groped blindly for the leaden sky.

Men in leather-shouldered donkey jackets and helmets of scarlet with a gold logo humped and hammered huge planks, the form work for the next stage, and dumpers, pick-ups, fork-lifts bustled around them. Right in the middle stood Austen, he too now in a helmet; with him a man who looked, by his clothes, to be the site manager. They were chatting — animatedly, with good humour. The manager part-unrolled a plan, jabbed with a finger, gestured across the site to where one deep hole you could have dropped a house in waited to be filled, its sides scarred with two millennia of strata. Suddenly Austen handed back his helmet and picked his way back to the street; Cargill turned and read from the glossy boards printed out in fashionable sanserif, 'Slaker Towers — Citeecon proudly announces a new development in the heart of London Town . . . thousands of square feet . . . luxury flats, service flats, condominiums, office space, swimming pool, restaurants and squash courts . . . Contractors: Sir Jacob Upton and Associates; site clearance: Lord Down; Architects: Merry, Tricius and Savage; Solicitors: Screw, Krafft and Base. Citeecon is proud to be a member of the Slaker Group . . .' and Austen passed by him, quite close, crossed the road, headed on down past the tube station and into Russell Square.

Cargill saw him into the grill-room entrance of the Grand. Clearly the Housemaster would not allow a steak lunch on top of *The Burning Matrix* when he was still only playing a hunch, and so he set off briskly back to his pub in St James's for his usual pie with a half of bitter.

5

A tall thin grey-haired American sat perched like a mantis on a stool in the small cocktail bar. Austen paused in the low doorway for a second, eyes slightly narrowed, then stirred himself into the sort of movement that will make a waiting man look up.

'Richard!'

'Roy! How *very* jolly.'

'It's good to see you, it *really* is. Now sit down and have a drink. A G and T. *Fine.*' (Not the first today by the smell on your breath and you're not as young as you were.) 'Well, you look *fine*. Not a day older. When was it? Ten, twelve years ago?'

'Thirteen, I think. '67. Well, Roy, you don't look too bad yourself.' (Is that a toupee? His great nose sticks out like the prow of the *Victory*, and his clothes... a multi-coloured check jacket, an opalescent turtle-neck sweater in silk? mohair?) 'Well this is *fine*!' Austen glanced round the not-unfamiliar surroundings. 'One of my favourite watering holes. But I should have expected you to be at the other end of town.'

'Hell, no. I'm a businessman, not a tourist or a film star. This is just dandy — and not too with it either. Know what I mean? I mean, here you can almost kid yourself the *sauce diane* was made on the premises, not snipped out of a plastic envelope. Here we are then. Cheers.'

'Cheers, Roy.'

'Well, it *is* good to see you. One of your favourite...? Do you come here often?'

Richard Austen was amused by Newman's choice of the place as a businessman's venue.

'Twice a year or so. Fact is, our miners' and steelmen's union leaders use it, and when they're in town they ask me round for a drink or a bite.'

'What on earth do they want to spend union dues on you for?'

'I give free lectures to union branches and WEA's on Bronze Age mining and metallurgy.'

'Still the old red, eh, Richard?'

'That's right, Roy. Still the old red.'

'Well, you'll never convince me you can run an industrial society if you make the profit motive a dirty little secret like sex,' Newman said. 'That's why we'll win in the end: we accept the profit motive; we get it out in the open; we put it on a pedestal and we say, there you go, profit motive, go get us the goodies. You can't do without it. It's always been there. Attila the Hun had it. Genghis Khan. It's a part of human nature.'

Austen, neat and jolly, twinkled up at Newman: 'Let me tell you a story. At an international gathering of petrol chemists an American was talking to a Russian who had discovered a new catalyst. The American said, "Ivan, what did they pay you? What did you get out of it?" He was thinking of the millions the American companies pay for such discoveries. Ivan replied, "What do I get out of it? I get cheaper petrol for my car. That's what I get out of it."'

'Richard, that's the eighth time I've heard that story. But tell me,' the American's turn to twinkle, 'is it all right for me to call you Richard? Should it not be *Sir Dick*?'

'Oh, come *on*!'

'In days of old when knights were bold ... Richard, how *come* you're a knight?'

'Well, Roy. Back in days of old we had a PM whose idea of an honours list was something concocted out of a Royal Variety Performance programme and the Newgate Calendar. I was one of his more conventional suggestions.'

'And finally the old fraud got on the list himself. Under which heading? Why *both* of course. Come on, Richard, drink up and we'll have a nibble, what do you say?'

* * *

50

Roy Newman had half a grapefruit, steak tartare, a vanilla ice, and drank Perrier. Richard Austen had whitebait, a chop, cabinet pudding and half a bottle of Margaux.

'Well, why are you in town, old friend?'

'To see you of course.'

'Come on. No. Really?'

'Really. I really mean it. Oh, of course I have one or two chores to do, but really. Listen.' The tall American picked a crumb of red meat from his moustache. 'You know United Special Steels, the firm I work for.'

'Own by now, I should think.' Austen sawed away at the fatty bit along the bone.

'Well, not quite. But my name is on the letter-heading. Well, our president has put it to us that we should do something, you know, a bit special, for Jamestown, Pa . . . '

'You're pulling out, I suppose.'

'Diversifying. The new technologies, the chip, and beyond, lasers, the rest of it, that scene. But the company will always keep its roots there.' Since what Austen had intended as a joke had hit on the exact truth of the matter, Newman took him entirely seriously. 'And to mark this stage in our firm's progress we want to leave a lasting record of our achievement . . . in our birthplace as it were.'

'Go on.'

'Well, a theme park has been suggested. And a symphony orchestra. And, you know, I find the former a bit ordinary, and the latter will be too expensive. So. My idea is we should set up a museum of metallurgy. Like Gold.'

Austen's fork stopped on its way to his mouth, and went down to his plate. 'But that's *marvellous*, Roy. You want me to help?'

'Of course.'

'But why didn't you write? I mean, why . . . well! How wonderful.'

'To tell you the truth, the idea only occurred to me when my copy of *Blazing Matrix* . . . '

'*Burning.*'

' . . . arrived. I went straight to the president and he said, Roy, you're going to London anyway, look up this old friend of yours,

51

sound him out, get some coarse costing done and estimate the appeal . . . so here I am.'

Roy had decaffeinated, Richard had black with Grand Marnier.

'Really we want to spend some time over this — I mean, I need a detailed briefing.'

'Have you got a day or two to spare?'

'For this, of course.'

A small, soft-leather black book. 'Could you come down to the Farm for a day or two? At the end of next week, say? Tell you the truth, Gold runs itself now — I'm in the way if I'm there more than two days a week.'

Roy's diary. 'I should be through my chores by Friday week. My flight stateside is pencilled for Saturday. But I can make that the Sunday, even Monday.'

'Well, that's fine then. And maybe we'll have time to chat over the old days, eh? I'd enjoy that.'

'The days at Bletchley Park? Why not. And you know there are one or two things in *Blazing Matrix* I think you have wrong? And one or two you left out?'

'Roy, why do you get that wrong?'

'Hell, Richard, it's just a joke. Richard, tell me, why did you crack on you were *chums* with Riversdale? His sister yes. As nice a bit of tail as a lucky man is likely to find. But her brother! Once, when you were drunk, you told me you were going to kill him.'

The grill room of the Grand lurched as if it were the dining room in the *Poseidon Adventure* (which it resembled), then slowly righted itself.

'Oh, it was one of those love-hate things, you know?' Austen's fingers gripped his thighs, the nails tearing into the flesh, his stomach heaved — sweat, he was sure, must be visible on his forehead. 'Maybe a touch more of the one than the other, but the publishers like these things kept bland.'

'Say no more. Sorry I brought it up . . .'

They parted in Russell Square with a firm arrangement for Newman to be at the Farm on Friday week in time for a late lunch. Splendid. Fine. Apart from that one nasty moment, Austen was pleased. He felt that, if he played his cards right, United Special Steels would take him in just as the Slaker Group had, and that would be fine. He needed a change, and at sixty-six years old there was time for one more project.

6

Riversdale's a cad, Riversdale's a cad, Bridge or Riversdale, Riversdale or Bridge is a cad, is a cad, is a cad, Riversdale's a cad, Riversdale's a cad, Riversdale's a cad...

Woking.

Usual routine. Get second G and T before the train picks up to some ridiculous speed — over a hundred (*a ton* they say but why?). Inter-City madness and no hope of keeping one's feet and not much of retaining the drink in the glass.

'Just the lemon, isn't it?'

'That's right.'

'I thought so. I never forget a customer.'

I piss on the obsequiousness of the *lumpen proletariat*, I piss on it.

Back to the drab seat at the narrow coffin-shaped, Formica-topped table, clutching a plastic glass with its sliver of lemon, a miniature bottle of Gordon's, a rip-off tin of Schweppes.

Riversdale's a cad.

Riversdale's a cad.

Ooops. This really is ridiculous. So bloody clumsy and uncomfortable. There used to be service on this train. Of a sort. Not any longer. Now it is squalid, nasty, grubby, noisy... I doubt if I've been in such squalor since The Meads.

Riversdale, Riversdale, Riversdale.

'... be amongst us and remain with us always. Amen. Mr Baker, kindly take the names of the next three boys who cough. They will attend my bathroom at Wakes tomorrow morning for a supervised cold bath.

'Now boys, I have an important announcement to make. All my announcements are important, but this one particularly so ... Mr Baker, did you get that boy's name? You did? Splendid. Don't forget, Austen, five minutes after Wakes, tomorrow morning in my bathroom and we'll share a cold bath. One way or another I'll make a man of you. Now. Pay close attention. Many of you will remember that throughout last year form six was graced with the presence of a lively, pleasant lad called Bridge. Yes? Right? Greenhalgh, do you remember Bridge? Of course you do. Equally, Greenhalgh and most of the rest of form six will be aware that for the first four weeks of this term Bridge has not been with us. And those of you who sleep in Nelson dorm will know that there is a vacant bed.

'Well, boys of form six, boys of Nelson dorm, I have good news for you, indeed good news for all of us at The Meads. Bridge will be amongst us again, at seven o'clock this evening, if, as I am sure will be the case, the London and North Eastern Railway performs with its customary exemplary punctuality. Mr Barber. There is a boy with very fair hair, snivelling, to your right... his name please. Jefferson? Ah yes. Jefferson, accompany Austen to my bathroom tomorrow morning.

'And now boys I come to the point. Bridge has been most unfortunate. In September, just before we reassembled here he lost his father. That is to say his father died. In fact, he was brutally murdered by some of the most cowardly, dastardly rogues ever to have trodden the blessed soil of these islands. Bridge's father laid down his life in County Wicklow for his country just as many of your fathers and brothers did in Flanders. Jefferson, if you must snivel, then snivel elsewhere. Mr Barber, kindly conduct him to the locker room.

'Now, as a result of this wicked tragedy, Bridge is no longer Bridge. He is now Riversdale, having succeeded his father to the title of Earl of Riversdale. I should like you all to bear that in mind. However, following our custom here, he will not be called *Lord* Riversdale by my staff, nor by you boys. But simply and straightforwardly *Riversdale*. Now is that quite understood? Has the meanest intelligence amongst you grasped

that? Austen, when Bridge returns what will you call him?'
   'Please, sir, Riversdale, sir.'
   'Right. Now to more mundane matters. Matron informs me
that the Tower dorm lats have again been misused...'

'Austen?'
   'Yes, Jefferson?'
   'You've never met Bridge, have you? You weren't here last
term.'
   'Riversdale.'
   'Riversdale.'
   'No, of course not, dope. I wasn't here last term.'
   'That's what I mean. You've never met Bridge.'
   'Riversdale.'
   'Riversdale. Austen. I wish Brid... Riversdale wasn't coming
back. Austen. He's an awful cad you know, an awful cad.'
   'Riversdale's a cad?'
   'Yes, Austen. Riversdale's an awful cad.'

Riversdale's a cad, Riversdale's a cad, Riversdale's an awful
cad. But I did not kill him. I should have, but I did not. I wish I
had. I wish I had.

Basingstoke. A million terraced houses built of Minibrix.
   'Just the lemon, sir, that's right, isn't it? And no tonic this
time?'
   I piss on you, fat woman with permed grey hair and spectacles, I piss on you and on the *lumpen proletariat* and *petite
bourgeoisie* of Basingstoke.
   Well anyway on the railway line that separates your horrid
modern little houses from the bare fields, unhedged now, on the
other side. Bridge, Riversdale, Slaker. Bridge, Riversdale,
Slaker. Slaker House, Slaker House, Slaker House, Scales.
Bridge, Riversdale, Slaker, Slaker House, Scales.

As he turned on to Mountbatten Way with the Millbrook docks
(timber, containers and Renaults) on the left of the six-lane
road, the last chords of Brahms's Tragic Overture faded away.
G and T, the warm memory of his lunch with Roy, and the

possibility of a new Gold Museum to be set up in America had shifted Riversdale and Slaker House to the back of his mind from which they only occasionally reappeared in dreams or following some sudden reminder. The Jaguar cruised effortlessly past a huge truck labelled *Mitsui O. K. Lines* and he took in the fact that a beautiful evening, a really perfect evening, was developing: there was just enough cloud to make the sunset lovely but not vulgar. The fifty years of the BBC Symphony Orchestra. Beethoven's Sixth. Conducted by Arturo Toscanini, recorded over two days — 21 and 22 October 1937. Well I'm blessed!

Sir Richard Austen chuckled, sang along, and talked aloud over this coincidence: what *about* the wakening of pleasant feelings on going into the countryside, he crowed, as the Totton roundabout dropped behind him and the fields of Ashling and the first woods of the Forest opened up beyond the villas and bungalows. 21 October 1937. As the maestro, magician, anti-fascist god conjured such warmth, such delight, such finesse out of the lads and lasses of the BBC SO, he, Richard Austen, was limping down the grey and brick-red expanse of the Strand, leaning every now and then on the stout, rubber-shod ashplant he had bought the day before in Above Bar, Southampton, looking about at the dismal banks, hotels, shops and between each block the side roads that dropped to the Embankment. D'Oyly Carte at the Savoy, just as it had been when he went at Christmas with his mother and Slaker cousins, the clattering news vans bustling up past him from Fleet Street, and just where the hell was King Street? He walked the wrong way round Covent Garden — at three in the afternoon a wasteland of dropped shutters, strewn cabbage leaves, and orange dahlias crushed in the gutters — before he found it.

'I want to join the Party...' Then unaccustomedly humble. 'That is, if you'll have me. I was at Guernica.' And I still have the scars rippled and ribbed like sand or mud all down the inside of my left shin to prove it. (Over the railway now into the Forest proper; oh my goodness how gorgeous the oaks, now the only ones left, the birches long since shed their frippery yellows, fool's gold, the oaks only get it right, not always bright, but always more than just yellow, the tints of the true, the real...) And it had been all right. Of course, they had been expecting him, in a sense he had been sent . . . Later a tall thin man in a grey suit — Reginald, call me Reggie — had taken him to a pub in Denmark Street. Reggie wore a trilby with brim pulled down all round and had owlish spectacles. He affected a slang that put Richard in mind of Wodehouse's Psmith. That he was in the company of someone who had actually been at Guernica seemed to have been the greatest thing that had ever happened to him . . . spiffing!

With peasants merrymaking, the Jaguar crunched to a halt in gravel in front of the Farm — a large late Victorian house with rhododendrons and trim lawns, set in the heart of the Forest but with its own fields around it. It really was a marvellous evening. To the left, the east, pale pink and violet above the great oaks still robed in old gold; to the west, almost buttercup yellows sank into peach. He'd take a turn before going into the house; no need to change, there had not been enough rain to make the ground miry — and still he had his ashplant, the very same, shod now with brass not rubber, standing in a tall ceramic tub in the porch.

Daws cackled above him, floating like sheets of burnt paper, and a grey squirrel scampered up a holly tree. Statue-still, he watched its progress marked by the swaying branches, then its flight, yes flight, as it launched itself across a twelve-foot gap on to the lower limbs of a beech, its few leaves a foxy red. On out on to the heath — cleared during the Napoleonic Wars to provide timber for the men-of-war and burnt to black earth four years ago during the drought when the heather had caught. They had had to evacuate the Farm, though the Hampshire Fire Brigade saved it — a dramatic day: the clouds of thick yellow smoke, the bellowing horses, Charlie the Arab stallion getting in an unscheduled and ultimately productive fuck on a mare in heat . . . now Austen marvelled, as he always did, at how quickly life had come back to the roasted earth — not heather yet, but mosses and coarse bog grasses. A pair of lapwings threw themselves across the opalescent sky and nearer, on a gorse bush that marked the limit of the fire's invasion, a stonechat clinked — exactly the noise of two flint cores tapped

58

together. Russet ponies with white bellies moved ponderously across the flat, their breath hazing the air about their heavy heads.

Leaving the plain where the fire had been below him, Austen climbed on to the low ridge that ran above the Farm and tramped along the wide gravelly ride cut through the heather by the Wainwrights' horses. A quartet of larks scurried low away from him, their plumage merging almost instantly back into the brown scrub they had come up from. Imperceptibly the evening had deepened — though the sky was still alive with colour, the air was darker and more chill. For a moment only he stood by the barrow, gorse-crowned, that he often made his turning point on an evening stroll, then he struck back to the trees that wrapped themselves snug round three sides of the Farm in the hollow beneath him. He had a sentimental ambition for that barrow — one day, next summer perhaps, he'd get George Partridge over from Lewes, and John Wainwright up from the bungalow he had retired to near Lymington, and together they'd do one last dig, repeating their first. There was no record in the county archives that it had ever been opened, though a low mound nearby suggested spill. Nevertheless, it would be worth a go — and it would have to be soon if a new Gold Museum in America really was on the cards.

The brass ferrule of his stick tapped on the tarmac of the narrow road that took him back. Soon, in front of the stables, he could see the Wainwrights' Land-Rovers and trailers, and the cars of their customers. His own red Jaguar was in front of the house. To the right of the stables was the large bungalow where Brian Wainwright, John's son, now lived with his not un-attractive but rather pushy wife — she who had suggested the switch from agriculture to up-market riding stable when Grandfather Wainwright finally succumbed to the throat cancer that had started with gas on the Somme.

And to the left, out in the woods again and underground, was the tiny and absurd fall-out shelter Austen had been told to buy and instal. He could not think of it without a smile; in its way it was touching that someone somewhere hoped he would survive the next holocaust, thought even that he might be useful after it . . .

Dum-de-de-dum-da-da
Dum-de-de-dum-da-da

The farrier was in the yard. A small man, very Iberian, darkish, balding, deep-set eyes, he came every Tuesday in a small van and set up a portable forge. Austen loved to watch him — he was still so much part of a very ancient past, for all he used Calor gas instead of charcoal and bellows, for all the shoes he brought were modern alloys not iron-cast then hammered into toughness. The anvil was the same, with its horn for curving the shoe, the hammer and the tongs and his leather apron; so was the magic broken ring of glowing metal shifting from orange gold to ruby to garnet as he placed it against the patient hoof and smoke pumped up around it in clouds above the horse's solid rump. And so was the rhythm of hammer on shoe on anvil...

Dum-de-de-dum-da-da
Dum-de-de-dum-da-da

...just like the opening of *Siegfried*, one thing that awful old fraud Wagner had bothered to get right.

Dum-de-de-dum-da-da

'Sir Richard, I've two letters for you in the office.'

Sandra Wainwright, Brian's wife, John's daughter-in-law. She was wearing a heavy sheepskin coat and fitted boots, blond hair that bobbed, a smile that almost always flirted — unless there was another woman around.

'The postman left them with our lot by mistake.'

Nothing significant in this, it happened often.

Austen took the envelopes, one small brown manila, the other white thick, expensive, addressed with a carbon-ribboned electric. He thanked her, put them in his pocket, walked up the flagged path and round the house to his own front door, dropped his ashplant in the ceramic tub, and then took out the envelopes again.

Later he was to say to himself that, in the second before he opened it, he knew. From the brown manila he took a single sheet of blank note paper, folded once.

Dum-de-de-dum-da-da

60

Automaton-like, he turned to the second; he had to read it twice before it made sense, and then of course he realised that they went together... they must.

Dr Olivia Shapiro of Milton University, Iowa, is doing a study of seminal importance on the intellectual climate of Cambridge (UK) University in the 1930s with particular reference to its interpenetration by Marxist ideologues... may I take the liberty of asking you to receive her... a matter of two or three interviews... a man of your eminence I know must ration his time most carefully... Dr Shapiro has a reputation as an entirely serious yet brilliant scholar... The Dean of Arts, Milton.

And, attached, a note written in such meticulous italic that it was difficult not to think that it also had been typed on a machine with a fancy letter face, asking him to ring the above London number... her time was his, but Monday through to Wednesday, the 17th to 19th... she would stay at the local hotel of course.

Christ, that's next week.

Austen moved into his large house and paused at the telephone in the hall. It is axiomatic that you should cooperate in every possible way — he had no important engagements before Roy Newman's visit at the end of that week, perhaps they knew that.

Who 'they' were was not clear. CIA presumably, since Shapiro was American. But one thing was sure. The folded page of blank paper taken from the other envelope signified danger. Control had told him that nearly half a century ago. He thought on for a moment. Slaker, Lord Slaker, his cousin and patron, was, he knew, on the point of signing computer contracts with the Soviets. He should be told. Austen lifted the phone, took three deep breaths to compose himself, and dialled.

7

There was, after all, more to Registry Three than Cargill had seen on his previous two visits: though much of it had no doubt been cleared of paper and re-equipped as a fall-out shelter for middle-grade civil servants, there was still quite a little complex of cubicles, small rooms, a canteen, cloakroom and so on placed at the end of the short corridor which now made up the core of the archive — the core for built into the walls were sixteen hundred drawers each containing fifty microfiche wallets. It was into this complex that Sally took him when he returned the next day, putting him in a small cubicle with its own VDU. There was a small stack of microfiche wallets beside it and two chairs in front of it.

For an hour or so she explained what she had discovered, flipping the dark blue rectangles of celluloid out of their wallets, into the tray, manipulating the tray back and forth, stabbing at the display with a thin gold pen to make a point, meticulously but briskly replacing each fiche as she finished with it. Clearly she was as familiar with this new technology as, say, her great-great-grandmother had been with her hand-loom two centuries before. She was a pretty girl too: about twenty-five, blonde, blue eyes, dressed in a pale blue nylon overall which entirely covered whatever she had on underneath. Only a short gold chain round her neck with a tiny gold cross swung and sparkled as she leaned forward or twisted sideways to make sure Cargill was following what she said.

She was not a bit like either of his real daughters — who were dark-haired, ochre-skinned shrews — but she was very

62

much the daughter he would have liked to have had...

She explained how, using the cross-referencing systems, she had first established that all ninety-six of the second-stage Bletchley Park suspects had been investigated, that therefore there had initially been files on all of them; later, when pressure of space became acute but before the microfiche process had begun, twenty-eight of these had been conflated into five files and material common to each had been shredded. Austen's was not one of these, but that it had happened had caused her some trouble — for a time she had thought a really quite substantial number of files had been lost. The next thing she established was that four files, three plus Austen's, had definitely been removed from Registry Three, and that in three cases anyway this had been done before they were put on microfiche.

There had of course been a procedure for removing files legitimately — a specially prepared microfiche explained what this had been. First, you had to get the proper authorisation in the proper form — a chit signed by both the Director and the junior minister of the day. One of the duty clerks then issued the file, tagged the space with a small plastic tab on which she or he carefully printed the number of the file, the date and the reference number of the authorisation; then the transaction was recorded on the index card in the catalogue, and finally logged in the logbook. There had always been two duty clerks on duty at once, and the second had to initial the whole business at each stage. With three of the missing files this procedure had been properly carried out and they could be traced to Registry One, the Director's private archive. The relevant index cards and pages from the logbook were all there on microfiche. The tabs, Sally said, would be with the rest of the B-P archive in the abandoned coalmine.

Cargill asked whose files these had been: it turned out one was of a politician who had reached cabinet rank in the Ministry of Defence; the second had become chairman of the Atomic Energy Commission, and the third was that of the man who was now Director of the Service.

'Wouldn't it be fun to know what was in them?' Sally chortled, 'I mean they must be jolly sensitive to be tucked away in Registry One, where only C can see them.'

Cargill was amused to find that clerks of Sally's grade still called the Director 'C'.

And so back to Austen's file, and the reason for all the meticulous work Sally had put into the business. The plain fact was that, as far as she could see, and she had been as thorough as she knew how, it was missing. That is, it had been stolen or lost, probably before the tagging procedure became operational — she believed it had been set up in the early fifties. The first reference in the logbook was dated August 1951.

'Why before?' Cargill asked.

'Well, it's almost foolproof. Whoever took it would have had to forge authorisation, suborn two clerks, remove the index card from the catalogue as well as the file itself, and at the end of it all the Johnny on the door would have gone through his briefcase. But, before August 1951, anyone, as far as I can make out, who was of station commander rank or above could have just come in, signed a chit and taken out what he wanted. And I don't suppose it was that difficult to remove the chit later. People were awfully slack in those days.'

'What's to stop anyone going off with a microfiche or two now?'

'Well, of course we check that everything anyone has been using is back in its wallet and the wallet back in its drawer before they go. And there's an electronic warning system too.'

'Bells ring, nerve gas pumps into the lift, portcullises drop, if you pass beyond a certain point with one in your pocket.'

'Something like that,' she laughed.

'Unless your briefcase is lined with lead. Which mine is.'

'Oh, go on with you.' She giggled this time, and both moved together to turn off the illuminated screen — the switch was above eye level — and in the confusion the back of Cargill's hand just brushed the side of her breast. He blushed and said nothing, but a smile as subtle as the Mona Lisa's momentarily relaxed the muscles of her face.

She went, and Cargill sat in the semi-darkness of the cubicle playing slowly with a pencil — passing his fingers down the barrel, reversing it, and so on.

The disappearance of Austen's file was, he was tempted to

believe, conclusive. Something there must have been in it which had, at the time of the investigation, seemed innocuous but which, in the light of later evidence, implicated the knighted archaeologist beyond reasonable doubt. Now, the only evidence to come to light since Riversdale had been accepted as the spy and the whole business had been closed were the Abwehr telegrams — the ENIGMA coded messages sent by Gehlen to the Americans indicating the Bavarian farmhouse codenamed Misery Meadow where the German Secret Services' Russian files were hidden in April 1945. These had been monitored and decoded by the British at Bletchley Park; Austen had presumably realised their importance and passed them on to his Russian control. And all this had come to light only a matter of a week or so ago, thanks to the American computer PSIKE: say, at the most — allowing for the Housemaster to have put the matter to a committee or two before calling in Cargill — a fortnight.

It was, therefore, at least as likely that Austen's file had been removed *not* from the old paper Registry before 1951 but from the microfiche one in the last few days: in other words, he was still protected either by someone very senior in the Service or there was a Russian agent in the Registry who had got the microfiche out, or who had suborned the Librarian or one of the girls to do it for him. Of course the simplest way to keep it out of Cargill's hands was simply to lose it: anyone with access to the catalogues and the drawers could remove the microfiche from its wallet and slip it in another somewhere else. With something over eighty thousand wallets, each with fifteen fiches, it could remain hidden for a long time without even leaving the building. The same too could have happened to those elements in the Riversdale file that connected Austen with the case against him.

It was surely ninety percent certain that whoever had removed or hidden the microfiches or arranged for it to be done was of Cargill's rank or higher: he would have to be, to know that the Bletchley Park case had been reopened. His mind went back to his earlier visit to Registry Three, the day the Housemaster had first briefed him. There had been a delay then. The Librarian had not been able to produce the Bletchley Park Suspects file straightaway. Why not? Because in it was the reference number which would locate the Austen file? And someone was already using it to do just that?

Cargill smiled grimly. There was more to all this than exposing Austen — who surely was old news anyway, even staler than Blunt had been. But someone was protecting Austen, and doing so because if Austen was exposed then that someone would be exposed too. In fact — and here Cargill suddenly longed to smoke (this was surely a two-pipe job), already he was wrestling with the cold, noxious bowl and occasionally sucking on the cracked mouthpiece — was it not really most probable that there was a lot more to this whole business than met the eye? Rumours of a mole still in the very top ranks of the Service had never been entirely stilled, and the fact that the Hollis thing was going to break out in two or three months' time — everyone from deputy assistant director upwards had already been briefed that it would — had started an epidemic of paranoia that left no one unaffected, least of all Cargill.

Might not this whole Austen business be a way of smoking him out? Might it not even have been initiated with that end in view? With Cargill himself as the tool, manipulated in ways he could not understand? He would, he now saw, have to move very carefully, as if in a minefield or a booby-trapped house. Clearly, to start an enquiry into who had had access to the Bletchley Park files during the last week apart from himself would instantly alert the mole. He would have to think of a subtler approach than that.

Austen himself was still the line to follow, and the safer one too. After all he was meant to be investigating Austen (assuming, as he did now, that Austen was the real B-P leak), and the ultimate enemy knew that. For a day or two he would continue with Austen and see if he could not turn up another thread, another pointer, which might lead back from Austen and into the Service again.

His mind made up, he slipped on coat and muffler, picked up his hat, rammed his pipe into his outside pocket. As he stepped out of the cubicle, he heard girls' laughter — a decrescendo of chiming crystals ending on a snigger.

'The dirty old man,' a voice said, and he hurried on past the small cloakroom where Sally was touching up her lipstick while two of her friends, already in outdoor clothes, stood waiting for her.

He strode down the darkening streets — grey trim, pumping out smoke behind him like a steam-powered frigate — and the hurt of what he had overhead quickly faded as he planned his next steps. A glance at the illumined face of Big Ben told him that the Housemaster would have gone home, that a duty officer with rank equal to his own would be in charge. This was all to the good, for he had now decided to order a grade-one surveillance on Austen — a phone tap, a full team of trackers equipped with cars and radios, a black bag job on his house and office at the Gold Museum involving miniature TV cameras, the lot. The expense of such an operation is of course enormous, but he felt he now had enough on Austen to justify it, or at any rate to give a reasonable defence of his decision if or when it was challenged. And that really was the point. Cargill did not really expect to learn anything from the surveillance, but it was a good way of testing the water, laying groundbait. If Austen did have an uncle in the Service, then sooner or later the order would come from on high to drop the surveillance, and that in itself would be a pointer.

Meanwhile, there was the dossier on Austen he had requisitioned from Research to pick up, and *The Burning Matrix* to read. By the time he reached St James's he was almost high, humming to himself the tenor line from the Hosanna of Berlioz's *Grande Messe des Morts* (for fifteen years he had held his place in one of the big London choirs, losing it in the end when professionally trained singers finally took over) . . . he'd get the nasty little sneaks yet, he thought, the sneaks.

8

An hour and half later he was at home — a large, sprawling, and, in the last few years, far too expensive Victorian flat in a block off the Brompton Road, not far from the Oratory. He had grilled himself a chop (he did all his own housework), played the first movement of one of the simpler Mozart piano sonatas on the baby grand that stood in the window of his living room, and was now at his desk with the heavy curtains drawn. A very weak Scotch and soda stood at his elbow and in front of him was Research's dossier, with *The Burning Matrix* beside it.

Richard Hugh Austen: born 17.9.14. Father: the Reverend James Austen, Rector of South Meon in Hampshire. Mother: Augusta, née Slaker-Fox.

'My father, like his father before him, was a High Tory of the old School, that is to say of the school of Lord Liverpool and the Duke of Wellington rather than Disraeli. Through his maternal grandmother he was descended from the Earls of Oxford. He did not mention this often — perhaps only twice in my hearing over the twenty-eight years I knew him — but that was enough. We had our place in society and it was sufficiently near the top of the heap for it to be important to maintain it — that is, to work for those above us and against those below us. Already it will seem that he and I did not always hit it off, and that I am afraid was indeed the case. Nevertheless, he had his qualities: he was abstemious, narrowly learned, had what he thought were the best interests of his flock at heart (they almost never agreed with him as to what these were) and had for a time a residual or embryonic social conscience. Through which he apparently met my mother.

'She was, is — well not a different kettle of fish; she's not at all like a kettle of any sort — but *very* different. They met in 1912 at one of those East End missions which were so popular then: tea and buns, soup even, and two pennies for the doss house provided you attended Evensong sober and reasonably clean. The whole administered by ladies and gentlemen of substantial means. I think it a dreadful comment on the neediness of those times that the poor of the city actually did turn up — I should need to be very hungry indeed to sit through an ill-performed service with a sermon exhorting patience, promising me my reward in heaven, and hymns emphasising that the Lord God ordered my estate. Thank... not God, but better directed efforts than those missions, that things are better now, in England anyway.

'My mother was much younger than my father. He was already fifty when they met, she only twenty-three. He was handsome, well connected, and in the context of the mission she presumed he shared some of her beliefs and tastes. This was mistaken. It turned out that they had almost nothing in common at all; but those being the times they were, and their position in society being what it was, they were stuck with each other and that was that. They remained on sufficiently close terms to have me and after that were intimate only as much as the conventions demanded — which was very little. They ate together, talked about money matters, my education, household affairs when they had to, and for the most part were polite to each other even when no one else was around.

'My mother was, is, a Slaker-Fox. That is to say, on one side she is connected with one of those splendid, enterprising, tough business families that built up out of ruthless trading the wealth of Victorian, Imperial England — oh, dear me, how my poor father despised them — and on the other side she comes from the Warwickshire squirearchy with a coat-of-arms almost as old as the Austens, and that my father tolerated. But she is far more Slaker than Fox. She has taste, intelligence, is well informed when her memory allows her to be. If she had married almost anyone else she would have been one of those jolly, bustling country ladies who know everything — all about the flowers in Shakespeare, how to bake, who is the most exciting painter at the Academy this year, and so on. In fact, come to think of it, away from my father, that is much how she was. Ruskin was an idol — Grandfather Slaker used to entertain the Prophet when he passed through the Midlands; needless to say, he thought Ruskin was sounder on Giotto than on social reform.

'She is alive but unfortunately, since I am not a trained nurse, is now in a home where I visit her at least twice a week...'

Education: The Meads School, Old Biggin Bay, Northumberland, 1922-27.

'... so long as I made it to the College, preferably as a scholar, my father had no deep feelings about prep schools. Slakers, however, had had the dust of ledgers washed out of their hair, and the Liverpool, later Birmingham, nasality out of their vowels at The Meads since the 1870s; my mother's father and brothers had been there, so I went too. It was not a happy time. If the place still exists, then I apologise. I'm sure it's much better now. It could hardly be otherwise and escape prosecution on a variety of charges ranging from corruption of minors to assault and battery.'

Beaufort College, Wintoncester, Hampshire: 1927-32.

'My time at the College was, however, not a bad time, not bad at all. The most awful thing about the prep school was home-sickness, which never really wore off. At Wintoncester I could look across the long roof of the Abbey and see a spur of the downs, my beloved chalk downs of Sussex, Hampshire and Dorset, and know that ten miles on the other side was the dear old rectory of South Meon. Although weekend *exeats* were not encouraged, they could be arranged, especially at half-terms, and anyway it was just the knowledge that home was so near that made all the difference. In fact, of course, Wintoncester already was home: and the part of that lovely town the College occupies, which had hitherto been a walled-off mystery, soon merged into the rest and I made little distinction between them. I think most Collegians do the same.

70

'Of course, in the early days, there were still unpleasantnesses to be put up with or avoided: fagging, beating, compulsory sport, which I detested, and an approach to teaching, especially in Latin and maths, which was positively medieval. It is still a matter of considerable surprise to me that the College has produced so many great classical scholars and scholars in other fields such as my own where the classics are an asset if not an essential. I can only think that the masochism that was so much part of other aspects of public school life affected them intellectually as well as... well, emotionally, shall we say?

'I was no Latinist, and Greek remained a mystery, and one of the real rows I had with my father was when I failed this *sine que non* of matriculation at what was in those days known as School Certificate. However, a second try took me over that hurdle, and from then on I breathed the freer air of an *urbanus*, as we were called once safely in the Lower Sixth. From now on, the College was a delight. I found academic areas where I could excel, particularly in History and German; I could ignore the dreaded Rugby Football field if I registered my presence adequately often in the Squash Courts; in the summer I surprised many people and not least myself by developing a respectable talent as a left-arm slow bowler. But the greatest delight was to be found in the various societies and clubs that flourished — some officially, some tolerated, some very much underground. One of these last had initiation rites which would have made those of Hell's Angels or Solomon Islanders seem like Anglican Confirmation by comparison.

'Through the more respectable of these, I developed my abiding love of music; I learnt to draw a little, which stood me in good stead in my chosen profession (and may I, in parenthesis, refer anyone who thinks photography has ousted sound draughtsmanship as an essential in the complete archaeologist's battery of skills to what Sir Mortimer Wheeler has to say on the subject?); and I came through the offices of one remarkable man to an initial understanding of the two principal obsessions of my life: socialism and archaeology. The man in question was Herbert Heath, surely one of the best masters ever to usher at the College, a man of whom more anon. But first let me say that he did not introduce me to archaeology and socialism. That

71

came about in the summer of 1929 and in this really rather remarkable way.

'One hot day at the end of July my mother came upon me listless and bored as adolescents so often are and on the spur of the moment organised the gardener, the gardener's boy, and two out of work lads from the village (there were many such at that wretched time) to assist me in opening what I now know to have been a bell barrow with ditch, but until then had been nothing so grand — just a lump of Wealden sand covered with gorse, known as Jacob's Tump...'

The mandarin prose continued to trundle along at its self-congratulatory, bland gait. Cargill, who had won a scholarship to a very minor place in the north of England run according to progressive principles by Unitarians — short corduroy trousers, cold baths, estate management high on the curriculum (a way of cutting out labour costs) — and which invariably prompted the reaction 'Where did you say? I don't know that I ever heard of it before' whenever he was asked where he was at, was already finding *The Burning Matrix* a bore. Clearly, if it was going to reveal anything at all significant about Austen, it was going to be through what it left unsaid, rather than through anything explicit. For instance, he did not actually state whether or not he had been a member of the secret society with the *grand guignol* initiation rites... Cargill rather thought that the implication was that he had.

He filled and lit his pipe and set himself to re-read what he had already gone through, only this time noting the points where he felt there were lacunae. If this was drudgery, never mind: it was part of the job in hand.

9

'Burgess and Maclean?' Dr Olivia Shapiro asked briskly. 'Did you know them?'

Richard Austen set down the blue and white porcelain cup and saucer he had been drinking coffee from, put his head on one side like, he hoped, a cheeky sparrow or a spaniel puppy, and said, 'Well, no, not really. Should I? I mean should I have known them?'

Dr Olivia Shapiro drew in her breath sharpishly — not quite the sigh of a teacher irritated at the obtuseness of a pupil, but near enough. She looked around, turning camelish eyes on the bookshelves that surrounded her, on the cases filled with fragments of stone, metal and pottery, at the large Purbeck stone fireplace filled with blazing logs. Her camelish teeth chewed on fragments of chocolate mint and her tongue, camelish too, but moving with the brief suddenness of a snake's, gathered in a green crystal from the corner of her mouth.

'Well, yes.' Her Virginian drawl was more obvious than ever. 'Well, yes, I should have thought so.'

A log dropped an inch or so and sparks flew up the chimney.

Sir Richard cleared his throat.

'Guy I did know. Maclean I never met. But not at Cambridge. I ran into Guy during the war. Mutual acquaintances, you know. Parties and that. *You* know — the Blitz and after.' He waited hopefully, listening to the noises of the fire and beyond that a steady chorus of birds. But Dr Olivia Shapiro just waited — her eyes fixed on the Edwardian brass electric

73

lamp-fitting above their heads. 'Well, you know,' he went on, 'that scene's well enough documented — Waugh and Powell in fiction, Connolly, Goronwy...oh, you *know*. At least, you should.'

Dr Shapiro's eyebrows rose a fraction at this. The implication was clear. If she was, as she said she was, researching into the intellectual left of the thirties and forties in Great Britain, then presumably she had done the required reading...

'Sure. But you were at Cambridge. Let's see...' She didn't glance at notes, but applied some mnemonic instead, a mental retrieval system — the sort of technique, Austen imagined, typically advertised in the *Reader's Digest*. 'October '32 to June '35. So you overlapped with all of them.'

'All of them?'

'Oh , come on. You know. All of them.'

'Dobb? Dutt? Haldane?'

'If you like.' She refused to be baited. 'But Maclean, how do you say, went *up* in '31; Blunt got his fellowship in '32; Philby...'

Austen stood up. Slowly, unbaited — he hoped. But the cup clinked in his saucer as he carried it to the French window. He looked down a gently sloping meadow to oak trees, a small pond, another field, and so to more oaks, an occasional ash, and then heath climbed to a crest of gorse and conifers. Twin chimneys beyond this pumped white vapour into a grey sky. Nearby, in the fields, ten or fifteen ponies and horses nibbled at muddy grass.

'Just hark at the sparrows and chaffinches,' he said. 'Just hark. I mean, well. Could do with a drop of oil, eh? I suspect Bronze Age carts in Galicia sounded like that. Certainly the ones they used in 1936 did. Bringing in the second crop of hay in July. Pipe playing in front, some cheerful ditty or other. And General Mola on the wireless.'

Perhaps Dr Shapiro sighed again. Austen set his cup down on the sideboard, eyed the decanters and thought, no, I won't. I'll wait till this hag has gone.

'I never knew them. None of them at all. Not, that is, at Cambridge.'

'But you were a communist. I mean you joined the party.'

74

'In '37. Two years after I went down. Yes. And left it, with many hundreds, in '39.'

'The Molotov-Ribbentrop pact.'

'Quite.'

'But why join...'

Suddenly he was irritated.

'My good woman, I was at Guernica. Actually there. I mean, it's in my memoirs... I make no secret of it. It's there in...'

'In *The Burning Matrix*. Chapter Four. Yes, of course I've read it. But I don't believe in Conversion on the Road to Damascus.' Dr Shapiro paused, plucked a large glossy bag from the floor by her chair, fixed a cigarette a yard long between her lips, and lit it from a large gas-fuelled lighter. Austen's nostrils wrinkled at the sudden assault of menthol flavoured fumes. 'So, if it wasn't Cambridge, *what* was it?'

Maybe she is writing a book. Maybe she is not CIA after all. She has a thesis, a theory. Cambridge in the Thirties. Well, all that's too simple, Austen thought. I won't play.

'Listen,' he said. 'At Cambridge I spent very little time on politics. I had a sad and silly love affair; sexual ignorance in those days was quite unbelievable, and I tried to get on at the ADC.'

'Amateur theatricals.'

'Not so bloody amateur. James Mason, Michael Redgrave, George Ry... as you see, the competition was a bit stiff. Anyway I was a swat.'

'Double first. History, and Archaeology and Anthropology.'

Austen inclined his head ironically.

'Still there must have been a preparation. A background, I mean, to your conversion. Really, Sir Richard, I would be most awfully in your debt if you could give me the benefit of an insight into all that...'

1926. On the pavement of Bedford Place, Southampton. Father, tall, gaunt, dressed all in black, apart from his clerical collar, with his hand on the small boy's shoulder. 'Good fit then, are they?' 'Oh yes, sir.' 'Good. Should be. Made to fit. Made on your own last... Oh, I say, well done.' The Reverend James Austen took off his homburg in a wide salute as a maroon corporation double-decker chugged by. 'Show those loafers a thing or two,' he crowed. And he waved his fist at the pickets on the opposite pavements. One of them, in a red muffler in spite of the heat, and a flat hat, spat back.

1922. A small boy, seven years old, hair fair, almost white, his hands over his tiny genitals, weeping, weeping. 'It won't come off, Austen. I can't get it off...' And later Austen said, 'I don't know, I don't know.' He had turned away. Gone and played marbles. Or conkers. Or learnt *The Lay of the Last Minstrel* for prep. But turned away. 'Austen. I can't get it off.'

1931. The lodge the College had in the Hampshire countryside for musical weekends, Anglican retreats and so forth. The local hunt meeting on the gravel forecourt. Red-faced, pop-eyed men; women pale in black, side-saddle, with veils — every one a Medusa; hounds snapping at hooves and the whippers-in doing just that. Cherry brandy lifted on silver salvers to shoulder height by little grey men in green aprons. Cacophony of horses neighing, dogs yapping, and foul language from the men on the horses. 'Well, Austen,' Herbert Heath had said to him, 'there they are. They are our rulers now.' And one of the horses opened its round anus and dropped hot yellow turds at their feet.

... Austen drank whisky and then set the tumbler by his now empty coffee cup. Dr Shapiro smoked away, definitely and positively refusing to admit that a small display of bad manners had happened.

Refreshed, and pleased that he had poured drink for himself and without surrendering to the social pressure to offer her one too, Austen cleared his throat and reached for the bookshelf.

'In 1930 my mother gave me this book.' He read from the spine. '*The Bronze Age* by V. Gordon Childe. A year or so later a teacher at school who was in love with me, but that was not the reason why, the reason was... well, he gave me this one. *The Coming Struggle for Power* by John Strachey.' He concealed a tiny burp behind his hand and mentally noted that really he had much better not drink any more. Not, at any rate, until this frightful woman had gone. 'I found them both most... (steady now)... influential.'

'Oh, really?'

'Yes, really. Let me see. How about this... "military requisition and monopolistic control of ores further restricted the supply. At the same time the state of universal war increased the demand to unprecedented proportions. In continental Europe we witness not only the struggle for land but also one for the control of ores..." Sounds familiar, eh? But that's Childe writing about the Late Bronze Age. Not the Late Iron Age of the 1930s. It was illuminating to a boy of sixteen with a curious mind and an already deep-seated distrust of whatever those in charge had to say about anything.'

'Ah. There we are, Sir Richard. Just why this distrust...'

'Or this,' bearing down over her interruption, '"the sacrifice of neolithic self-sufficiency was only possible when certain sociological and economic conditions had been fulfilled... the effective demand for and use of metal is only possible when a certain stage of development has been reached..." Do you know, in that, lurking like a virus, is the evil doctrine of Historical Materialism? In spite of half a century of treatment ranging from the mystifications of an Academe that has plunged its head into the sand and us into a new Dark Age on the one side, to the temptations of money, prestige, position on the other...' He gestured vaguely with the cut-glass tumbler at the book-lined room, the Turkey kilims, the fields filled with horses beyond. '... I remain infected.

'Or take this...' stopping again her opening mouth and picking up the Strachey. '"All sorts of devices are resorted to in order to induce the native peasants, who own their own simple means of production, to come and work on the white man's plantations. The most common is the well-known imposition of a hut tax. A tax of a given amount is placed on a native's hut in order to make it necessary for him to earn money. He is then enabled to earn the sum of money which he must subsequently hand over to the tax-gatherer by working on the plantation of a white landowner. It is one of the triumphs of the League of Nations that its jurists have been able to detect a difference between this procedure and the imposition of forced labour..." Now I read that in 1932. And there was a programme on TV only two or three nights ago which showed exactly that process

77

at work in Brazil now — except that, in this case, the peasants found that through some legal trickery the palm trees they thought they owned had been stolen, I mean acquired, by a giant coconut-processing firm...'

'You *still* believe all that?'

'Oh, yes.' The excitement, enthusiasm, that had made him such a popular lecturer had hold of him now. Dr Shapiro watched with wary, slightly amused eyes as the little man bounced round his warm rich room, slopping very good-quality Scotch, spitting slightly on plosives, really working himself up into quite a state.

'You see, that's still the sort of thing that underpins the British Way of Life. And yours too. Cheap tin from Bolivia. Cheap copper from Zambia. Cheap sugar, cheap coffee, cheap tea, cheap fruit. Cheap shirts from sweat shops in Seoul and Taiwan, cheap toys from Hong Kong. And what little we do pay goes, after the bosses have bought their Mercedes and topped up their Swiss bank accounts, to pay for arms bought from us to prop up corrupt regimes who rely on murder and concentration camps to stay in power. What else? Even our universities, schools, libraries, research foundations that our liberals find such a comfort only represent the accummulated capital of three hundred years of looting...'

'Sure. I know the line of argument...'

'Do you? Really? What else? Millions dead through famine and civil war from Biafra to Namibia, from El Salvador to Tierra del Fuego, so client and compliant states can be maintained where colonies were before. And these things not only pay our masters, they also serve to keep our honest, reforming British workers in slavish contentment — with a level of class consciousness that can scarcely rise even as high as an occasional worry about the right to picket...'

'Oh, really?'

'And then there's the back-up, Dr Shapiro. The Special Patrol Groups, and those johnnies who murdered everyone that moved in the Iranian Embassy, what are they called? Yes, the SAS. And surveillance of everyone who dissents. Complacent coroners and vetted juries. Well, I mustn't bore you, but these are just a few of the things, of my favourite things, that underpin the good old BWL.'

Dr Shapiro felt that he was less coherent now. And, like most of her sort, she found what she called the bleeding-heart syndrome in socialist apologetics distasteful.

'What you're saying then, Sir Richard, is that you are still a Marxist, a socialist...'

'Yes. Absolutely. Never denied it, made no secret of it. It's all in the record. In *The Burning Matrix* and elsewhere. I've stood by it all my life, and it's got me into trouble often enough.'

'But you've never worked actively? I mean not since you left the party in '39. How do you equate that with Marxist theories of praxis?'

Suddenly he sat down in the large armchair. His face glowed, perhaps from the firelight, perhaps from drink. Perhaps, Dr Shapiro realised with a faint twinge of excited alarm, he was angry.

'I've done my bit.' The tumbler, now almost empty again, turned between his palms. It too, like his eyes, glittered. 'I've done my bit. Oh, not in any fancy way like all those fancy boys you were on about earlier. Just by the way I have taught, developed my discipline. By using my position. A nudge here, a little pressure there. But you brought up Marxist theory, and you must know that individual action counts for very little. It is the collective will of the proletariat that will change things... Ha! That sounds like claptrap to you, but you wanted to know so let me go on. Bourgeois intellectual sympathisers like me have never done much. Got in the way really, if the truth be known. Althusser, New Left, all that nit-picking. By and large our sort have done more harm than good.'

The fire crackled, and then there came a tiny little knocking noise that Dr Shapiro had heard before but failed to trace; now she followed Austen's gaze, turned her head and saw two blue-tits pecking at a half-coconut suspended on a string from the lintel of the French window. As they pecked, the shell tapped on the glass of the highest pane. She moved again, and with a tiny whirr of wings they zoomed back into the cypress tree that stood ten yards away — tiny toys of azure and dusty yellow, white and black.

'And you have been to Russia, which is more than most members of the New Left can say.'

'Yes, indeed. Indeed. I've made seven trips in the last ten years, developing links with the Leningrad Archaeology Institute and so on. I've even learnt enough Russian to get round GUM without making a fool of myself. But that's got nothing to do with what you are meant to be interested in.'

Dr Shapiro nodded her head minutely.

'Back to the thirties then. To what extend would you say the position you took up was a response to fascism?'

But Sir Richard had had enough. He stood up and quite bluntly said so.

'Perhaps then we can go into that tomorrow?'

'Tomorrow?'

'I'm booked in at the Hythe Road Hotel for at least two nights. My letter asked for at least two interviews.'

Austen made a show of consulting the small black leather-bound notebook. He sighed, ostentatiously. 'I'm afraid I can't manage tomorrow. Three thirty, Wednesday, all right?' I'm not giving her another lunch. And he pencilled it in with a gold pencil. 'Three thirty. Shapiro. Anti-fascism. Tea. Fine.'

At the front door he ignored her hand and her thanks but then took her elbow and led her to the corner of the house where the view was the same as from the large study they had been in.

'Those two chimneys. You see? They are Marchwood power station. In a direct line between us and them, just over the ridge, there is a concealed American base. Mostly underground. Probably stuffed with nuclear warheads. Something for you to think of until we meet again. I mean, if you feel homesick. There is some corner of a foreign land, you know?'

Silly man, she thought, as she got into her hired Renault. Silly little man.

10

There was a yellow Post Office van outside the gate; two men, one of them up the telephone pole. A week earlier they had spent four days laying a cable right across the Farm, up the hill, and across the heath on the other side. Austen was sure it was part of the American web of telecommunications that now stitches together their bases in Britain. At all events, yellow vans were a familiar part of his landscape and he gave this one no further thought.

He cleared away the coffee things to the pantry where one of the stable girls would find them when she came in at six o'clock — that this happened was part of the symbiotic relationship he had with the Wainwrights. The girls worked for no money in the stables, just for the dubious pleasure of managing horses and getting advanced riding lessons free. They were grateful to earn actual cash doing Austen's housework.

Back in the study he put *The Coming Struggle for Power* back on the shelf and sat down in his big chair with a fresh Scotch in one hand, and *The Bronze Age* in the other. Dear old mums. Her way of saying sorry. Sorry because she had landed him with such a pig of a father.

An old film, edited over the years no doubt, played back in his mind — the fire burned low and the darkness silenced the birds; outside the grey sky came closer, touched the distant chimneys of Marchwood and as night fell a steady drizzle came on.

A morning in late July, already hot, the sash windows of the

81

Rectory school room open top and bottom and all the distractions imaginable washed in on heavily scented billows of warm air. A boy, a youth really, sat at a desk too small for him and struggled disconsolately, inaccurately and sporadically with *The Times* fourth leader for the 27th. With the aid of *Kennedy's Eating Primer*, North and Hilliard, and a gradus, it was to be put into Ciceronian prose by lunchtime. Pinned like a notice of execution to the tiny blackboard at his shoulder was a sheet of paper he had come to hate — his school report:

'I can hold out no hope at all that Austen will have passed the School Certificate in Latin this term. I most earnestly suggest hard disciplined study between now and December when he will have a possibly last chance to gain this *sine qua non* of matriculation. His translations into English are adequate, his mastery of the set texts less so. However, it is his prose that is so disastrous, and this, with concomitant revision and instruction in grammar, is where most strenuous effort should be made.'

Outside, a murmur of voices — female — his mother's gentle, careful, and that of Mary, the new kitchen maid, chirpy, bright, anxious to please.

'Of Ur Mr GADD says that its "history ends in grosser darkness than it begins". The gaps, he points out, in its chronology are enormous, inviting the rash to play with centuries of millennia as with days ... and Mr WOOLLEY, as these columns have recorded, has found an alluvial deposit which can be none other than a consequence of the Flood... the new knowledge of empires, dynasties and cultures, unsuspected a generation ago, has been largely if not mainly the gift of Englishmen — among them in particular EVANS in Crete, PETRIE and CARTER in Egypt, and WOOLLEY in "the Land".'

Whatever did it mean — 'the Land'? Was *ratio temporum* really the Latin for 'chronology'? Wearily he recited the third-declension noun endings, but before he reached the ablative a large bumble-bee that had been blundering around for some time thundered against the windowpane.

Surely the Reverend James Austen, man of Christ, would deem it a necessary act of mercy to help the foolish creature back into the sunlight?

Richard held a wooden ruler horizontally across the path of the bee. Laboriously it clambered aboard. Then he turned the ruler through a right angle and watched the silly beast haul itself upwards. It managed an inch, seemed likely to fall, so the boy gave a quick flick of the rule and launched it into the open space above the window catch. He watched its lurching, zooming flight out across the kitchen garden and wondered if he had condemned it to death in a swallow's maw. But they were nothing but circling, wheeling, inaudible specks in the hazy violet sky, hundreds of feet above the sleepy elms, the odoriferous lime tree, and the copper beech that stood in the corner nearest the churchyard just to the left of the Wilderness and Jacob's Tump.

'Oh, mum, be they peaches on that wall? I've never seen peaches on their tree before, I'm sure. Not often anywhere else, come to that.'

'Nectarines, Mary. And this year we shall have a reasonable crop, I think.'

Richard pulled himself to the side so the brown velvet curtain and a clump of virginia creeper grown unruly hid him. Below, almost directly below, stood his mother, small, trim, dressed neatly in a summer frock, almost concealed from where he was by the sunhat she wore, and Mary Partridge, a girl about his age whom he had always thought rather wild, but now, on her first day as second kitchen maid to the Austens, very clean and neat in black trimmed with *broderie anglaise*.

'There, Mary, I think I've shown you everything...' The young girl bobbed her head, and her short reddish hair lifted to show white, oh very white, skin across the nape of her neck. She had freckles on her face and on her arms; Richard knew this because he had seen her at the village shop buying a screw of tobacco for her father, the blacksmith, and once also giggling and larking with two girl friends in the water meadows by the river amongst the yellow flags and dragonflies. And freckles where else? Where else, he thought, and felt a sudden explosion of excitement in his diaphragm which left him dizzy and hot.

'Of course you must take only what Cook tells you to — I expect today she will want broad beans and perhaps raspberries...'

'Yes, mum.'

'And you will always be most particular with the bird-netting, won't you?'

'Yes, mum.'

Each time she bobbed, the skin of her neck and even her shoulders flashed white again.

'I'm sure you will. You seem a very sensible girl.'

'Thank you, mum.'

'Well, off you go, back to Cook.'

'Yes, mum.'

For five minutes Richard wrestled with an evil mixture of Latin gerunds, fantasies about Mary-by-the-river, and feelings of desperate, seering guilt — a mixture which blossomed like some foul black flower as the potency between his legs grew and throbbed, stabbing into the dark, hot spaces left by loose-fitting cotton underpants and flannel bags. It would not go away. It would *not* go away. Not unless ... but God said ... father said ... mother, your mother, if your mother knew you could fall so ...

'Richard. Richard? Have you forgotten it is usual to stand up in the presence of... Oh. Oh dear me. I am sorry. I will come back in ten minutes. Yes.' He heard the door close then open again, but through tears of grief, rage and pain — for at that very moment he had clenched every muscle in his lower abdomen into a most fearful cramp and his rebellious fist too to hold in a gush of semen that would not for all that be dammed. His mother stayed on the landing this time and pitched her voice higher. 'Your father has gone out. He has gone to Wintoncester. Richard. I'm sure you need not be distressed. Please do not be distressed. I will come back in ten minutes. Do you understand? In ten minutes.' And the door clicked firmly shut.

Not wishing to be too exact, she left him for twelve, then came in very briskly and walked past him straight to the window.

'Don't be silly,' she said as he struggled dutifully to his feet. 'I was silly. No need for you to be. Richard — I've had an idea. A jolly good one. Too silly for words for you to be stuck up here on such a lovely day ... your father lacks imagination sometimes.

I'm sure your Latin will be all the better for some fresh air and healthy exercise.'

From his cramped desk Richard looked at his mother with growing puzzlement — suicidal shame ebbing away.

She kept her back to him, her dark hair, the brown fading to grizzle, bobbing in its fashionable waves above the slightly mottled skin of *her* neck, and the slightly stubby fingers of one hand played with the window catch. She wore a thin gold watch which glinted on her bony wrist, and a flowered dress which hung from rather than enclosed her body. Dimly, it occurred to him that she was thinner than she had been.

'I think you should do some digging.'

This — because it echoed one of the school chaplain's preventatives against masturbation — provoked a sort of subdued snort from him, and at last she turned. Her brown eyes beneath dark eyebrows scrutinised him for a moment, then she turned back to the vista in front of her: the well-stocked, well-cared-for, well-walled kitchen garden, the small wilderness with a lump in the middle, the stand of large trees clustering round the church, and so to the chalk down.

'I think you should do some digging. It's quite the thing now you know. King Arthur's Small Change and all that. The Wretchley children have been doing it, so I suppose your father won't object on grounds... Well, he won't think it necessarily *low* of you. To go digging.'

It began to dawn on him what she was about.

'So. What I think ... I mean, how you should spend the rest of the day is opening up Jacob's Tump. It's a *barrow*, you know.'

Relief, excitement, even a little love, trickled through the ducts of Richard's numbed mind — but slowly. Repression, disappointment, and worse still betrayal, had left a deposit that all but clogged up the springs of affection he wanted to feel for his mother.

'I know. I know it's a barrow. Herb, the history master at the College, has been telling us about them.' Once, just once, the dull horror of life at the Rectory had betrayed him into saying *home* instead of the College in front of his mother... she had scarcely spoken to him for a week. Ever since, some device in his

85

head had signalled warning when he spoke of the place in front of her and he sat on the words heavily. *At the College.* In case he made the same blunder again.

'Quite.' Herbert Heath, who occurred in her son's conversation too frequently, she vaguely identified as a threat. But just now, she resolved, just now I shall not be diverted. 'King Arthur's Small Change at Lydney. And now *The Times* says they are to dig at St Alban's.' The briskness had returned to her voice. 'So I'm sure it's all right. Now. You can't do it on your own. So this is what I propose...'

At half past ten, less than an hour later, a procession left the small stable-yard — now merely a garage for the Morris Cowley the Reverend James Austen had taken to Wintoncester, a potting shed and a shed for tools — and zigzagged its way up right-angled paths to the wooden door at the end of the kitchen garden. It consisted of: first the Reverend Mrs Austen, her straw hat resumed; Richard Austen with a cotton sunhat of the sort one can still see worn in the members' stand at Lords; then Mr Wainwright — gardener — carrying one spade, his own; on his heels John, his son, the gardener's boy, carrying a short-handled pick; finally, two more lads took up the rear — Eric and George Partridge, twin brothers of Mary and a year older. They pushed wheelbarrows laden with a further assortment of shovels, picks and rakes.

Mrs Austen led them through the door, which her son held open for the rest, and so into a half-acre of scrubland, briars, broom and gorse, that lay in an awkward triangle between Rectory, churchyard and the down beyond. It was called the Wilderness at the Rectory, and Jake's Garden by the villagers, who were thought to hold it in awe as a place of ill repute, and refused to be buried on it, though it went with the church and was sanctified ground. Moreover, since it was in fact an outcrop of Wealden sand and sandstone, no one bothered to rent it for agricultural purposes either.

Its real function in village life, hitherto kept from the transients who passed through the Rectory (the Austens had been there for less than two decades), was as a courting place. Richard discovered this and much else during the next eight hours, which were to be the most educational of his life until then, and the most entertaining too.

In the middle of Jake's Garden stood Jake's Tump, a low mound about six feet high surrounded by a shallow ditch and largely overgrown with etiolated gorse, which, once penetrated, provided a canopy above springy and, in July, thyme-scented turf dotted with scabious and daisies. Mrs Austen sent Eric Partridge to the top, where he held a rake above the bushes which almost submerged him.

'There. I want you all to dig a trench. Let me see — about a yard wide? Wider than that?' Her voice was pitched high again, was intended, Richard with some embarrassment realised, to be commanding. 'Wide enough for you to work in. It will run from where I am standing to where Eric now is, but its floor will always be level with my feet now. Do you understand?'

'That's a lot of dirt you're asking us to shift, mum.'

'But there are five of you, Mr Wainwright, and I'm sure such a trench would have seemed very little to you when you were doing so tremendously well for us all on the Somme.'

'Five, mum?'

'Certainly, Mr Wainwright. You are in charge. You will treat Richard exactly as you treat John. And I mean exactly. He is to work just as hard as he is able.'

'Mum, what are we doing this for?'

'You are right to ask, George. This is a barrow, that is to say the burial place of a king born ten thousand years ago. You are looking for his tomb, which is almost certainly below Eric's feet. When you find it, you will send John for me. If I am busy and cannot come immediately, you will then, and only then, be instructed by Richard, who will take out carefully everything you find, dust it off as well as he can and note each item in his notebook. Is that all clear? You may take a break between half past one o'clock and two, when I shall see that lunch is sent out to you. I have given Eric and George half a crown each and, if Mr Wainwright is satisfied at six o'clock that they have done as well as they are capable, they will get another half a crown each. Is that all clear? Right then, Mr Wainwright, you may begin.'

She turned and began to pick her way through the broom, some of which still flowered, though most of it was now in pod,

87

back to the door of the Rectory garden. Richard caught up with her.

'Mother?'

'Richard.'

'Father will be most awfully angry.'

'There is no reason for him to discover. As you see, I have directed that the trench will be out of view of the house and I very much doubt if anyone will tell him about it.'

'But if he comes back?'

'He won't. He is attending the consistory, who are examining a curate from Eastleigh suspected of preaching socialism. He will dine with the Dean and possibly stay the night.'

'Mums, thank you.'

She held his gaze for a moment, her brown eyes serious again, her thin mouth held tight. Then briefly she touched his arm. 'You may well not feel so grateful at the end of a day spent doing real work,' she said.

Mr Wainwright was almost forty but looked older — broad-backed, bow-legged, large-handed, sandy Saxon hair gone from the top of his head and grey over his ears.

'Right, sir. If you'd be so good as to take this shovel...'

Richard suddenly experienced that awkward combination of rage and terror that comes when adolescence is faced with adult stupidity and is determined to overcome it.

'Mr Wainwright. You heard my mother. You are to treat me as your son and you will not "sir" me.'

The gardener flushed too, eyes narrow and bright, knuckles whitening on his spade.

'Very well. Very well. George here is picking. John is barrowing. You are to shovel.'

'Yes, Mr Wainwright.'

It was an hour at least before the others felt properly at ease — not with him, that was an impossibility — in front of him: but bit by bit they forgot he was there and began to talk, for the most part village gossip put in perfunctory phrases punctuated by thud of pick and rasp of shovel, but beneath it Richard became aware of strata of deeper significance.

Until then he had known only two very limited registers for

social intercourse: on the one side, the barbaric camaraderie of boarding-school common rooms and dormitories which allowed no rights of privacy or even individuality; respect there was in this essentially competitive world, but only for money, family, sporting achievement, and at the College, which was not the most philistine of such places, for academic and artistic competence — not for individuality as such, as a right. The other world was one of cool 'good' manners, whose conventions suppressed all expression of feeling or original thought: even laughter was limited to amusement at quiddity — the oddness of being caught in the rain without a hat, the strangeness of the lower classes. Wit was 'showing-off' and the truly comic was 'low'. Opinion was not allowed — one merely reiterated the unquestioned assumptions of one's caste. Communication was constrained by the absurd poverty of allowable language and gesture, and so — while respect, of a sort, ruled — intimacy, even friendliness, was virtually an impossibility.

There was respect, even reticence between Wainwrights and Partridges too, and Richard guessed this was due to the fact that, while all had been part of the landscape of each others' lives since birth, gaps in age and differences of occupation had never brought them as close together as this before. A new relationship had to be worked out — *worked* out because they lived in a freer world than Richard's, where rigid conventions existed for each new acquaintance or social situation: thus he knew exactly how to behave in the company of a married aunt, a bachelor uncle, a female cousin of his own age or a male one before they actually appeared.

But the Wainwrights and Partridges had to work things out, first on the level of work itself. Mr Wainwright was to be obeyed not because Mrs Austen had put him in charge, and only partly because he was older, but mainly because he knew more about this sort of work than the others. Yet it was soon acknowledged that Eric and George were quite definitely stronger than John; and to Richard's amazement not only did Mr Wainwright respect George and Eric's strength — which was predictable — but George and Eric respected John's weakness. Thus, after the first three barrow-loads, they indicated to Richard that he should leave John's barrow two thirds full. And, while for the

89

most part they followed Mr Wainwright's directions, when a gorse-root system proved especially intractable and he ordered John to go for an axe, they goodhumouredly ignored him and working together dragged and tore the thing bodily out of the sandy earth.

Once these relationships and the rhythm of the labour itself had been established, the range of their conversation widened to include what was, for Richard, a marvellous multiplicity of topics, differences of opinion, and occasional touches of real emotion. They discussed the rival merits of different sorts of wood used in making tool hafts, whether or not gorse flower was a suitable addition to ginger beer, the battiness of the village schoolteacher the three younger ones had all been under and that of her predecessor who had taught Mr Wainwright — and there was no condescension or impatience in their laughter when the older man described her antics at some length, though like all their generation in the village they had surely heard it all countless times before.

They disagreed with complete amicability over churchgoing (Wainwrights for, Partridges against) but with some heat over the morals of a girl who lived at the end of the village — Mr Wainwright thought she was a 'bad'un'; George insisted that she had a loving nature and a husband who was melancholic and ignored her. Mr Wainwright eventually allowed George might be right — and Richard realised he had given way because he valued the friendly atmosphere of the moment more than his own opinion.

At half past one George threw down his pick and let out an extraordinary crowing whoop — half laugh, half shout: 'Eh, Eric, look, look at this, it's not our Mary is it? Is that our Mary, well, well, well,' and he slapped his thighs and hooted again as she came tripping through the broom carrying a basket and a cloth.

She set these down, blushing and dimpling, then let her brothers turn her around and finger the black stuff of her uniform, showed them how she'd have to take it in here and let it out there, and how the lace required repairing at the back of the collar. Richard meanwhile felt an obscure shame that he had allowed this person to become an object of sexual fantasy, while at the same time feeling the power of her prettiness more than ever.

Then she said, 'There's pasties for you all, and barley water, and beer for Mr Wainwright,' at which George and Eric turned scoffing and sent her back for beer for them.

'Well, I'll ask,' she said. 'I'll ask, but I'm sure I don't know.' Yet she was back in five minutes with another jug.

Tired and hungry they ate and drank most of what there was in silence — then came for Richard the one wretched moment of the dig. He thought at the time that it was the beer talking, for George was no more than a year older than him, if that. Later he realised George could not have said what he did without the beer — but it needed too to be said.

The stronger of the Partridge twins was lying back on the pile of spill they had heaped up and was picking his teeth with a straw. Then he belched — not loudly or offensively like boarding-school boys showing off, but because he needed to.

'Pardon,' he said, 'but that's cooked-over meat for you. Can't be helped. Reckon you had a tasty leg of mutton for your dinner yesterday, Mr Richard. Redcurrant jelly and all, I shouldn't wonder.'

'The day before, actually.' He was glad to have been spoken to — it was not something that had happened often during the morning.

'Come now, George,' said Mr Wainwright, 'show some respect.'

'No disrespect intended, Mr Wainwright. But that makes it twice cooked-over and my stomach won't take it. Not that it can remember when it last had fresh-cooked meat. Pass the jug, Eric.'

Richard was on his feet, face red again. 'Mr Wainwright, I'm sure George meant no disrespect... and I don't see why he should show me respect anyway; I mean, no more than he does to Eric and John.'

'Because you're gentry, Mr Richard. And we'm not. And there's an end to it.'

To his alarm, the image of the older man, who was now pulling on a very strong-smelling pipe, suddenly blurred with tears and he turned away into the Wilderness. He stayed there on the edge of the broom, looking out over a low stone wall up the down to the Iron Age ramparts, until he heard the thud and rasp of pick and shovel again. Then he silently rejoined them in the crevasse they had cut. It was already deep enough to cast some shadow. The sandy soil now seemed chill to touch though still dry, so deep in were they. They had left a pile of loose earth for him — this seemed at first a reproach, but then he realised it was a favour, an invitation to him to rejoin them. As he stooped into it, George, in front of him with a pick, turned and winked.

The afternoon wore on and Richard realised that a more real acceptance had been accorded him — for, if the grunts and rejoinders became more laconic between thrust and heave, they were also less self-conscious, more personal, and where they reflected on his mother and father not, as far as he was aware, censored by his presence.

Thus he discovered that the Wainwrights, who had worked for his father's predecessor, had no liking for his father. Not that they said so . . . it was just that Mr Wainwright was ready to reminisce about the genial ex-army padre who had happily stuck pig in Poona and was happy to chase foxes in Hampshire. The Partridges concurred but were more direct. The Reverend Austen was to be feared. He could employ in his own right, and, more important, potential employers amongst the landowners around looked to him for advice.

Mrs Austen, however, was allowed by all to be well meaning though odd. This surpised Richard. In spite of the appalling severance she had apparently consented to when he was sent to his distant and vicious prep school, she still remained the most familiar element in his emotionally starved life . . . therefore not odd. Though perhaps only intermittently well meaning.

Not just odd — but well meaning. It was like her, all assented, to have found the Partridges a half-sovereign's worth of labour at such a particularly bad time for the family, just as for sure she had no need for a second kitchen maid — yet she had given Mary employment.

Richard felt secure and bold enough to ask why it was a bad time.

They were not really surprised that he did not know — why should he?

'Becuz ower vather a' clozed ower smithee, iz whoi,' said Eric — lapsing, perhaps because of embarrassment, into yet deeper dialect.

'But why?'

Pick and shovel thudded and rasped on; one of the wheelbarrow's wheels had developed a squeak.

'Thairz no varryin to be 'ad no moarr. The djendry 'avin gone over to they mo'o caaz.'

''n moast varmers a' goin' o'er to they tractuz.'

'Zo dang all varryin'.'

'An smithin's been vawlin away vor a decud an moarr.'

'Whoi, e'en Mester Wainwright 'ere'll boi a noo pick'ed if ol'un break. Zeems it be djeeber 'n a'un ol'un fixt.'

'Not cheaper,' said Mr Wainwright. 'But a new one lasts a whole sight longer than one fixed by your pa.'

'Anyway, we'm goin' to Zo'owt'on next week — but they zay there'z no work there neither.'

'Vather's all ri'. He'll get boi chimbley zweepin'. No chance the djendry'll stop burning coal in their grates be the times never so bad.'

Disconsolately they dug on. The afternoon heat settled about their heads, the soil at their feet was black now, dank and oddly evil. Richard started hot and cold when a very large orange centipede slithered down over a root at shoulder height and dropped at his feet. George found the skull of a cat.

Eric said, 'No tomb then, oi reckon. We'm well past the spot where Rector's wife made me stand.'

Mr Wainwright pulled the knotted handkerchief from his head and wiped his face with it. 'You'm right. And reckon we'm shifted a ton and more of dirt and no tomb.'

'More nor a ton,' said George.

They were puzzled as well as disappointed; puzzled more than disappointed, Richard realised, and what was confusing them was that they did not know what to do about the situation they were in. They liked Mrs Austen and, even if they thought her odd, foolish even, they still flinched from making her seem foolish in her own eyes. He was embarrassed again for her sake.

93

He would have to do something. He walked into the cutting, stooped where it crossed the middle of the mound. Eric was right. The sides now sloped down a yard or so from a zenith, where the walls were just about six feet high.

He knelt. On his left, there was an irregular curving patch of very slightly paler soil and under it a band of very black stuff. Above the pale stratum was a layer more solid, more impacted than the rest, more peaty. But on the right there was nothing. The soil for many feet in every direction was uniformly the same blackish sand.

'Mr Wainwright?'

The gardener grunted — he was not allowed to 'sir' the boy, would not call him 'Mr' for he was a youngster, and would not presume to use his unadorned Christian name. He grunted.

'Mr Wainwright. Before we give up I think we ought to dig it out a bit more on this side. Down here, do you see?' The excitement he felt was quite unlike anything he had ever felt before — for until then the only commensurate thrills he had experienced had been sexual, and therefore corrupted by guilt. At this moment there was no corruption.

Yet it was George who actually penetrated what had been a turf cyst — the peaty layer.

'Vanzee this now. I rekun this to be ol' Jake hisselv. I thought it was kindlin' at first — but mebbee it be bones... ol' droi brown bones. An' funny thing too but this 'ere death's'ed come from higher up than all the rest. Like 'ee was sat here, instead a laid down like a Christian person.' As George lifted out the skull, Richard's excitement overflowed and from that moment he was an archaeologist for life.

With the skeleton they found: a beaker, slightly waisted just below the brim and scored horizontally with fine lines; a round-heeled dagger made of copper with holes for rivets; two very fine arrowheads, tanged and barbed, and knapped from flint; and an almost flat rectangular slab of greenstone with holes at each corner.

It was while they were passing this last from hand to hand, speculating as to what it could have been and waiting for John to return as instructed with Mrs Austen, that the village constable appeared with the gardener's boy behind him, like Jesus in the inner room or the Angel Gabriel. Certainly angel-like, he bore messages and commands. The Wainwrights were to gather up all the tools and return to their cottage; the next day would be time enough to fill in the trench and put Jake's Tump to rights. Richard was to go to the school room and wait there until sent for. As for the Partridges, first they must turn out their pockets, for the Reverend knew them to be out of employment and therefore subject to temptation...

'Come.'

Richard took a breath and pushed open the heavy oak door to the Reverend James Austen's study. I am nearly fifteen he said to himself — I am too old to be whipped.

His father sat behind the large desk at which he wrote his sermons and from which he attempted to rule his parish. Sixty-eight years old, white-haired, chapfallen, beak-nosed, an old testament prophet gone to seed: bitter where once he had been scathing, cantankerous rather than wrathful — still capable of spite though, and ready to scheme where once he had bullied. Hence his tactic in sending the constable to the Tump instead of appearing there himself. Not that he would not try bullying when he felt he could get away with it.

He looked up over his spectacles, pushed back the heavy throne-like chair he was sitting in. It moved easily on brass casters which the maid-of-all-work polished every day at dawn together with almost every other shining thing in the big house.

'I shall not invite you to be seated, Richard. And kindly keep your hands by your sides and your feet together. Now. What have you to say for yourself?'

Richard of course said nothing. The problem was his mother — whatever had passed between her and his father between his unexpected return and the sending for the constable he never discovered. His worst fear was that under pressure she might have revealed why she had got him out of the school room and into the sun with hard physical work to do: but if she had his father said nothing of it. It was possible that he could not trust himself to mention it.

'Nothing. I see. Well, I wonder just how much of the harm,

the wrong-doing, the evil you have been connected with today you are aware ... of.'

He made an odd brushing gesture with his hand — perhaps irritated that the powerful emotions of the moment had led him to end a sentence with a preposition.

He enumerated: filial disobedience in failing to finish his Latin prose; idleness — connected with the same; encouraging the servants in idleness ... 'At times like these I need hardly say it is, more than ever, our most solemn duty to set the right sort of example'; sacrilege and blasphemy for the Wilderness was sanctified ground; grave robbery. Most serious of all, it seemed, was consorting with the Partridges. They were idlers, scroungers, discontented stirrers of trouble. It was known for instance that their father had attended a Labour Party rally in Southampton in 1928. Moreover it was now clear that George Partridge was a thief.

'Why do you say such a thing?' Richard at last blurted out. 'I am sure that he is not, sir.'

The expression on the Reverend James Austen's face twisted into a caricature by Leonardo. One bushy white eyebrow shot above the other; beneath it his mouth twisted up in a grimace that was nearly a grin. Yet on the other side of his beak he contrived to hold his face severe, minatory. Nevertheless, he could not keep a note of senile triumph out of his voice as he hitched himself up on one hip, the better to delve in the black worsted of his jacket.

'Here, sir. Here is why he is a thief,' and four gold discs spilled from his palm across the vast blotter in front of him. 'Constable Wilkins found him in possession of these.'

They were the size of halfpennies, as thin as silver threepenny bits, and each was marked with four notches forming a cross. Undoubtedly they were gold — they shone as clear and as bright as when the Beaker Folk put them in Jake's Tump three and a half thousand years earlier, sealed in a cyst of turf with their chief, his archer's wristguard, his arrows, his dagger and the cup he always drank from, and then heaped up a mound of sandy earth, easier to raise with antler picks and hafted celts than the chalky clay around.

'You were robbing a grave, my boy. And Partridge was

robbing you... So much for your *low* friends,' and the old man's hand came down on the blotter so the gold discs jumped a little and glinted again in the light — like fish snapping for insects at evening. 'I shall take a severe view and I make no doubt Sir Lewis will too. In these times sentences must be exemplary. Six months is what I look for...'

'Sir, I gave them to him.'

'Eh? What?'

'Well, not exactly...' Richard struggled to think coherently — he must, he knew, be convincing, not contradict himself.

'Now sir, tell the truth, if you can.'

Richard breathed in deeply and out again. 'George discovered them, sir. He was ... pleased with them. Their beauty perhaps ... Well, anyway, I said he could keep them. And sir...' Inspiration came at last. 'He may be entitled. The law relating to treasure trove. Would not a coroner have to sit...?'

This was indeed inspired. The local justice of the peace, Sir Lewis Dax, might well have been in the Rector's pocket (or rather the other way about), but the coroner, a solicitor from Romsey, most definitely was not. The upshot was that the Rector thought on the whole he would not press charges of damage to property, trespass, blasphemy, sacrilege and the rest against the Partridges. He would, because of what he saw as his son's misguided sense of chivalry, even drop the charge of theft. What other actions he would take he would give some thought to... At this point he suddenly looked older, more tired, and his speech became a little confused... But anyway — pulling himself together — Richard would, for the rest of the summer holiday, do two proses a day, and 'spends', his weekly allowance of half a crown, would be cut off *sine die*...

Sir Richard stood up a little stiffly, a little unsteadily, and put *The Bronze Age* back in its place.

Many upshots, outcomes, side-effects and spin-offs had come from that day, he reflected. Not least that, from then on, he had rejected, or at least questioned very closely, everything his father held to be true on any subject whatsoever — from politics and religion to sex and common honesty.

More important was the fact that he had discovered in perhaps not untypical members of the lower orders a humanity that he rarely encountered within his own class. There, insensitivity and even downright cruelty, however tempered by the conventions of 'civilised behaviour', were the rule. It was disturbing, moving also, to be led to suspect that these might not necessarily be characteristics of human nature in general, but only of a particular group at a particular time — so Herbert Heath, the history teacher had argued, and Richard was now ready to believe him.

That night, in moonlight and breathing the scent of stock and honeysuckle, he masturbated joyfully, albeit with blistered palms; in December he passed Latin with the aid of a crib of *Aeneid Book II*. He also arranged for the prose to be smuggled out of the exam room, where a swot translated it and sent it back in for the fee of one guinea — an expense the other candidates shared. Matriculated thus, he eventually *went up* to Cambridge. He was not the first and by no means the last to slip into that establishment by such means.

If his conscience troubled him in this and other peccadilloes, it was always eased by the memory of his father's claw-like hand scooping up the four gold discs and returning them to his coat pocket — where, to all intents and purposes, they remained until the old fraud died fifteen years later. On that day Austen returned three to George Partridge; the fourth, which his father had had mounted on a ring, he kept.

11

St John's College, Cambridge: 1932-35. History Tripos I, First;
Archaeology and Anthropology Tripos II, First cum maxima laude.
Apart from high academic achievement, which also included two college
prizes, subject was a member and for a short time a committee member of
the University Labour Club until it closed in 1933; a member of the
Amateur Dramatic Club; and of other smaller societies including most of
those with archaeological or historical aims. Once the Labour Club closed,
he apparently took no further part in political societies. There is nothing on
record to suggest he joined the CP at that time, nor that he was on intimate
terms with those of his contemporaries that did. He must have been
acquainted with Philby, who was treasurer of the Labour Club when it
folded, but we can find no indication that they remained in touch later. He
seems to have had only one emotional attachment, with Maud Lawson,
now Dame Maud Lawson, Principal of St Bridget's, Oxford. As far as
can be ascertained, they no longer communicate. Other friends from this
time who have remained in touch include Geoffrey Slaker, now Lord
Slaker of the Slaker Group; Sir... the eminent archaeologist; Professor
... and so on.

Cargill thought, it can't really have been just a matter of a
couple of books, a schoolteacher in 1930 — then nothing until
Spain in 1936. There must be something in between. Research
has left something out — intentionally or not (he had in mind
the protector he believed Austen still had within the Service)
remains to be seen — let's see what *The Burning Matrix* excludes.
He turned again to the book.

'The worst that has been said of me is that I am a *flâneur*; one

99

who strolls on the pavements of life, haunts its arcades and *galeries*, and never gets out into the street; one who gets the best of both worlds and belongs to neither; one who runs with the hare and the hounds; one who is not committed, not *serious*.

'It's a damnable charge, not one easily answered. Only jesuitical attention to my own conscience can clear me — it's not a charge that anyone else can acquit me of — or make stick. In work at least I have not, I think, been a *flâneur*, though that was of course the context in which I was accused ... but the petty jealousies of Academe are not my concern here. Suffice it to say that I am satisfied that I have done my job as an archaeologist, whether as digger, teacher or administrator, well and seriously, and no more need be said about that, except let history be my judge.

'The area where I do feel vulnerable is of course politics; and the period in which I was possibly less than serious, did less than required of me, was during my time at Cambridge.

'I have my excuses. And I suspect they will be dismissed. They are not serious enough. Let us say they are reasons, explanations, rather than excuses. First: when I went up I was determined to qualify and ultimately make my way as an archaeologist. Now this was no mean ambition in those days. Although our art/science was already popular, even fashionable, it still provided only very limited openings: either you had to be an extremely wealthy amateur (and I was not then wealthy — very comfortably off, if you like, but certainly I did not then expect ever to be able to finance my own digs), *or* an extremely gifted polymath — like Childe or Wheeler. To get into that class I had to train properly, I had to work. In short I had to be a swot, and politics for a time were put to one side.

'Alas for me — I did not then realise how important politics are — that was to come later, in Spain. And that is matter for a chapter on its own — the next but one.

'My second reason is this. I fell in love. No great matter, the young of today would say, and I daresay they are right. But things of that sort were not arranged so well in 1932. Not at Cambridge, not amongst the public school classes. For the first time, at the age of eighteen, I was let loose in a community where members of the opposite sex also existed — albeit in the favourable (to them) ratio of twenty to one. There were girls there to meet, to flirt with, to fall for, and I suppose everybody did: the point was this — if you happened to be the fortunate twentieth whose undying passion was tolerated, even oh heaven!, reciprocated, then one had a clear duty, a *biological* duty, far more potent than mere political or intellectual duties, to *hold on*.

'The lady in question, who is still with us, and whom I still admire albeit from a far safer distance, and whose name wild horses would not drag from me — nor even well-trained shire horses who would surely do the job much better — was *not* a socialist, not a socialist of any sort at all. She was, however, a swot, like me, so our early romantic days of walking hand in hand along the Backs, checking to see, in the approved fashion, if there was still honey for tea at Grantchester, spooning on the doorstep of Newnham College before the door closed at nine sharp, and later our sad, bungling, ignorant attempts to make love, were never allowed to interfere with actual work. She got her First too.

'Socialism, however, was out. She knew too much about it. You see, her people were not landed gentry, nor upper professionals — if they had been she might, like so many then, have felt a *frisson* of excitement in flirting with socialism or even, horrors, bolshevism. But her parents were cotton-mill owners in Lancashire and they knew what socialism meant, first hand. It meant the Union, it meant organised labour, it meant the criminals who put pickets on the factory gates, and actually paid them to be there, to discourage hands from working for two pounds a week when in the boom years they had got five for the same labour.

'"But," I once asked her, "if you once paid them five pounds a week, then surely that is what the job is worth?"

'"Oh, you don't understand," she'd say with the exasperation of one trying to describe the colour red, or rather blue, to a blind person, "you don't understand."

'I think I did. Especially when she added that their second house, a converted farm in Eskdale, had been sold to a specialist in piles from Liverpool who, to make matters worse, gave his services free to the unions in industrial-accident cases. I

101

understood, but also I knew that to argue would mean an end to afternoons spent with her in front of the gasfire in my Whewell Court rooms, and, as I said, biology is more powerful than politics — at any rate to a conventionally brought-up public-school boy into whose unbelieving and clumsy hand the apple has dropped at last.'

Cargill sighed, chewed on his pipe, made a note. He's hiding a lot here, he thought. I wonder if this Maud Lawson would throw any further light. He turned back to the document from Research and checked: yes, Principal of St Bridget's Oxford, and a Dame. Maybe he would give it a try, but meanwhile. . .

The next section of *The Burning Matrix* described how Austen had spent the Long Vacation of '33 under Wheeler for the final season at Verulamium, making his way in the pottery shed, and then again in '34 for the opening season at Maiden Castle. The account was anecdoted and entirely reverential to Sir Mortimer (Riki, he called him), and it did nothing for Cargill at all. As far as archaeology was concerned, he felt at one with the Reverend James Austen, who, according to his son, continued to fulminate against grave robbers who spoiled good farm labourers by over-employing them and over-paying them.

Then on the last page of the chapter a name caught his eye: 'But the best of finds for me at Maiden Castle, was the Maid herself — a small, dainty, blue-eyed blonde — vivacious, a flirt — you name it she had it, working as one of three small-finds recorders. As soon as I saw her, I knew I must strike up an acquaintance at least. As the rest of the gang downed tools in the gorgeous West Country sunset and repaired to bread, cheese and scrumpy at the "local", I scooped her into my Alvis and in two shakes of a billy goat's tail there we were, satisfactorily ensconced in the cocktail bar of Dorchester's grandest road-house. "A gin and it," Lady Kitti Bridge demanded, and I hastily scrapped my plan of having a pint of the best, and went along with her.'

Cargill, his interest caught, his mind back to the crone's mask set above a young woman's body, to the yapping terrier and the huge whisky, stood up, poured another weak one for himself, restuffed his pipe, and then dutifully sat down, not to *The Burning Matrix*, but, following what was now his established procedure, to Research's document first.

From summer of 1934 through to winter of 1944 subject was an intimate of Lady Kitti Bridge and her brother Edward Earl of Riversdale (see below). Apparently the connection was initiated at the Maiden Castle Dig, although subject was already acquainted with Riversdale, who had been with him at both The Meads and the College. Following the apparently chance meeting, subject was invited to spend the following summer (1935), after taking his degree, at Scales, the Riversdale residence in Co. Wicklow, where the family intended to begin excavations on a Bronze Age site within the boundaries of the estate. Dr Fernando González, a Spanish archaeologist, was in charge.

At this time the Riversdales were actively though not publicly involved in right-wing politics, particularly the politics of appeasement. Riversdale was a member of the Anglo-German Fellowship and corresponded with similarly minded people in France, Hungary and Spain. Dr González was a member of JONS, the Spanish fascist group. Subject's own political beliefs at this time remain uncertain until he became involved in the Spanish Civil War on the side of the Basques. As a result, he later claimed, he joined the CP of Great Britain on his return, suffering from wounds received during the bombing of Guernica. He joined so he could more effectively propagandise the loyalist cause in Britain...

That, thought Cargill, is too slight. Let's see what the man himself made of this period.

'Again I must plead guilty to a certain degree of political *flâneurism* (is there such a word?), and again my excuse is in part biological, but coupled this time with what had already become a more attractive and demanding mistress than all the ladies of flesh and blood I have ever known — and, if that sounds ungallant, well so be it.

'For not only were the charms of Lady Kitti herself well nigh irresistible, even more so was the chance to be deputy director on a properly organised Bronze Age dig; for it was the Bronze Age I was by then (thanks in the main to dear Gordon Childe) totally committed to, and I would do anything for anyone to get into it on my own account. Iron Age and Roman Britain, under

103

Wheeler, had been well established, and through them, as I have already made clear, I really began to learn my trade, but it was the Bronze Age I wanted to get my teeth into and the chance of a virgin site in the gold-bearing Wicklow Mountains just simply could not be set aside; no not for any reason on earth.

'And let me, in the first instance at any rate, plead ignorance too. I had no idea then just how far committed my charming hostess and host were to the most deeply evil creed that has ever flourished on this planet. How should I? They did not goose-step about those blue hills of Wicklow with swastikas on their arms and jackboots on their feet; there were no camps or short-haired lads stripping off brown shirts to bathe nude in the River Slaney; and when one of their dinner guests exclaimed that he was sure James Joyce was a Jew I put this down to Philistine ignorance, nothing worse.

'Of course the more sinister truth dawned in the end; indeed, after a time I realised I was being proselytised. Well, then there was the most almighty ding-dong of a row which could well have ended the relationship on the spot. But those were strange times. However clearly the lines were drawn later, then they were confused, and, fascism apart, I was more than a little in love with Lady Kitti, much in love with our Bronze Age dig, and also I should add that I got on very well with the two other members of the family.

'Teddy Riversdale I had been at school with, but he was two years older than I, and so until then we had been little more than ships that pass in the night. At Cambridge I came across his first collection of poems, written while he was at Oxford, and out of curiosity I read them. I found them striking, both for their passion and their use of language, and if they are as imbued with fascist ideology as some latterday critics have argued, then I was not by any means the first or last to fail to see this. Becoming re-acquainted at Scales, I found a tall, straw-haired young man, a sort of neurotic, underfed Rupert Brooke, but he could be very charming when he wanted to be, and very clever too, one of the sharpest wittiest conversationalists I have ever met. Once that row was over, and we had all agreed to differ, I grew to look forward to his company.

'The other member of the Riversdale family was in many ways the most enchanting of all, and no fascist either, far from it — I mean the Countess herself, Kitti's and Teddy's mother. Enchanting, but terribly sad too, being already almost blind from inoperable cararacts and with legs infected and swollen. Whenever I hear the word "stoicism" I think of her. We took it in turns to push her along the terraces of Scales and describe to her what we could see — the formal gardens now restored after the ravages of "The Troubles" that had made her a widow and her children orphans; then the park, and beyond the park the hills where, five miles away, our dig was under way. She was so interested in everything, so kind in spite of her afflictions, and yet so full of common sense and practicality too.

'Alice was, of course, a Slaker — the connection that made the Bridges distant cousins of mine through *my* mother — being the aunt of Geoffrey, the present baron and chairman of the group, and also my very good friend and patron of the Gold Museum. And that meant that courage and common sense had to be dominant parts of her personality.

'But the important thing about that summer was the dig. A series of gallery tombs and passage graves, late neolithic, had already been excavated, and these suggested the presence of a very early (by the standards of these islands) metallurgical industry...'

Cargill's eyes began to droop. Pulling himself together, he looked over it all again, and again felt that the whole thing was flannel. Whatever had happened at Scales, whatever it was, could not have been this airy-fairy agreement to differ between a committed Marxist and a bunch of really way-out Hitler-lovers. Perhaps, he thought, I should try her ladyship again, as well as Dame Maud.

Really, he thought, as he went to bed, one thing about this job is that I am mixing it with the nobs, I really am. Father would have been pleased.

Cargill's father was a Bradford pharmacist whose success with a small chain of shops, later bought out by Sir Jesse Boot, had enabled him to send his son to his Unitarian public school and his less than significant college at Oxford.

105

12

'Come.'

'There was a memo saying you wanted to see me.'

'That's right, William. That's right. There was. Park yourself, there's a good chap.'

The Housemaster, head on one side, ears straight out, face grey with thin lips set in their usual smile of calculated bonhomie, waved him into the chair in front of his desk.

'Well now. Let me see. We are looking into the Bletchley Park file, the Riversdale affair, all that lot, aren't we?' He turned a typed page in front of him, and squinted down at it as if it was the first time he had seen what was on the other side. 'That's right. Following product from PSIKE showing there was a B-P leak post-dating Riversdale's assumed demise.' He looked up. 'Funny if the old bugger turns out to be alive and well and in Gorkiy or some awful gulag, eh? Serve him right.'

'He's hardly likely to be in Russia if he *wasn't* the B-P leak.'

'Oh, quite. Absolutely. And that brings us to the point old chap, doesn't it?'

It was said in this particular department that, if the Housemaster called you Old Chap twice at one meeting, you ducked. Apparently, at the College, it had been his custom to use the same phrase before inviting you to kneel on his pouf with your elbows on the low armchair in front of it.

'The point?'

'Well, William, have you any ideas? Come up with anything yet? If it wasn't Riversdale, who was it?'

106

'It's early days yet. I have a lead or two. A pointer. I'm checking it out.'

'Quite. And being very properly cagey about it. Early days, eh?' He stood up now — unfolding long thin limbs like a stick insect from outer space or the Bellman in the illustrated *Hunting of the Snark*. He went to the window and remained apparently lost in the swirl and snarl of traffic below. Then he turned back, the grey light of the London sky behind his tilted head, behind his ears. 'Yet the fact is that half London knows who you've fixed on. Knows, because he's been telling everyone.'

Cargill felt this in his diaphragm like a blow, suddenly aware that what was happening was indeed far more serious than the request for a progress report he had been expecting.

'I hardly think...'

'I put it to you, Cargill. You think your man is Sir Richard Austen FBA, FSA. Am I right? Oh, don't beat about the bush, there's a good chap. Austen? Yes?'

'Yes.'

The Housemaster sighed. The confession (to what... smoking? buggery?) extracted, he could now move on to execution. He returned to his desk, stirred the papers, looked up. 'Wrong track. Quite the wrong fellow. Definitely not Austen.'

Cargill remained grimly silent.

'Let's look into it. What put you on to him? What first led you that way?'

Cargill, using as far as he was able words of no more than two syllables, explained how there were lacunae in the files, how there was no record of how the information against Riversdale had first been laid; of how the evidence against him had been found in private papers, but there was no record of why his private papers had been looked into in the first place. He finished by saying that it was on record that the papers had come from Lady Kitti Bridge, and that in a personal interview she had said she got them from Austen.

'Ah. A-ah. And you believed her.'

Cargill shrugged. Belief or not, it was clearly something to be followed up.

'You were not to know, I suppose. Scarcely your scene. But, amongst those of us who do move in... certain circles, Kitti is

107

known as an inveterate and malicious liar. She is particularly famed for her spite against each and every one of her numerous past lovers, all of whom, or almost all of whom, gave her up rather than the other way about. Austen came fairly early on the list. Not to be held against him; whatever one thinks of her now, she was damned attractive once. You know she has been a registered heroin addict? No? Well then.'

Cargill was conscious of a prickling emanation of sweat at the back of his neck, of dryness in his throat, of forgotten anger burning up like a newly erupted peptic ulcer. Gripping his pipe with both fists, he explained as evenly as he could that the file on the investigation of Austen was also missing — and completely missing, not tagged to the Director's own archive, Registry One, like the other three that were missing; that too was surely a significant piece of evidence?

'I'm not quite sure why that should follow. Unless you mean Philby or even poor old Hollis removed it? But be that as it may your whole hypothesis is vitiated by this.' The Housemaster lifted and then dropped a fattish pink folder with treasury tags. 'This *is* Austen's file. It was in Registry One all the time. If something went wrong with the tagging and logging when it was booked out, or when Registry Three went on to microfiches, well, it won't be the first time that's happened. It's all here. Austen is clean.'

Desperately Cargill burst out, 'He's an admitted Marxist.'

The Housemaster crowed. 'Oh really, Cargill. Really. Don't be so naïve. Do you think the KGB would really employ a known, self-confessed Marxist as one of their spooks? Is it really likely? Apart from anything else, there is one thing your average senior Russian bureaucrat cannot abide and that is a western intellectual Marxist. No. Come on. One third of our academic establishment would be under surveillance if we took that sort of thing seriously.'

Cargill restrained himself, just, from replying that he knew, and the Housemaster knew, that rather more than one third of our academic establishment is subject to random checks of mail and telephone.

The Housemaster went on, 'No. Take it from me. Austen is clean. Right through from the Bletchley Park enquiry, through his trips to Russia, right up to his vetting six years ago when Harold put him up for a K. So be a good chap and lay off him, will you?'

It was not easy to think quickly and sensibly and yet Cargill knew he must. There would be no further opportunity. He was already aware of approaching *esprit d'escalier*, what he should have asked, what he should have said, coming to him just as soon as the heavy handsome door of the Housemaster's den (his name for it) clicked behind him.

Eyes on the ceiling, on the rose from which a plain lampshade hung, he asked, 'Who did the Bletchley Park investigation on Austen?'

Traffic hooted and grumbled.

'Lay off, Cargill. I said, lay off.'

The tone was now coldly venomous.

The pipe twisted and turned on Cargill's knees.

'There is one thing I do have the right to know.'

The Housemaster waited — patience on a monument.

'You started this interview by asserting that half London knows I am, all right, *was* investigating Austen: because he's been telling everyone. I don't see how that can be so. The only way he could possibly know he is under scrutiny is if someone in the Service leaked it to him...'

'Oh, come on. You ordered a grade-one surveillance. With the standard of tradecraft currently available to this department, he'd have to be deaf and blind not to realise something was up...'

'I put that order in late last night. It could not have taken effect yet, not possibly. I doubt if even the briefing is under way.'

'No, it's certainly not. I cancelled it.'

'So. How did he know?'

'William. I had not meant to bring this up. But you force me. On Tuesday morning you ordered Research on Austen. Then, having nothing better to do you went to the Gold Museum, and hung about there for nearly an hour. Right? You know, William, your days for this sort of thing are over. You must have stuck out like a banana in a coal scuttle. I can just imagine. The hat, the coat, the muffler, the...'

The pipe broke with a crack like that of a living bone. For a moment Cargill looked at the two pieces, one in each hand.

'He didn't tell half London,' he said at last. 'Who did he tell?'

The Housemaster's voice was now slow, emphatic though quiet. He was making his last statement on the business. 'Sir Richard has impressively important friends; the sort of people who can get to our Director, the sort of people our Director listens to, for in effect they are as much our paymasters as the Home Office. In this case it was Lord Slaker. Chairman of the Slaker Group. Officially the man with the second highest sal . . .'

'I know about Lord Slaker.'

'I doubt if you do Cargill. I doubt if you do. Nobody does.'

PART TWO

13

Cargill was at breaking point. It had been coming for years. He had joined the Service partly out of idealism, partly because the only alternative with a second-class degree and no pull was teaching. So when the invitation came, in the traditional way through his rather shabby tutor who had been in military intelligence in the Middle East during the war, he had been ready to fall. Nevertheless, of the two, idealism had been the stronger. Cargill, in 1950, believed in God, the spiritual significance of music, the British Way of Life. This last he believed was founded on the inalienable rights of the individual protected by a tradition of honesty, fair play and a rather cool sort of comradeship. Dunkirk, the Blitz, El Alamein had all occurred during the most vulnerable period of his life — amongst the first films he had seen were *Desert Victory*, *The Way to the Stars* and *The Way Ahead*. After the defeat of fascism, the enemy was clearly communism. Bolshevism was what it had been called at school. Since he would never be more than a third-rate amateur at music, since religion in the creed in which it had finally crystallised for him — a personal mix of his family's Methodism and his school's Unitarianism — offered no career, it seemed right and just, almost a calling, to dedicate his life to the security of Britain.

Over the thirty years, God had withdrawn; the three or four friends he had in the London Mozart Players, including the one he had married, let it be understood that he had become something of a bore, an embarrassingly middle-aged groupie, and he had been sacked from the Philharmonia Chorus; the

113

British Way of Life disappeared as if it had never existed, which, of course, it never had, except in the minds of those of us brought up on Arthur Mee, the Dunkirk Spirit and Olivier's *Henry V*.

Meanwhile, through the nature of his job, he knew more than most of us of thirty years of political chicanery, double-dealing and downright treason. He had actually had to work on the Rhodesian sanction-busting cover up 'in the national interest', and had had to connive at deliberate misrepresentation to the media of the facts about nuclear waste: these were only two of the areas where he knew more than most of us about what goes on, what really happens.

He felt he could guess why the investigation into Austen had to be aborted: someone higher in the Service, as senior at least as the Housemaster, would be threatened by Austen's exposure; that Lord Slaker had an interest was no surprise — over the years one thing had become very clear: 'in the interest of national security' really means 'in the interest of the big corporations'.

The Housemaster had told him a childish lie. The pink file on Austen contained simply his vetting for a knighthood, and possibly accounts of his recent visits to Russia. The reference numbers on the cover made that clear. It had come from Registry Two, not from the Director's archive. There was no reason at all to suppose that it contained the missing account of the Bletchley Park investigation.

Cargill had had enough. That afternoon he spent an hour on Hampstead Heath, out in the cold grey air, always keeping at least two hundred yards from the nearest third person, and with him was Desmond Sleight, the newspaperman he had previously consulted about Lady Kitti Bridge.

Sleight had been a contemporary at university and a friend — until, in the sixties, he made a name for himself and money too as an investigative journalist. For Cargill that had been not quite cricket. Then, towards the end of the decade, he had found himself overtaken by the class of '55, the glitterers he called them, the whiz-kids who went on from scripting TW3 to the grittier parts of the *Sunday Times*, and from there spread out until most of the plum seats in Fleet Street had fallen to them. Sleight hated them, because, he said, they had come in on a tide of spurious slick protest which made them look like radicals, when in fact they were timeservers and arse-lickers to a man — and woman. They exposed things like thalidomide and asset-stripping, but when it came to the really big things, they pocketed their pride with their salaries and held on to their jobs while Sleight was back in the reporters' room. Mind you, he was not doing badly — after thirty years in the job his chapel saw to that.

Sleight was tall and thin, bald on top but long-haired else-where, had glasses with black rims, and wore a duffel coat, but a good one — lined, thickly woven fine wool, bone toggles, the latest in a long line that stretched back to the loose, thin thing he had affected in his last year at Oxford.

At first Cargill, well aware of the efficiency of long distance eavesdropping devices, kept the conversation on the level of personal trivia. He asked after Sleight's family.

'To tell you the truth, old friend, not too good. Jason, the sprout, you know? Well, I sent him to the local comp because, damn it, I believe in these things; state schools just have to match up to the private sector, or else we're getting nowhere. And this particular comprehensive used to be a direct grant school with very old traditions. But, you know, he's twelve, only twelve, and the other day he brought a joint home. A Jamaican had given it to him. I mean, you and I were swapping stamps at that age, not dope...'

Cargill tutted sympathetically. 'And Jane?'

'Trouble in that sector too. She's into Women's Lib. Now, I don't mind getting my share of washday hands and housemaid's knee, but, you know, she spends more time down the pub of an evening than I ever did, while I stay at home baby-sitting and worrying if Jason's having a quiet high under the bedclothes. It's a bit much. It really is. And she's knocking around with our nextdoor neighbour's bint whom I never could stand, and I suspect is more than a touch of a Les, know what I mean?'

But now Cargill was satisfied that they were alone and he began to explain why he had arranged the meeting. For ten minutes they hiked across the grass away from the trees, to the boundaries of Kenwood, then Sleight stopped, forced Cargill to turn and face him.

115

'Bill, let me see if I've got it right. You're saying you've been pulled off a job when you were about to pinch a Soviet spy, now highly placed, but not actually in the Service. And you think mission has been aborted because someone-up-there, in the Service, is going to get his come-uppance if you pull in the non-Service bastard. Right?'

'Right.'

'And you're peeved about this; you want to go right ahead and shake all the rotten apples off the tree at once.'

'Right.'

'And you think I might be able to help.'

'Right.'

'Fine. But I'm not quite sure I see just how.'

Cargill turned away, they turned together, made their way through the gate and began to climb the long green slope towards the white palladian façade nestling amongst rhododendrons and chestnuts. A cold draught from the north-east blew almost in their faces now and Cargill pulled up his collar, turned away from it, and coaxed life out of his pipe. This one, a reserve, had a bent aluminium stem.

'Research (puff), research in the (puff) first place.'

Again they began to move.

'Been cut off from the Registry (puff), you see. If I put in requisitions for relevant files, the Housemaster will soon rule that I'm out of order. Now, your rag has got the second-best archive in Fleet Street, and I think I could use that. I don't need much more. I don't think I do. Then, when I've got it, second stage starts.'

'I think I can see what that would be.'

'I'm sure you do. Shall we sit down for a moment?' They had reached the first of the long lines of slatted seats set between the rhododendrons and the path. The grass now fell away below them to the pond — its water black, bordered with dead remnants of rushes and water-lilies like frayed old trimmings on a widow's weeds. The false bridge and the inverted half-bowl of the concert platform hung their reflections like shoddy beads on her bosom. Above, four gulls, looking cold against the grey sky, flew purposefully west, getting away from the sea before night fell.

116

'Yes, I can see what that would be. The Blunt routine. Fly a kite or two in *Private Eye*. Touch up a couple of Labour backbenchers who don't mind abusing privilege in the House...'

'It would not be abuse. It would be in the national interest.'

'Of course it would. But you know the scene. "Let them say that sort of thing outside and I'll sue," that's your man's next line. But if he's got insurance ... in the Service, or wherever, it may not work out too well.'

Cargill shifted impatiently. 'We've not got that far yet. Time to work out that when I'm sure I've got him. You know, you might be able to do a Chapman Pincher — I'm sure you know he's bringing out a book on Hollis to be published against extracts in the *Daily Mail*. He'll make a bomb. Well,' Cargill's voice was dry now, 'you could too. The point is, are you on board?'

'Yes. Tentatively. Anyway I'll dig what I can for you out of the Morgue. What do you want? Have you got a shopping list?'

'Slaker. Lord Slaker. The Slaker Group.'

Sleight leant forward, hands fiddling with a dried stem of grass he had plucked lower down the hill, head up, glasses flashing in a transitory gleam of sun that went on over the next ten minutes to touch with brief magic the Post Office Tower, New Zealand House; finally a patch of river glowed like white gold, then faded back to grey.

'Come on. I'd need a truck to give you all we've got on them. That's the first thing. The second is that an envelope folder would hold most of what we've ever printed. There's a sort of self-imposed, self-perpetuating D-notice on Slaker. Now Kitti Bridge is another matter. I suppose your ringing me about her the other night is connected with all this?' He turned and looked at Cargill puffing away beneath the pulled-down brim of his trilby. 'And that brings us to the third thing, old friend. You can't tangle with that lot. You really can't.'

'I'm not tangling with them. Yet. It's just that at four different points in my investigation the name Slaker cropped up.' He didn't add that it had been the intervention of Lord Slaker himself that had led to the shut-down of his enquiry. 'And I'll narrow the field for you. Riversdale. Not the present one but his predecessor. His mother was a Slaker. The Gold

Museum. Lord Slaker. And Sir Richard Austen. Just get me what you can on the points where those names intersect. That'll do for a start.'

'Well. Can do. But...'

Briefly they discussed ways and means, whether Cargill was being watched, should they use a cut-out or dead letterbox when Sleight was ready to deliver.

'No, no. Not really necessary. When you've got a file together, give me a ring at home. At seven o'clock. It's still the old number. Let it ring seven times and I'll be in the Granby round the corner in twenty minutes.'

They stood up. Long lines of seats, each with *in memoriam* notices cut into the larger piece of wood in the back, hundreds of them, stretched away down every path.

'Like a flaming cemetery,' said Sleight, waving his hand. 'Myself I blame the proximity of Golders Green Crematorium.'

Malcontents both, they stumped off, he this way, the other that.

Half an hour later, with a chilly darkness already closing in over Bloomsbury, SLA 1 drew up on the double yellow line outside the Gold Museum. A square-looking, hatless man trotted up the steps. He had grizzled hair, balding, brushed across a high, round, dome of a head, a face like one of the better-looking Roman emperors, ruthless but fine-featured; he wore a coat of blue so deep that five yards away it looked black, but yet seemed to glow with the fineness of the wool: all in all he was dandyishly but unostentatiously immaculate.

The guards, the lady at the kiosk, almost bowed as he surged past, a procession of one — his dark keen eyes momentarily relished the glamour of gold in the showcases, then he span up the lovely curve of the spiralling staircase and so out of sight on to the gallery above.

A moment or two later Lord Slaker sat in the large black leather chair opposite Austen's desk in the converted organ loft, with a glass of Austen's Scotch in his hand.

'Well, Geoffrey.'

'Cheers, Richard.'

They drank. Slaker was a presence: physically solid, hard,

118

with the glossy look of a man whose diet is red meat and crustacea, very fresh salads, French cheeses and the best in booze — but it wasn't just that. He was concentrated like an impacted astral body, like a piece of electronic machinery so well designed that it is half the size with double the capacity of its nearest competitor. One was not sure which to admire more — the power or the control; yet the dichotomy is meaningless, for what is one without the other?

He had his faults. Where other men with his wealth, power, coupled with the strength of character to resist the temptations of physical vice, are often over-bearing, bullying, dictatorial, mean, melancholic, or whatever, his fault was — detachment. He surveyed the world with an eye that often twinkled; his mouth too easily smiled; one felt, and one may have been right, that what kept him going, what made him tick, was the fun of it all. 'You know the trouble with Geoffrey,' someone had said... a Prince? a President? 'he's not serious. He doesn't care.'

You know the board game Buccaneer? You sail little boats over a chart, you pick up treasure and crew, you attack other boats, you take chance cards and so on. Yet it is a game of skill, or ruthlessness anyway. The unprincipled cheat (cheating is built into the rules; it always is where the rules include penalties for breaking them) wins. Lord Slaker plays like that; but his game is called World Market.

'I thought I'd drop by,' he spoke quietly. No one had ever failed to hear what Lord Slaker said. 'And let you know I had a drink with Humphries last night. The Housemaster, you know? I put him in the picture. He rang me this morning. And that really is that.'

'It was one of his chaps then.' Austen frowned a little as he said this. He believed Slaker — who wouldn't? All the same, there were questions.

'Oh yes. I don't know the details. Even in the Club one doesn't gossip too readily. Especially in the Club,' Lord Slaker gave his little laugh — very infectious, 'but he admitted he had a chap reopening the Bletchley Park file, and that, he was sure, was the source of the bother. And now he's called him off. Once he knew it would all lead back to you, he was quite happy to shut the thing down.'

'Geoffrey! Did you have to...? Oh well.' Austen laughed nervously and drank. 'Did he say why? Why they reopened it?'

'Not overtly. But the Americans come into it. Some computer they've got churning away in Illinois or wherever.'

'Could the Americans be working on it independently? I mean without Humphries knowing?'

'I don't think so. You know they have this agreement. Share and share alike. Be an awful stink if they started messing about on our patch without letting on. Why do you ask?'

Austen explained about Shapiro — how he had given her an interview, how a second one was scheduled for the following day, how she had said she was writing a book on the Cambridge Left.

'It might just be true. I should think there must be dozens getting grants from one foundation or another to do just that after poor Tony got clobbered. I'm surprised they're not all camping on your doorstep.'

'Oh, come *on*.'

'Why not? No. For the moment I'd take her at face value. Play her along, be nice to her, tell her as much of the truth as you can. You know the style.'

Austen grimaced. 'I suppose I must.'

'Yes, I think you must.' For a moment there was a hint of steel in Slaker's voice. 'There's a fair bit at stake at the moment. If she's CIA, I'm sure the way to play it is give and give and give and hope they'll go away. And if she isn't, no harm done. Anyway, thanks for the drink. And keep in touch, won't you? I mean, let me know the moment you feel queasy again.'

At the door he turned, the twinkle very much there.

'Humphries was your fag at the College, wasn't he?'

'The Housemaster? Yes. That's right.'

'He'll behave. That relationship is *indelible*.'

Outside, the traffic warden opened the door for him and saluted. SLA 1 purred away into the dusk.

14

Dame Maud Lawson's desk was pale green with mouldings picked out in white; it had a bottle-green leather blotter. Its setting was even more bizarre: there were huge cushions covered in shantung silks; the velvet curtains, one green, one pink, could be fastened together by pushing large green pom-poms through braided pink slits, and so on. The whole business was thought to have been rather a feature in 1958 when two bright young men called Merry and Tricius unveiled their re-vamp of St Bridget's Principal's Lodge; it was rather hoped that in 1988 the whole interior might be moved to the Victoria and Albert Museum. Dame Maud was in awe of it — not daring to admit even to herself that she hated it; in constant subdued terror that she might chip the brittle corners, stain the unprac-tical fabrics.

Nevertheless, it was where she had to work, for another year, until she retired.

With a gold pencil she was now in the process of cannibalising an old lecture on *The Morning of Christ's Nativity* by John Milton, for a talk she had been invited to give on Radio Three over the Christmas period. She read, beautifully, into a microphone, the lines:

> 'Nature that heard such sound
> Beneath the hollow round
>   Of Cynthia's seat, the airy region thrilling,
> Now was almost won
> To think her part was done...'

She paused; played back; yes, she had said, 'wun', 'dun'; she rewound and read again, this time returning to the Lancashire vowels she was at pains to get back into her voice — 'w-*on*', 'd-*on*': she knew today's undergraduates respected her for this.

Then she went on. 'Eh awfen feel it is a shame that medieval cosmology is not taught in our schools, for, Renaissance Man though he was, the universe Milton depicts here is unrelievedly ptolemaic, the philosophy or science is of course neo-platonic — thus Nature's sublunar duty, beneath the moon (Cynthia's seat), is to maintain balance, harmony between the disparate warring elements which otherwise would collapse again into old Chaos . . .'

Dimly she recalled her first days as a full lecturer, thirty years earlier, and the sudden gale of laughter from a predominantly male audience that had greeted her recitation of 'such sound, Beneath the hollow round of Cynthia's seat', laughter that had become hysterical with the words 'the airy region thrilling'. Apparently the word 'thrill' in those days had strong sexual implications to young people . . . that much she later gathered, but why laugh at 'the hollow round of Cynthia's seat' . . . ? She shook her head.

A knock.

'Come.'

'A Mr Cargill to see you, Dame Maud.'

'Ah yes. Of course. How exciting. Do show him in.'

A dumpy woman she was, in sensible tweeds, brogues, permed grey hair close to her scalp, a long inquisitive nose with just a hint of blue beneath the powder at the tip; a silver and imitation amethyst brooch in the shape of a thistle was pinned to her lapel. She looked utterly incongruous in that room: a health visitor checking out a classy brothel.

But no more incongruous than Cargill, who found himself perched on the edge of a very oddly shaped armchair upholstered in watered dove-grey and scarlet silk.

'Very good of you to give me your time, Dame Maud,' he muttered.

'Not at all. I generally have a glass of something about now — sherry? Scotch? G and T?'

'A G and T would be very nice.'

'There then. Now, what can I do for you? You said in your note that you are in the Security Service — that's MI5, is it not?'

'Well, Dame Maud, that's what the general public like to call us. In fact, MI5 has no official existence, as I'm sure you're aware...'

'Nevertheless, how very thrilling.' She frowned — should she have said that? She hurried on. 'And you want to know about my acquaintance as a Cambridge undergraduate in the thirties. Well, I am sure you know I have never been any sort of a socialist, let alone bolshevist; indeed, to a limited extent you could say I have been something of a crusader the other way. I knew only one person of that persuasion...'

Suspense hung in the air and then toppled like the sort of orgasm bee-fumbled flowers may be thought to feel as they release their nectar. In unison, they said, 'Sir Richard Austen.'

In silence they drank.

'Dame Maud...'

'Of course, I... Do go on.'

'Have you read *The Burning Matrix*?'

'No. I can't say I have. Is it a novel?'

'No, Dame Maud. It's Sir Richard's autobiography. It was published only last week, so I don't expect... I have a copy here. I wonder if you would mind reading these pages — see, here — while I sit quietly.'

She took the book and sat for a moment with it on her knees, not looking at it. Cargill became embarrassingly aware that she was blushing, then she gave a quick shake of her head, and said, 'Well, of course. That was just a little bit of an untruth. I have read these pages.'

'What do you think of them? Are they truth — I mean, of course,' he hurried on, stumbling over the words, 'about his political activities?'

'Oh no, no, dear me no, not at all. Pack of lies. But Dickie always was a fibber — I really have not read much of his book, but I'm sure most of it is fibs.'

'Can you remember, can you tell me just where he is fibbing at this point?'

'Let me see. Here we are. Well, he contrives to give the impression that largely on my... on account of the girl he talks

123

about, he gave up socialism, or shelved it. All this *stuff* about biology. It really won't do.'

'He wasn't a party member until 1937.'

'Wasn't he? Are you sure?'

'No. Not sure. That is really what I am trying to find out about. He says he wasn't. We suspect he was.'

'I too think he was. For instance, he knew Philby. I'm sure of that. I never actually saw them together, but then I wouldn't have recognised Philby anyway. But he knew him through the Labour Club; they were both committee members. And then he was always reading those slim green books, Marx and Engels, you know, published by Martin Lawrence...'

'Lawrence and Wishart.'

'That's right. First, though, the firm was Martin Lawrence. That man Dutt, who actually edited them, fed them into the university and asked all his nasty little acolytes to pass them on, pass them on. And Dickie was on the chain.'

'Intellectually he has never tried to conceal that he is a Marxist.' Cargill, sensing emotion here, and wanting to keep the adrenalin and the information flowing, injected a note of boredom into his voice, as if nothing really convincing had come out so far, as if, unless it did, he might draw the interview to a close. 'He says so in that book often enough. What I am trying to establish is whether or not he was as politically inactive as he says he was. I mean, did he go to meetings, did he picket, did he sell the *Daily Worker* on street corners?'

Dame Maud frowned, absently bobbing the slice of lemon in her drink and letting it float up through the mauve-tinted liquid.

'No,' she said at last. 'No. He didn't do anything like that.' Her voice hardened again. 'But the lie in that book is that he tries to give the impression that he had lost interest for a time, given it all up. And that's *not* true.'

Cargill this time allowed himself to sound exasperated. 'As I said, he never denies it — he went on studying the basic Marxist texts so he could develop archaeology on the lines already being established by Gordon Childe. But was he *doing* anything?'

A half-smile, very sad, touched with bitterness, played over Dame Maud's prim, careful mouth, and the lemon slice bobbed down and came up again. Then her head lifted and she spoke very quickly. 'For a time, over most of the Hilary Term in 1934, and at the beginning of the Trinity Term, he went up to London once a fortnight. We argued about these trips. He would not tell me why he went. To anger me he told me he went to a prostitute, and that you may imagine silenced me, but' — the words were tumbling out now, she was very breathless, hectic little touches of pink glowed in her cheeks — 'I found an address in his diary, a London address, it was 3 Rosary Gardens, South Kensington. There.' She ended triumphantly.

Cargill was nonplussed.

'I'm sorry, Dame Maud. I don't quite follow.'

'But you must. You must know. It was an OGPU safe house. Everyone knows that.'

'They do?'

She was exasperated: 'It's in all the texts. In *The Climate of Treason*; in...'

Cargill, in spite of himself, was excited. 'Are you sure about this?'

'Quite sure. Look. I'll find it for you,' she swung enthusiastically back to the wall behind her desk which was lined with books, and knocked her glass flying. G and T splashed over the shantung silks.

'No, no, don't bother now. I'll check later. I mean are you sure about this address? That you saw it in Austen's notebook? It was a long time ago...'

The moment had gone. On her knees, dabbing away with a pathetically inadequate slip of a handkerchief, she looked up through spectacles now ever so slightly askew. 'No. I'm not sure. Actually I made it up. In fact, you see, I made it up. About 3 Rosary Gardens. He *did* go to London. He did say he was visiting a prostitute. I am sure he wasn't. I did not see the address. I made it up about the address.'

To his horror, Cargill realised that there were tears behind the spectacles, tears in the voice too. What he did not know was how the unfortunate moment had intercut two areas of Dame Maud's life about which she felt particularly vulnerable — her long-past affair with Austen, and her neurosis about the ghastly room she had to work in.

125

Brusquely, gruffly, he offered to go. Dame Maud nodded and went on dabbing. But, as his hand was on the door handle (artfully shaped to suggest an abstraction of a banana or a cucumber), she spoke again; he turned; she was standing up amongst the absurd cushions, against the crazy curtains, twisting the handkerchief in her fingers.

'He was active, Mr Cargill. He really was. And you are officially looking into him now. I won't warn him. You can trust me for that. No. I won't warn him. One more thing, Mr Cargill — may I wish you, wish you Godspeed in your work? Godspeed!'

Fresh-faced, cheeks even a touch too rosy partly through natural youthful bloom, partly through the nip in the February air, and not a little because she had drunk a large gin and tonic, but mostly a delicious, trembling dread, young Maud Lawson pedalled gamely round the Backs, into Magdalene Street and across Magdalene Bridge. She spun the pedal back on to the curb, propped the bike on it, gave her scarf a fling, and resisted the temptation to look at her watch. She had left Newnham at three, it must now be ten past; men were allowed to entertain unaccompanied girls between three and five for tea, so she was all right. She almost sang to the porter 'Maud Lawson, tea with Mr Austen. Whewell Court' and tripped on through the lodge, round the lawns, and so to one of the middle staircases of the grey building, which, for all its neo-gothic extravagances, remained as much like a prison or barracks as anything else, and as she went her bike crashed unheeded to the pavement behind her.

His oak was unsported; she burst in without knocking.

'Here I am then,' and took off coat and gown together, dropping them over the back of the leather armchair. 'Here I am. Aren't you glad to see me?'

Austen looked up from the table beneath the leaded window. It was a dark, dim room, wood-panelled; the only light came from an orange-shaded centre light or through this one inadequate window.

'Of course I am, Tootsie.'

Short fair hair, small but robust, a teddy-bear — a *tough* teddy-bear, no doubt, of that, but cuddlesome.

126

'No, but really glad.' She stood behind him, put her arms round his neck, her cheek on the top of his head; thus she had seen it done in a flick she had been to with a friend from Salford High over the Christmas Vac.

'Of course I am, Tootsie. Just let me finish this.'

He had deliberately put his finger on the spot where he was reading when she came in, and it still rested there.

'"If economists,"' she read aloud over his shoulder, '"in support of their optimism, cite the example of the English workers employed in the cotton industry, they see the latter only in the rare moments of trade prosperity. These moments of prosperity are, to the periods of crisis and stagnation, in the proportion of three to ten. But perhaps also, in speaking of improvement, the economists were thinking of the millions of workers who had to perish in the East Indies so as to procure for the million and a half workers employed in England in the same industry three years prosperity out of ten..." Oh, what *stuff* is this, what stuff...?'

Austen put his hands firmly on the book so she could not lift it.

'What *is* this?' She prized up his fingers. '*The Poverty of Philosophy* by Karl Marx. Well I never. Well titled, I'd say, pretty poor philosophy.'

He caught her by the waist and pulled her on to his knee (he too had been to a flick or two in his time): 'You should say ex-ah-mple, not ex-a-mple, K-ah-l not K-a-l, and you must *never* say "well I never". Give me a kiss.'

His accustomed hand slid up silk to the top of her stocking.

'No, Dickie.'

'Why not?'

'Because I've decided. You can have me. I'll give myself to you. You want it and I do too. Now. Properly.'

'You mean now? Properly?'

'Yes!'

'Oh dear Lord. Dear God.'

But the logistics of it all defeated them. First, she would not go to bed — the tiny room that completed the set was cold, the bed as narrow as a coffin; so he must turn up the gas fire and look the

127

other way. When he turned back, expecting to see her naked on the hearth rug, he saw no change.

'Aren't you going to undress?'

'I have.' Blushing terribly now, she pointed to the chair. Sensible drawers and silk stockings hung neatly next to her coat across the arm.

This nonplussed him. He felt to leave his bags on, do it through the fly (which is how they had always finger-fucked in the past), would be quite wrong, yet he knew he would look a fool in shirt tails and suspended socks. He also realised she was now very near tears, and a spasm of pity soured his lust.

'I'm going to take mine off.'

'No, Dickie.'

'Please.'

'Suppose someone comes in.'

'I'll sport the oak.'

'You mustn't. They know at the lodge I'm here.'

'Oh Lord. Well, all right. Just my bags. But don't laugh, I'll look a fright.'

'Of course I won't laugh. But do hurry.'

Awkwardly he lay on top of her, pushed her skirt up round her waist and then felt a sudden shock of terrible joy as he actually got his fingers between her buttocks and suspender belt and felt her hands sliding over his bottom. One fear he had had was now quite gone.

'Oh, Dickie. It feels bigger than ever before. Be gentle.'

'Of course, Tootsie.'

'Do you love me?'

'Of course I do, my love.'

'Dickie. Will you put on one of those things you showed me? For me. Please.'

'Oh Lord. Do I have to?'

'Yes. Please.'

He knelt above her, sweating, heart pounding, a savage warmth spreading out from his loins. His member pushed up his shirt tail in front and pulsed. He fumbled in the drawer of the shabby little table that stood by the chair, and found one of the three square packets he had bought at a barber shop near

128

Liverpool Street Station. Paper crackled, rubber snapped, and the smell of it filled their nostrils.

'Geoffrey,' he said, 'says it's like going for a swim in an overcoat, oh, oh, oh . . . oh hell, oh damn,' and covering himself with his hands he turned away, stood up, and ran to the bedroom, snatching up his trousers as he went.

'Dickie, Dickie, what's the matter?'

'It happened, Maud. You know. It happened. When I put that bloody thing on.'

She turned her cheek to the hearth rug and wept.

'And what a marvellous catalogue it is,' Dame Maud said into her microphone, 'the Devil and all the pagan gods defeated by the birth of the Christ-child; the old dragon swingeing the scaly horror of his folded tail, Apollo leaving his shrine with hollow shriek, the brutish gods of Nile, Typhon huge ending in snaky twine. I wonder, if Milton were writing now, what other hollow idols he would include in his list; Marx perhaps? Engels? Lenin? Lukács? Marcuse? Even my colleague here in the English School at Oxford — Terry Eagleton — might rate as an imp, if not a devil. It's a thought, isn't it? And wun, w-o-n I'm happy to close with, for "See, the Virgin Blest, Hath laid her Babe to rest, Time is our tedious song should here have ending."'

She stopped the tape, and sat for a moment looking out across the green table and the huge silk cushions. On the floor lay *The Burning Matrix*, back cover up — a photo of Sir Richard Austen.

'I'll get you, Dickie,' she murmured, 'I'll get you yet.'

And she poured herself another G and T.

15

At the college gate Cargill realised he had left his copy of *The Burning Matrix* behind, but he could not bring himself to return for it. Shire horses would not have dragged him back. He walked to Blackwell's and bought another, and this time he threw away the receipt.

Briefly — the Inter-City gave him no more time than 'briefly' — he glanced at it again and skimmed through the chapter on the Spanish Civil War. It did not interest him, except in so far as it reinforced — by what it left out — his suspicion that Austen had been a communist in the hands of the OGPU, KGB or whatever, long before the conversion that appeared to have taken place while he was in Spain.

It was *Boys' Own Paper* stuff, Buchan with the ideologies reversed, *For Whom the Bell Tolls* told by Dornford Yates. If Austen was to be believed, there he had been, digging away with the Mephistophelian Dr González, up in the Asturian hills, painfully endeavouring to relate shards of pottery to Beaker 'B', when suddenly all hell broke loose. General Mola on the wireless, the workforce (mostly unemployed coalminers) deserting to a man and joining the loyalist militias; the sudden disappearance of Dr González himself — presumably into safety behind the rebel lines along the coast at Vigo — a confused period, a phony war, then the appearance of Junkers and Heinkels 'black as crows out of hell', according to Austen, heralding the steady advance of the rebels from the west.

News came that they were cut off, that the mountains and plains that separate Madrid and the Castiles from the Atlantic coasts were in the hands of Mola, that Irun had fallen, then San Sebastian. Slowly the perimeters were eroded, the lines inexorably contracted on Bilbao; the Asturias fell, and Austen's moment of heroism came, told without overt modesty.

He had, it seemed, been working as first-aid man, stretcher bearer, that sort of thing — it having been decided that his inability to speak or understand Spanish made him more dangerous than useful as an actual combatant. A sudden push from the enemy had left him with a churchful of wounded on his hands; a rebel officer marched in accompanied by a section of what looked like Moors and began systematically to shoot each of the wounded in the back of the neck; Austen had a revolver, three hand grenades, and a sound defensive position behind the altar. He shot and blew up the murderers and in the confusion contrived to escape. In the hills he stumbled on a column of refugees, mostly old men, women and children, and with them, after more appropriately heroic exploits, regained the Republican lines.

In April 1937 he was working in the hospital at Guernica and was bombed — his left leg was fractured and badly lacerated. He was invalided to Bilbao, leaving the bombed town in the back of a requisitioned Hispano-Suiza only moments before the rebels entered it. In the Bilbao hospital a British member of the CP, unnamed, discovered him; they talked with all the intensity of committed youth, and the upshot was that Austen allowed himself to be evacuated in one of the courageous British merchant ships that had broken the rebel/German blockade, with the mission of touring Britain's industrial heartland, speaking at factory gates, in working men's clubs, telling the story as it really was. This he did, only stopping off at King Street on the way to join the Communist Party. Liar, thought Cargill, he's been a member for years.

The chapter concluded thus: 'As an intellectual I have been, since pre-university days, drawn to that wide body of thought, more a method than anything else, a way of looking at things, loosely called Marxism. As I grew older, study of both the basic texts and those more narrowly concerned with my own field, coupled with research and thought within that field, led eventually to the state of affairs where I would no longer dispute

131

the point when I was labelled "Marxist"; my only reservation being: have I really studied it all well enough, have I really achieved the control, discipline, thoroughness in my own thought processes without which that title is not merited?

'To my shame, as I wrote earlier, I have not been what is called a "political animal". For two brief years I was a member of the Communist Party but that had little to do with Marxism, though the fact that the CP claimed to be Marxist was definitely an added inducement. But I joined because I had by then developed a very deep, a very passionate, hatred of fascism, which has not, in the forty odd years since, abated one jot. My experiences in Spain were not isolated; they were the culmination of a process that had begun many years earlier — perhaps at my prep school, perhaps at the dinner table at home when I heard members of my caste categorising fellow human beings as animals, louts, sluts and worse because they would not accept reduced wages during the recession.

'I joined the CP in the autumn of 1937 because it seemed to be the only organisation which was strenuously, effectively and with utter conviction combating fascism. Hence all the greater was my disillusion when Stalin and Molotov made what seemed then to be their hideous pact with Hitler and Ribbentrop. Like many hundreds of others, I impulsively tore up my card; and I have remained outside politics in the narrow party sense ever since, apart from campaigning for the Labour Party whenever the local candidate seemed a man of principle and intellectual substance — a rare enough conjunction.

'However, I have, to the best of my powers, fought fascism wherever and whenever I could. In the war that followed I was called, through no choice of my own, to serve not as a combatant but nevertheless in an organisation which contributed much to the downfall of Hitler: that is the subject of my next chapter. Since then I have done what I can. Only the other day, as I write this now, I discovered in the Hampshire village I most frequently visit, a "charity shop" selling swastika armbands and Nazi uniforms. Enquiry revealed that the "charity" was an organisation calling itself the "Vigilantes", which recruits adolescent boys ostensibly to train them in rescue and survival techniques. I remonstrated with a spokesman wearing a paramilitary uniform, who made facile excuses for the presence of these foul insignia and uniforms in a shop window in a village high street, and, when I said that I and many other local residents found them profoundly nasty, he called me "a silly little man".

'A small incident, but not a day passes without some such portent. The Nazi alliances in Britain today have a membership comparable with that in Germany in 1930. As the playwright has it, "The bitch that bore the bastards is in heat again."''

For all the tone of this was more serious than anything he had yet read in *The Burning Matrix*, Cargill remained unmoved, indeed unimpressed. Two words only caught his attention, so much so that he underlined them. They occurred in the sentence about the Non-Aggression Treaty between Germany and Russia — '*seemed then* to be their hideous pact'. And now, Cargill thought — almost aloud — as the train slowed through North Kensington past walls scrawled with racist slogans, swastikas and the NF logo, what do you think of it *now*, eh, Austen?

Back in his hutch of an office, Cargill turned on the light, took off coat, hat and muffler and hung them on the coat-hanger (his own) that swung against the door. With a sense of weariness he sat in the broken office chair that fell apart if you leant too far back in it, relit his metal-stemmed pipe, checked the air-extractor was open, and returned to *The Burning Matrix*.

For half an hour he read through the opening pages about Austen's spell at the Government Codes and Cyphers School at Bletchley Park between 1940 and 1945. It was chatty stuff: how he had been recruited (Long time no see, Richard — spot of lunch in my club in order, eh? — Actually been hoping to bump into you, fact is I've been asked to look out for bright chaps for a rather hush-hush sort of job...and so on). For a moment Cargill thought there might be a lead here — if Austen was the real leak (and he was now convinced of this), it was very probable that his recruitment to Bletchley Park had been organised by the NKVD. But here he identified his recruiter as the College chaplain, a man now dead, but who had died mitred and croziered as bishop of a major see. No doubt

133

someone less irreproachable had suggested to *him* 'why not try that chap Austen?' but it was a trail too old and cold to be worth pursuing now. Cargill read on.

Bletchley Park itself: an amusing amalgam of styles — Victorian panelling overlaid with rather gaudy art-nouveau decoration; a park, a pond with ducks. The complex of huts put up behind the house; the informality of it all yet its efficiency too; a brief description of the basic routine — how the German wavelengths were monitored, how most of the messages on them had been encoded by their machine ENIGMA, how the 'chiefs' at B-P cracked ENIGMA and passed on fragments of decoded messages to the 'indians', who then tried to make sense of them; the thoroughness with which this was done — the card-indices cross-referenced with hundreds of thousands of entries; the specialists in all things German; the people with extraordinary memories — one man, a railway freak, apparently knew every inch of Europe's railways down to each last coal and dock siding and was clearly invaluable, though Austen mocked him: 'One imagines him in the thirties, manically using every spare week-end or holiday trundling from the Urals to Bordeaux and back again after spending the long winter evenings immersed in the European equivalent of Bradshaw.

'It was,' Austen went on, 'jolly hard work, perhaps the hardest intellectually I have ever undertaken. I quickly established that my particular skills as an archaeologist had their place there. The trick of mind that observes an apparently meaningless trace of black in the soil at one point in a trench and relates it to a shard in another, and out of them produces the site of a kiln; that out of what is *not* there, conjures what *should* be there by the very shape and contours of the gap — as when we project a missing wall because a ditch of soil differently impacted from that around it suggests that it is a filling replacing stones or bricks that have been taken and used elsewhere; these and others of our skills I found could be applied to make sense of the ceaseless flood of, as it were, fragments, shards, crumbled rust or specks of gold that dropped on our tables from the chiefs in Hut Six.

'At a later age, after such intense effort, one would have been only too grateful to stumble away to bed in one's digs but we were young and tension would have led to sleepless nights without some form of preferably riotous relaxation. In this context it was good to find that some old friends with whom one had trod the gowans fine in days gone by had now swum into one's ken again at Bletchley Park. Amongst these was dear Teddy Riversdale — now quite recovered from his brief but ugly flirtation with fascism, and, in a spirit of contrition, only too happy to devote his very considerable skills as a wordsmith to the task in hand. His once regrettable connection with members of the finance aristocracy of the Third Reich also proved useful on occasion. He joined in 1941 as far as I remember.

'In 1942 our circle was enlarged and enriched by the arrival of the Americans who quickly gave our routs an edge they had hitherto lacked and who also had unlimited access to such necessities of life as Jameson's and Southern Comfort, even, on occasion, real Scottish malt. Amongst these Roy Newman, now a vice-president of United Special Steels, was a tremendous buddy — a tall, thin youth with a huge eagle-like nose, a fat wallet, and a line of talk that would have seduced a nun or persuaded a poteen producer to reveal his still. He was never actually required to do either — but ATS drivers and landgirls fell into his lap like cherries, and they usually had a friend around for Roy's hangers-on. When neither booze nor birds were available, he played poker, and brought to that game a level of cunning which almost convinced me that it could rank with bridge as a game of skill. His favourite variation was five-card stud. He has remained a good friend since and I look him up whenever I am, as they say, stateside, and he calls on me when business brings him to this side of the herring pond...'

Cargill pulled up, tapped the mouthpiece of his pipe against his teeth, leant back — just so far — and: 'Newman, Roy Newman,' he said to himself quietly but aloud, 'it strikes a chord. I wonder now. Roy Newman.' He got up, pulled open his filing cabinet and checked. Yes. He had been an OSS operative even while he was at B-P, later worked for the CIA, while at the same time pursuing his career as export manager for USS. It would be interesting to hear what he had to say about Austen.

* * *

135

'Towards the end of 1944 Roy somehow or other got the use of a jeep and the necessary petrol to make it go, and this, you may imagine, enlarged our horizons considerably, though in the end with tragic results. Whenever we had time off together he would run us — that is Teddy, me and perhaps a girlfriend or two — up to town, where we would meet Kitti, Teddy's lovely sister, another old friend I was only too happy to see again. After a spot of nursing, she was now driving for a rather grand desk-flier at the Air Ministry. There would follow thirty-six hours of... well, never mind that ... but we kept ourselves very well entertained before returning to B-P with minds refreshed and ready for work, however exhausted we may have felt in other areas.

'The fact that this was the period of the V2 assault on London added a wild, nightmarish spice to these junketings — I think it is material that we knew better than most that the war was on its last legs, that when it was over many of us might feel a sort of regret that we had not actually seen action. That, I think, lay behind the fascination the darkened metropolis held for Teddy and Roy — not for me; I had supped my fill of horrors in Spain.

'One night in December 1944 we were split up by some accident of the party we were attending. When, next day, we reassembled at Roy's jeep, parked if I remember rightly in Brook Street — no Teddy. We waited for as long as we could before returning to B-P, heavy hearted and fearing the worst, for bombs had arrived that night, two exceptionally within the West End. He was never found, but was eventually posted as a casualty presumed dead. A tragic waste. A tragic loss. He showed promise of being a major talent and I mourn him still.

'When all's said and done, B-P, fascinating though it was, was an interlude only, and just as soon as those who dispose of such things were ready to release me I was off — eager to get a PhD under my belt and an academic base from which to pursue my career. I chose to enrol at what was then Southampton University College for various reasons. First — on my father's retirement in 1937, at the far too advanced age of seventy-five, we had moved to a small place in the New Forest, taking with us the Wainwrights, father, son and daughter-in-law, who managed the Farm for us. Then, in 1943, father passed away at last, leaving mother surrounded by trees, heath and cows. Naturally enough, she wanted me near her, and now the old dragon was out of the way I felt I could enjoy her company in a way that had not been possible before. I have never regretted that decision. As I said earlier, she is now very old and is well cared for in an excellent home in Lymington, where I visit her at least twice a week; the Farm is still my home and main base and a delightful spot it is. Old Man Wainwright died long since; John Wainwright, who helped me in my first dig all those years ago in South Meon, has retired to a bungalow at New Milton, and his son Brian now manages the farm which he and his wife have converted into a highly prosperous riding stable.

'But I digress. Back to 1945 and my other reasons for not returning to Cambridge or giving the "other place" a chance. The fact is London University, through the Institute of Archaeology, had a lot more to offer and Southampton University College, besides having a small and vigorous department of its own, was then of course under London.

'A stronger reason was the antipathy I had begun to feel for Oxbridge generally, an antipathy which has grown ever since. I shan't go into this now — I have written about it elsewhere: just let me reiterate that almost everything that is wrong about England at the moment is in part at least due to the smugness, arrogance and complacency that emanate from those two seats of learning ('seats' here may be taken as a euphemism, and 'emanate' too); to the way they have been appropriated by the ruling class as a means of perpetuating itself and its privileges; and, in no little measure, to the narrow-minded, hidebound ignorance about almost everything that has happened in an intellectually important way in the last hundred years: believe me, that is, with several honourable exceptions, still the main characteristic of most of the so-called academics who live (forgive the expression, but I feel strongly) on the loot of empires (Ruskin's phrase) like pigs in shit...'

Cargill nearly tipped himself out of his chair at this. That, he thought, really is fouling one's nest — this man's got a nerve, he really has. For Cargill to have thought otherwise was impossible. Austen had attacked unquestionable assumptions which

137

were as much part of Cargill's mental physiognomy as his nose was part of his face.

He rubbed his eyes with the balls of his thumbs and flicked on over the next pages. He was very tired; it was gone seven o'clock, and he should have been at home in case Sleight rang. The next section seemed to be archaeology, primitive metallurgy, and who knows what all: Austen had developed a doctoral thesis on just how new techniques of smelting copper and tin had revolutionised bronze production in the Middle East, all of which apparently related to the title of the book — *The Burning Matrix*; he had at the end of it been delighted to get the chance in 1948 of directing a dig on his own for the first time, in Anatolia, at a place called Sherefhisar in the Konya Plain, Konya being St Paul's Iconium...

The phone rang. It was the Housemaster. 'Look, Cargill, I thought now you've dropped that B-P business you'd be back on your Windscale signalman. No? Well, listen, a nonsense has occurred. Rather a serious nonsense. Fosdike has cocked up his arrest and the signalman is holed up in a farm somewhere in Cumbria with a shotgun, his wife and two children, and he's going to shoot the lot if he isn't given access to the media... Be a good chap and sort it out, will you? There's an SAS chopper waiting for you at the Heliport, and Andrews will brief you on the way. All right, William, I can leave it with you? Fine!'

Wearily, Cargill pushed away *The Burning Matrix*, pulled the Windscale file out of his pending tray, checked pockets for pipe, matches and keys, and, after one last look round his bleak office, switched off the light.

16

'Sir Richard, I don't think we can get any further until we
understand each other over just what constitutes fascism. We
have a semantic difficulty just here, I believe. I equate fascism
with Mussolini's party in Italy, with National Socialism in
Germany, with the Falange in Spain, with parties or groupings
with similar aims in other countries. You, if you'll forgive me'
(God — she's being charming!) 'seem to equate it with anything
you don't much like from liberalism through ant-tie communism, ant-tie Marxism, to the downright reactionary. Now,
I'm not going to understand too well just what it was about
fascism made a left-orientated person out of you, unless you
choose to be a little bit more specific.'

Dr Shapiro, off the record you're pretty sure I'm a spy; off the
record I'm not going to give away anything that might help you
to prove it, so let's just stop fucking about, shall we?

'Another muffin?'

'Thank you, no.'

'You haven't drunk your tea.'

'No. Actually I don't much like this Chinese stuff.'

'I could make you some coffee.'

'Hell *no*. Sir Richard. Pardon me. Fascism. Please.'

The evenings are drawing in. Brian's got the floods on over his
all-weather riding surface. There'll be a frost tonight. Fat out
for the tits and nuthatches. Mustn't forget.

'Sir Richard?'

'Sorry, sorry. Wool-gathering. Fascism? Yes. Fascism is one
of the methods which may be adopted by the capitalist class

139

when the threat of the working class to the stability of monopoly capitalism becomes acute: it is the attempt to create a popular mass movement for the protection of monopoly capitalism.'

Shapiro shifted haunches closer to the edge of the deep armchair he had put her in. Her hands, capable, sturdy (I expect she knows karate), gripped the arm rests.

'I would say, Sir Richard, that you have defined your European Social Democrat parties right there, and to some extent the Democrats of the United States too. Now, they may fall within your earlier, rather *catholic* definition of fascism, as they do within this apparently more *considered* one. But it won't do.'

Austen fumbled, then recovered; really it was intellectually quite stimulating disentangling the camel's verbosity off the cuff as it were. 'Difficulties too obvious to be described as semantic, here, Dr Shapiro,' he said waggishly. 'None of the parties you have mentioned can, in any interpretation I would put on the words, be described as a movement, none is popular, none has mass following. The membership of all is very small — it is only at elections that they could be said to have a mass following: and that, quite clearly, is a following that is merely choosing the lesser of two evils. You know what I mean. National Socialism in Germany had mass popular support. And it was financed by monopoly capitalism.'

'There was no such popular mass movement in England.'

'No.'

'So there was no immediate, direct reason for being an ant-tie fascist.'

Oh dear. This really is going to be very difficult. I had forgotten how pig ignorant most liberals are. Austen had also forgotten momentarily that he believed the serious, rather ugly lady in front of him was a CIA agent come to trap him into indiscretion or worse. Now his only concern was to demonstrate the rightness of his thought and to demolish hers.

'Monopoly capitalism is international. True socialism, through which capitalism will cease to be the dominant mode of production, is also international. In the thirties, the chief threat to monopoly capitalism, apart from its own inbuilt contradictions, was the Communist International and its support of socialist movements across the world. Where these seemed likely to succeed they had to be countered. The next country most likely to become socialist was Germany. International monopoly capitalism created, or anyway supported, the fascist movement there. North Italy was also a threat. Czechoslovakia and Hungary too. In all these countries monopoly capitalism created or endeavoured to create popular mass movements devoted to the crushing of socialism. It began to lay the foundations for similar movements in countries where it was not so obviously threatened — England, America, France. It did this no doubt partly as a precaution against worse times ahead, partly to provide a focus for support of the fascist movements in the directly threatened countries. It gave support in other ways too. Now, as a young man just down from Cambridge, I came into personal contact with elements, high up people you understand, influential, wealthy, who were giving just the sort of support I am talking of. It disgusted me. A year or so later, my convictions were confirmed when I saw their beliefs in action in Spain. It's in my book. These were the experiences that made an anti-fascist of me.'

'*The Burning Matrix.* Yes. You describe Guernica most dramatically. And how you joined the CP on your return. You describe too how the Molotov-Ribbentrop Pact caused you to lose faith in the internationalism of Soviet socialism, how you renounced the British CP as being Soviet-dominated. Then in a later chapter you express doubts about that renunciation, argue that history may yet show Stalinism to have been the correct response to international capitalism at that stage. But you do not, as I recall, mention this earlier ... confrontation with ant-tie socialist, pro-fascist, upper-class elements.'

The small, dapper man looked suddenly weary; he twisted away from her, stood up and walked across his Turkey kilims to the windows in the side of the house.

'But I do,' he said. 'I mention how I became friendly with the Riversdales and stayed at Scales, how I had — what did I call it? — an almighty row with them and agreed to differ.'

He stayed still for a moment and beyond his reflection in night-blackened glass she could see lights, heavy fencing, sand and horses, riders practising dressage under the direction of a

141

sheepskinned, booted lady. Then Austen abruptly drew the curtains.

'I went no further into it than that since one at least of the protagonists is still alive. There is no call now to rake up that sort of muck. One doesn't want to hurt people unnecessarily, the whole thing has been well aired, and from the Windsors down the main culprits exposed. No need to throw mud at the smaller fish.'

Shapiro could not recollect when she had last witnessed such transparent insincerity in the flesh (though familiar enough in the media). Feeling sure that the delicacy of feeling Austen was laying claim to was just not part of his make up at all, she threw out more ground-bait. 'Most of that sort of person was in the Anglo-German Fellowship. I suppose you are talking about that circle? Were the acquaintances you spoke of in that?'

'Yes, yes, I've no doubt they were.' He was abrupt, dismissive.

She laughed — she supposed lightly, gaily, but her insincerity was as transparent as his had been. 'And Kim Philby was a secretary for a time. For the Anglo-German Fellowship — that's right, isn't it?'

'There's no secret about that. It was his cover. It's all in Boyle. But I didn't come across him then.'

'Boyle? Oh yes. *The Climate of Treason.* Fascinating. But you did later?'

'Later? Did what later?'

'Met Philby. Later, not before, for on Wednesday you told me you knew none of that group at Cambridge. So later.'

'Why are you so sure I did meet him?'

The retrieval system again. She would never need to use a recording device — every word she had ever heard or read could be recalled: 'You said, and I quote, I didn't come across him *then*. More important, in your book you have an anecdote about how he cut you in Beirut only days before he defected. Now you can't cut someone you don't know.'

She's no fool.

'Well, well, Dr Shapiro, you've caught me out. I could say, and it would be true, that I knew Philby very briefly at

Cambridge when we were winding up the Labour Club. But you're right. There was another meeting. It's a story few people know. Would you like to hear it?'

'Of course, I'd love to.'

Of course you would. It's what you've come for. I've never mentioned it to anyone before because I was told not to. But it must be on their files that he came to me, they know it. Probably through the Turkish Third Section. So the best thing is to admit it — otherwise they will read into my reticence an admission of collusion. The best way to defuse this one is to make a clean breast of it. A tolerably clean breast. But I must go very carefully.

'It's quite a good yarn. Can't think why I have sat on it all these years. Well, I can, actually. With my known beliefs, no one would have believed me when I said I had no idea at all that Kim was with the KGB. But it's true. No idea at all . . . It was on my first dig abroad actually, '48. Sherefhisar, a small tel in the Anatolian steppe, about ten miles from a town called Konya, and a bloody hot place in July, I can tell you. Well, one day, just as we were knocking off, a taxi trundled into our camp and out got this rather suave sort of chap — we of course were looking indistinguishable from our Turkish workmen — and announced he was First Secretary at our Embassy . . .'

'Oh, Gee! And it was Philby. He was then head of the SIS station in Turkey.'

'That's right — you've got it!' She really does know it all.

'He introduced himself, said he was passing by, thought he should look in to see how we were coping.'

'Wasn't that a bit odd? I mean, checking on the welfare of nationals is consular work, not diplomatic.'

Steady now. She really is quite shrewd. I wonder how far I should go with this. Tell the truth always, as much of the truth as you can.

'Of course. Deuced odd. And it became odder when it transpired his taxi had gone back to Konya without him, and I had to take him back in my jeep.'

'Why odder?'

'Because he made me have dinner with him, got me drunk and pumped me.'

143

'My. What about? This is really fascinating, Sir Richard.'

'But off your subject: Cambridge in the Thirties.'

'Oh sure, but what a good story this is. I'll get it in some-where, even if it's only in a footnote. So what did he pump you about, Sir Richard?'

She looks like an adolescent hearing about sex from a friend — excited, but butter wouldn't melt... Now for it.

'Well, Bletchley Park, naturally. You know I worked there in the war. It's in *BM*.'

'Sure, sure. Go *on*!'

'It seems there had been a leak; they, that is MI whatever the right number is, had found out the Russians knew all about it. So all known lefties that worked there were questioned, and Philby was sent to check me out. Of course, I've no doubt, he knew who the leak was all along, but he had to pretend he didn't.'

'It wasn't you then.'

Jesus. She has a nerve.

'God, *no.*' That was too emphatic. 'I think I've made it clear that if I have a fault it is that politically I like to stay on the touchlines.'

'Yes. You call yourself a *flâneur*. But did *you* know who the leak was?'

This is tricky.

'I didn't know then. I've been told since. Unofficially of course. Club gossip.'

'Who?'

'My dear lady, I wouldn't dream of telling you. Not even in the cause of accurate scholarship. But I can tell you he is dead.'

'So it was somebody on the left. University and on the left?'

'No, no. My lips are sealed on that one. Our chaps sorted it out in the end, even without Philby's help, or in spite of his hindrance... and that really is that.'

In the silence a dog barked and horses' hooves, chump, chump chumped in coarse sand.

'So that was your main meeting with Philby, Sir Richard?'

'That's right. That's the interesting one. The couple of occasions at Cambridge I really don't recall. And the snub in Beirut is in my book.'

Austen got up, stirred the logs into life in the big stone fireplace, threw on another. His eyes wandered over the wreckage of their tea... cucumber sandwiches, fruit cake; she had hardly eaten a thing and hadn't touched her Earl Grey. Damn it, he thought, but I think I've got away with it, and I need a drink.

'Care for a Scotch?' he said.

She looked at her watch... she's one of those idiots who won't touch it until the sun's below the yard-arm or whatever.

'All right. Yes. I'd like one.'

He retrieved tumblers from the sideboard, unstopped the decanter. 'Soda?'

'Fine. Sir Richard,' her voice was contemplative, questioning, as she took the proffered tumbler, 'Sir Richard, when you were speaking of Philby, you referred to him as Kim, and there was even a sort of admiration in your voice.'

Damn this stupid woman. I should never have given her a drink, tea, the time of day. I don't care who she is, the head of the CIA's favourite *whore*, I must get rid of her.

'Listen. You know we have an honours list, a system of public honours...'

'Of course. You yourself...'

He gulped from his glass, then waved it dismissively. 'Quite. Discredited. So many rogues and charlatans K'd, OBE'd, all the rest of it. Well. If Mrs Thatcher wants my advice on how to bring a touch of respectability back to the whole charade, here it is. Make General Kim Philby of the KGB a Companion of Honour. How about that?'

Quite soon after that, she went.

Austen cleared away the tea things into the kitchen, where one of Sandra Wainwright's stablegirls would wash up (they had a rota, called it 'mucking him out', and reckoned he was more trouble than Charlie, the Arab stud); then he topped up his glass and sat by the fire in the chair Shapiro had vacated. He looked around, trying to force himself into seeing the over-familiar room with fresh eyes — since, one way or another (Jamestown for Roy's steel firm; the Leningrad Institute of Archaeology where, he had been assured, a Bronze Age niche

145

awaited him should he ever need it; or, just possibly, Parkhurst top security wing, Isle of Wight) he now had presentiments that he would not be there much longer.

He would not be sorry to go. The room had been his father's before it had been his and — though the theology, the Loeb Classics, the Buchans and Dornford Yates and Bulldog Drummonds had gone from the bookshelves; and kilims replaced the Axminster; and drawings by Ben Nicholson and Victor Pasmore the prints of stately homes owned by distant relations — the ghost of the old fraud still lurked.

He had not done badly with the Camel, he thought. Tell as much of the truth as you can. He'd really got very near it. He stirred sparks and heat out of the largest beech log, then leant back in the sudden warmth...

17

A wide flat plain appeared in his mind's eye, yellow soil, sparse yellow stubble, whiter yellow dust devils whispering up in the hot wind, floating a yard or two, then sighing away again. Thorn bushes on the stony outcrops, teazles that clatter. Tiny blue flowers on desiccated stems — immortelles. And beyond the hills — stratified red and green with minerals, then grey, violet, snow — a limitless blue sky, out of which a red kite casts a purple shadow that drifts across the stones and stubble, lurches suddenly and magnifies as the fork-tailed predator slides down the wind, then recovers. The movement scuttling beneath it was a ball of straw, not the rodent it needs.

A great cloud of dust, far larger than all the dust devils put together, an isolated fog of dust a mile or so to the right, marks a hundred or so skeletal sheep just down from the mountain pasture, scavenging across the stubble, policed by two large grey dogs with spiked collars and a shepherd in an untreated sheepskin cape whose stiff shoulders rise in a crescent across his back.

Austen heard the dogs and hoped they would not come too close.

Then another noise above the wind, straight out of a cowboy picture, the distant blast of a steam whistle and a bell. Further off than the sheep, balls of black smoke roll away across the plain and through a defile between low rises comes the Ankara/Antioch train — a large black locomotive complete with cowcatcher, six passengers coaches (one first class), and an interminable string of cattle-trucks, wagons and tankers. Austen looked

147

at his watch. A quarter to four. As usual the train is punctually four hours late — a reliable signal to his workmen that the worst heat of the day is over, that work should begin again.

He turned. Sure enough, a short line of men was making its way across the stubble from the village of square, dried dung shacks half a mile from the tel he was standing on. They would have spent the middle of the day in the one tea-house drinking from small tulip-shaped glasses, dipping rectangles of sugar, eating grapes, grey bread, halva. They were all dressed alike in waistcoats, collarless shirts and baggy, black trousers, and all wore western flat hats reversed so the peaks protected their necks and allowed them to touch their foreheads to the ground in prayer. At first sight they had been indistinguishable, though as he got to know them better Austen had come to recognise their dour individuality. Murteza was a joker; Ali, who had two wives, was morose and easily angered; Davut was older than the others — had white stubble on his sunken cheeks and only three teeth. His back had gone but his hands were like vises, could straighten iron bars. Fifteen of them there were, glad of the work now the harvest was over, and all incredibly tough.

The train was disappearing into the foot-hills, would be at Konya in five or ten minutes; the flock of sheep was moving on. Time to get on with it.

Austen picked his way down the loose earth to the exploratory trench they had already cut across the periphery of the mound. It was eight feet wide, carefully pegged out and posted, and at its deepest point the walls were ten feet high, a straight chord linking two points on the circumference of the tel. In this trench George Partridge was dismantling his camera and tripod, and young Mehmet from Ankara University was carefully taking down the labels identifying the eight main strata: the workmen invariably displaced them and then stuck them back any old where, thus causing endless confusion.

The afternoon's work went well. By six o'clock, when the unblemished blue of the sky had begun to deepen imperceptibly, the wind had dropped, and the snow-capped mountains seemed nearer, they had cleared enough of the floor of what Austen had hoped would turn out to be an Early Bronze Age hearth for him to feel sure that he was right. For such a small team they were doing well. George wore three hats at least — deputy director, site supervisor, photographer. He had been foreman too, but this post Davut had taken over — the villagers respected his age and character. Mehmet was small-finds recorder, pottery assistant, and attempted to be draughtsman, a function George saw no reason for — he had a Leica and a Rolleiflex: what was the point of scribbling away with pencil and paper? Almost all other jobs essential to a well-run dig Austen himself contrived to fulfil — save of course for the most important of all, without which nothing was possible, that of actually shifting muck. Davut and his fellow villagers did that.

Now, as they began to pack up for the day, he walked well-trodden stubble across to the small compound of tents and two jeeps, where he, Mehmet and George cleaned, labelled, bagged, wrote up each succeeding day's history, and, if and when they had time, slept and ate. Austen reflected that he was happy, although never far off exhaustion. It was his first dig, the first he himself had directed. They had identified the strata where the first local metal objects were likely to be found, had recovered a gold fibula, and three studs probably off a belt or dagger hilt. If only they could hit the forge. He turned. With the westering sun falling across the tel, it now looked mountainous, though it was small by Anatolian standards, less than an acre. But still huge if you had only fifteen workmen, probably only one season, and a most unprofessional ambition to find one particular thing: the site of an Early Bronze Age forge.

Following Gordon Childe, he knew that the metal workers always lived apart from the rest of the community and usually on the outskirts of the settlement. Their occupation was arduous, highly skilled — a craft, a mystery. Alone amongst the community they had nothing to do with food production; they were fed in return for axes and adzes, swords, rapiers and spearheads, pins, buttons, crowns — and, most important of all, so important that the importance of a king and of his tribe would be measured by the number he possessed: cauldrons. But that was going ahead to the Hittites themselves. It was the first forge Austen was after — the moment when the division of labour became absolute.

149

Not for the first time, his obsession sidetracked him from the small-finds tent and out into what was virtually semi-desert. *Then* it had been a steppe of fertile grassland and the inhabitants had quite recently learnt to cultivate the grasses with plumper seeds, thresh, grind and bake them. They had driven sheep — much like those climbing the rise three miles off now, but probably fatter. And they had had timber. The present village had none, or very, very little — relying on dung for fuel, dung and mud for building. When they had to have timber, they bought it with the pitiful few pence they got from raising salads and sunflowers round their well and selling them in Konya market, or earned in return for gruelling labour on behalf of the distant landlords who owned the fields and the rights of pasture — though this labour barely covered rent and taxes. But their remote ancestors had had timber. There must have been a river supporting a belt of forest, and Austen believed he had found its course marked by a winding declivity, a very gentle slope answered by another, and in the middle a trial hole had discovered gravel at no great depth. So he had struck his trench, his chord, across the edge of the tel nearest to this river, rather than on the other side facing the copper-bearing hills ten miles away — smiths need wood and water, and may well have panned alluvial gold from what had been a wide, shallow riverbed.

But *how* isolated from the rest of the community? 'A class apart, a distinct society, excluded from the ranks of those entitled to ceremonial burial, detribalised...' Childe had posited. Perhaps even the very outskirts, the periphery of the Bronze Age settlement, were yet *too* close.

The sun was now throwing longer shadows, the slightest undulations in the stubble were becoming clearer every second. (Dimly, in the background, Austen heard the throb of a car — he looked up, marked a column of dust tracking a dark blue pre-war Buick — a car for Capone, but in fact one of the two taxis Konya then boasted. He guessed but avoided verbalising the thought, so irritating was it, that whoever had hired it to come out here in the early evening could only be coming to see him.) It was like, very like, cracking a code. You had enough information to be sure something was missing. The same information or, more probably, a quite different set of data — if only one could jump to it, guess the connection — would provide clues as to the nature of what was missing.

Water. Timber. Timber was surely the clue. Heavy, awkward to handle — would it have been easier to move the forge rather than the timber? After a time it would become easier. As the timber was exhausted nearby you moved . . . up or down, even perhaps to the other side. There might have been several sites . . .

'Hullo there. Your man told me you'd be down here somewhere. Austen? My name's Philby.'

'What? You mean George Partridge? Yes, my name is Austen.' The interruption was bad enough — but the assumption that George was *his man* was distasteful. He looked up and was instantly, instinctively, aware that the point had been taken.

The man in front of him was only a little taller than he, about the same age or only a little older, compactly built, dressed in a linen jacket over an open shirt with a Trinity scarf round his neck. Immediately recognisable, Austen thought, as the more relaxed sort of diplomat — an impression Philby confirmed: 'I'm at our Em-m-mbassy, you know.'

It was the smile that got through to Austen — it was open in the sense that it held nothing back, promised fair shares; complicit too — not fair shares all round, dear me no. Just between us two.

'But don't think I'm here in any official c-c-c-capacity. I'm on leave and just pottering about, you know? The consul told me he thought there were a couple of our chaps out this way and the Archaeological Institute confirmed it. So I thought I'd drop by.'

'That was kind of you, but really no need. Everything's fine.'

The smile again. 'I intruded, didn't I? Broke a train of thought. Unforgivable, I should have stayed at your dig until you came back.'

Austen's resentment finally melted. He explained to Philby what he had been pondering, and was finally captivated by the other man's enthusiastic appreciation of the problems: 'Would they have had to drag the timber — would tracks have been necessary? What about tributaries to the river? I suppose a *flat* site for each forge would have been essential . . .'

151

In the end Austen showed this charming, intelligent visitor over everything they had done so far — exhibited the shards, the fibula and gold studs, the flakes of bronze...and entirely approved the way Philby treated George — not as anyone's man after all, but as a social equal, and, as far as archaeology went, as an authority.

'Well, just one,' said Philby, when in the swiftly falling dusk Austen offered him a Scotch. 'I mustn't deplete your store — I imagine you treat it like liquid gold out here. Then I must get back.'

George, who had perhaps been a shade less enchanted than Austen with the intruder, asked sharply, 'How?'

'Why, in my taxi, of course.'

'It went, while you were over in the fields with Mr Austen.'

'Oh Lord, did it really? How awful, I was s-s-sure the Johnny Turk who was driving it had understood.'

'Odd he should go off without you paid him.' George was relentless.

Philby's eyes narrowed, his face for the briefest second cold, calculating. Was there after all something a touch reptilian...?

The smile came back. 'Well, of course I paid him something in advance — only way to get them on your side at the outset, you know. I suppose I underdid it and he thought he had done his bit. I say, this is a most awful bore. All my stuff is in that squalid little hotel, I don't know what I shall do.'

Naturally Austen said he would drive him the ten miles to Konya in one of the jeeps — but only, Philby insisted, if he allowed him to buy him a dinner when they got there. 'A slap-up one. Turkish cuisine really can be very good, even out in the wild. I'll show you.'

George elected to stay behind — with his cameras; and Philby, for all his earlier camaraderie, did not press him.

'The *dolmas*, stuffed things, you know? are very good at this time of year. Peppers, tomatoes, but the best are the courgettes and vine leaves. Let's have a couple of each, shall we?'

Nervously Austen agreed. For a month he had lived on tomatoes, grey bread and eggs — meat was unobtainable in the village and the other things the locals ate looked too frightful for

152

words. Not that the dolmas appeared much better — they had the dull green of rotten vegetables, were oily, and barely warm. He admitted, though, that the filling was delicious.

'And we'll start with *raki*, the ideal aperitif. It's a bit like Pernod, goes white not yellow, and it's not so bland. More of a bite, snakebite perhaps. You can add water, but it's best just poured over ice. I don't suppose you remember, but we met briefly at Cambridge. When the poor old Labour Club was on its last legs.'

'You know, it's been bothering me. I was sure we had met, and you're right, that was it.' Austen took a swig, and felt better.

He looked around. They were in a restaurant next to Philby's hotel. The room was large, bare, dully lit; a large fan like a helicopter's propeller stirred the air above them. The chairs and tables were dark brown bentwood, the linen grey and damp to the touch. At one end a tiny stage flanked with ferns promised entertainment of a sort later. Inevitably there were two large portraits of Kemal Ataturk and Ismet Inonu, his recent successor. The only other customers were four army officers, smart in well-pressed uniforms, already boisterous from raki, and a tall young man with a serious, even gloomy, expression with, in spite of his youth, deep lines in his cheeks.

Philby whispered conspiratorially, waved his fork in the young man's direction: 'That is Nur bey,' he said. 'A policeman from Istanbul. He follows me everywhere — I'm not quite sure why. Is he a bodyguard? Is he spying on me? I don't know. But I've learnt to live with him — he's quite a comfort really.' The diplomat laughed. 'Poor Nur. The other taxi was already bespoke so he couldn't follow me to your tel... That really was fascinating this afternoon, you know. These Anatolian villagers are incredible workmen, aren't they?'

The meal moved on. Really it was very good. Philby certainly knew the cuisine, even though it was only the second year of his tour. The next course was large lumps of leg of lamb, still on the bone, stewed with aubergines — after five meatless weeks, it was delicious.

'They're so marvellously strong. The Anatolian peasants, I mean. A colleague of mine had a piano sent over. It arrived at Galata, the port in Istanbul, and he tried to hire a donkey and

153

cart to get it up to his flat. Well, the porters there are unofficially organised and they insisted it was a one-man job — the donkey owners are their class enemies, you understand; they have more to sell than just their labour, a donkey is capital — so my colleague had to entrust his piano to one man, one much like your Davut, I should say. Golly, this stew is jolly good, don't you think? And... let us call him Davut, this Davut had the piano — only a small upright, but all the same — strapped to his back and like that he lugged it up the hill into Pera, and then, when it wouldn't go in the lift, up three flights of stairs. Well, when they struck the bargain there was no mention of stairs... another drop of wine? Why not... I think we might order a second... and Davut wanted an extra ten liras. Less than a quid. But my colleague is a mean old bugger and refused. So what do you suppose Davut did? He just carried that piano back down the stairs, down the hill, back to the dock at Galata. And there the matter rests, as they say.' Philby chuckled, dabbed at gravy stains round his mouth, and drank. 'Not bad this *Kavaklidere*, is it? Not unlike a not unsound Beaujolais. We'll have some of those marvellous Turkish pastries for pud, shall we? They give them the most marvellous names — Lady's Thigh, Lady's Navel; you can see how their minds are working towards the end of the meal.'

After the pastries Philby ordered coffee. He stretched out, seemed to expand, brought out a pipe and lit it.

'Can't recommend the brandy — *kanyak* — sure way of getting a very nasty head. So let's have another quarter of snake-bite, what do you say?'

Austen was now filled with well-being and benevolence. The lights in the room seemed brighter, more people had come into the restaurant, a piano trio were playing something vaguely slavic *con brio* amongst the ferns, and Philby himself seemed like a splendid combination of a Cheeryble brother for generosity and a Noel Coward for wit. He assented to another quarter of raki.

'Have a good war, did you?' The smoke swirled around the enigmatic smile. Austen acknowledged the ironic note.

'Did my bit. But there's more to a war than bang-bang you're dead.'

154

'Too true, old chap. Someone's got to keep things going back in Blighty. Make sure the chaps have the wherewithal for going bang-bang. Keep the home fires burning and all that.'

'No, no, no, no. Not anything like that.' Austen was a touch miffed. 'Look. Put it this way. The chaps have to know where to go bang-bang. Right?'

'Ah, I'm with you.' Philby touched the side of his nose — again the gesture was clearly ironic; all the time he maintained the implied criticism of the conversation they were having, a detached sense of the absurdity of it. 'Intelligence, spying, all that sort of thing.'

'Not exactly spying. Intelligence yes. Actually, the lot I was with got more information than any of your common-or-garden spies ever did.'

'Sounds like Bl-bl-bl-bletchley Park, if you ask me.'

The return of the stutter was like a warning bell.

'Careless talk...' said Austen. And then another memory too:

'...Offizzle Shecrets Act.'

'Oh, don't mind me,' said Philby expansively. 'I was in much that line myself during the war, and we knew all about the Golf Club and Chess Society at Bletchley Park. You're right though. You chaps did a damned good job.' The mockery had gone now. For a moment the diplomat seemed to be absolutely sincere. Austen was mollified. 'Let's f-f-f-finish the snakebite and then see what else this town has to offer.'

On the way out, Austen gestured magnanimously at the band. 'Splendid lot,' he said. 'Habañeras, baccarolles, Hungarian fantasies produced to order.'

Philby was abruptly dismissive: 'White Russians. Don't like them. Istanbul simply crawls with them.'

The next five or six hours were remembered by Austen only in snatches over the next two or three days — and he never was quite sure that he had pieced it all together. There was more raki drunk, and later beer spiked with vodka; some of the time they were in a café or tea-house and he recalled trying to play backgammon with one of the Turkish army officers and arguing over the rules; then choking on a hubble-bubble. The officers had some English, were very friendly; inevitably they all went together to the town brothel. Nur bey, the policeman from Istanbul, remained discreetly outside.

Austen had not been to a brothel anywhere before and was agreeably if very drunkenly surprised that it was not as awful as he had expected. In fact, let's admit it, he said to himself the next day after facing George's implacable anger, I really rather enjoyed it, what I remember of it. Which wasn't much — carpets and cushions lit by dull reddish lamps, curtains and huge floppy mattresses on a floor, a fattish lady only dimly seen and reeking of cologne who was prepared to go to a lot of trouble getting him up to the mark, and didn't seem at all to mind when eventually and regretfully he gave up attempting the impossible and went to sleep.

His first clear recollection was sitting naked in a very hot steam room. Philby, a touch paler than he had been, but otherwise surprisingly familiar, was in chummy mood, wanted to chat.

'Funny you should have been at the Golf Club and Chess Society. There's a bit of a stink on about it at the moment, you know.'

Austen grunted, tried to sound interested but he had never felt so weak in his life, worse than the day after being bombed at Guernica, worse even than the night . . . the day after . . . He pushed *that* memory back to where it belonged, shut well out of harm's way. This, however, was a marvellously euphoric, warm, light-headed weakness.

Philby went on, 'Oh yes. Seems the Ruskies know all about it. ENIGMA, ULTRA, the lot. How you were organised there, who did what, the whole works. So there was a leak.'

The euphoria vanished. The weakness remained. Austen very nearly fainted, had to put his head between his knees.

'Bit hot for you? Best to hang on as long as we can. Sweat it out, you know.' Philby's voice remained entirely casual. 'Not surprising really. I mean, you were a pretty high-powered bunch — the cream of the cream. Bound to be some odd-balls in a set-up like that.'

Dripping water, a hiss of steam, blood thundering in his head.

'Philby, I think I might be sick.'

'I doubt it. You were earlier, you know. I don't suppose you have any idea who might have been the Bletchley spy, do you? Any far-out reds, homosexuals, that sort of thing?'

They were sitting on a narrow wooden bench, feet in wooden clogs. Austen had his hands beneath his hams, was sitting on them. Now he dug his nails as hard as he could into the hidden flesh, forced them deeper till the pain became the scream he would not let himself utter. Then slowly he relaxed, and his head cleared — a cold lucidity replaced the awful flux of panic. A beam of sunlight pierced a clouded pane in the small dome they were sitting beneath, played on the billowing steam, threw an egg-shaped blob of light on the cracked marble of the curved wall opposite.

'Well, there were one or two,' he heard himself say.

'Off the record — you can swear blind later you never said a word...who?'

This was it. It was, after all, the moment he had been told to prepare for. It was a dreadful thing to do, but the worst, the very worst was already past and could not be undone. It would be foolish beyond everything to waste all that through a failure of nerve now. He ran his tongue over his lip, tasted the strong salt of his own sweat, and said, 'Teddy Riversdale was one.'

Philby's head turned slowly until his face appeared above his slightly plump shoulder. Runnels of moisture ran over the pallid skin, giving it the look of polished alabaster — a dissolute buddha: the smile was utterly beatific.

'Riversdale. Lord Teddy Riversdale?'

'Yes.'

'C-c-c-can you... I m-m-mean... if, if we send a chap round to you, when you get back to London, will you be able to i-i-indicate...'

'You mean — could I give you...well, pointers to real evidence.'

Philby now seemed to have lost the power of speech, he could only nod his head up and down so vigorously that the wetness flew off.

'Yes. Yes, I could.'

The diplomat began to shake, seemed to be in a fit, his head swayed from side to side, shoulders bobbed, he chewed on his bottom lip — but finally could not control himself, and at last it came, the one word 'Riversdale' burst out in a shout and then its echo was drowned in a giggling, gurgling burst of helpless laughter.

Bemused, then relieved, infected, Austen relaxed and began to laugh too. The small, stone-lined round room reverberated with the wild gaiety of the two men.

At last they calmed down, though small eruptions of giggles recurred for several minutes.

'Better get to the cold room before we stew,' said Philby at last. They were both now a pretty shade of salmon pink. Austen stood up — and farted.

'Oh, *pardon* me.'

It was too much for Philby; he doubled up again and cried out, between chokes and gasps, 'Better out than in, Austen, better out than in,' then, 'Riversdale, oh my sainted aunt, Riversdale.'

An hour later, Austen accompanied him to the railway station. Nur bey, the cadaverous policeman, had rematerialised and was again in discreet attendance. The huge engine hissed, whistled and clanked, spewing grit and grime, leaving a greasy deposit over everything. Philby climbed on to the stoop of the first-class carriage. Down the platform, peasants loaded live chickens tied by the legs into one van; ten sheep were picked up and thrown like sacks into another.

'Austen, I don't think we'll meet again. But . . . er, if we do . . . well my friends call me Kim.'

They shook hands. Very British.

'And here's a tip. From a Turkey hand of fifteen months' seniority. Every town large enough to have more than one minaret to its mosque will also have one good restaurant, a tolerable brothel, and a real *hamam*. Bye now. Take care.'

A log moved, his head came up sharply, then he chuckled. Call me Kim. Perhaps the chance would come. And that bit about making him a Companion of Honour had really got to the Shapiro woman.

'Sir Richard,' she had said, 'either you are entirely frivolous
— in which case I shall not be able to trust a word you have said;
or you are mad.'

She had been tenacious and astute. She might have gone on
for hours producing questions requiring more and more wrig-
gling and eventually fatal invention, but she had drunk up her
Scotch like a good girl, and gone.

Austen stretched, yawned. He had dropped off for a moment
and felt better as a result. He looked at his watch — time for the
news; he reached for the television control. As the screen
flickered to life, a tiny tremor of misgiving wriggled in his mind
like a touch of gas in the stomach heralding indigestion: had she
been ready to go because she had, after all, got what she came
for?

'The Cumbria farmhouse siege came, only two hours ago, to a
dramatic and tragic end...'

What's this, he thought, and the premonition of personal
danger faded.

'... for almost twenty-four hours John Tyler, a labourer from
Cockermouth, remained on the first floor of this empty holiday
home of a Lancashire businessman. There, armed with a
shotgun, an axe and a carving knife, he held his wife and two
children, threatening to kill them and himself unless his de-
mands were met. These apparently were never made clear but
related to his dismissal some time ago by the Central Electricity
Generating Board.

'Throughout this morning and the early hours of this afternoon Cumbrian police attempted to talk to him, first through
loud-hailers, and then courageously approaching nearer until
Tyler told them to stop — while he was thus distracted two
specially trained men managed to occupy the ground floor from
the back. However, Tyler probably became aware of their
presence, for suddenly either his wife or his eldest child began to
scream. The two men stormed the stairs. What happened next is
not quite clear, but it seems Tyler shot his wife Mary in the
head with the shotgun before himself being shot down by
one of the police marksmen. It is believed that Mary Tyler
was dead on arrival at Whitehaven hospital, and that Tyler
himself died instantly. The two children are being treated for

159

shock in Whitehaven hospital but are otherwise unharmed.

'The Chief Constable has issued a brief statement regretting the killings but praising the courage and skill of all the police who took part...

'In Poland the strikes continue in Lodz, in spite of reports of Russian troops concentrating on the border near the garrison town of Lvov...'

Austen's attention sharpened. Events in Poland excited and confused him: he was exhilarated at the realisation in practice of what theory had long prophesied — that the greatest threat to the Eastern bureaucracies was a genuine mass proletarian movement, and that only thus would the revolution move on from post-Stalinist stagnation; he was amazed and hopeful at the patience and skill with which the Kremlin had so far handled the crisis; fearful that the time was not yet ripe, that the ferment of a proletarian revolution in Eastern Europe (for it would surely spread if not stamped out) would so temporarily weaken both the economy and central control that it would allow the West to destabilise the East and make pre-emptive strikes against the Soviet bloc... Clearly, his thinking ran, this would do more harm to socialism than Russian armed intervention in Poland — yet even Austen admitted it would be a tragedy if they did go in.

18

'Well, that was a near-run thing, eh, Bill? Park yourself and smoke if you feel like it. I must say I think Ashley did rather well, in spite of it all.'

'It was a bloody mess and the fault was Fosdike's.' One crumb of comfort in what had been hell was that Cargill could see no way in which Fosdike, a cocksure young man from Rugby, whose father was a general, could escape a severe reprimand, at least.

'Oh?' One eyebrow up, then the eyes narrowed, head even more on one side. 'It's not usual for a head of section to blame a subordinate. As I see it, Ashley Fosdike managed things rather well. Of course, if you are entering an official complaint...'

Cargill shrugged. Because permission to smoke had been made explicit, he kept his hands firmly on his knees.

'Well?'

Pressed, Cargill still remained silent. The Housemaster stood up, went to the window, turned.

'As I see it,' he repeated, 'the operation fell into three phases. The first was a perfectly normal investigation into a leakage of classified information, and that went precisely as it should, following normal procedures, using well-tried techniques, the marked fiver and so on, and there's no doubt that you and your team quickly and efficiently hit on the right man.' He came back to his desk, leaned forward with his hands on the back of his chair. 'Things, I grant you, went a little awry in phase two. Ashley Fosdike, left to make arrangements for the arrest, did get his knickers a wee bit twisted. No doubt due in part to

161

inexperience, but also because you yourself were elsewhere. My fault, this last factor, if anyone's.' He was expansive now, magnanimous. 'It did seem at that time that the Bletchley business needed looking into, and you were the man for the job. Still. That's water under the bridge, no use crying over spilled milk.' He came round the chair and sat in it again, pushing it back, tucking his knuckles beneath his lacerated chin, crossing his knees, exuding bonhomie. 'But in the end it worked out well, no doubt of it. Fosdike, Ashley, played his part in the initial planning and you arrived to set your seal to it. Thank God,' he concluded, and slapped the top of his desk, 'thank God at least that the end was carried out cleanly, decently, and above all efficiently. As I say, the right man was in charge for the showdown.'

Momentarily Cargill relived the clammy cold of the farm-house bedroom with its incongruously expensive furniture — the Lancashire businessman had done himself well. In one corner, a five-year-old boy stood in cataleptic shock; his sister, at less than eighteen months mercifully less aware of what had happened, sat under the dressing table and howled. Their mother lay across the vast satin-covered bed with half her head shot away but yet contrived an entirely horrible, because not in the least human, flutter of one hand; their father was properly dead — the hole between his eyes was a neater business and the exit wound behind was hidden. There were smells of cordite in the air, of human excrement, and blood.

The tableau fragmented as a policewoman, a doctor and ambulance men pushed their way in behind him, and he withdrew. On the landing a masked man in police uniform unscrewed the components of a large machine pistol. A second man, also masked, looked on.

Now Cargill looked up at the Housemaster and his large fists slowly bunched on his knees.

'They were in police uniform: but they were masked. They were not police. Not even Special Branch.'

The Housemaster waited, head on one side.

'They were SAS. Why wasn't I told?'

The Housemaster lifted one finger — briskly it touched away the spittle from his mouth. He stood up, came round to the front

162

of the desk. 'Come on now, Cargill, come on. Tyler was a madman, a homicidal madman. The police are well trained, granted; dedicated certainly; and courageous to the point of foolhardiness — but why risk lives in an operation of this sort when there are men available so good at it that one can be sure they will do what is necessary; and do it without coming to harm.'

'Why was I not told?'

'You were told what was going to happen, and you approved.'

This was so far from the truth that Cargill momentarily lost the power to breathe.

'The Chief Constable told me what had been planned, agreed between him and Fosdike, and I approved that. He told me two men would get in at the back while Tyler was kept busy in the front. That they would use flash and bang devices and smoke. That this was thought to be the safest way of dealing with the situation, the way least likely to cause bloodshed.'

'Quite.'

'But that is not what happened.'

'No. As I understand it, Mrs Tyler began to scream. The men, SAS or not is immaterial, believed, correctly as it turned out ...'

'Just one moment, please.' Cargill was pale now, and moisture gleamed in a sickly sheen on his forehead. The Housemaster may for a second have been alarmed — at any rate he shut up. Cargill spaced his next words carefully, emphatically. 'I ... heard ... no ... scream. Not before the first shot.'

They faced each other, Cargill still seated, but breathing heavily now. The Housemaster sank away, settling his backside on the front of his desk, hands out to either side: it was not a retreat, more the drawing back of a snake preparing to strike.

'My dear chap. My dear chap, I hope ... no. I know. I know you won't put down anything so absurd when it comes to your own written report of the matter. I'm sure you won't.'

He turned again, this time to his case of pistol trophies — perhaps in the glass or in the polished surface of the cups he could still see Cargill's face. He spoke briskly, giving orders now. 'You've had a bad time. A rotten week or so what with ... take the rest of the week off. Spend the time planning that report

163

properly and bring me a draft on Monday. Is that clear? Fine. Mind, to me only, the draft. Till Monday morning then, old chap,' and to make quite sure his meaning was taken he came round the chair Cargill was already half out of, and opened the door for him.

At Oxford Cargill had read History and had been much impressed by one lecturer in particular who was even then already gaining a reputation as a maverick; a man who, in the face of older traditions that sought pattern and meaning in history of one sort or another, denied that any of that was the historian's business, the historian's only duty was to the facts — to finding out what happened and recording it as honestly and completely as possible. This seemed to Cargill highly laudable, especially as the historian in question made it clear how difficult this duty was when interest of every sort has always compromised the records of every event to obscure, fudge or blatantly deny what really happened.

In this case what had happened was this: the SAS man's pistol shot had preceded the shotgun shot by at least ten seconds, during which Mrs Tyler had screamed. And screamed. But if enough people reported it otherwise, often enough, with enough conviction, not only would they be believed but most of them would in time come to believe that what they said happened did. For what is the subjective recollection of a sequence of dramatic sounds over a wretchedly short few moments of extreme confusion in the face of newspaper reports, police reports, evidence given under oath at an inquest, and so on, and so on?

There had been cases before. Cases when Cargill had eventually decided that what his senses had told him had happened could have been wrong. The difference now, though, was this: he had lost the motivation to believe what he was told to believe; he had lost his faith.

Indeed, as he made his way back to his tiny office to pick up his things, including his papers on Austen and *The Burning Matrix*, one uncharacteristic phrase repeated itself in his head like a mantra: 'I'll get the bastards. I will. I'll get the bastards yet.'

19

'You look grim. Are you all right?'

'Yes. Tired. But all right. I was at the Cumbria farmhouse siege.'

'Good God — I had an idea that I caught a glimpse of you on the telly. I said to Jane, hey that's Bill Cargill, but then thought no, you're on to something else at the moment, it can't be. What'll you have? This bitter isn't bad.'

At Cargill's suggestion they moved out of the saloon bar into a more secluded snug, arranging themselves round a glass-topped table — hat, gloves, Sleight's scarf and briefcase; two pints of bitter, one in a mug, the other in a straight glass. The bleeps and roar of Space Invaders were barely audible here.

'That was a shambles then, from the look of it. Care to tell me the inside story? On yesterday's events in Cumbria, I mean.'

'And have the SAS crashing in on us? You must be joking.'

'Jesus. Dear Lord.' Sleight had really lost colour. 'We had a chap covering it and he said there was a rumour you'd brought in the Milk Tray brigade — but no one was going to print it: the press briefing explicitly said a police marksman, and that was that. Our man also said the scream came between the shots...'

'Oh, really?'

'...yes, well. It's not what we came to talk about, is it?' Sleight was now quite alarmed — Cargill looked...well, like death, his face grey, the skin round his eyes even darker than usual, his hand as he drank shook a little. And quite clearly he regretted he had mentioned the farmhouse...massacre?

Sleight's mind had almost automatically rewritten the headline. 'I think I'll have a packet of nuts. I'm rather gone on these dry-roasted ones.'

Cargill seemed calmer when Sleight returned from the bar with his packet of Planter's. He watched as the newsman dribbled six or seven into his palm, and from there to his mouth, and then, chewing on them busily, undid his briefcase. He had five folders, each filled with sheafs of photocopy paper. 'There's not a great deal, as you can see. As I said, there's a sort of unofficial, self-imposed permanent D-notice on Slaker. This first lot is a potted history of the group. Shall I leave that? You can read it at home.'

'No. Give me a run-down now. The overall picture.'

'OK,' Sleight drank, opened the folder, stabbed at succeeding paragraphs with his finger. 'They were originally Lancashire merchants, Liverpool, slave-trade. And one thing I'll say now is that right from the start they've always known when to diversify — they've seen changes in the weather a decade or so ahead of everyone else and got out at the top of the market each time. It's still a gift they have, as you'll see in a moment or two. Anyway. By 1790 they had switched from slaves to cotton: only the Rathbones were ahead of them in that. In the 1850s they saw the American Civil War on the horizon and so began to open up the African Horn, Arabia, even down to Kenya and Madagascar, making lots of connections with the sheiks, and probably doing a bit more slaving on the quiet, gun-running too, I don't doubt. And this led to their first ventures in manufacturing: they opened an arms factory in Birmingham in the 1870s and from then on they really expanded very fast. Anything that was about to boom they had their fingers in. Arms led to munitions, led to chemicals, led back to arms. And it all moved in Slaker ships. When Kaiser Wilhelm went into East Africa, Slakers stayed on and married their daughters into the right German families. They kept up their connections with the Arabs too, though I doubt if they actually sent any Slaker ladies into the harems. Unwanted domestics perhaps.

'By 1914 they were too big, the family had got idle too, the way such families do. Some enterprises were sold off, one or two actually went bust; because of their German connections, they

166

were now a touch unpopular. By 1930 they were half the size they had been; the group had to all effects and purposes disintegrated into seven or eight separate enterprises whose only connection was that substantial holdings still remained in the hands of the Slaker family. And that was by then a pretty diffuse affair. Trusts had been set up, the capital was entailed, but though it could not be sold it could be split. A hundred cousins all over Britain lived comfortably on income, even in the Depression, and weren't too bothered so long as the trustees — a Slaker firm of course — sent in their cheques.'

Sleight finished his pint, all but the bottom inch, put his first folder on one side and opened the next.

'Enter Hugh Slaker. In 1930 he was only forty, but in so far as anyone was he was the head of the family, the direct male descendant of Hugh Slaker, the slaver. He was also one hell of a whizz-kid. He set about drawing the whole thing together again, rounding up the family as it were, denting the trusts wherever his lawyers could find ways of doing it, stripping assets in the areas that were trading at a loss or near it, building up a central power base once again. He lived in style too, refurbished Slaker House in Bloomsbury — it had been built by them in the 1840s — and he went in for the whole salon bit for a time: then he got on the wrong side of Lady Ottoline, the set stopped coming around, so he dropped them and took up the St Ives group instead. Usual canny instinct. He's got more early Hepworths, Moores, Nicholsons and Pasmores than the Tate has. And incidentally his son has started selling them, so I expect that too is a peaking market.

'In real business too, he followed in Grandad's footsteps: mainly because he never allowed any narrow-minded prejudice to stand in his way — in this case he opened up what is still a very profitable trade with the Soviets; yet he kept in with and revived the German connection. Along with Dunlop, Unilever and Guinness, the banking side of the Slakers were corporate members of the Anglo-German Fellowship. Meanwhile, he was unloading almost all the group's holdings in heavy industry — some may think he was a bit premature there with the war coming, but he knew what he was up to — he put it all, or most of it, into fine technology, electrics, instrument making and,

167

cheeky bastard, pharmaceuticals, and those still form the main
base of the Slaker Group, except now it's also one of the three
world front-runners outside Japan in computers, microchips
and laser technology. But that's anticipating a bit. Shall we
have another?'

'Of course.' Cargill stood up, took their glasses to the bar. 'Do
you want more of those nuts?'

'Why not?' Sleight had unbuttoned his duffel coat, was
sitting back against the plush-covered upholstery. Clearly he
was enjoying his exegesis. 'It's the bitter from the pump.
Marston's.'

'File number three,' he said, as Cargill came back with the
beer. 'Short one this, not much I could dig out. The Riversdale
connection. Hugh Slaker's elder sister, by five years, Alice,
married the seventh. Earl of Riversdale. He was killed in the
Troubles and her son Teddy inherited. Her daughter is Kitti
Bridge, you remember you asked me about her — sex fiend and
junkie. Bad blood there. Teddy would probably have turned
out worse, the way he was going. A sadistic homosexual and a
poet too, would you believe? But all blood, roses, dark heroism,
the worst of Yeats and the worst of Lawrence, and a fascist to
boot, but he got to be missing during the V2 emergency and that
was that. Or almost.' Here Sleight threw what was meant to be
a canny or penetrating look at Cargill. 'He worked at Bletchley
Park in the war. Don't have to tell *you* what all that was about.
And it's *said* he leaked it all to the Russians, who no doubt had
something really nasty on him. Anyway, you know what truth
there is in that, if any. If there was, then it was well hushed
up — and that's probably the hand of Slaker protecting its own.
Anyway, he was dead before it came out.

'That's it for the Riversdales — the present peer has nothing
to do with the Slakers, not being in the clan. So on to the fattest
file of all — Slaker and Austen.'

He drank deeply.

'Only this time the Slaker is Geoffrey, son of Hugh. Hugh got
a peerage from Churchill — war effort, and all that: more likely
for smoothing the way with Joseph Stalin Esquire than anything else. He was probably a Hero of the Soviet Union too on
the quiet. He went to Yalta, you know. In the background of

168

course. And by then most Russian tanks had Slaker gyros in them. Anyway, Hugh Lord Slaker died in 1953 and Geoffrey Lord Slaker, after a decent interim with some chap from the Prudential as figurehead chairman, took over.

'Geoffrey. Well, he's in it for laughs. He's said so. And he's run pretty close to the wind three or four times, and at least once Richard Austen was there or thereabouts. Austen has Slaker blood, through his mother, all those cousins, and Slaker money too. He's two years older than Geoffrey and they went through the same mill — prep school, the College, Cambridge. Austen at St John's, Slaker at Magdalene. Well, Austen, you know, is a Marxist, and that started early ...'

'I know about Austen. That part anyway. Cut through to the period when Slaker seemed to be, what did you say? sailing close to the wind. If there's anything earlier I need, I'll find it when I read your notes.'

'Right. Well. Two things. Or three, depending on how you look at it. In the 1950s, just after the Korean thing, and with the cold war rather warm, Austen made his first trip to Russia. Chatting up the archaeological establishment and getting permission to look at their Bronze Age digs in Moldavia. Eastern spur of the Amber Route and all that. Ostensibly. But a year later Slaker signed contracts in the USSR whereby he was to provide instruments for monitoring nuclear-reactor experiments, and similar hardware. Nothing illegal — it was just the wrong time, so they kept quiet about it.

'The next big Austen/Slaker connection is the Gold Museum. In the late fifties, with McCarthyism throwing its shadow this way and so on, Austen's career was a little shaky. He had had hopes of the Archaeological Institute here in London, and didn't get it. Maybe he was still a bit young, but all the same. Then suddenly cousin Slaker comes along and sets up Gold. Enormous expense, bombed church in Bloomsbury rebuilt, and a really good job for Austen ...'

'I know. I *know*. But what was fishy about it?'

'Well. Once the idea was off the ground, Austen went to Beirut with a blank Slaker cheque. The idea was that there's precious little Bronze Age gold around not already in public hands except in the Levant, where a lot of it started and a good

169

bit got high-jacked between the digs and the museums. But it was also the time when the Palestinian liberation organisations were really getting going, were short of funds, and hadn't then the sort of respectability that they have now. There's no proof of course. What I'm now saying is absolute hearsay and guesswork and I'm sure every possible trace of evidence was obliterated years ago — but what the whisper is is that the Gold Museum was a cover: it really operated as a bank for the PLO and whatever. A way of getting funds to them, and something arms dealers could trust too. Remember Slakers have been doing business with Arabs since the late 1800s. God knows how else it worked but it's not beyond possibility that the Kremlin used it too — as a means of getting aid through to the Palestinians in an untraceable way.'

'And the third?'

'Right. The third. The first repeated. Austen's last visit to Russia was two years ago. Any day now — it could be tomorrow or in a month's time — Slaker Laser and Allied Technology, SLAT, is going to announce a computer contract with the Soviets. It's still in the balance on two counts: the new administration in America is going to be much tougher about deals of this sort and may pressure Thatcher to put the boot in. And a cabinet committe has to be convinced the computers can't be put to military uses. However, Reagan is still at the stage of testing the water, and advisors to cabinet committees can be bought. I think Slaker will get his contract.'

'Do you know what these computers are going to be for?'

'Advanced versions of PSIKE, as far as I understand it. In the first instance, they'll be data banks on every man, woman and child in the Eastern bloc, but with enormous capacity and ability for almost instant multiple cross-reference. You know — you feed in a selection of apparently random parameters: subscribers to the *New Statesman*; blue eyes; fell behind with National Insurance contributions in 1965, and two minutes later out of the three hundred million or so files up pop the ten names that fit, with their addresses now and what they had for breakfast.

'That's it in outline. You'll find the details there.'

He sat back and drank, but kept his eyes on Cargill's face.

'I'm very grateful, Desmond. That's a good start. I'm sure it will be very useful.'

'Yes, well, Bill. That's what I wanted to say.'

'What? What do you mean?'

'Well, as far as I'm concerned, it's not just a start, that's *it*. That's as far as I'm prepared to go.'

It took Cargill a moment or two to catch on.

'You mean, if or when I do get enough to start a press campaign, you won't help.'

'That's it. In a nutshell. It's too big, Bill. It's far too big. I mean I can already see where you're heading. You've got your sights on Austen. Well, OK. On his own that would be fine. On a par with Blunt. A good story, a good bit of clean fun establishment baiting — and I'm sure normally it would turn out the same way. We'd be told Austen turned Queen's evidence years ago and got a pardon . . . in other words, he's fixed up with insurance: you can't actually prosecute me because if you do I'll spill such a load of shit on Lord this, Permanent Under-Secretary That, and Prince So and So too . . . Well, that's how we reckon Blunt really got away with it.

'But this is different. The Slaker connection makes it different. As soon as we begin to hint Austen might be the man we're after, they'll track the rumours back and I'll be right out on my ear, just like that.' He snapped his fingers. 'If I'm lucky. I wouldn't work on the Street again. And if they're feeling really paranoid I wouldn't work anywhere — or only from an invalid chair. I'm sorry, Bill. I've talked it over with Jane and she agrees. From here on in I'm out.' It was a lie: the only thing he had discussed with Jane in six months was the sort of financial settlement he'd agree to if she decided to divorce.

Cargill began to stuff his pipe, but with his big head held up, eyes seemingly on the rows of bright liqueur bottles on the top shelf of the bar. His face was almost impassive, but the muscles were very tight, the corners of his mouth below his heavy grey moustache pulled down. To Sleight's horror a moistness appeared in his eye.

'Hollis. You know Pincher's bringing out a book on him. If he can . . .'

'But that's just it. Hollis is dead. Austen may be smaller fry as

171

far as the Service goes, but he's alive. Anyway Pincher's just flying a kite. Your lot will be able to get away with flat denials and that will be that.'

Cargill nodded. He knew this to be true.

The newsman rushed on quickly. 'There's one way, just one. When you're sure you've got him, then set about it in such a way that *you* are the news. You are what has to be reported. I'm putting this badly because I haven't properly worked it out, but if, say, you did a civil arrest on him, brought your own case — oh, I know the law on all that has been tightened up, but something of the sort. Or you could straightforwardly libel the bastard and make him sue. That would be even better.'

Cargill's lighter flared, smoke billowed round his head, drifted into the light of a pink spot that was directed on the bar. He seemed to be under control again.

'Libel's out. From what you've said, I'd never get anyone to publish it. There might be something in the other idea. But it would have to be planned. Could I rely on you to be there if I moved in on him on my own? Would you report it? Make sure that why I had, say, arrested or kidnapped him got reported? I mean, get some *real* coverage.'

'Well, I'd do my best, of course I would. And I can't really say fairer than that. You can be sure, old chum, I'd do my best.'

Cargill nodded slowly, as if weighing up just what sort of a best he could expect.

'Well anyway, Des, you've done a good job for me with all this. I'm sure it will be useful. Many thanks.' He drank some beer but did not empty his glass. He pushed it to one side and said, out of duty, 'How are Jane and Jason? Things any better at home?'

'No they're bloody not. I went up to the school to see the Head and he told me I was a racist. I could not get him to see it was the joint I was objecting to, not the colour of Jason's friend's skin. I'll have to get him out of there, but Lord knows I can't afford a fee-paying school.' Not with Jane after half my assets plus maintenance. 'There's a fifth file you haven't seen.'

'Oh?'

Sleight pulled a last folder on to the table. 'All we have actually printed on the Slaker Group over the last twenty years.

172

It's ninety per cent gossip-column stuff: Kitti Bridge cited again; HRH opens the Gold Museum; Lord Slaker with friend at Klosters. About twice a year our financial editor does his piece about solid base for future expansion despite recession, good investment.' He riffled through the sheets. Clearly Cargill was now bored. Sleight was hurt. No newsman can bear thinking he's a bore. 'This very last item, early last month, is a bit of a curio though.'

Politely Cargill read it.

BODY FOUND ON BLOOMSBURY BUILDING SITE

Site workman Michael Collins had a shock today when his pick knocked down a screen of bricks at the prestigious Slaker Towers development opposite the Brunswick Centre. First he saw racks and racks of old bottles — port, claret, champagne. And the second was a skeleton sitting there with a cut-glass tumbler between its knees.

Although he felt he could do with a drink, Collins did the right thing and raised the alarm — 'Never a drop did I touch,' he told a *News* reporter later.

A spokesman for site developers Citeecon later said that the unfortunate tippler was almost certainly a caretaker seeking more congenial shelter from the Blitz than that offered by the Russell Square tube. The bomb that had destroyed the house had exploded only yards from him and he was probably killed instantly by the blast.

And as for the choice of wines, they must belong to Lord Slaker — for at the time of the bombing Slaker House belonged to the present peer's father. Perhaps he'll give Collins a bottle or two!

20

'Herman, for God's sake stop yapping. He is Herman the fifth. I have always had a Herman, ever since 1936. And yes. The first was named for... Yes. I have read *The Burning Matrix*. And really it is a most dreadful pack of lies. You do drink whisky, don't you?'

It was ten thirty in the morning.

'I know what you're thinking — everyone does.' The glass chimed, the whisky gurgled. 'How do I do it? My doctor even wonders, and heaven knows doctors should know — every one I ever had was a drunk. The secret is simple.' She came towards him, holding out the glass with almost perfect control, but leaving the distance between them just a touch short so he had to lift himself slightly from the chintz-covered chair to take it. In the grey cold light of a late November morning Lady Kitti Bridge looked older than ever — though just as immaculately turned out as before. 'It's quite simple. I eat sparingly. Take plenty of vitamins B and C. And what I drink is always the very best. Most important of all, I sleep. I sleep more even than when I was... well. Never mind.'

'*Burning Matrix*, Lady Bridge.'

'You know, you should call me Lady Kitti. I am not the wife of some trumpery baronet or whatever. Yes. Pack of lies, what I've read of it.'

Cargill recollected that Lady Kitti Bridge was not the first person he had interviewed who had read only the parts that concerned her and none of the rest. Vaguely he supposed that this was how such books got an assured sale ... and

174

that explained too why they were always so full of names.

'As far as we were concerned, there was not the slightest hint in anything he said or did during the summer of '35 that he was in anyway a bolshie or sympathetic to them. There was never an almighty row or an agreement to differ. In fact, we all got on like a house on fire and had a very jolly time of it indeed.'

This was so much what Cargill wanted to hear that he felt he must beware of over-evaluating what this alcoholic harridan was saying.

'Lady . . . Kitti. When did you first become aware that Austen was, is, sympathetic to Marxism?'

' Bolshevism. I'm not really sure. I think I may have heard he was behaving in a silly way over the Spanish business. But quite a few of one's chums were, and one didn't particularly notice one more or less.'

'What about during the war?'

'You mean, all that bit about parties and so on when poor Teddy got killed? No. It didn't come up then. Why should it? Oh, except for one thing — one thing he jolly well doesn't mention in his silly book. Those parties often enough started at Bentinck Street and ended there too. Yes. I met them all there you know. Guy, Donald, Tony. And I'm fairly sure it was through Rich . . . Austen in the first place that we went there. But *then,* I mean during the war, being a bolshie didn't signify, did it? "For dirty reds, read Our Glorious Allies", that's how it went, didn't it? And in every other respect it was an entertaining circle. Circus, perhaps one should say. And, well, Teddy could always find *rough trade* there when he felt the urge.'

Cargill was still bothered by her disdain of propriety — he supposed it was aristocratic.

'Could we go back to Scales, Lady Kitti. In 1935. Austen was there because of the dig. Did he stay at Scales or outside?'

'He stayed at Scales, of course. He was one of us. You know, actually related. Besides, he was besotted with me.'

'He says that no one wore swastikas or anything like that. Yet he became aware that he was among people who sympathised with the extreme right.'

'You mean fascists. Let's call a spade a bloody shovel, shall we?'

175

She stood up and walked over to the fireplace, turning her back on him. Again he had the absurd idea that by doing so she had transformed herself — like the witch in the *Wife of Bath's Tale* — into a woman half her actual and a quarter her apparent age. Then the illusion was again replaced with the reality. She put a photograph into his hands — the frame was heavy, plain, undecorated, not silver-gilt but gold.

'That's Unity. That's me. I think you know the chum in the middle. Bayreuth. '36. The Valkyries. That's what he called us. His Valkyries. Certain historic interest, don't you think?'

'Lady Kitti, what was Austen's reaction at Scales when he found he was among fascists?'

'Oh dear. Mr Cargill. I think you're beginning to bore me. And Herman too. Just what is it you're getting at?'

No one likes to be thought boring, least of all to a Nazi border terrier.

'I'm sorry. I'm trying to satisfy myself that Austen was a clandestine communist, a spy indeed, before he openly joined the party in '37. I already have evidence of a sort that in '33 and '34 he was passionately interested in Marxist texts and so on; and possibly had a Soviet control in London; although during this time he was not involved at all in overt political action.'

'I'm not quite sure I follow.' Lady Kitti took her glass to the decanter, refilled it, and then moved to the window. The lapdog snuffled; briskly she told it to shut up. She sipped, then gulped, seemed to contemplate the gaunt plane trees. Then she turned, holding the large tumbler in both claw-like hands just below her chin — a sybil inhaling trance-inducing fumes before prophesying. 'Perhaps I do. You are saying that he was sent to spy on us. If that's the case, then when fascism was discussed, or the Anglo-German Fellowship, he would have been sympathetic, even enthusiastic.'

'Exactly.'

'Well, he was. I think you are right . . . ' She drifted into a held silence, then spat, 'The cunt. The fucking cunt.'

Cargill was shocked. Then alarmed. The glass was now shuddering as if the claws would crush it, the face was deathly white, and he realised that her small frame was vibrating, and on top the high, back-combed silver mane which caught the morning light in a nimbus was more upstarting than ever. He had never been in the presence of such rage.

With an effort, a real physical effort, for it seemed the convulsion had deprived her of the ability to move, she got the glass to her lips, where it juddered on her teeth. At last she drained it. Then she came back into the room, sank on to a chair, faced him and spoke.

'We have to nail him, Mr Cargill. We must do our utmost. He must pay.' She breathed in very deeply, then let out a long slow sigh. 'He was spying on us, and he was a spy later. He was a spy at Bletchley Park. He *framed* Teddy. Is that what you think, Mr Cargill?'

Silently he assented.

'Then we must get him. He must pay.'

He assented to that too. And if he had any qualms or scruples at having to work with this horrifying and repulsive ally, he gallantly suppressed them.

But she was too far gone to be any further use that morning. He tried to get her to remember details of Austen's acceptance or support of fascism and the Hitler régime; but she mumbled that it was all too long ago, her memory had begun to let her down, and so on. He asked if there was any chance of her turning up documentary evidence, photographs or letters — and suddenly she giggled. 'You know where the cunning bastard says we didn't parade about in swastikas, or go swimming in the nude? Well, actually we did both. And there were photos and I bet he was in them.'

But when he pressed her to find these, she shrugged and tossed her head (the gesture had by now lost its classiness — looked merely tipsy or worse), and said they had been lost, all lost, when Slaker House was bombed.

'I've only got that,' she said, pointing again at the Valkyrie photograph, 'because I begged it off the Mitfords when Unity finally snuffed it.'

He stood up to go; then what she had said stirred alive a question that had been niggling in his mind since leaving Sleight the evening before.

'You mean Slaker House in London?'

'Yes, of course.'

177

'I'm sorry but this might be important. Did you live there? I mean, you must have been using it for your stuff to have been in it when it was bombed.'

'Yes, we *used* it. Actually Uncle Hugh got bored with it roundabout 1935, or '36, and mother was bored with Scales. She was born in Slaker House and wanted to die there. So Uncle Hugh let us live there whenever we wanted to, and we spent more time there until the Blitz than anywhere else.'

'What happened then?'

'Oh dear. This is a bit of a bore. Is it really important?'

He was aware that her thin claw of a sparrow hand was shaking, that her eyes were fidgeting. Clearly, coherence was an effort.

'Well, it may be.' He put his case on top of a hexagonal table whose marquetry top depicted with remarkable skill Raphael's *Triumph of Galatea*, and pulled out the last file Sleight had given him, the last item in it.

'Did you see this?' He handed her the cutting about how Michael Collins had discovered a skeleton in the cellars of Slaker House.

She looked at it, tried to steady it in her hand, then smoothed it on the table. At last she lifted her head.

'I . . . I can't really read it just now. Leave it here, would you?'

He felt sure that she had read it, but equally that no reaction could be expected on this visit. He refastened his case.

She came halfway across the Aubusson with him and then stopped, leaning heavily on a wall table which supported a large urn-shaped vase of long-stemmed dark roses.

'Well, Inspector. I have your phone numbers. Meanwhile, what will your next step be?' The question was a politeness. She was not interested in his answer. However, he explained that at some point in 1945 or '46 Austen must have undergone a long and thorough debriefing, that *The Burning Matrix* suggested he had at that time been living in some isolation with his mother in the New Forest, so he was now going to go down into Hampshire to see if there was anything there to be uncovered. Long before he had finished, her attention had wandered.

As he moved to go, she flung up an arm at the dark roses.

'Nice, don't you think? Vulgar but nice. Like their, um, source. American you see.'

Cargill contrived a politely curious noise.

'Old flame. From the war years actually. Roy Newman. Never forgets me when he's over here. Never. He came round for a chat last night. About old times. Ha! Had to hope no other old flames turned up at the same time!'

21

Austen bent to his mother's cheek.

'Hullo there, how are you?'

It was soft like a crumpled poppy petal to touch, the colour of an end-of-season apple kept in a cool loft.

'I wish you woudn't say that, Richard. I get asked by the staff at least six times a day. I'm rather tired. I have been visited once already this afternoon.'

'Oh really?' He turned away, responding quickly to the signals: she was in a tetchy mood; probably the silver pin in her hipbone was playing up. After his father's death, they had lived quite contentedly together at the Farm (though he of course was often away) for nearly twenty years. Then she caught pleurisy following a soaking in the garden and the next five years were bad — as a semi-invalid she had become broody, demanding and quarrelsome. At nearly ninety she had a fall and broke her hip. When she came out of hospital, he took her not home but to Heartsease in Lymington, where a room filled with her furniture and her favourite books had been prepared for her. He had even persuaded a cousin to part with a pair of Ruskin sketches of Venice and the Lagoon . . . and still she had been furious, had refused to see him for two months. When she did eventually let him in, the Ruskins had been remounted and reframed.

He looked at his favourite now — a deliberately Turneresque presentation of late dusk, and thought again, as he had thought before, that the man who could pull that off was entitled to go for Whistler's rubbishy *Nocturne*. And his mother had been right about the frame.

180

'You've never forgiven me, have you, Richard?'

He turned wearily. She was sitting up against pillows in the one ugly thing in the room — the bed, which was a hospital bed. Heartsease insisted — they did for all nursing cases. Her hair, purest white now but still wiry, was fluffed out around the top of her head; her eyes were as bright and beady as ever, though she was very thin. Occasionally she looked like Ruskin's last sketch of Rose La Touche and it was possible she encouraged the resemblance: the difference was that Rose had been a mad girl in her twenties dying of anorexia nervosa, whereas Mrs Austen was already seventy years older and apparently indestructible.

She hated Heartsease and felt guilty because she did. No doubt they could have afforded to keep a nurse living in at the Farm, with a relief on standby, and paid a doctor a retainer large enough to make him jump when called, but it was not the sort of house, nor was Richard the sort of man, to support such a permanent intrusion. Heartsease really was the best solution, and she knew it and she hated it. Her most usual way of coping with all this was to insist that in the past she had inflicted on Richard some utterly unforgivable suffering — hence his readiness to *slough her off*, as she sometimes put it. What exactly it was she had done changed from occasion to occasion: the irony was that he did hold one thing against her as unforgivable — the fact that because she was a Slaker he had been sent, at her insistence, to The Meads Preparatory School for Boys. Once he had tried to explain this to her, but she had dismissed what he was saying as rubbish. The fact was that the separation had hurt her too — until then, in spite of Nanny, they had had a close and loving relationship. The eight-year-old who returned withdrawn and thin at the end of his first term had been a stranger. And what had been lost had never been recovered.

She repeated, 'Never forgiven me.'

'What for, Mother?' He made little attempt to sound other than irritated and bored.

She shifted on her buttocks and the inner tube-like contrivance beneath them squeaked. She may look like an old apple, he thought, but she doesn't smell like one.

'That I was a socialist before you were. A communist of the old school — reddest also of the red.' She was quoting Ruskin.

'I don't mind that at all. I never did. I'm glad you were. I hope you still are.'

'*That* remains to be seen,' she said cryptically. 'No. You resented it. Whenever you came back from the College with the books that Moore man gave you...'

'Heath.'

'Eh?'

'Never mind.'

'I said Heath. And read bits from them to me, I was foolish enough to say Ruskin had said it all before. The same again with *My Struggle*.'

'*Capital*, mother.'

'Just so. And *The Condition of the Working Class in 1844* by Frederick Engels, published in England by...'

'All right, Mother, all right.'

'Anyway. I did not mince matters with my visitor this afternoon. I told him the whole truth about the whole business.'

A warning.

'Mother. Who was your visitor?'

Her old knotted fingers picked at the edges of her bed-jacket exactly mimicking the actions of embroidering on a framed sampler.

'A gentleman from MI5, that's all. A gentleman from MI5.'

'Geoffrey? Listen Geoffrey. Your action the other day with that Humphries man doesn't seem to have achieved a thing. No, really. First of all that Shapiro woman came back... Geoffrey, do please listen. Of course she's genuine; they're not sloppy about cover, the Americans — if she says she's writing a book, then she bloody is. But that's only the first thing. This afternoon my mother was questioned by a man called Catkin from MI5. No, don't laugh. I expect she got the name wrong. No, she didn't make it up to annoy me — she described him to me, and when I got back just now he was sitting in a car outside the front gate. He's driven off now. Look, there are the pips — ring me back, the number is Ashling 3180. Geoffrey? Good man. I'm at the pay phone in the stables. Because, yes, you're damned right I'm afraid my own phone might be bugged. Listen. She, Mother, told him I had Guy and Igor staying here in 1945,

182

Christmas and into the New Year. Yes, of course I bloody did. No, of course I don't know this phone isn't tapped as well. They're probably listening in on every phone within ten miles. All right. All right. But have another word with Humphries, will you? Get this Catkin off my back. No, I won't. Roy Newman's coming to stay for a couple of nights so I'll be down here. An American, that's right, with United Special Steels. Didn't you? Well, he's been a buddy for donkey's years. Ever since the war. All right. But it would be a relief to know just what's going on. Why they're doing it and what they imagine they'll get out of it. Fine. Many thanks. Yes. And you. Take care.'

22

'In January 1948 I sent my thesis, which had just been accepted, to the Turkish Institute of Archaeology, with a request that I might be allowed to finance my own exploratory dig of an Early Bronze Age site somewhere in the Konya area. I made it plain that my central purpose was to put to the proof my theories on bronze-casting technology, and that I was therefore looking for very specific evidence — a practice not normally approved by field archaeologists. However, someone in Ankara was on my side, for only a month later back came a letter saying that in principle the project was approved, that there was an untouched *tel* of no great importance at Sherefhisar, and it was mine for the asking. I've little doubt that my offer to finance the dig entirely played its part in all this — the fact was that my father had lived well within a very comfortable income for the sixty-odd years since it had been settled on him: not only had I now inherited the continuing interest off that capital, I also found a very substantial sum unentailed which he had been steadily accumulating over the years. It was this that I decided to use to finance my digs, and so I did, and the last penny of it went at Sidon in the Lebanon in 1963.

'But again I anticipate. My delight was unimaginable and for the next three months all was hustle and bustle, involving three trips on the Orient Express, endless struggles with Turkish officialdom, and almost as many persuading George Partridge to leave his family and the garage he had bought in Sussex so that he could be my site foreman. Ever since that July day back in 1929 he has been the man I have chosen for the job, if I could persuade him to come.

'But where there's a will there's a way, and by the end of June there we were on the Istanbul-Ankara-Konya-Antioch express trundling across the wide, sun-baked, wind-swept Anatolian plain, and there, three miles from the permanent way, was the tel we were to attack.

'"Bigger'n Jake's Tump, eh, Mr Austen?" said dear George as I pointed it out to him. "And hotter too, I daresay..."'

No less great was Cargill's joy, as illumination dawned, than that of Archimedes when the level of water rose in his bath, than that of Newton when the apple landed on his head. Philby. The key. He had to be. Preliminary investigations into Bletchley Park suspects had been carried out by Heads of Station where the suspects were abroad. Philby was Head of Station in Instanbul in 1948. He *must* have been instructed to investigate Austen...

Cargill set his pipe down, went quickly to the index at the back and yes, there was a reference to Philby, but much later in the book, much later in time.

'One interesting little episode occurred about now — my one brush, as far as I know, with the cloak and dagger world of spies and agents. I had just finished one of our finer deals with Sheik Ben Khameen for the gold oak-leaf wreath that is now one of our most cherished exhibits at the Gold Museum, and I was feeling rather chuffed — in short, ready to celebrate. So, as soon as I was back in Beirut, off I went to the Hotel St Georges — where else? — where I ordered a bottle of bubbly; then, feeling this was a touch greedy of me, I cast around to see if there was anyone there I could share it with, a friend, an acquaintance... I wasn't fussy. And lo and behold who should be there, I was almost sure it was he, though it was many many years since we had, very briefly, been friends, but none other than the *Observer*'s Middle East correspondent, Kim Philby. I knew he was around — I read the *Observer* — and that was another reason I was sure it must be he. Well, I stood up, waved a hand at him, at the silver bucket beside me — the meaning was surely unmistakeable —

but to my dismay the fellow gave me a most fearsome scowl, stood up and vanished at a rate of knots.

'I must, I decided, have been mistaken, and I thought no more of it. Not that is until six months later, when the news of his defection broke at last — though in fact it had taken place just two days after I had asked him to share my bottle of Bollinger: the poor chap must, I suppose, have had a lot on his mind just then; not the moment to spend an evening drinking with a wild archaeologist who thought a handful of gold leaves the most important thing in the world...'

Not the moment, when he was under very close surveillance, to tar by association a fellow spy, thought Cargill.

But when had they very briefly been friends? At Cambridge — in the last months of the Labour Club? Perhaps. Certainly that would be what Austen would say. But when both had infiltrated the Anglo-German Fellowship too? Why not. Lady Kitti might know something about that. But also when Philby came to Konya to question, *warn*, him about Bletchley Park — that was for sure. Cargill bumped his forehead with his clenched fist. What a fool he had been — distracted by his need to find an agent in the Service protecting Austen *now*, he had ignored the obvious possibility that there had been one then.

But how to prove it? Or anyway find something supportive? The fact that Philby's report on Austen had been 'lost' was an indication. Moreover, it must have been Philby who had instructed the London end of the enquiry to look at Riversdale's private papers, and told London that Lady Kitti had them in her possession, and all that had gone missing too. That these documents had been removed, possibly by Philby himself, would infallibly implicate Austen. But there had to be evidence that this is what had happened. There should be a copy of the instruction to Philby to investigate Austen...

If only I could get into the Registry — just once more.

Cargill thumbed tobacco into his pipe, strode up and down his room from the window which overlooked the brickwork of one corner of the Oratory, back to the bookcase filled with scores, topped with his metronome and bust of Mozart. I can do it once, he realised, with a touch of bluff, and provided I haven't been warned off the course by the Housemaster. He sat down again to work it out, and to make a list of just what and how much he could look at during what he was fairly sure would be his last visit. Smoke billowed round his head.

He got in — by giving a two-day-old password and pretending it was what the duty officer at Head Office had given him. 'A nonsense at the other end,' he insisted, 'look, you're not going to send me all the way back to get the right one, are you? Why not have a word with the Librarian — he'll vouch for me. This is a bit urgent; frankly, time is running out...'

The delectable Sally was quick too with six wallets of fiches, and he worked for an hour almost uninterrupted — the only occasion being when Sally borrowed back one of the wallets for another customer: the American, Mormon-like youth who had been there before.

Cargill did well, very well. First, he found the signal instructing Philby to ask Austen — believed to be on a dig near Konya — certain specific questions about Bletchley Park, and to give a personal assessment of subject's political views, etc.

He worked on, sending the pages and pages of telegrams, memos, reports, and minutes scudding over the screen of the VDU, and finally hit on this too: the defector who had in 1948 revealed what the Russians knew about the Government Codes and Cyphers School had actually brought with him the Russian file — that is, the file in Russian — on film. This had been translated back into English. With him Cargill had *The Burning Matrix*. At one point the leak had said this: 'There was no escape. Security laid down the rule: once in, never out. Application could be made to a committee for an alternative posting, but applications were almost invariably turned down. Even a girl who had been seduced by a superior, and consequently was in danger of mental illness, could not get release.' Sir Richard Austen in his autobiography thirty years later had this: 'Of course once you were in Bletchley Park that was it. For the duration, as we said in those days. The rule the security chappies had laid down was absolutely adamant on the point — once in, always in. Of course there was machinery for dealing with those who wanted out, but it was cosmetic, for it always

187

turned you down. Even a girl who was on the point of nervous breakdown following an affair with a married man from King's (no names, no pack-drill) was given the usual brush off.'

The sequence of thought was the same, the example was the same; what further similarities might there not be if only the original English version of the leak could be found?

Then, a few pages on, this: 'Bletchley Park's success depended to a great extent on the close-working between cryptography and intelligence, the fact that they were working together on the same material in the same place. Those who produced the material and those who consumed it were cheek to cheek, and it was easy for them to communicate with each other, often verbally.'

The Burning Matrix had this: 'Success arose, I am sure, from the closeness with which code-crackers and intelligence co-operated. Those who turned the stuff out and those who gobbled it up lived cheek by jowel — easy, free interchanges were always possible and often by word of mouth.'

This, surely, Cargill thought, would stand up in a court of law: and what would a thoroughly professional analysis of the two, preferably confirmed by a computer since juries tend to believe computers are infallible when in fact they think, even more than the English newspaper-reading public, what they are told to think...

This not altogether relevant train of thought was attenuated and finally snapped, first by the scented presence of Sally, then by the light touch of her finger on his shoulder.

'Mr Cargill. The Librarian would like to see you for a moment.'

She lied. The Housemaster himself had come over from St James's. He was very angry. Cargill tried not to look at him — not out of shame as a naughty schoolboy caught cribbing or shagging might have done, but out of deep distaste, an emotion almost too lofty to be called hate. Instead, he studied Dame Peggy Ashcroft as Hermione; the fantails and angelfish in the aquarium; the averted head of the Librarian (the *sneak*); he even speculated on just what preserved delicacies the silly little man had stashed away amongst the Heinz. Bottled gulls' eggs, no doubt, thought Cargill, and if the Librarian could have heard him he would have been withered by the corrosive intensity of the scorn.

But enough of what the Housemaster was saying (head on one side, long fingers picking at his jacket, at the Librarian's blotter, thin long lips bloodless, snarling) penetrated. Gross breach of discipline. Insubordination. Dead against the standards of conduct that made the Service the best of its kind in the world (Cargill's mouth twitched at the ritual declamation of this myth: with an insider's knowledge, he rated us about seventh or eighth). And so on. And so on. There would be an enquiry of course. A tribunal in effect. Meanwhile, Cargill was to consider himself under house arrest. That is, he was to go back to his flat and, apart from essential shopping, stay there. There would be chaps around to see he did. For the time being he was suspended. For a fortnight, in the first instance.

'Your warrant card is all I need before you go,' was the concluding shot. Kneel on the pouf. Put your elbows on the chair. Swish!

23

'Body found on Bloomsbury building site,' read Kitti Bridge, later that same evening. What's that doing here? 'Prestigious Slaker Towers Development.' Oh yes. That boring man from MI5 whatever left it here. Thought I might be interested. Ha! 'Perhaps he'll give Collins a bottle or two.' Why should he do that? Who is Collins?

She forced herself back to the beginning of the cutting and read it through again. 'Skeleton sitting there with a cut-glass tumbler between its knees.'

For a moment she thought she might faint, or worse, for the words had brought back the past with the vividness of a drug-induced vision...

A stone chamber at the end of a narrow passage, lit by flickering candles, a smell of old earth and dust, the air warm, the night outside hot June, *Walpurgisnacht.*

A pantomime, Teddy had said, a bit of fun, a jape. Seven or eight house-guests, men and women, pushed in with her, around her, all young, all much of an age: they had left the older members of the party playing bridge, relaxing after a day spent planning the future of fascist Europe. Behind her was a German, an Aryan Wonder Boy in white shirt, breeches, boots, duelling scars on his cheeks. And his name? Could she remember now? It didn't matter. Siegfried probably...

Kitti Bridge gave her hard laugh again, drank, leant back into the chintz armchair, and allowed memory or fantasy to unroll another turn or two.

190

... Siegfried had pushed up against her in the flickery gloom and she had pushed back feeling the warmth of his chest on her back, of his loins against her buttocks, then they had stumbled on, spreading out into a loose circle round the tableau that had been prepared for them. On a low stone daïs a naked man sat with his knees drawn up, his arms folded across them, his forehead on his arms. Between his feet was a large, shallow, terracotta bowl in dark brown smooth slip. She recognised it for a supposedly Hittite drinking cup taken from the house, and wondered if their mother would realise it had gone — she seemed to be aware of things like that even though she was nearly blind... The man was her brother, his thin shanks instantly recognisable, and faintly ridiculous.

A bell chimed three times (a brass shellcase — also from the house) and over its reverberations a voice amplified by Senger-phone boomed from somewhere behind them, 'Behold, the King. He awaits his destiny, in the shape of his brother, his alter ego, his doppelganger.' The German, whose English was per-fect, nodded wisely at this. A hooded, sheeted figure passed through them and stood between them and her brother. 'He is come,' the voice went on. 'He is come and he challenges the King to mortal combat.'

The figure raised an arm and the gown fell to his feet leaving him naked too — the moment had an accidental look to it and someone sniggered — the voice went on, a little more quickly. Meanwhile, Kitti recognised the neat, stocky figure of Richard Austen and felt tremors at the sight of his tensed bottom and sturdy thighs. 'They will fight for who shall rule from this night of solstice for a year and a day, to decide who shall take the King's sister as Bride and Queen.'

'Oh, will they indeed,' she had heard her own voice say, clearly ringing beneath the corbelled-stone roof (and smiled now over her half-full tumbler to remember it), 'surely the Bride herself should have some say in the matter.'

There had been a moment's silence as most of those there wondered whether this was or was not part of the show, then Austen's shoulder had begun to shake and one or two more began to snigger again. Teddy lifted his head. His thin, twisted faced looked scornful, he sounded angry: 'Blast you, Kitti, you

191

always spoil our games,' and the laughter became, as they say, general.

Nevertheless, they had had a party, there in Round Grange as it was known, for of course champagne had been carried out earlier. Teddy got over his sulks more quickly than she had expected and had thought up other games — purification ceremonies he called them, in which three of the men undertook to be birched by the ladies present and not cry out even when blood was drawn. A Scottish laird bit off the head of a live cock and the blood was scattered on everyone; a wild music of a sort was set up by banging the shellcase and various bits of wood, stone and emptied bottles, and they took off their clothes and danced, eventually spilling out into the moonlight on to the daisy-strewn turf.

It got colder and by dawn most had gathered up their garments and drifted back to Scales: Teddy alone remained in the tomb, drunk now or high on cocaine, apparently unconscious, blood and vomit streaking his chest and loins. Kitti came on him there, lit by one guttering candle that threw black shadows over the dressed stone, and a moment or two after her Richard, also drunk, returned too. 'We must keep him warm,' he said, pulling the poet's thin knees up to his chest. Then he covered him with what odd bits of clothing still lay scattered about.

'In case he dies we must leave him a drink.' Miraculously the Hittite bowl was unbroken. Richard slopped champagne into it. 'And gold. They always did.' He took off his ring, with the Austen crest, and dropped it into the bowl.

Then he had straightened, swayed in front of her and said, 'It's as well you stopped our fight, you know.'

'Why?'

'I could have killed him.'

'Because I fuck with him sometimes, I suppose.'

'Oh no. Not really. Not that at all. But since you've mentioned it, why don't we?'

But Kitti had had enough of being messed around for one night.

Later she bathed in the lake beneath rising mists and Siegfried appeared too. He admitted he had found it all quite

192

interesting, jolly good fun. But not real. Not like Nuremburg. This she could believe, and she made him promise to get her in next year, or at Berlin for the Opening of the Games. He might even do much better than that, he had said, swimming along sedately, breast-stroke, an introduction was a possibility, especially if they were able to take back favourable reports following their tour of stately homes...

But that's *not* it. Kitti banged her tumbler on the *Triumph of Galatea* in an effort to force her mind back to the significance of the newspaper cutting. But she was empty. She needed a refill. She hauled herself upright and on legs bird-thin tottered across to the decanter. Empty too. With Herman snuffling behind her, she carried it carefully, using both hands, out of her drawing room, through the door and into another world — a short passage took her to a filthy kitchen, littered with empty bottles, half-eaten food some whiskered with mould, half-empty tins of dog-food one of which Herman now licked at. In the reeking pantry she unstoppered a bottle of Glenlivet Malt and, using a plastic funnel, poured it into the decanter. Herman lapped at a bowl of brackish water, peed on the doorpost, and trotted back after her to the immaculate front room.

There was something, she knew. But what? Yes. A piece of newspaper. Now what had it been about? Oh yes. Dickie and Teddy. Well, of course Dickie had this hate thing for Teddy, which he kept quiet about. Something from their kids' school. Too silly. But a killing hate. Yes.

Here's the newspaper. But no mention of either of them. Just Slaker House and a skeleton. With a cut-glass tumbler between its knees. Too absurd. Can't hold a glass between your knees when you're dead. Difficult enough sober. Must mean on the floor. Probably with a gold ring in it...

Almost everything about Lady Kitti Bridge was frail — her physical frame, her hold on sanity, her desire to live: yet, if the shock of revelation nearly snapped the threads, it also cleared her mind as if swathed cobwebs had been torn down, dusty drapes thrown open. Passion, not light, flooded through her consciousness like a hot destructive wind tossing aside the bricà-brac of thirty years spent pursuing oblivion in other women's beds, with junk, in bottles.

Certain she had been for most of those thirty years that Austen had framed Teddy, made it appear her brother had been blackmailed into cooperation by the KGB, and that he had done this by getting Teddy's poems and papers into the hands of MI5 through her. Then, the other day, that old man with the moustache, who smelled of old clothes and pipe, had shown her how Austen had come to Scales in 1935 as a spy, a bolshie spy, not at all because he was obsessed with her. And now she knew Austen had killed Teddy, and she knew how . . .

Feverishly aware that her powers to move and think were slipping again, but also conscious that there was still a steeliness in the dissipated core of her being, she rummaged for and found Cargill's telephone number; she dialled it, heard with relief that he could not be at Fennimore Gardens for two hours at least (he did not explain he would need so long in order to slip the watchers the Housemaster had left on his doorstep): relief, because she could sleep out the time between, and then with caffeine, ascorbic acid, orange juice, vitamin B, raw egg, and so on, perhaps draw together again the ragged fabric of her mind.

24

Two middle-aged to elderly gents, both with that healthy shine
that only sustained good living over many years can give, one in
an old-fashioned tweed deer-stalker, a longish tweed coat, plus-
fours, and very shiny shoes; the other in an Austrian hat with a
feather, a coat of much louder check than the first (Roy, the last
time I saw a garment like that was on a silver-ring bookie), and
borrowed yellow wellies, tramped (their word for it) across Yew
Tree Heath. They waved their sticks proprietorially at anything
that took their attention: a pair of lapwings; the chimneys of
Fawley Refinery; the Island's distant hills, blue beneath a
wintery sky; the sullen browsing ponies.

They paused in front of a gorse-covered lump.

'There,' said Austen. 'Austen's Last Dig.'

'Oh, really? What did you find?'

'I haven't done it yet. But I will. As far as I can see from
county records, it's never been opened. I'll get John Wainwright out of his New Milton bungalow, and George Partridge
over from his garage in Sussex, pick a nice, warm weekend in
July...'

'And end up on your back with a slipped disc.'

Austen laughed and they tramped on.

'See those chimneys over there.' A pair of white ones with
black tops — well away from Fawley. 'That's Marchwood
Power Station. And between us and it are *two* of your bases.'

They tramped on.

Newman said, a little drily, 'You shouldn't believe everything you read in the *New Statesman*.'

'No? And here's another thing.' Austen paused, and with his stick tapped a short white concrete post that stuck up out of the heather to a height of about half a metre. 'The Post Office has just finished laying a heavy cable; it needed a JCB and a special digging gadget to get it under, and this post marks a junction box. The engineers said it was to satisfy extra demand for telephones on the Ashling exchange. Now Roy,' he took the American's arm, 'Ashling is that way. And the cable runs that way. And that way, between here and the next exchange at Brockenhurst, are six houses and they all have telephones. And this is a National Park which means no more houses can be built on it.'

'Richard. What are you trying to tell me?'

'It's really part of *your* communications network. We'll turn left here and have a spot of lunch at the pub, good idea?'

'Fine. Well, you know we try to do our best. And I sometimes think we should advertise ourselves more, and get the credit we're due to. I sincerely do believe our American deterrent is what has kept the peace these thirty years.'

'Roy. Back home, do you have your personal fall-out shelter?'

'Well, Lena and I certainly gave the matter some thought. But we decided that on the whole, taking a chance though it might be, it would, at this particular point in time, be counter-productive. You see we, that is Lena and I, sincerely believe ...'

'Roy. I know why you don't have a fall-out shelter.'

'You do?'

'Yes. Because the British Isles, on which we now stand, are your aircraft and missile carrier — as one of your generals recently said, and I quote, "We've fought and won two world wars in Europe and that's where we'll fight and win the third."'

Newman looked angry, kept silent for a moment or two and then said, 'You, of course, do have one.'

'Actually I have. I'll show it to you later. I think it's rather • neat, but I'd like your opinion.' He forebore from adding that he had bought and installed the absurd thing on instructions from his Control.

'Are you ribbing me, Richard?'

'Perish the thought, Roy. Perish the thought.'

* * *

On the way back from the pub, Austen showed Newman over the Farm. Sandra Wainwright smiled as effortlessly as a plastic flower and went back to the clipboard from which she was directing six insecure-looking and wrongly dressed customers on to six totally bomb proof hacks. Charlie, the chestnut stallion, watched everything with an alert eye, nodding his raffish head over the door of his loose box.

'You're a fine fellow, and no mistake. Do they still ride him?'

'Oh yes. He'd kick the place down if he didn't get exercise. He's thirteen years old. Doesn't look it, does he?'

They passed on. Two stable cats slinked, then darted away in front of them. In the hay barns at the back Brian Wainwright and a friend were laying a new concrete floor. A mixer powered off a David Brown tractor churned away. He barely acknowledged the two visitors' presence.

'I admire him, you know. He's really made a go of this place. And he manipulates the black economy for all it's worth.'

'What do you mean?'

'Well, that man with him is paying for his wife's pony she keeps here. And this tarmac we're walking on was paid for in much the same way. I would guess that the turnover of this place is about twice what the books say.'

'Well, I expect the same is true of ICI.'

'And not of United Special Steels?'

'Say, Richard, I thought you were meant to be some sort of a socialist. All for state control and zapping the entrepreneur. Am I right or am I right?'

'Only so the state can wither away and the individual find freedom in free association with individuals. Meanwhile, I like to see the spirit of individualism kept alive against the day. Or look at it another way — it's an example of capitalism's inner contradictions, which will bring it down in the end.'

'Oh shit. Anyway, those people hate you, you know that?'

They stopped — on a path between two fields, horses one side, cows the other. Austen looked at Newman, put his head on one side, and became suddenly conscious that he was gripping his stick quite hard.

'There was no need to say that, Roy. No need at all. And it's not true. Indifferent, I'm sure. Damn it man, I have no strong

197

feelings about them. And they get it all, as theirs, they have it on lease already, as soon as I hand in my dinner pail.'

'Why leave it to them if you're indifferent to them?'

'Why not? Their labour has made it what it is. They haven't had a penny from me or anyone else.'

'I suppose you call that socialism. Just ask yourself who'd get it if you had a family of your own.'

'Stop needling me, Roy.'

'OK, OK. I'm sorry. Forget it. But you needled me about our deterrent and bases here. What do you say? *Pax*. Is that it? Pax it is. Anyway where *is* your shelter?'

'Over there. In that patch of forest. Just about under where all those rooks are making such a shindy.'

In the evening Austen took Newman to a hotel a couple of miles away and gave him a dinner. It was meant to be rather a good place, exclusive, very expensive, right away from the main roads, but Newman claimed that whatever was in his game pie was off.

'We like our birds well hung, you know, Roy?'

'Well hung! This is as high as a kite. Leave it until tomorrow and it'll be a case of on the third week it rose again. Oh, never mind. Tell them to burn a steak for me and forget it.'

They had coffee and armagnac back at the Farm. Austen stirred up the fire and they settled into armchairs, glasses, cups on the wide arms, coffee pot in the hearth, decanter on a table between them.

'Well, Richard. What do you think of it? What do you think of coming to USS and doing a Gold for us?'

The tall American was stroking the long curve of his extra-ordinary nose: dimly Austen recalled that an ATS girl had annoyed Newman by saying he inevitably did this when what he was saying had more motives than were immediately obvious. 'If your friend offers a girl a drink or even a cigarette and doesn't stroke his schnozzle, she's safe — but if he does, watch out; he'll have them down before the evening's out.'

'I'd like to very much. But does that mean you've settled on the idea? I thought you were going to pick my brains first. Work out costs and appeal and so forth.'

198

'Oh sure. But I think in principle it will go ahead.'

'It won't be cheap, you know. Not if it's to be as good as the London one.'

'No, I'm sure it won't be cheap. But you are on board, are you?'

'Well yes, I think so. London Gold runs itself now so I won't be letting anyone down by going. Anyway, it's time I stopped hogging it — it would be a great stepping stone for a younger chap, and they need it these days. These cuts in government spending, you know, they've just about shot the academic career structure to pieces...'

'Richard.'

'Sorry. Yes. I'm on board.'

'Fine, fine. I take it you'll want to be paid?'

'Well, yes...a modicum. I mean, you know, I'm quite well off, but one doesn't...'

'What does Slaker pay you now?'

'It's not Slaker. It's the Foundation...'

'Crap. It's Slaker. What does he pay you?'

'Eighteen thousand.'

'That's chicken shit. We'll give you fifty. And a big bonus if you pull off what we have in mind.'

Silence. They looked at each other across the glasses, the cups — the tall American wary, one eyebrow cocked; the small neat Englishman suddenly alarmed, poised, alert, head on one side, eye bright: the one ready to shoot, the other to fly.

'What is this, Roy? What are you on about?'

Newman turned away, drank off his brandy, poured himself another without asking.

'I wear two hats, Richard. You must have guessed that. Always have. At Bletchley I was OSS, keeping an eye on you all. And just at this point in time you could say I represent Uncle Sam, rather than United Special Steels. Now. For some months we've had an operation set up against you and all ready to go. And with Ronnie safely past the post we don't need to wait for the Inauguration.'

'Roy. For Christ's sake, what is all this about?'

'Well, Sir Dick, we aim to turn you or blow you. That's what it's about. If we turn you you get good compensation — a new

199

Gold in Jamestown, you write your own cheque. If it's the other, then it's straight to Parkhurst Top Security Wing and you don't pass Go.'

Austen stood up, moved towards the french window. He felt tired, which was, in a way, a disappointment. He had always know that this moment would come — at times of boredom, *taedium vitae*, he had almost willed it, expecting it to bring with it excitement, a sudden rush of adrenalin, challenge. He raised his hand to the curtain thinking to let in a breath or two of frosty air, to look for a moment at the half-moon, at the stars.

'Hell, Richard. You must have realised something of this was in my mind when I offered you a new Gold Museum. You must know that we know what you do for Slaker, and why Charlie trusts you.'

This riled Austen simply because his vanity had concealed from him what was now so obvious. The fact of the matter was that he had done well as an archaeologist, that he had become a public figure as an archaeologist, a successful author, a talking head on television. Even in so far as he was a socialist, a Marxist, he still thought of himself as a Marxist archaeologist first, as a Soviet agent a long way after. Therefore vanity had had its way — he had sincerely believed Roy's offer for his services as an archaeologist was no more than what it had seemed to be.

He came back into the room, poured himself brandy and sat down.

'You really are a rotten bastard, Roy. You know?' In response, Newman pasted a broad humourless grin across his face and then tore it off. Austen went on, 'But why? Why me?'

'Oh, it's not *you* we're after. Of course not. It's the Slaker computers. It's just not in the interests of the free world for the Soviets to have those computers.'

'Why not? They're not military. Have no military application.'

'Don't be naïve, Sir Dick. The next eight years are going to see the completion of our final strategy — the internal destabilisation of the Soviet régimes. Stepping up the arms production cycle, retuning climatological patterns, well, I won't go into all that. But as their economies go bananas they're going to need every aid to population control they can get — far more

200

even than they have now. That's what those computers are for. And if they are as good as Slaker says or only as good as we in USS know them to be, they could still lengthen the lives of those régimes by three or four years. And that is just not acceptable.'

Austen bit his knuckle in an effort to clear his head.

'If I'm exposed, one way or another, there will be a huge scandal here. A much bigger business than Blunt. I mean the fact that I've worked between Slaker and the Russians all these years will be made to seem that all the time I was working for my masters in the Kremlin.'

'That's it.'

'Yes. I see the, what do you say? scenario. Public outcry, backbenchers, the government would be forced to forbid the contract.'

'That's the idea. But right now *you* have to decide how it's done. In spite of the expense we'd rather buy you: it's quicker, more certain, has great propaganda value, and it's more humane. You retain dignity, soft job, title too if it falls out right. The other way will be just hell. Well you can work it out for yourself and in the morning tell me you're bought. But one thing I think you ought to know is this: this house is so wired up with every bug known to man — well, known to USS, which comes to the same thing — that on a dark night it *glows*. And it's been like that for some time. Now think of that. Just think of that. Now that's enough for starters.'

'Why? Are *you* afraid you might say something you shouldn't? And it'll be on record?'

25

Three hours later, when Austen was as sure as he could be that Newman was asleep, he tiptoed out through the frosty night to the stables — he had a torch, but scarcely needed it: the moon was bright in a clear sky. Horses snuffled round him, puffs of vapour pumped rhythmically out of the loose boxes, hooves clumped on concrete. The pay phone was in a box that had been converted into a cloak/first-aid room. As he pulled back the bolt in the top part of the door Sparta, the Wainwrights' Alsatian bitch, began to bark down by the bungalow a hundred yards away, hauling at her chain as if she'd drag the whole building after her rather than let the intruder get away.

Austen passed a hand over his head and leant against the stable waiting for her to stop, praying her to stop. But she wouldn't. She was too good to. At last a door opened, a torch shone, and he heard Wainwright's voice — instantly Sparta quietened, but then her chain rang on stone, a footstep crunched on gravel, and here they came out into the moonlight — the bitch still straining in front, Wainwright ready to let her slip with a shotgun broken over his other arm.

'Brian, it's all right. It's only me.'

'Sir Richard?'

'Yes. Look, I'm terribly sorry I set her off. I have a phone call to make, to America, which is why I'm so late, the different times, you see.' Austen's ability to improvise a fib on the spot was something he was privately rather proud of. 'And the blasted phone in the house is on the blink again.'

'You'd best come into the bungalow then. I'm sure ours is all right.'

'No. No need.'

'You'll need a deal of ten p. pieces to get through to America.'

'Oh, that's all right. I just have to give the operator my Barclaycard number.'

'All right then, Sir Richard. But I'll have to stay out with Sparta till you've gone, else she'll start up again.'

'I'll be as quick as I can.'

He was very quick. All he had to do was leave a message for Lord Slaker. It ran: 'Something rather sticky has cropped up, and I hope to be at Briar Rose Cottage early tomorrow, by midday anyway.' He then put on a charade to convince Wainwright that he really was speaking across the Atlantic; finally he rang off. During the interim the sight of the sturdy figure, inevitably in his hat and coat as if he kept them by his bed for just such eventualities — and his shotgun too, had given Austen a glimmer of an idea of how he might yet cope. He didn't like it at all; he would have to think it over very carefully. He had already rejected the idea of making a bolt for it straightaway — it was important to find out more of what Newman knew and was up to — but later he would want to make a getaway, and the sight of Wainwright with his gun had given him a clue as to how this might be done.

He let himself out of the box and called that he was going in now, he'd finished. Wainwright gave a barely visible wave, the chain chinked, and he strolled back to the bungalow with Sparta obediently at heel. Inevitably cigarette smoke hung in the moonlit air behind him — Austen wondered if he slept with a cigarette in his mouth: awake, he was never seen without one.

The first part of his plan apparently worked well enough. And later Newman quite readily accepted that Austen would not want to talk things over in a thoroughly bugged house — so readily that again Austen wondered if the American too would prefer for some of the time at any rate to be off the record.

The two polished, tweeded, middle-aged gents set off once more for a tramp, not this time out on to the heath, but, at

Austen's suggestion, through the Forest. The rooks cackled and cawed over their disintegrating nests in the tracery of oak twigs high above their heads, the frosted leaves crunched beneath their feet, the air was still crisp and as they talked the vapour of their breaths gusted above them. Ponies moved stolidly out of their way crackling through the holly, and the noise of the Farm's generator slowly receded.

'If,' said Austen, 'I am not bought, you have, I think, only one option. That is to make public the fact that I was for a time a KGB agent.'

'That is correct. And since you are still here this morning I assume you would rather be bought and confess than be exposed.'

'The assumption being that either way Slaker will have to drop the Russian end of his business. Well then, two questions occur. I should, in parenthesis, make it clear that what I am trying to do is estimate the strength of your hand should I decide not to be bought . . . I think we'll head off to the left a little here. Sometimes one sees deer round here, awfully pretty and not to be missed if one has the chance.'

'The hand is strong, be sure of that. I should not otherwise be playing it this way. No bluff at all. I'm showing one king and three aces; and you need an ace or a nine to make a straight. You can't win. Your two questions?'

'One. If I choose, as you put it, to be bought, just what do you expect of me?'

'You come over to the States. Once safely tucked away out of sight you issue a statement. A resumé of your career as an agent of the Soviets, how in recent visits to Russia you have seen the light, the persecution of the civil rights movement, Afghanistan, we'll give you a script. How, particularly, you think the Slaker computers are a terrible mistake, instruments of oppression for an already intolerably oppressive régime. That sort of thing. Of course what happens next is anyone's guess. It'll depend on what HMG decide to do about it. My guess is, not much. Similarly, Slaker's best bet will be to keep cool, hope it all goes away. But whatever happens you can be sure we'll find enough on the Statute Book to keep you stateside should they try extradition. Then when things are a bit calmer you cash your cheque — that is USS employ you to set up a Gold in James-town. If that's what you want. But, as I said last night — *you* write the cheque. And your second?'

'Well, obviously, just what is it do you have on me? I mean what do you lay down if I call you.'

'Enough. And incidentally your security people have most of it by now as well. We gave them a lead, and they put a sound guy on to it. And the interesting thing is he was called off as soon as he got near you. *That's* going to be egg on your people's faces when the shit hits the fan. But that's by the way. Here is what we've got. It's enough. We know someone at Bletchley Park passed on the Abwehr telegrams to the KGB a full four months after Riversdale was killed. Incidentally, making Riversdale the fall guy never washed with me, but never. And I've now got a pretty shrewd idea of just what did happen that night he was meant to have been killed by a V2. You see, I've been to see Kitti and I know *you* went to Slaker House — and I think it can now be shown Riversdale went there too. Yes.' He stopped. Austen stopped too. The Englishman was white, running his tongue over dry lips. Newman went on, 'But that's not a lot of use to me. What we've got to get you for is being the spy, the guy who passed on the Abwehr telegrams after Rivers-dale was dead. Now I should say that in all this we have been greatly helped by PSIKE, a USS computer on lease to the CIA. That's how good our product is. She threw up something else the other day. What the Russians got in '45, '46, is one lot of material, passed back to us in Russian, of course. But what you say about B-P in *Blazing Matrix*...'

'*Burning.*' Steady now. The ground falls away and there should be a holly bush with a fresh mark on its trunk.

'...is another. And you know, there are matching idio-syncracies of vocabulary, style, what's left in, what's left out, even though the languages are now different. You see, when you wrote *Blazing Matrix*, you couldn't help echoing some of the report you'd done thirty years earlier and virtually forgotten. We know about Briar Rose Cottage too, and when you opened it up, and we can guess why.' He was checking the points off on his fingers. 'We have it straight how you were recruited in 1932 between the College and Cambridge, and all that romantic stuff

205

about hobbling up King Street after Guernica is hogwash. Say, are you looking for something?'

'Only deer. I thought I saw one that way, down there, beyond that very big beech tree the other side of the dip. Do you see where I mean?'

'Sure. We'll head that way. But what clinched it for me was this. You know all your SIS files are now on microfiches? Well, I've had a couple of guys, good boys they are, going through that sector for the last few weeks, oh very discreetly — actually their cover for SIS was that they were weeding out more material for PSIKE to look at — and they found there was no record of your having been investigated over Bletchley Park. And there should have been. A known leftie like you. But nothing was ever filed; or if it was it was later removed. So then we asked ourselves . . . what was *Sir* Richard doing when the preliminary investigations were made, where was he? Uh-uh. Check. In Turkey. So. Just to be sure, I sent you that folded piece of paper, to give you a fright, and followed it up with my very good friend Dr Olivia Shapiro. And because you were sure she was an agent and had something on you, you followed the standard routine — tell the truth for as long as you can. But you went on too long, Richard. Comes a point, *old boy*, when you're meant to start lying. But you went right on and told her Philby came to see you on your dig; you assumed that she knew that already, that Philby would have filed a record of his interview with you. Well maybe he did. But sure as hell he got it out again later. And that wasn't the only one. You know we've caught people through Philby like that before, over what should have been somewhere but wasn't because he'd moved it. Incidentally, if the hunting gun I saw you leave the Farm with before first light is behind that beech tree, you won't mind if I'll be the one to pick it up, all right?'

He now had a heavy automatic in his hand which he pointed straight at Sir Richard's stomach.

'Oh, *shit*. Oh, damn and blast you!' Austen actually stamped — and this was too much for Newman who exploded into a high hoot of laughter: 'Oh boy,' he struggled to say, 'if you could only see your face. If only . . .' He stumbled slightly on his backward progress to the tree, took his eye off Austen, recovered and . . . 'Hey. Come on. Austen? Austen!'

26

From behind his tree Austen could see, just, the heavy black automatic slowly traversing the terrain in front of the tall American who was still only fifteen yards away. Absurdly, Newman had adopted the style of TV police, holding the gun in both hands out in front of him, and his body weaved with it, but the muzzle was aimed high, chest high, and instinctively Austen had dropped to a crouch. It reached its furthest point in its arc from where he was, and he scurried off again, still as low as could be, to the next tree away, adding a further ten yards to the range.

'Don't do that, Austen, there's a good fellow. This thing will blow you in half and I know how to use it. Now, why don't you just step out from behind that tree, and let me see you good and plain, and I'll try to forget this happened.'

Austen kept still, surprised that his breath was back to near normal so quickly, one corner of his mind assessing his performance, aware that he was doing quite well to have got so far. If he could, in one more dash, get a further thirty yards off, he'd have a lot of trees to play with, should be able to begin leading Newman, to control the pattern of their movements through the forest.

'Hell, Austen. I'm coming for you.'

As the American stepped towards him Austen ran again, hard and low across the fallen, rotting branches, through the drifts of leaves, and stumbled over a root as the gun went off.

The noise was appalling. Colonies of rooks rose vertically from their high stations above them, their hysterical cackle drowning the reverberations of the shot; two hundred yards off, six fallow deer became briefly visible through the holly scrub as they moved away smoothly, speedily, and without a sound. Austen rolled into cover: he was petrified now, but shocked too, stunned by the outrage of it. How *dare* he!

'Now hear this, Austen. I put that high on purpose. I want you to understand. If I wing you, then I have to kill you: obviously I can't take you to hospital. And that'll be all right if I do. Kill you, I mean. Messy, I know, but with you dead we can still blow you, we'll still stop Slaker... *Goddamn* you, Austen.' Two more shots rang out. At this further assault on their eardrums, the rooks too seemed to feel outrage as much as anything — in a great cloud they rose again, wheeled purposefully, soared, and made off. Austen had no idea how close the bullets came (nor for that matter had Newman) but he was now a clear sixty yards away — and that, something from the back of his mind told him, was enough to make the pistol if not harmless then certainly very inaccurate. Only a very lucky shot would hurt him now — so long as he kept his distance.

He knew these woods well. Where a stranger would see only endless vistas of beeches with broad smooth trunks interspersed occasionally with oaks and scattered holly bushes — all spaced over undulating ground littered with fallen timber and leaves, he knew that over the rise to his left one suddenly came on a clear grassy ride with a plantation of young conifers beyond; that behind Newman the ground fell away into a swampy area of rivulets and shallow pools and so to the tiny Beaulieu River; that if he could move in a careful semi-circle, using a small clump of very tall pines as a landmark, he would come back to the beech tree where his shotgun was, and that behind that...

He moved off obliquely and as he did was aware that the American was following, but cutting across the arc, seeking to shorten the distance between them. The difference, though, was that Austen understood the geometry of what was going on whereas Newman did not. Lapwing-like, he allowed himself to limp a little, drew the American closer, and then suddenly put on a very fast spurt indeed, covering forty yards in less than five seconds, and drawing, as he expected he would, another shot after him. Really the American had no other option but to fire — it must have seemed to him the only chance of preventing the complete escape of his quarry.

But escape was not Austen's prior aim; not, at any rate, until he had closed off the possibility of immediate pursuit and also given himself at least one counter to bargain with in the wheeling and dealing he foresaw must lie ahead: a sleepless night of intense thought had produced more than a shotgun planted out in the Forest.

Not that the shotgun was not still foremost in his mind, even though Newman had seen through his first attempt to get to it. It, and the huge beech tree against which it was propped, were now about forty yards away, at right angles to the line they were moving on, for they had now completed a rough semi-circle. It remained to be seen whether Newman had realised this. At any rate, Austen did not feel he could risk a sudden rush to it — he was aware that even with it his fire power would still be inferior to Newman's: something more was needed to give him a decisive edge.

Newman was sidling from tree to tree fifty yards or so away, quite ignorant of where his prey now was but still moving in something like the right direction. Austen stooped, silently rummaged in fallen holly leaves ignoring the sting of their sharps, and pulled up a small flint core, irregularly shaped but about the weight of a cricket ball.

It was awkward — he must not attract attention by the action of his throw; the flint must travel clear of branches a good fifty yards and not make a sound until it fell.

The slow left-arm bowler of College days had also been a tolerable Third Man, with a fast, accurate throw guaranteed to take the bails off three times out of five. He had been turning out in the summer for Lyndhurst Academicals until five years ago, and although he had given up squash he still played badminton; Sir Richard Hannay himself could not have done better, Sir Richard Austen thought, as the flint landed with a satisfying clunk on a fallen branch twenty yards the other side of Newman.

The American reacted, and began to move warily towards the sound, his back three-quarters to Austen, who now also moved away towards the beech, but always keeping the

American in view. Suddenly he too was gripped with an urgent desire to shout with laughter. The long, loud check coat in front of him swayed from tree to tree; occasionally he caught a glimpse of his old friend's Punch-like nose, but the black, lumpish weapon in his hand and the memory of those terrifying reports kept him quiet. At last he had his hand on the stock of the hunting gun — a twenty-bore Purdy that had been his father's . . . then nausea flooded back for, for the life of him, he could not remember if he had left it loaded and he did not dare risk the noise of breaking it to see. For twenty minutes in the pearly dawn he had agonised over the choice and he rather felt that he had eventually unloaded it, and put the two shells in his coat pocket. But his pockets were empty. So, after all, he must have broken the last tabu of all, and left the gun loaded, the breach closed, the firing mechanism cocked.

Now it only remained to bring Newman back to within lethal range — preferably still with his back to him. A judicious cough; a twig carefully cracked beneath his shoe; sidling round the tree at the right moment soon achieved this.

'Drop your gun, Roy. Roy? Drop it. Please.'

Newman had frozen satisfyingly enough, his right arm faded to his side and the pistol pointed at the ground. But he held on to it.

'Listen, Roy, the muzzle of my shotgun is about a yard from the back of your neck. Now, I know that this sort of weapon is unreliable, it *may* not kill you . . . ah.' The pistol thudded to the leaves. 'But sure as anything it would have hurt. There. No. NO. *Don't* turn round.'

'You're a son of a bitch, *Sir* Dick. You know that.'

'Oh quite. Now listen and I'll tell you what I want you to do.'

'I don't know how you did it. Crafty bastard.'

'Actually I stalk deer — just to photograph them, you know. Jolly good fun, actually. Now listen Roy. Ten yards in front of you there's a slight mound of freshish earth, nothing growing on it, not overgrown. Right? Right. And a declivity to the left of it. Yes? Now at this end, under the leaves, you'll find a manhole cover. Find it and lift it. I promise you, if you mess me about I really will do my best to blow your head off, but play fair and you'll come to no harm.'

210

'"Play fair,"' Newman mimicked. 'God, you British. I suppose it's your fall-out shelter.'

'That's right.'

'Christ, can't you get *anything* right?'

'What do you mean?'

'The war starts. A high one goes off over Southampton and this whole forest goes up in a fire-storm. Do you know what sort of temperatures that will mean, have you any idea at all? There's a Chubb lock on this cover.'

'It's not locked, but I do have the key. You just lift it and go down the ladder. I think you'll find everything you need down there. There's a torch to your left on a shelf at the bottom.'

Still shaking in weary disgust, Newman's head, nose, close-cropped grey hair sank out of sight.

'I hadn't thought of fire-storms,' Austen said as he lowered the square cover into place. 'Let's hope Jimmy Carter doesn't decide on one last fling before he steps down.'

He pocketed the pistol, broke open the shotgun and discovered that after all it wasn't loaded. With a sick feeling of dismay, he remembered how, after that twenty minutes of internal debate, he had recognised that a gentleman simply *can't* leave a loaded gun lying about in the open. The cartridges were of course in his pocket. No they weren't. He'd put on a darker coat foreseeing the possible need of camouflage.

He rubbed and rubbed at his eyes. The trouble was that he was exhausted. At sixty-six years old a night without sleep is an appalling imposition. He looked at his watch — still only half past nine. He could give himself an hour before moving on to Briar Rose Cottage.

On the way back to the Farm, he took a short cut across a corner of heath — and a curlew flew up ahead of him trickling its liquid cry into the frosty air. The noise cheered him, and he began to hum, then whistle, the last movement of Dvorak's Violin Concerto, and his small feet twinkled in a tiny pattern of dance-steps. Really he'd done very well. He'd turned up a nine to complete his straight, and a straight beats three of a kind. He would leave old Roy in the tiny shelter (a cylinder ten feet long, six feet high) for as long as he possibly could, and pay him out for the fright he had suffered.

As he turned into his gate he saw, leading away from it, a dead-straight line of mole hills. Distracted for a moment, he reasoned over this aberration in nature, and then cheerily concluded that they had followed the loose earth left round what he took to be the American communication cable recently laid there. Inevitably he chortled to himself, 'Well grubbed, old mole. Well grubbed.'

PART THREE

PART THREE

27

His mood had changed for the worse when, later that day, soot
fell in the tiny fireplace of Briar Rose Cottage. He started up,
eyes smarting from the smoke that suddenly billowed out from
the fall, stomach dropping as the awfulness of his predicament
came back at him like an incompletely digested gobbet of
unpalatable food. Blindly he felt along the mantle for his
tumbler of ancient whisky. He found it, tipped back half an
inch, then banged the tumbler down on the small, solid parlour
table, where Newman's gun still lay. He rapped it again, almost
as if he wanted to break it, smash it in his hand. A brusque turn
on his heel brought him to the low window — it would be a silly,
futile thing to start breaking glasses, but he felt angry, not far off
despair...and terrified. There was a car parked behind his
Jaguar. No, not a car. By standing on tiptoe he could see over
the trimmed privet — it was a small lorry, what do they call
them? a pick-up with a hoist on the back. Relief flooded back as
he recognised even after a quarter of a century the large dark
figure of his old site-foreman.

'George. Oh, how good to see you. Come in, won't you?'

Dark brown eyes, set beneath lids that drooped now, looked
squarely into his, then edged away.

'Sir Richard. You should have warned me you were coming.'

'I know, George, but I couldn't and there it is.'

'That fire needs attention. Shall I look at it?'

George Partridge, not one for warm displays of emotion,
evaded Austen's handshake — even, horrors, embrace, and
knelt in front of the smoking fireplace. Richard surveyed his

215

broad back, clad in a donkey jacket, and the greying, dark hair wispy over a lined and wrinkled neck with an almost filial affection — for, although George was less than two years older, there had been problems and scrapes when Richard had had to rely on him utterly: from relatively trivial matters like checking pilfering amongst Syrian workmen to shifting half a hundred-weight of Basque bricks off his broken leg at Guernica.

'It's a matter of the damper, you see. And this cowl is adjustable too. There. It'll draw now and the smoke's going up the chimbley where it should. When it's burning too hot, just close down the cowl again.' He stood up, smoothing large hands down the sides of heavy cloth trousers. 'I brought you what'll see you through until tomorrow, and I'll come with summat fresh, or Madge will, before dinner then. It's not fancy, but it's enough.'

'George, I'm sure it is. You are a wonder.'

'Well, Sir Richard, you should have told me.' He looked greyer, thinner than Austen expected. Not just old, but worn down, harassed, ill even. But he stumped about the tiny house capably enough checking all the things Austen had checked already.

'You'll be all right then. Until tomorrow.'

'Yes, George. Of course I will.'

They faced each other in the tiny hall. George's breath was sour.

'Well, many thanks, as always. I say, George, don't rush off yet. Stay and have a drop with me.'

'No, Sir Richard. I told Madge I wouldn't be more than half an hour.'

'She's all right then?'

'She's fine. Apart from a pair of Mormons we rented the spare bedroom to have made a Latter Day Saint of her. They won't catch me, though. The children and grandchildren are fine too.' Pre-empting the inevitable catechism.

'Business?'

'Not so good, not so good really.'

'I *am* sorry to hear that. What's the matter?'

George's voice hardened. 'Bloody bypass is the matter. Took three quarters of my trade out of the town. They gave

216

compensation, and see, well, I reckoned I'd have to make up by going more into maintenance and repair like. So spent it all on electronic stuff. Compression tester, tuning. New-fangled gadgets. Made the repair shop look like Emergency Ward Ten.'

'And it hasn't worked out?'

'Not yet. But it will. It better had because I can't sell up and retire until it does.'

'If it doesn't, let me know.'

'You've done enough for me and mine, Sir Richard. Let be now.'

Austen watched him stump up the short path to the wooden gate. He half expected him to turn and wave, but he did not. Presently the pick-up engine fired, and Austen closed the door.

What was in the bag he had left? Six eggs. Half a pound of bacon, half a loaf, cheddar, butter, a tin of beans. And a bottle of White Horse. Good old George.

He switched on the wireless — Rhine Maidens in golden harmonies filled the tiny warm room again: the sheer sensuous beauty of it held him for a moment and he shuddered, then grinned at the soppiness of his reaction. It would do well enough as, what do they call it? aural wallpaper while I fry up some bacon and eggs. He turned up the volume so Wagner's specious myth-telling would rise above the hiss and spit of the frying-pan.

Good old George. But I should not have suggested helping him with the garage. Even if I do manage to get money to him, it will be spotted and traced, and he'll be harassed as an accomplice. I suppose I just wanted him to think well of me. A fault that has got me into trouble often enough, the desire to be thought well of. Perhaps after all he didn't like *The Burning Matrix*, and that was why he had been well, not surly, but near it. If he does need money, I can probably get it to him through Geoffrey.

He trimmed four rashers of bacon and set them in the pan, pushed them around, turned them, and cracked in two eggs. Finally he pulled the sheet of the *News* clear of the half-loaf and cut himself a slice. Then he topped up his whisky and sat down to enjoy himself.

Inevitably he smoothed out the sheet of newspaper. His mother had once said, 'Richard can't even buy a penny's worth of toffees without reading the wrapping.' That had been when

217

shopkeepers twisted a cone out of half a sheet of newspaper instead of selling loose sweets in a bag.

Body found on Bloomsbury Building Site. Michael Collins had shock. Skeleton sitting there with a cut-glass tumbler between his knees . . .

Austen pounded up the narrow wooden stairs and into what would have been the second room back — was in fact now a bathroom — and there was violently sick. Wagner, magnified by the stairwell, washed seas of golden sound round him as he cleaned himself and the porcelain with soft toilet paper torn from its original wrapping, and as he did another terrible doubt grew like a boil and burst in his mind.

The wrapper had an offer — colour-films, development, that sort of thing, allow three weeks for delivery, closing-date 31 March 1981. George had asked, 'Sir Richard, you should have warned me you were coming.' So why put in new toilet paper? Who had he been expecting, if not Austen? And then surely it was a huge coincidence that he had wrapped the bread in the one sheet of paper that would throw such a terrible scare into him: so *not* a coincidence. He had been put up to it — to frighten him into some silliness. A tactic that smacked of Newman, and Newman had said that they knew about Briar Rose Cottage. More than ever now Austen regretted that he had told Geoffrey that this is where he would be: he thought of bolting again, but what would be the point? If they were on to him they would follow him. Best to sit tight, and see what happens.

They *can't* have turned George but Madge, perhaps. Those Mormons. That bloody music. Austen went back to the sitting room and angrily switched the wireless into silence. The blood stormed in his ears. I've had far too much whisky — and there's a nightmare stage you can go through before it clicks, and that must be where I am now. Not George. That fool game I played when I arrived — dating the previous occupations — and because I knew what I was looking for, I missed what I did not expect to see.

With the methodical thoroughness of the paranoid and the near-drunk, Austen opened every cupboard and drawer, examined lining paper, checked the dustbins, and found nothing else to suggest that his arrival had been expected, and as he did a

218

sort of sanity began to return: George and Madge came in every autumn. They swept and dusted and aired the place, and George cleared the garden. What more natural than that they should have a crap during all this? And end up replacing the toilet paper?

He was back in the front room downstairs and it came to him then that when he had first put the wireless on it had been tuned to Jimmy Savile, Radio One. Well again, so what. Madge would like a bit of music while she dusted and swept. The evidence was not that they had been expecting him, but simply that a month ago they had done their usual clean-up. So the sheet of newspaper was a coincidence. Yesterday's paper, and like it the paper of six weeks ago, becomes today's wrapper. But what were the odds against George or Madge pulling out that sheet, that actual sheet for bread? It *won't* do. It won't *do*. Someone has got at George, Newman for sure, and the poor bastard needs money for his garage.

Still. So what. Oh Jesus, there's that gun on the table, he must have seen it. He will have reported that. Escaped spy holed up in Sussex cottage with . . . with what? He turned the heavy thing over. A Browning apparently. I'll end up like that poor bastard on TV the other night if I'm not careful.

I wish Geoffrey would show up.

He gulped more whisky, and suddenly exhaustion gripped him, actually gripped and twisted the muscles in the back of his neck, across his shoulders, across his stomach, sore from the sudden bout of vomiting. Let them all come, see if he cared. They can sort it out between them. It's not my business anymore. Leningrad or Parkhurst, it's all one with me. Almost without knowing, he clambered up the steep, narrow stairs again and taking off only his jacket threw himself into the huge down bed which filled the tiny room almost from wall to wall.

But the russet stains by his head were still there — with an outstretched finger he traced the contour of the larger and he remembered that Kitti too knew Briar Rose Cottage. She could lead them . . . who? . . . why, *them*, everyone's implacable enemy, to this door.

28

He lay with the light on, too tired to turn it out, his whole body suddenly leaden. If he slept, he dreamt; if he was awake, then memory had a hold of him of its own, like a dream's: it went where it wanted, not where he directed it...

They had met, he supposed fortuitously, at an Archaeological Institute dinner in honour of Professor Sir Somebody or Other, who was to receive the Institute's Gold Medal. It took place in one of the livery companies' halls in the City, he could not now remember which, but there was a lot of dark oak, candles, portraits, old silver in glass cases. She sat opposite him. Her fair hair had been shortish then and curled, tinted very slightly with reddish gold and she had worn an emerald-green dress that shimmered. In 1951 she looked magnificent — opulence surrounded by austerity: most of the other women there were in black, even though Winston Churchill, with the promise of better things to come, had returned to power a fortnight earlier. She was thirty-five but looked less — her figure had lost the slightly pasty plumpness it had had at the end of the war, her skin was clearer, her pale eyes, green from the dress, bright in the candlelight: altogether, she recalled the girl before the war — except there was now an alarming coolness, steadiness about her when then she had been fey, nervy. Through the dinner she hardly spoke to him, but in the intervals of swapping archaeological gossip with the men on either side of her, her eyes met his and held them. He drank more than he should have.

As soon as the speeches were over she stood up, and her eyes again caught his: 'Come out with me now, Richard. There's something I have to say to you.' Obediently he followed her past the long tables, aware that they were already causing a stir. In the small world of archaeology they both had their reputations. In a darkened ante-room, through which waiters moved with trays of coffee cups and petits fours, she turned and said, 'Richard. I want to go to bed with you again. While I get my things you must decide where. Private please. Not a hotel.'

His Jowett Javelin irritated her — it was a cosy car and its little luxuries were, she said, middle class, but she told him to ease up as he drove through the Elephant and Castle (no spaghetti junction then): 'You are behaving like a schoolboy.' Nevertheless, they reached the cottage in only just over an hour. On the way she talked laconically about nothing much in particular and smoked continuously. He realised, as they approached Lewes, that the confused emotions she had set up were crystallising out as apprehension—acute and wretched, rather than unsatiated passion, and this was sharpened when, stubbing out her cigarette, she said, 'What about Burgess and Maclean then? Do you remember Guy? His party, the night that V2 got Teddy? They say there's another one too who tipped them off.'

'Anyone we know?' He struggled to keep his voice calm.

'"We",' she repeated scornfully. '"We" hardly know the same people any more, do we darling?'

'All right. *Knew*, then.'

'Oddly enough, yes. Well, Teddy knew him before the war. I never met him. He was a secretary to the Anglo-German Fellowship, so perhaps you did come across him.'

'I shouldn't think I did. If he was in that lot, he could hardly have been a leftie.'

'No. One wouldn't have thought so.' Her voice as she said this became harder, dryer. 'But then you didn't exactly broadcast you were a bolshie then, did you? No more than this other chap.'

'Anyway,' she went on, 'his name is Philby and a KC friend of mine has been given the job of breaking him down. Do keep your attention on the road, please.'

She kept him up drinking whisky for most of what was left of the

221

night while she lit the fires, waited for the immersion heater to get the water bathable, aired sheets. She did all this in almost complete silence, efficiently, as if she were a nurse again, as she had been for a spell in the early part of the war. She seemed to approve of the cottage: 'Nicer than your nasty little car anyway. I suppose you often have girlfriends here.'

'No, not actually. You're the first.'

'Almost I believe you. There are no signs. If you have had any, they must have been very well brought up. But if not why on earth have a place like this? Well?'

'I . . . like to be on my own at times,' he said lamely.

At last he heard her leaving the bathroom, then she called. He went up, a little unsteadily, and stood in the doorway of the little bedroom with its plank door. She was standing on the other side of the large down bed — she had turned down the rose-printed bedspread — and she now let drop the towel she had wrapped herself in.

Her skin was touched with pink from the bath, her breasts, small and pointed, were as perfect as ever, her stomach was flat.

'Yes,' she said. 'I look very well, don't I? Don't you think?'

He couldn't speak.

'You, however, are drunk, and you smell of whisky. So you can sleep it off in your armchair by the fire.'

He was as angry as no doubt she had hoped he would be. If he had been able, he would have raped her. As it was, for a moment he did not know what to do. In the end he had a bath too — the water was now only luke-warm — and then, dizzy with tiredness rather than alcohol, slipped in, in the darkness, beside her.

Aware of her in the down but not daring yet to touch her, he remembered:

Lady Kitti Bridge standing on the Mayfair pavement — black-out, but enough light to catch the glitter of falling drizzle in her hair and on the shoulders of her long fur coat and he halfway up the steps from the basement, his hands on the wet pavement. Behind him, in the tiny area, Edward Lord Riversdale, tall, thin, etiolated, with hair lank and a little long for those days. Finally Roy Newman, almost as tall as Riversdale, but far more sturdy, in American Army Air Force uniform — a lieutenant or rather 'lootununt'. Jazz — thin, muffled, as black and sharp as the night around them, male voices, laughter, glass breaking.

'Guy was amusing,' she said. 'He always is. But I will not be insulted by drunken louts.'

'No one, I'm sure, has ever called Tony a lout before.' Her brother was sulky. 'And weren't you rather rude to him?'

'I don't think so. He asked for it.'

'Richard, what exactly did she say to Tony?' Newman sounded petulant.

'Tell him, Richard.'

Austen turned his face up into the darkness, seeking the blessing of the rain. Be he never so drunk, wild horses would not drag from him what Kitti had said to Tony.

The tip of her black shoe came close to his face and he wondered if she would kick him.

'All I said was, would it help him to get it up if I offered him my bottom?'

'Jesus,' said Newman.

'Silly of you,' said Riversdale. 'And now we have lost our only chance of any more to drink. The only drink in town lies behind my back and we are excluded. I want more to drink.'

'And I want to be fucked. And not backwards by one of Guy's boys.'

For a moment three of them were motionless, Medusa-struck by twinned desires for sex and wine. Austen, Perseus-like, improvised a step further on a situation that he had engineered out of the events of the evening. ('On your next trip to town.' Control had said, or someone speaking for Control, for the voice at the other end of the line had been very English, not Russian at all, 'get Riversdale out on to the streets on h-h-his own.') 'I have an idea,' he now said, 'Kitti should go back to Fennimore Gardens and then the first of us to join her with a decent bottle of wine can give her the fuck she wants.'

Above their heads her laughter rose and fell like a *feu d'artifice* of grace notes. 'Two bottles or a drinkable whisky, and may the best man win.' Her shoe touched his mouth and he felt the grit from the pavement and tasted it too. He felt elation: she like the others was answering to the strings he pulled.

223

Her footsteps, sharp squeaks on the flags, receded, her shape became part of the night. From behind, a hand moved up the inside of his leg to his groin, firmly not painfully it squeezed on his balls, and the presence of Riversdale suddenly close leant weight to the damp air. He felt breath, felt rather than heard a whisper.

'My sins confirm your desecration.'

He turned his head and his mouth was kissed; pain exploded as the caress between his legs became a vice; then he sensed rather than saw Riversdale lope over his twisted body, and so up the stone stairs and on to the pavement above him, saw his thin stooped figure against the night, heard the confident steps diminishing down the street.

The old hate flared like a blown-on coal — he chose to follow (although the mysterious Cambridge voice had warned him not to). As he went, he heard Newman behind him say, 'I of course have PX privileges, and that's my baby. It'll be six hours before they open and that's the start you fellows have.'

She stirred in the downy billows, already nesty from her warmth, and he sensed that she was awake. He found her thigh, but fingers caught his wrist and moved his hand away. A sparrow chirped in the eaves disturbed by dreams or conscious of the distant dawn.

As Riversdale crossed Oxford Circus, the first of the night's arrivals thudded somewhere south of the river — a brief blossom of warm pink against the roofs, then the whisper of the rain again. In spite of the blackout there was more light here — the wider street perhaps; and more people too — cigarettes glowed by the lamp-posts, and Zippo lighters flared as GIs bargained with girls. For a moment Austen thought he had lost his quarry, decided he could risk being closer, and so quickened his pace, though cat-like his feet made scarcely any noise.

Across St Giles they went and so into New Oxford Street; two ambulances lurched by, headlamps reduced by slitted visors, and suddenly it occurred to Austen that he knew, knew quite for sure, where Riversdale was heading. He ducked away up Bloomsbury Street, determined to get there first. What, though, he had missed was the fact that he was not the only person on the track of his old enemy.

By the time Riversdale was coming up Grenville Street, Austen was crouched in the deeper shadow cast by the hoardings that fenced off the ruin of Galsen Yard. He watched him walk round two sides of Brunswick Square, and then marked how he squeezed his thin frame between the boards that shut off from the pavement the eyeless façade of Slaker House. And as he watched a second figure, short, stocky, clad he rather thought but could not be sure, in a short, dark top-coat and bowler hat, crossed the road in front of him. With more difficulty, this stranger followed Riversdale through the narrow gap. Austen moved up the side of the square and sheltered in the bombed doorway of the house where Ruskin had been born. There he waited, but his heart pounded with dread.

First she woke up his sex with firm caresses, then just as she had once before, just as he hoped she would, she neatly wriggled herself on top of him and ground with her loins on his until he found his way inside her. Only then did he dare open his eyes and he found he could see her, her head and short curls against the grey panes of the small window (the sparrows were more confident now that day would come, fluttered brittly and cheaped). Her neat hollow frame on his chest gave him a sense of his own size and substance. He sighed with satisfaction and in anticipation. Her head came closer and he felt her breath, the touch of her breasts, her arms sidling behind his shoulders, into and beyond the pillows. He stirred, brought his hands towards her buttocks, then:

'Don't move.'

There was a throatiness in her voice, and an excitement too — very intense. She felt chilly now, clammy, and she was breathing very fast. Her hands slipped out from behind his head, her elbows came back on to his chest, and her head and breasts receded as she raised herself up above him again. She wriggled her loins, he felt a tightening round his sex, her breath came yet faster — then she swallowed, shook her head, and in his ear he heard a quite clear *click*.

225

Cold steel touched his jaw along the line between ear and chin and fear so instantly gripped him that he was barely aware of how his shrunk member dropped out of her.

She laughed.

'This,' she said, 'is poor dead Teddy's razor. Did you guess?'

He remembered the implement — an old-fashioned 'cut-throat' but smaller than a barber's, the handle mother-of-pearl mounted in silver, the blade not stainless and worn by stropping into an almost straight line. It was, he had once supposed, quite old.

'First I want you to appreciate that I am in earnest. Keep absolutely still or I might hurt you more than I intend.'

She nicked him on the very corner of his jaw and he had to clench every muscle in his body to keep himself motionless. Presently he felt the warmth of blood slipping round his neck and so, he supposed, on to the pillows.

'In this light it still looks black.'

She wriggled into a more comfortable position, though her hand and the blade, laid now like a feather on its flat, never left his cheek.

'What the hell are you up to?'

'You must know very well. I'm sure you do. But I'll tell you. Then perhaps you will tell me what *you* are up to.' She breathed in, and in his fear he felt irritation too that she was so sure of herself, so sure she had control of the situation. 'Well. This is it. Three years ago, almost exactly, a gentleman insisted on seeing me in my flat. He was, he said, from the Special Branch. He said he had been ordered to investigate the wartime activities of everyone with a fascist past. He was polite, careful not to be offensive. And I believed him.' She shifted again and sighed, and Austen realised that her anger was tinged with old despair. 'He came back two more times and on the third asked if he could take away any papers of Teddy's I might have. I gave him . . . ' She breathed in deeply and held it for a moment and the silence of a November dawn settled around them like a sea-mist composed of the ghosts of drowned sailors, then: '. . . I gave him the papers you had taken from Teddy's room and brought to me. His poems, notes, and . . . well, you know.'

'I know.'

226

It was like a lover's caress after rapture, the gentle stroke of a contemplative finger, the way the blade drew a line along his jaw.

He gritted his teeth and shut his eyes.

A small bubble of laughter rose from her chest, was born dead.

'You're frightened, aren't you?'

'Of course.'

'I know. I can smell it. The blood looks red now. Look.'

He opened his eyes. Still holding the razor she lifted her hand momentarily from his cheek and briefly dabbed one finger in the centre of her forehead. It left a blob like a caste-mark. Cat-like — quickly and smoothly — she altered her position, rising so her knees were on either side of his chest, her buttocks on his diaphragm, her body straight as a pillar, her breasts, her neck, her implacable face above him.

'So. Last night, on the way here, you remember I said I knew a barrister who is questioning that man Philby?'

'Yes.'

'He was given all they had found out about Teddy and asked to apply his legal mind. He told me all this, you see? He looked it all over, two, nearly three years ago; he didn't know me then, and he decided that the evidence pointed at Teddy, that Teddy told the Russians all about Bletchley Park. There. Now. *That's* what all this is about... *Austen?*' The name left her mouth as if someone had tricked her into eating something foul. 'I could cut that vein beneath your ear and you would be dead in less than two minutes.'

'They'll hang you.'

'Quite. So probably I won't. But every time you look in a mirror, I want you to know...' — she was gasping now, gulping in draughts of cold air after every phrase — '...I want you to know that I'll pay you out, Richard Austen, one day I'll pay you out.' She raised her hand back and up towards her own shoulder and a level beam of watery sunlight glinted along the blade, transmuted steel to gold. He twisted and heaved, her body lurched towards him as she struggled to keep her balance and he felt the skin above his collarbone part like silk...

29

With rain at nightfall the temperature outside rose perceptibly and in the billows of the feather mattress Austen began to feel too warm. Thus he was already almost awake when, a half-hour or so later, that is at about five o'clock, the small brass knocker in the porch below him was hammered peremptorily. In a moment he was wide awake, alert and thinking.

It should be Slaker, he thought. Not Geoffrey himself perhaps, but someone from him. It could just be Control or someone from Control — recent events could well have stirred his interest enough to provoke one of his rare manifestations in Austen's life. And it could be whoever it was had prompted George or Madge to wrap his bread in that dreadful sheet of newspaper: and that probably meant CIA or USS — Newman's lot anyway.

The knock — more a clatter really — again.

Enough of the whisky still ran in his veins to give him a sort of Dutch or Scotch courage and he felt quite cheerful as he stumbled down the narrow stairs, tying the belt of his dressing gown as he went. It could, he thought, even be the persistent if enigmatic Catkin.

And so it was.

It was raining quite heavily by now. Cargill stood outside the porch and had contrived his position in such a way that a steady run of water from a stopped gutter was spilling down one side of his trilby and on to his left shoulder — in the dim light thrown through the doorway it looked almost like a bloodstain spreading across his nondescript coat. Behind him stood a taller figure clad in a duffel coat. Owlish, black-framed spectacles flashed dully.

'Sir Richard Austen?'

'The same. And...'

'William Cargill.'

'Ah. Not Catkin. Never mind. Mr Cargill, do come in. And your friend too.'

He stood aside to let them pass and for a moment the tiny hall seemed impossibly crowded. He sidled between them, aware of alien smells — of wet clothes, stale sweat, pipe.

'Do hang your things on the pegs.'

Dutifully they did so, then awkwardly, not knowing quite where to go, ducked under a lowish lintel into the front room. Austen in flannel dressing gown (c. 1950) was on his knees trying to coax fire out of cold embers.

He stood up, stocky, close-cropped grey hair upended, and shrugged apologetically.

'It's quite gone, I'm afraid. Never mind. A Scotch instead might do the trick — I mean, chase off the colds you must both be in danger of. Meanwhile, do, both of you, try to find somewhere to sit. Mr...?'

'This is Sleight. Desmond Sleight. A...colleague.'

Of Cargill Austen carried out to the kitchen a brief impression of heavy black shoes, a grey suit with wet turn-ups, a heavy face with heavy lines on either side of a thick grey moustache — an inspector or chief inspector in the Sir Robert Mark mould, he would have placed him as, had he not known better. A sound man, Newman had said — and he had obviously been wrong to suggest he had been called off. The implications were serious: Slaker had less pull with the Service than he supposed. The other man seemed more of a nonentity. Stooped, thin, dressed, now the duffel coat was off, in corduroy with a sweater. He had longish hair below a quite large bald patch.

'Would you care for a bite to eat?' he called, and without waiting for an answer added George's cheese and bread to the glasses, water and whisky on the tray.

Much of his bonhomie leaked away as he returned to the small front room. Cargill had picked up Newman's heavy

229

automatic, broken out the magazine, and was now sniffing at the open breach.

'This has been fired. Recently.' He snapped the thing together again.

'Yes,' said Austen, and then, somewhat lamely, 'at me, not by me.' He put the tray down on the round table where the gun had been.

Cargill ignored the tray; instead he sat in the only armchair on the other side of the fireplace. Keeping the automatic across his knees, he took out pipe and pouch, and began the elaborate ritual of lighting up. Austen, from one of the two high-backed cottage chairs by the table, watched with distaste and apprehension: he disliked tobacco smoke and the heavy stuff Cargill was thumbing into the large bowl looked particularly noisome. Sleight, meanwhile, perched himself on the remaining chair against the wall between them. He now had out a pad and pencil.

'Best if I keep the gun,' said Cargill. 'After all, I know you're a killer.' What was left of Austen's good humour evaporated. Cargill went on. 'Really, I know a lot about you. One way or another, there's very little I don't know.' The pouch was slipped away, a large lighter took its place. Dark brown eyes were raised to Austen's for a moment and held his. They were entirely serious and direct, and Austen had the strange feeling that, whatever might come from this Cargill, one thing he could be sure of was that any deceit the man might attempt would be transparent. 'Odd to meet you at last. Face to face.' The lighter flared. 'Odd to know somebody *so* well, before you actually (puff) meet him.'

I must not bluster, thought Austen. But I can't let them have it all their own way.

'I take it you are in Intelligence. The Service.'

Two puffs seemed to signal assent.

'Then you are not a policeman. You have no authority to arrest.'

Two more puffs.

'So this must simply be an interview, an interrogation even — but at this stage nothing more.'

Cargill took the pipe out of his mouth. 'You seem familiar with the procedure.'

Austen was irritated. 'Oh, come on. A hundred best-sellers, both fact and fiction, can't all be wrong.' He poured himself whisky, sliced cheese on to the bread. Sleight shifted in his seat. Blast him, thought Austen. Let him ask if he wants some. He went on, 'You had better tell me what you think you know.'

To his surprise Cargill did just that. In dry, colourless tones, without referring to notes, pausing only to knock out and replenish his pipe, he recited a detailed account of Austen's life as a Soviet agent, naming names and giving dates. Recruited on Herbert Heath's recommendation at the early age of eighteen in 1933; instructed to drop all overt political activities at Cambridge while simultaneously undergoing training given in fortnightly sessions at a London safe house. First mission in 1935 — to infiltrate influential pro-fascist groups based on the Riversdale set, and so on. Meanwhile Sleight, rather to Austen's surprise, scribbled it all down in shorthand.

'But then there was a switch. I imagine your masters realised with war inevitable it would not do for all their well-placed agents to seem to have pro-fascist pasts — some at any rate, if they were to get posts with access to really useful information, would have to be known as anti-fascists. So your presence in Spain in 1936 was used to convert you to a brief spell of anti-fascism and even overt party membership — something that could be ditched when it had served its purpose, and the Hitler/Stalin pact of 1939 provided the opportunity. Thus there were no black marks against you when they set about slotting you into Bletchley Park.'

For a moment Cargill's eyes did flinch away. 'I must admit that's one point where I'm not quite sure... I mean, I don't know *how* you were got into B-P.' He resumed, but Austen's attention had been diverted. He began to observe Cargill more closely, pay more attention to the how of what was being said rather than the what, and gradually he realised that things weren't quite right, not quite what they seemed to be. Some time before Cargill had finished, he began to ask himself *why*, why was this heavy-jowled, heavy-fisted, rather awkward man so completely and thoroughly going over all he had discovered, so openly revealing his whole hand. And why was his unprepossessing sidekick relentlessly recording every word?

231

But soon his attention was dragged back to the content of what Cargill had to say, mainly because the voice had become a little louder, a little harder, more measured and emphatic.

'Every spy lives in danger of backtracking. The moment when it becomes known that the information he has passed on has been passed on is bound to come, and then begins the unravelling that may lead back to him. There is no foolproof insurance against this, but the best is to arrange for an innocent person, or an agent of lesser importance, to be saddled with the blame. Again, whether Lord Riversdale's presence at B-P was merely a fortuitous matter of which you took full advantage or whether he was recruited by your masters is something I have not been able to establish. He may well have been recruited under threat of exposure of his homosexual activities, purely with his ultimate end in mind, that is, as a scapegoat for you. In either case you made the best of it, no doubt preparing your ground carefully before his death, and then, when that happened, making quite sure the opportunity was not wasted.'

Cargill's voice fluked up a tone — at last he set down his pipe. Both large hands gripped the arm-rests of his chair; the gun remained across his knees. Austen guessed what was coming a moment before it did, and the knowledge caused a cold sweat to break out on his neck and forehead, and nausea rose on the sudden tide of acute anxiety.

'That brings us to the actual matter of Riversdale's death. Throughout most of my investigation I accepted the official version. But I now know better. On the night of the eighteenth of December 1944, you followed Riversdale into the bombed wine cellars of Slaker House, Bloomsbury, and there you broke his neck. Then you sat him in the posture used in some Early Bronze Age burials, with a glass instead of a beaker between his feet, and a ring, your ring — and this can be proved — on which a Bronze Age gold disc had been . . .'

All Austen could hear was the thunder of blood in his ears, then at last he did bluster.

'What the hell are you talking about?'

'The murder of Lord Riversdale.'

Austen in sheer petulant chagrin pushed all the glasses and plates but his own to the floor.

232

Cargill appeared to remain calm, or at least in control. 'I am not able,' he said, 'to arrest you as a spy, since only the state may initiate proceedings against people who have endangered the state. Such is the law. But I am able to arrest you for...'

And then the telephone rang.

It rang five times, ten beats, before Cargill nodded. Austen lifted the handset but covered the mouthpiece. In the moment's silence, he hissed, 'I did not kill Teddy Riversdale.'

'Yes?'

'Austen?'

'Yes.'

'I'm speaking for Lord Slaker.'

'Fine.'

'That is, it is on information laid by him that we rather thought you must be, ah, where you are.'

'Oh, right.'

There was a pause.

'Austen?'

'Still here.'

'Is there a fellow called Cargill with you?'

'Yes.'

'Is he armed?'

Austen hesitated — then: 'Yes.'

'And menacing you?'

'You could say that.'

'Fine. I'll ring again in half an hour.'

The line clicked shut and the dialling tone purred. Austen replaced the handset.

For a full half-minute the three men in the cramped room sat almost still, eyes only flinching from each to each and then away. Then Austen stooped to pick up the glasses and plates he had pushed off the table — none had broken — and as he straightened he and Sleight spoke together.

'For Christ's sake, Bill.'

'Just what is it you're playing at?'

Cargill chose to listen to Sleight, who also was now pale and sweating.

233

'Aren't you going to ask him about the phone call? I mean, shouldn't you know who he was speaking to?'

For a moment Cargill looked puzzled: he passed his huge palm across his forehead, then it dropped to his side to delve for his pipe.

'Yes. Yes. Well.' Head on one side, pipe stem now jabbing the air towards Austen. 'Who was it? Sleight's right. We should know.'

The gap had given Austen time. At last he realised that, after all, Newman had it right — Cargill was not acting officially. But just what then was he up to?

'An aide of Lord Slaker's. I told him I was coming here, he was ringing to check I had arrived.' He pulled himself straight, contrived to jut out his jaw while he assumed to the manner born (which of course he was) the tones and style of the topmost drawer. 'Now what is all this? I don't believe you have any official right to be here. I am not at all sure you are what you say you are. And I shall not be badgered with this... *stuff* about Teddy Riversdale.'

Cargill's bushy eyebrows rose a millimetre and his expression turned sardonic, even sneering. Austen fleetingly wondered if the bullying tone had not been a mistake — until then, Cargill's emotions seemed not to have been much engaged: now Austen sensed revulsion, hate even. The lighter flared, and smoke billowed again. Austen knew that Cargill was enjoying his obvious dislike of it.

'I think before we go into all that we had better finish the story. There's not much more to tell.' He nodded at Sleight, who, however, was still on the edge of panic.

'Bill. Did you believe all that about Slaker's aide? Don't you think it could really...?'

'Yes, yes. But *you* don't have to worry. Let's get on.'

Sleight shook his head, sighed, but took up his pad and pencil.

'The murder of Riversdale turned out to be premature. Up to December 1944 your main duties as a spy at B-P had been to record and pass on the methods by which B-P functioned, the organisation and so on, the personnel. Most of the product relevant to the Soviets was being passed on to them anyway. However, as the war drew to a close, and as the nature of the

confrontation to be known as the Cold War was better understood, the official flow east of ULTRA-derived information
dried up and you were doubtless instructed to pass on clan-
destinely anything important that was now being withheld. In
the last weeks of the war, the Americans were in touch with
Gehlen and the Abwehr, particularly the section that dealt with
the eastern front and Russia. Their communications were
encoded by ENIGMA, and fortuitously intercepted and decoded at B-P. When the B-P interpreters and assessors understood what they had stumbled on, they of course classified it
immediately as not suitable for transmission to the Soviets, but
since you yourself were one of those assessors, this precaution
was scarcely effective.'

Cargill paused, took a deep breath and let it out in a long sigh.
He was very tired, was struggling to master and present what he
had to say.

'The importance of all this now is simple. It demonstrates that
the Russians were receiving information from B-P after Lord
Riversdale's death, information to which few people had access
and Austen was one of them. None of this came to light in the
original investigation, which pinpointed Lord Riversdale as the
leak. It came to light only a few weeks ago, and it was backtracking from this point that led me to him.'

Austen looked up sharply, glanced from one to the other.
Everything Cargill was saying was not to and for him, but to
and for Sleight. Again he adopted the tones of an aggrieved toff.

'Now, look here. I think it's high time you told me just
what . . . '

But Cargill ignored him. 'After that, after passing on the
Abwehr telegrams, he, you, became fairly inactive. You were
debriefed at your place in the New Forest by Burgess and a
Russian attaché at their embassy here. You bought this place,
and a garage for your man George Partridge in Lewes, so he
could be near here. You came here at the time of Burgess and
Maclean's defection and at the height of the investigations into
Philby in 1955 — no doubt, you were a safety net if the arrangements made for them went awry . . . '

Damn, thought Austen. They have got at poor old George.

'. . . then in the sixties your masters found an entirely new role

235

for you, one which did not I suppose, break the law. From then until now, you have acted as intermediary, trusted by both sides, in commercial operations between the Slaker Group and the Soviets. Your reward for this work was the Gold Museum, your post as its director, and the not inconsiderable salary that goes with it.'

Cargill leant forward, steadying the gun with his left hand, and with the other knocked ashes into the fireplace. Then he looked up from Austen to Sleight and back again.

'I should add that Mr Sleight here thinks the Gold Museum was used in the sixties to pass Russian funds to Palestinian liberation groups. But I've found no evidence of that.'

Let us be thankful for what may turn out to be a quite large mercy, thought Austen. He looked sharply at Sleight, whose watery blue eyes dropped to the mottled hands that lay across his pad. But I'd like to know where *he* got it from. And who he is. Then it came to him. He slapped his hand on his knee, then jabbed a finger. 'I've got you, Sleight,' he cried. 'You're not with the Service at all, are you? You're just a hack. A newspaper hack. Let me see. Yes. That's it. You're on the *News*.' He swung back to Cargill. 'Now, look here. It really is high time you told me just what is going . . . '

The phone bell again, cutting across his voice like a cheese-wire.

'Austen?'

'Yes.'

'I take it Cargill can hear you?'

'Yes.'

'So you can't describe what sort of gun he has. Is it a revolver?'

'Er, no.'

'So an automatic pistol. Large?'

'Yes.'

'Is the magazine in front of the trigger or in the butt? Sorry. Is the magazine in front of the trigger?'

'No.'

'So *not* a machine pistol. Let me think. A Browning?'

'Actually yes, I think so.'

'Fine. Well, anyway, not as bad as it might have been. Now listen carefully. We're going to get you out of there. In something between twenty and forty minutes the telephone will ring again. Just one beat, and when it does I want you to get on the floor, behind furniture if possible, and stay there. Very quickly. Because that telephone beat will also be the signal for our chaps. Right?'

'Yes, Mother, I understand.'

'Mother? Oh, ah. I get you. Very clever. Fast thinking. Well, you've clearly got your wits about you. I'm sure we'll get you out.'

'Yes, Mother. And you take care too.'

30

He turned back into the room and said, with a smile that felt as false as a hallowe'en mask and probably as white too, 'That was, er, my mother. You've met her, I believe.'

Cargill was embarrassed to have been caught using a man's aged parent to gain damaging information about him, and this probably prevented him from noting Austen's unusual failure to fib convincingly.

Sleight was less credulous. 'Oh, come on. Come on. Bill, I was near enough to hear that wasn't a woman he was talking to. There's something going on and frankly I don't like it. I'm scared. Actually shit-scared. I think we ought to get out while we can. Take him too if you like. But let's get out...'

Austen pushed a glass half full of Scotch under the newsman's nose.

'Here,' he said. 'You never had a drink. Cold got into you, I expect. Have some bread and cheese too. I tell you that was my mother. She knew I was coming here and when I'm travelling she likes to know I have arrived safely. It's as simple as that.' He was about to add that old ladies often develop deep voices, but remembered in time that Cargill actually did know what her voice sounded like. 'It was a bad line, distorting, you know?' he concluded.

The weakness of his performance was due in part at least to the fact that really he had no idea just who it was was now planning to get him out of his predicament. Someone Geoffrey had contacted: yes, the voice had said as much. Surely not the Service, the very people Cargill belonged to? That would be a

238

nonsense — the Special Branch or this new lot of heavily armed psychos, what were they called? the SAS, yes — a nonsense for them to come bursting in to rescue a Soviet spy from one of their own investigators, however maverick. That left the Russians. Geoffrey was certainly in touch with them, was friendly with the commercial attaché and so on, and knew personally industrial management close to the Politburo. They would too be quite reasonably anxious to get Austen out of any fix he was in — but fireworks were not their style, for all James Bond *et al.* would have you think so. Blackmail, wheeling and dealing, a discreet exchange, that would be their way, not fireworks, and, Austen thought with a scarcely suppressed shudder, it seems pretty clear that fireworks are what is planned... poor Catkin, or rather poor Cargill.

Who, meanwhile, had gone on relentlessly to bring the story of his investigation to its conclusion.

'Three years ago Citeecon, a member of the Slaker Group, obtained planning permission to redevelop the bombed site of Slaker House, off Brunswick Square, in Bloomsbury. It is usual in such developments where deep excavation is required for a member of the GLC archaeological department to be on stand-by if not in continuous attendance. This was not the case with the Slaker Towers development. Instead, on the grounds that you worked nearby in the Gold Museum, and that you are an eminent archaeologist, and finally a member of the family, a cousin of Lord Slaker, County Hall agreed to give you first sight of anything that was dug up. On paper it looked a simple, pleasant little arrangement, but I spoke to a member of the GLC archaeological department who was able to say that at first they had resisted the suggestion, and only given way when very considerable pressure was brought to bear.

'On the sixth of October Michael Collins, a labourer on the site, pick-axed his way through a brick wall below street level and discovered a skeleton in the cellars of Slaker House. The site manager closed off the area and sent for you. Eyewitnesses say that you seemed very disturbed indeed — as, if I may say so *Sir* Richard, you are now — but that after a few minutes you pulled yourself together, offered the suggestion that the corpse was that of a servant caught by a bomb whilst tippling his master's port,

239

and there was no archaeological matter of importance involved. You suggested that the proper people to be looking into it all were the police, and you left the site.

'Mr Sleight's paper, the *News*, carried a brief item about the discovery of the body, but made no mention of you. It was withdrawn from later editions, and when a junior reporter suggested he should follow it up, he was told firmly to keep well away.

'An inquest followed. Purely a formality. Lord Slaker gave evidence through his solicitor that the body was that of a senior footman who had been left as caretaker in 1940. It was decided that, pending tracing of next of kin, the few possessions found attached to the fragments of clothing and so on should remain at the coroner's office. There, yesterday, I presented myself, armed with a statement from Lady Kitti Bridge that identified me as next of kin, and what there was was handed over to me.' (Austen heard her again: 'One day I'll pay you out, Richard Austen, one day I'll pay you out.')

'There wasn't much. A handful of small change, a bunch of keys — but not the sort you expect a caretaker to have, an ordinary set. Almost everything organic had been rotted or eaten away, though no doubt an archaeologist, or forensic scientist, might have been able to make something of what had been left, but you see Lord Slaker was given permission to see that the corpse was decently cremated at his expense — the least he could do, he said, for a valued servant of his father.' This last was said with bitter distaste. Before going on, Cargill relit his pipe.

'Two things remain. First the corpse itself. Collins will swear that it was sitting in a crouched position with a glass between its feet. He will also say that the head lolled back off the shoulder in a totally unnatural way. None of this was mentioned at the inquest — for it was you, Richard Austen, who gave evidence of discovering the body, not Collins. All right, a pathologist said the neck injury was in keeping with the body having been thrown across the room by bomb blast and a verdict of death as a result of enemy action was entered by the coroner. But you see it was not mentioned that the body had been found in a sitting position.

240

'The second thing is this.'

Here Cargill hitched himself up, raising one buttock, the better to delve into his jacket pocket, and for one terrifying moment Austen involuntarily recalled with visionary exactness his minatory father, seated behind his enormous desk at the Rectory. It was a premonitory flash as well as regressive, for on Cargill's palm now rested the gold ring on which his father had had one of the disks from Jake's Tump mounted, and which Austen had worn for eighteen months between his father's death and Riversdale's. Entranced by its lasting brightness, he slowly reached out for it, but Cargill's palm closed, and it disappeared back to his pocket.

'I've read *The Burning Matrix*, Sir Richard, and in the context of everything else I have discovered about you, I think it reveals more of you than you perhaps realise. At all events, I detect in you signs, symptoms, of a sort of decadent romanticism, knight errantry, what you will. Difficult to describe. Not my province putting that sort of thing into words, but I have a feel for it, for it is a fairly common characteristic amongst men of your age and background, and my work has brought me into contact often enough with your sort of people. I suppose the word your sort of person would use to describe what I am talking about is "honour", but it's a far way from what I mean by the word. Anyway, it is this I think that prompted you to arrange Lord Riversdale's body like that of a Bronze Age chief, and leave him with gold so he could pay his way on the other side. Even though, or perhaps actually because, you had just killed him.

'Let us now go back to that night in December 1944 . . . '

But quite distinctly a car door had shut — not noisily, but near to.

' . . . when, together with Lord Riversdale you left . . . '

'Bill. Shut up. For Christ's sake.'

A gate latch clicked. Footsteps crunched on gravel, and a house door clicked shut.

'Next-door neighbour,' said Austen. 'Accountant. He's converted the other three cottages in the terrace into a house in the country. George, George Partridge wrote to me . . . '

'Oh Jesus, Bill, shut him up. Can't you hear?'

241

The throbbing clatter, not all that distant, of a helicopter. They listened. It diminished, then stopped.

'It's landed,' said Sleight. 'SAS. Special Air Service. They always use choppers.'

Austen coughed. 'RAF, I'm sure. Air-sea rescue. They keep up one of the old Battle of Britain strips for them, about three miles away. Often hear them.'

Cargill looked from one to the other, a grave but bemused expression on his tired, lined face.

'This is rubbish, Desmond. They don't need the SAS. They can just come and get me if they want to.'

'You're armed.'

Cargill looked down at the solid lump of precisely tooled metal in his lap.

'They don't know that.'

'They do if he told them. On the telephone.' Sleight jerked his head at Austen. 'Anyway, let's take no chances. Quite frankly I've heard enough, Bill. I'll follow it as far as I dare. It's a great story I grant you. I really will do my best. But now, just now, I've had enough. I'm off.' He made for the door, turned. 'Come on, Bill, best if you come too.'

But Cargill looked as immovable as he would have had he been the lump of granite he resembled. His shoulders merely shrugged minutely, his eyelids drooped momentarily in a gesture of dismissal. In the hall there were sounds of a brief struggle — Sleight getting into his duffel coat in the confined space — then the door latch and steps on gravel.

'Poor Desmond,' Cargill murmured. 'I never really thought he'd be up to it. Actually I'm surprised he's stuck it out so long.'

Silence again. Austen wondered how much of the telephone conversations Sleight had picked up. Certainly he had been better placed than Cargill. Then . . . there had been no sound of a car starting up, surely there should have been? Had Cargill noticed?

The large man shifted again in his chair. 'Well,' he said, 'I'll finish the story, having got so far.'

'Yes, do,' said Austen. His heart had begun to thump; he felt sure the moment was near now, almost he had it in him to warn Cargill, but the important thing was to learn just how much the

242

man knew, what he could prove and what was just guesswork. 'It's been quite fascinating. Do finish. December 1944.'

'Yes. You were at Burgess's flat in Bentinck Street. You left at about one thirty after a row with Burgess and Blunt. You, that is Lord Riversdale, Lady Kitti Bridge and an American called Roy Newman.'

Whose gun you now have on your lap, whose gun is going to be the death of you, and perhaps me too, if I don't warn you.

'Two and a half hours later you arrived at Lady Kitti Bridge's flat in Fennimore...'

'House. She had the whole house then.'

'...Fennimore Gardens. You had with you two bottles of vintage claret which could have been taken only from the cellars of Slaker...'

And the bell rang.

As Austen rolled to the floor, there were three deafening reports and a blinding flash, which left him stunned, almost unconscious, for nearly a whole minute. Of course he did not see the helmeted figure with tinted perspex visor, dressed in a black jumpsuit, who shot Cargill twice with a far more wicked and efficient-looking weapon than the one Cargill had allowed to drop. Nor did he see Cargill pushed as if by the hand of God back into the chair he was already rising from in response to Austen's tumble to the floor. The first thing he was conscious of was a tall man dressed in black short top-coat with a velvet collar over a striped suit, bending then crouching over him. An effort brought dark eyes beneath heavy brows, and crinkly short black hair into focus.

'Sir Richard? Sir Richard Austen? Are you all right?' The voice came as from a distance through the roar and the pain in his ears. He pulled himself to his knees, then strong hands hoisted him back into his chair. Now at last he could see what had been Cargill — a broken death-sized doll, legs spread, massively shod feet sticking up, head slung over the back of the chair. There was blood — not much — from a hole in his forehead, in the middle of his chest, and a dribble from his open mouth. But for that he could have been a tired businessman, fallen asleep by the fire after a hard day coping with a reduced

243

order book, high interest rates, and compulsory redundancy payments.

'A drink of water, Sir Richard? Er, no, I think you may be in shock, and I wouldn't advise alcohol. Oh, very well. Yes. But not much. Actually I think I'll have a spot too.'

Glass chinked. Whisky flowed.

'Cheers. Um. I should introduce myself. Fosdike. Ashley Fosdike. Jolly nice to meet you, sir. Always been a keen admirer, very keen.'

31

'Feeling better? Fine. Then I think we should be off.'

'Off?'

'I think so.' Fosdike was firm. 'Have you a coat? Wash things? In the bathroom? I'll get them for you.'

In the brief moment he was out, Austen looked round the shattered room, his eyes flinching from the body in the chair, finding at its side the large pipe with metal stem. It still smouldered. Should he put it out? No, let it burn down the whole messy business, a funeral pyre for Cargill, *Götterdammerung*.

'Right then. Here we are.'

Austen pulled off the old dressing gown and slipped on his jacket and camel top-coat. In the hall he ran a comb through his hair, and beside his reflection in the mirror noticed the grey felt trilby, the nondescript coat still damp, the grey muffler...almost he was sick, not from revulsion, but out of a sudden wave of far more complex emotions. Pity, anger and shame predominated.

He followed Fosdike, and out in the lane was helped by a Special Branch policeman into the back of a new black Daimler. The leather soughed at his side as Fosdike sank down beside him. At the end of the lane, blue lights flashed over a police car and an ambulance and then outriders on powerful motorbikes fell in in front of them. Past whispering windscreen wipers, the headlights picked up bandoliers studded with orange reflectors.

'Where are we going?'

'Not far actually. The Cosmopol at Brighton. In some ways a touch old-fashioned perhaps, but they do you really very well.'

'I like it. They know me. So it's not to be the Scrubs?'

Fosdike laughed with just the right touch of a young man's sycophancy at an older man's joke.

'Dear me, no. Not at all. I don't think there's any question yet of anything like that in the air.'

That too was well done. Just a hint of doubt left the matter imperfectly resolved.

As they approached the elms on the Level — amongst the last left in the south of England, they loomed above the street lamps like benevolent giantesses — Austen said, 'Did you have to kill Cargill? I mean, basically, he seemed a decent enough sort of chap, and the stun bomb on its own would have rendered him harmless.'

But on that subject Fosdike had nothing to say.

Brighton Pavilion lay like a dead and decomposing Chinese dragon to their right — no floodlights in off-season November; then they swung right at the Royal Albion and on to the equally dead promenade.

But the Cosmopol was bright, warm, comforting. The familiar feel of deep-pile carpet, the hint of good cooking on the warm air, the gleaming brass and sparkle of chandeliers, the deferential servants, were all in their way reassuring. Less so was the fact that, after showing Austen into his room on the third floor, overlooking the sea, and indicating that with his own bathroom and room service all his needs could be met, Fosdike told him not to leave it. Austen came to the door and the message was pressed home by the presence of another Special Branch plain-clothes policeman on a chair at the end of the corridor. Not, after all, the Scrubs — but a cage nevertheless, however well gilded.

He stood at the end of the large bed and looked around at the not unfamiliar surroundings. The walls and furniture were pink and cream with here and there gold-coloured mouldings. The fittings included a colour TV, a wash-basin with simulated gold taps, a refrigerator with a half-bottle of Black Label, a half of Beefeater's, tonics, ginger ale and ice. The room purred with the gadgets needed to keep it warm here and cool there. There was of course a Gideon Bible.

Overpowered with exhaustion, not far off despair, Austen sat, then lay, on the bed. Cargill's murder had shocked him more

246

than he willingly recognised, but not only that: he was bewildered by a sense, quite unfamiliar to him, that he had entirely lost control over what was happening to him — the feeling was literally vertiginous and he had to sit up again to master it. For a moment he rocked himself to and fro, hands clutching upper arms, face twisted like a child's on the point of tears. Then he kicked the bedside unit (shelf, drawer, built-in light) and splintered off a piece of moulding. 'Good,' he said aloud, and kicked it a second time. 'Good again. Dickie. This won't do. Get a grip. You need a drink.'

He drank a gill of whisky and felt better.

'And something to eat.' He groped for the phone. 'Ham sandwiches. No, I don't want smoked salmon, I want ham, ham, ham with mustard. No, I don't know which room. Austen. Sir Richard.'

Almost half the available whisky had gone by the time they arrived, so he ordered another bottle. The first mouthfuls needed to be held down; then he ate voraciously. With only half a round left, the phone rang, and anxiety struck again as he reached for it.

'Richard?'

'Geoffrey! Thank God to hear a sane voice.'

'Oh, really? As bad as that, is it? Now listen Richard. Where's Newman?'

'Newman? Ah. Yes. Well, it's a long story. He's in my fall-out shelter.'

Neither spoke. Then, Lord Slaker: 'Richard, are you drunk?'

'A little.'

'Well, try to do better. You said Newman was in your fall-out shelter.'

'Yes. I locked him in.'

Again the pause.

'Richard. Why did you do that?'

'He was shooting at me, Geoffrey. Trying to kill me. It seemed the right thing to do.'

'Is he hurt?'

'No. No, of course not. I'm not either.'

247

'Right. Now listen, Richard. Try to sober up enough to tell me what went on between you. Briefly. The gist.'

'He is planning to expose my naughty past. And he seems to have it off quite well pat, if you follow me. Because, he says, the American government, whose hat he was wearing, doesn't want you to sell your computers to Warsaw Pact countries. He says they'll delay the planned destabilisation of the Eastern Bloc by three or four years.'

'Rubbish. A decade at least. Did he tell you about his other hat?'

'United Special Steels?'

'Right. And with that hat on too he's messing himself over our Soviet contract.'

'Why? He can hardly have hoped for it himself.'

'No? Under Carter he might have done. But you're right, with Reagan, no. But the point is this. If we get six or seven orders from the Warsaw Pact, we'll be able to reduce our costs across the board and undercut USS in their markets. We'll get Latin America, South Africa, even the Far East and China. The possibilities are ... well. Very big indeed. I'm telling you this, Richard, so you can understand just how important it is we stop Newman from exposing you. I shall be working on it with Sergei, who sends best wishes, from this end. But I'd like you to give it some thought too. Sleep on it. Don't drink any more. Frankly, Richard, I haven't been exactly enthralled with your performance in this business so far, so see if you can't be a bit more use in the morning.'

'Why not just leave him in my shelter? No one knows he's there.'

'Don't be childish. Now tell me how he can be got out.'

Austen did as he was told. Then, wanting to sweeten his cousin and patron, regain a little favour, or at any rate pre-empt further rebukes, he attempted to warn him about Sleight.

Slaker cut him off brusquely: 'That's no problem. He's been taken care of. Anything else?'

'Geoffrey. What ... I mean ... ?'

But the phone clicked and the line went dead.

* * *

248

Taken care of. Like Cargill? Poor Sleight. Was he responsible? Were they his fault, the deaths of Cargill and Sleight? He shrugged with despair and drank.

Much later, he was awake again, in bed, naked, the light off, the room almost pitch dark. A breath sighed on the pillow close to his ear, and the warmth of the bed beneath the quilt held odours of perfume and woman. She stirred again and then a hand touched his shoulder, passed down his arm, linked fingers and gently pressured.

She whispered, 'You were crying in your sleep. Well, like moaning. Are you all right?'

'Yes. I think so.'

'Well, so long as it's not a pain. I had an old geezer a year ago had a pain in his chest in the night and woke up dead. Something bothering you, is it? Tell me, if you like. Lots do. I mean, they're unhappy, they talk. I don't mind.'

The depth of the sigh he breathed in and let out surprised him, but, dumbly, in the dark, he shook his head. Then he squeezed back on her fingers. She snuggled in more closely, tentatively put her knee across his thigh. Then she giggled. 'You weren't half pissed when I come in.'

'Really? I don't remember.'

'Never mind. It's happened before.' Her hair brushed his cheek, but he lay still and so then she did too.

Cargill. Sleight. He was not to blame. No sense in blaming himself, no sense at all. Except...

Except that this, like every other morally confused episode in his life, could be traced back, like Ariadne's thread in reverse, not to daylight but to the Minotaur in his pit of bones. Riversdale, who had been Bridge, had returned from his father's funeral at Scales, and had found Jefferson not as acquiescent as he wished in the rule of terror he had instigated on his first night back in Nelson Dorm. Indeed, this Jefferson, a small thin boy with almost white hair, the son of an academic, had threatened to go to Matron.

'Greenhalgh.'

'Yes, Lord Bridge.'

'Riversdale.'

'Yes, Lord Riversdale.'

'What's to be done with Jefferson? Something must be done.'

Riversdale's locker was placed on its side across his bed. He sat on it, tall for his age, thin, with dark circles round his eyes, his nose already beaky beneath the floppy lock of hair, and thus enthroned lorded it over five chastened and obedient eight-year-olds and Jefferson, who sat outside the circle and snivelled.

... the same Teddy, six weeks ago, still there, just as he had left him thirty-six years earlier, but now the beak of a nose fallen away, his eyes dried out, his flesh eaten by his own worms, a fardel of brown bones. Racked bottles white with dust or black where it had been smudged from them; four or five workmen with the gold SG logo on their scarlet helmets; the rumble of machinery as a huge hopper filled with conglomerate was swung through the air a hundred feet above — and Teddy, his brown skull tipsily lolling over one shoulder, Teddy hissing in Austen's ear as he stooped to retrieve his ring, but the voice his father's not Teddy's at all: 'Grave robbery, Richard. Grave robbery.'

'Something must be done.'

'Make him eat number twos,' a tiny voice suggested. A year later the same voice, singing *Oh, for the Wings of a Dove* moved the Bishop of Durham to tears.

'Let's,' another voice suggested, 'pour ink on his sixpence and on his bollocks.'

The girl stirred, whimpered, then sighed. Well, thought Austen, she has her troubles too. He slipped his arm beneath her neck and drew her head on to his shoulder. Christine. A nice girl. A year or so ago the waiter on night-room service had sent her up. Had he asked for her this time? Or had she come when she was told he was back at the Cosmopol? It didn't matter...

I should have killed Teddy. I could have done. I wish I had.

'Austen, Austen, I can't get it off.'

'Jefferson, you mustn't blub, really not, best not to blub.'

'But I can't get it off.'

250

Shivering on cold tiles in front of a cracked basin; knowing that in an hour's time the bell would ring when they were both due to be at the Headmaster's Bathroom for a cold bath; terrified Matron would hear, would come storming down the dimly lit corridor, he watched Jefferson, skeletal thin and shivering too, who had promised to be his friend and who stood now with his back to him and scrubbed at his tiny scrotum with a pumice stone.

'It won't come off.'

I wish I had, he thought, as he stood in the doorway of the Hunter Street house where Ruskin was born, his collar turned up against rain turned to sleet. Then there was the dark silhouette again across the road, lit suddenly by a flash of red above the roofs and the percussion was near enough to bend the air and shake the ground, a silhouette square, bowler-hatted, melting as the glow faded, into the darkness towards Coram's Fields.

Austen slipped across the road and between the boards, up shattered steps into the roofless hall of Slaker House. He knew the way, had stayed there with his mother on visits to town ("Get you kitted out for next term, take in a Gilbert and Sullivan at the Savoy..."); a door, lined on the reverse with green baize, then steps to the cellars. Feeling his way down, he became aware of a glow, dull and feeble, and the smell of coal gas.

A candle, guttering among high stacks of racked bottles, set on the desk where the butler had kept his ledgers, and Edward Lord Riversdale, who, presumably, had lit it, stretched on the floor beneath it.

He had died more quickly than Jefferson, who choked himself to death on the cord from his pyjamas, behind a locked lavatory door.

Austen lifted the candle and dared it to ignite the gas. Elation welled up and he capered and carolled, 'For in spite of all temptations to belong to other nations he remai-ai-ai-ai-ned an Englishman.'

Then he set down the candle, hauled the body into a sitting position and propped it thus, like the old chief in Jake's Tump, poured gold champagne into a tasting glass and set it on the floor beneath the lolling lock of Rupert Brooke hair. Finally he

251

dropped into it the ring he had taken from his father's finger not two years before — this last done a little grudgingly, but there, he needs gold to pay the Ferryman and it's all I have about me. Why do all this? Because it is more seemly thus: and seemliness was something his Ruskinian mother had taught him to value.

Halfway up the steps he remembered and turned back, took at random two bottles from the racks, and thus encumbered set off on the long walk through bomb-ravaged London to Fennimore Gardens, where he made love to Kitti with more strength and control than ever before and made her lose hers. She had believed him too — that Teddy had gone back to Bentinck Street with a bottle of brandy, expecting to find rough trade there in the shape of a grenadier who was also a boxing champion. He clinched the lie by saying he had bribed Teddy to do this with his ring. She knew her brother coveted it.

'And now he has it,' he had said. 'And I wish him luck with it.'

He had played his part, followed Control's instructions, only breaking them by following Riversdale through the dangerous city. He had played his part, but he had not actually killed Riversdale himself. He wished he had.

'Austen, I'm going to ask you a very important question. One I have already asked every other member of Nelson Dorm, and one to which all have given the same answer. So I want you to think very carefully about it. Think of your father and mother, of how they would like you to answer. Remember your cousin, recently returned from a terrible bereavement. Remember I have to punish you for being in the lats between Dim and Wakes with another boy. Now Austen. How was it Jefferson had ink on his person?'

'I don't know, sir.'

'Austen, everyone else in Nelson Dorm has said that Jefferson poured the ink on himself, of his own free will. A sign, which the coroner will note, that the balance of his mind was irretrievably upset. So. How do *you* say the ink got there?'

'I... I truly do not know, sir.'

It was the best he could do for Jefferson. It was better than the others had done. It was not good enough...

* * *

252

A little roughly he twisted away from Caroline or whatever her name was, stamped over to the window, and pulled back the drapes. Through grubby double-glazing he could just make out the greyness of the pre-dawn sea, the sprawl of the two piers fumbling out into it. The sky was grey too, bruised by heavy clouds trundling purposefully across it. That's when it started — at any rate, I became conscious of it then. No doubt it would have come any way, some other awfulness at school or at home — and there were plenty — would have triggered it, but that, in fact, was when it started. From then on, I knew I hated them, knew too that they were too much for me. So I went under. I played their silly games, passed their boring exams (apart from that hiccup over Latin), was known to be a good chap, sure to do well. And it's been like that ever since. Oh, there was the brief bliss of discovering that I was not alone. Herbert Heath, soon to be sacked from the College, Gordon Childe, Strachey, Brockway and Edgar Snow, Dutt, Bernal and Dobb — and a decade of certainty, of a sort. But they kept me under — along with Blunt and Philby, Maclean and silly old Guy, and . . . well, never mind. Under, in a confused twilit world, a world of cold, grey nightmare as often as not not so different from that of The Meads, a world where one was denied even the light of one's own conscience, one's own intellect, obedience was all, and one was asked to do some pretty dubious things; the only support offered was blind (apt word!) faith.

He turned from the window, went to the lavatory, paused in front of the mirror. Jesus. I look almost old. He snapped out the light, fumbled through the bedroom to the refrigerator whose interior of course lit up when the door was opened. There was still a measure of Beefeater's left.

Don't drink any more, said Geoffrey. Well, fuck Geoffrey. And this now is the most dubious position ever, will it never cease? Can it really be true that the stability of the Union of Socialist Soviet Republics depends upon these infernal machines produced by two of the most ruthless international trusts ever to have carved up the territories of the globe between them? Is it even true that rigid stability is still desirable in the USSR? Oh Lord, I don't know, I don't know.

That poor chap Catkin, Cargill. *He* was certain in the wilfully

253

blind, monistic universe he had created for himself out of the rags, the memories of the strong, proto-bourgeois non-conformism of . . . not the nineteenth, but rather the seventeenth century. He had no doubts about what was right, what was wrong. With his brain blown out through the back of his head.

'You really ought to come to bed, you know. You look quite poorly.'

Of course, my face is lit, by the light from the refrigerator, from below. Never a flattering angle. He smiled at her: she, Charmaine?, smiled a little back, then let her dark head fall back on to the pillow. He shut the refrigerator door and in the darkness thought: the Stalinist rump, my masters!, have nothing really to fear from the liberal bourgeois dissidents the western press make such a fuss of; nor plebeian windbags like Solzhenitsyn. They don't need computers to monitor that lot. And some elements, at least, in the Kremlin seem ready to recognise and bend to the stirrings of the industrial proletariat they have in large measure themselves created, as indeed they were bound to. The point is — Czechoslovakia and Hungary have shown it — things will not change in the east by moving right, by moving back to bourgeois parliamentary democracy. They will only change, as Poland seems to indicate now, by going left, by moving on out of Stalinist stagnation, to a genuine dictatorship of the proletariat. So. Let me once, just once, emulate the exemplary Cargill and make an unequivocal decision, illuminated by reason and conscience — unequivocal if negative. I will not assist, any further than I already have, Slaker Laser and Allied Technology in their project of equipping the reactionary, bureaucratic elements in the Eastern Bloc with further means of postponing the rule of the workers. Especially I will not, since if I do the client states of the third world will get their computers at knock-down prices . . .

'Come o-o-o-on.'

In bed again, he let Caroline fold herself round him and thus warmed and relaxed fell into a deeper more restful sleep than he had had for a long time. He awoke, as she no doubt knew he would, with a quite remarkably strong desire for love.

32

The phone.

'Fosdike here. Time you were up, Sir Richard. We have an appointment to keep in just half an hour.'

Austen looked at his watch. Half past ten.

'Lord. I haven't had any breakfast.'

'We'll rustle up some coffee when we get there. In the foyer in twenty minutes, right?'

Whatever of obsequiousness Fosdike had shown the evening before had gone. With stomach sinking, Austen wondered why. And an appointment with whom? The vertigo of being out of control of events seized him again and he sat down, his resolution of the dark hours almost forgotten.

'You all right?' Christine, Charmaine, Caroline coming out from the bathroom. She was dressed now in a tight black sweater with a golden thread, a tight black skirt and flame stockings — but it was a uniform, nothing more. She had a kind, pert face, not above twenty-five, and straight short, artificially glossy black hair.

'Yes. I'm fine ... I say, I don't know, but I think I might be here again tonight.' It was a sign of weakness, and she knew it, touched his cheek.

'Well, I shan't be, dear. Almost I could get fond of you, and that wouldn't do at all. I always watch you on telly, you know. All that lovely gold.' She took fifty pounds and went.

The big black Daimler whispered down the front, the grey sea to the right, a spatter of rain on the windscreen; to the left souvenir

255

shops, rock candy shops, and cheap restaurants boarded up for the winter.

'Where are we going?'

'To the nick, actually.'

Austen was alarmed. Fosdike went on, 'Well, it seemed the best place. For an interview. Just a few questions, you know, clear up one or two points.'

Austen looked sidelong at him. In daylight he liked this Fosdike less and less: his pale skin was pocked, his dark hair looked coarse yet was far too well cut, his lips, though thickish, had no generosity in them at all.

'Who with?'

Again Fosdike had nothing more to say.

The Brighton Police Station is a long modern building which, because it is set into the hillside above the town, seems smaller than it actually is. Brighton itself has more than its share of political extremists — a strong National Front, Trots of every sect, even a larger CP than most towns of similar size: consequently, the Special Branch has a corridor to itself and in it two rooms are kept for their masters in the Service. Into one of these, a large room with a desk, black chairs with chrome frames, and the Annigoni portrait of the Queen, Fosdike led Austen. He swung a chair in front of and facing the desk and indicated that Austen should sit in it, then himself sat slightly to the right and behind. In the silence Austen could hear children in the small school playground, then a bell and the voices were stilled.

He half turned and said, 'That coffee would be wel . . . ' but at that moment a side door opened. The man who came in was tall and grey — grey-suited, grey skin, with short lank hair plastered across the top of his head. Fosdike stood. Austen was damned if he would.

'All right, Ashley.'

The newcomer sat behind the desk, and with the light behind him the first things Austen took in were the large ears sticking out from the head at perfect right angles, the head itself set on one side as if the man suffered from some malformation of the neck. Yes, thought Austen. Humphries.

256

The Housemaster. He doesn't frighten me. I can handle him.

'Sir Richard. I suppose I should apologise for having you brought here, but frankly the conversation I want to have with you would be out of place in the public rooms of an hotel.' Thin lips lengthened in a gesture towards a smile, which faded abruptly. 'Right then. We'll not beat about the bush. The Slaker Group, having used you as a trusted intermediary, is on the point of signing contracts with the Soviets whereby they will supply them with computer hardware and the appropriate software to go with it. It is an extremely valuable contract, as you well know. A Roy Newman, who used to be a senior official in the CIA, and may still be on their payroll, and has at any rate maintained very close contact with old colleagues, has contrived to uncover the fact that for a time you were a paid spy working for the KGB...' (Austen's eyebrows shot up — he'd never been *paid*) '... If that were made public, the scandal here would be such that our government would have to refuse permission to the Slaker Group to go ahead, and the contract would be cancelled. That is the position.'

The head tilted further to the side, fingers met beneath the square chin, concealing the raw grazes and spots of cotton wool beneath it.

'We have to stop Newman from making your past public.'

At several points in his life Austen had faced this situation: first at The Meads; several times with his father; at the College, of course; at Bletchley Park; even once or twice in archaeological departments; and once the Head of BBC 2 had tried to tell him off for preaching Marxism on *The Gold Show*. He knew the scene, that the bullying, however smooth, was still bullying and almost always concealed, or revealed weakness. Thus the Head of The Meads was desperate to soften the scandal attached to Jefferson's suicide; his father had coveted the gold discs that had been found in George's pocket; and so on. So now he composed his face into his most Buddha-like smile, ostentatiously crossed his legs and relaxed.

True to form, the Housemaster blustered, 'I take it you do not want to be blown. That you do not want to face public execration, ostracism, humiliation, and very possibly jail.'

Austen knew that Humphries had something in mind, and he

had perhaps guessed what it was. He also knew Humphries wanted it to come from him, but non-cooperation was now his policy. He allowed the silence to lengthen. Outside, four powerful motorbikes were kicked into rowdy clatter, and over the windowsill behind the Housemaster's back he could see the white helmets swoop away. Humphries passed long fingers over his lank hair.

'You have insurance. This may be the time to cash it.'

'Insurance?'

Humphries tapped the desk with whitened knuckles. 'You know what I mean. Since the early sixties, all you chaps were issued with information which you could reveal to the media if we harassed you. Stuff detrimental to the public interest. Philby's idea, we think. It's his style. Oh come. You must know what I mean. That was Blunt's card. Of course he didn't confess, well not in any useful way. He bought his pardon with his insurance.'

'Ah yes.' Austen's grin became more cheshire-cat-like than ever. Behind it, his mind began to work with a sort of childish, impish delight. Humphries clearly deserved to be baited. 'I think I see what you mean. But it won't help in this case.'

'Let me be the judge.'

'I was sent photographs. Taken in Stephen Ward's place back in '62. The two-way mirror and so forth. Rather a giggle. But I happen to know Roy Newman rather well and I know he is in all senses a republican. I'm sure he would tell you where to put my insurance, as you call it.' He recrossed his legs, took, as it were, the second pair of *banderillas*. 'Nevertheless, there they are. And I promise you I shall produce them if I am exposed. And I don't fancy your chances of a K if ever it were discovered that you could have stopped them from appearing. There's yet another aspect to it all. I'm younger than Tony Blunt, I've led a more active life, mixed with all sorts. If the very worst happens, I'll end up in the Chair of Bronze Age studies in Leningrad with a summer dacha next to Kim's, and quite honestly the prospect doesn't appal me at all.'

Scarcely a word of this was true. He had received no photographs, though like many others he had heard gossip to the effect that the Dzerzhinsky Street archives had several hundred stockpiled against a rainy day; he wasn't at all sure about Leningrad and anyway was loth to go there, or to Parkhurst for that matter, while his mother was still alive. But it was pleasant watching Humphries's reaction.

The cold grey eyes filled with rancour, spite and even scorn — a very familiar part of the routine. Then the Housemaster sighed.

'Ashley,' he said, 'be a good chap. Go next door and see if you can raise Lord Slaker at this number.'

'And be a good chap — see to some coffee while you're at it.'

The shark-like mouth snapped, 'No coffee.'

The pettiness of this irritated Austen. 'For a time you were my fag at the College, weren't you? I seem to remember you cocked things up then, given half a chance.'

Minutes passed.

A knock, and Fosdike was back with a sheet of teleprinted paper. 'I haven't got Lord Slaker yet,' he said. 'He'll ring back in ten minutes or so. But this has just come through. It's Sleight's preliminary draft outline of the copy for tomorrow's paper. London want you to approve it.'

Relieved no doubt to have something to do, the Housemaster took the sheet, and began to go through it with a gold pencil.

'Sleight's all right, then?' Austen asked.

'Of course. Shouldn't he be?'

'On the phone last night Geoffrey said he'd been taken care of.'

'You could say that. Fact is, next term his son starts on a Slaker Foundation scholarship at the College.'

Austen nibbled his thumbnail for a moment. The gold pencil tracked, paused, tracked on again. 'Of course,' he said. 'Pity you couldn't think of something similar for that poor bugger Cargill.'

Humphries bridled. 'My dear chap...' he began, then faltered. Austen was not after all a social inferior to be "dear-chapped". 'Well, yes. A pity. But he had joined the Holier-than-thou-Club. And in spite of the Official Secrets Act you're never going to know where you are with chaps like that, even if you retire them. Really, nothing else for it. A ministerial committee set up the procedure after the Agee/Hosenball nonsense. You see, one knows where one is with your sort, but . . . ' His voice drifted into silence.

Austen brooded. I wish I could see what it is Sleight has produced, what it refers to. A whitewash on the slaughter of Cargill? Something on Slaker and the Soviets? He pondered. Am I doing enough? After all, Geoffrey has a lot at stake — not only a substantial investment with enormous profits to follow, but, what he values more, his reputation in the world market. He'll go to any length to prevent Newman from sinking this deal. Am I doing enough? Is simple non-cooperation sufficiently unequivocal? Is there not a positive step I can take? Perhaps there is . . .

'Lord Slaker is on the phone now, sir.'

As Humphries stood, Austen raised a hand. His heart was beating faster; he knew that what he was about to do was probably foolish or worse, but . . . well, apart from anything else his vanity was engaged. He wanted to reassert himself, to lose the awful sense of being a piece in someone else's game.

'Tell Geoffrey,' he said, 'I've decided it's up to him to silence Newman. And that, if he doesn't — that is, if Newman exposes me — then I shall expose the records I have kept of how the Gold Museum paid Ben Khameen for the Sidon Treasure.'

33

It was, apparently, enough. Austen was allowed to leave — at last unencumbered, at least overtly, by the Special Branch or whatever, though it seemed the Daimler was no longer available. As he walked down St James's Street,* he decided to stay in Brighton for a day or two. The Farm belonged to what he realised had become the past and he was reluctant to return to it — the past not only because it had been his father's first, but also because it was tied in with the Gold Museum and a routine unchanged for twelve years. And all that was now over. He had challenged Geoffrey, and the vague mutual convenience society that passes for trust between people of their sort had been destroyed for ever. He needed time, as he put it, to take stock, think things over.

Brendel was in Brighton that night with the London Symphony Orchestra, playing Beethoven's First and Fourth at the Dome. He bought a ticket on the way back to the Cosmopol, had a light but pleasant lunch, drank much but well, and slept into the late afternoon. Then, while the corridor maid sponged and pressed his suit, he took a long hot bath — and there the peaceful glory of what his life could now be, slowly expanded in his mind. The point was that he was free, free from Slaker, free from the museum, free from Riversdale and Kitti, free even from his past as a spy.

Through the scented steam his eyes traversed his stocky frame, tight tummy, small penis floating like a flower in the

*Not to be confused with the London thoroughfare.

261

water, passed down legs (well, yes, a touch spindly and varicose) to toes that toyed with the gilded taps. And he thought of gold.

I'll trace, he thought, the uses of gold from the burnished, annealed, twisted, stretched, coiled and hammered brooches, rings, and fibulae, the torques, masks and coronets of its first magical uses through to the brutal slabs banked up in electronic fortresses, and on again to a future of unmystified gladness when it will be worn by dancing girls and boys; and I'll show how these changes come about, relate them to the revolutions in production and society that cause them, yes there, there is something to be done, yes, there really I can get something done.

At the Dome, an hour or so later, they played for overture the Second Symphony and did it honestly, so that was all right. But with Brendel in the First Piano Concerto Austen judged himself to be less than enthralled. He distrusted the man's liberties with tempi, with rhythm even. He lingers, Austen thought, then he rushes on, especially in the last movement, the rondo. The left hand is . . . heavy? And the trills are so bloody quick they *buzz*. In short, isn't it a wee bit precious? I prefer my Russian recording with Alexei Nassedkine, a sound interpretation, yet not dull either.

He left during the interval: not in dudgeon at all, but doubting quite reasonably whether even Brendel would discover new insights into a concerto he must have heard five hundred times. Supper time too had crept up on him. It was all part of the jolly anarchy of I'll-do-as-I-please.

Only in the small hours did the doubts return.

Slaker is less than enthralled. And Kitti thinks I killed her rotten brother. Together they could make a great team. She's a loaded pistol — all Geoffrey has to do is point her in my direction.

She'll be waiting when I get back to the Farm, in father's study, with a silver pistol or Riversdale's razor.

'What will you do when you have killed me?'

'Set the house on fire with oil lamps.'

'And you?'

'I shall stay.'

'A sort of *suttee*. How flattering. Brunnhilde's Fire Music appropriate?'

262

'That would be nice.'

'Boulez or Karajan?'

At which Richard Austen broke the fantasy with a giggle, some last tension gave, he slept.

The morning was milder, the cloud had withdrawn, was scarcely more than a haze — burnished where it curtained the sun. Austen had kedgeree for breakfast, a treat, and then decided to walk up into the Lanes, to the rare-book shops, to see if one in particular had any of the volumes his mother still lacked from her library edition of Ruskin's works. They had been putting this together over twenty years or so, ever since they had discovered that some sets of the first, numbered printing, had been split. Their aim was to piece together a complete set and donate it to a university library that did not have one. If he found one of the four volumes still lacking from the thirty-nine, she would be pleased: not least because it would be proof he thought of her every now and then. She would be disturbed too — once the set was complete she feared it would be carted away: that she could keep it in her room at Heartsease until she died was a card he held in reserve. Always with her he was, however mildly, equivocal.

He turned left too soon, headed up from the sea and into the town before he meant to, and found himself in a wasteland of rundown squares where stucco crumbled, railings rusted, and windows were boarded up. Fascist slogans competed with anarchist: KILL THE NF — JEW SCUM OUT — NF SUCKS — GAS THE BLACKS. One house only had colour and life. The whole front had been painted crudely but brightly with doves, clouds, palm trees. A poster proclaimed: SUPPORT OUR SQUAT. EIGHT FAMILIES, ONLY THREE MEMBERS IN FULL-TIME EMPLOY-MENT. There was a plastic bucket on the step. Austen put in a ten-pound note, then added another. It left him rather short. Perhaps he should find a bank.

Notices at the lowest-level exits of a multi-storey car park, set against the side of the steep hill, announced access by lifts to Churchill Square. Walking across the wide, barren cavern, a maze of brutally square concrete pillars lit inadequately by strip lighting most of which had been smashed, the whole smelling of urine and car exhaust, he realised he was not alone. A pack — four, no five — were loping on a course at a right angle to his, but also heading for the lifts. Their heads were cropped to leave combs or crests like Hollywood Mohicans, but dyed puce or acid green; they wore black cloaks stuck with giant pins, and baggy tartan trousers; their legs were manacled at the ankles but the chains were long and looped up. One was draped in a huge Union Jack. They had style, Austen thought, but were dangerous too — their leader held a large screw-driver with which he scraped the side of each car they passed: clearly he would not like to discover that he had been seen. Austen stopped by a pillar and let them get to the lifts ahead of him.

As he waited, he recalled the Vigilantes — the organisation that sold Nazi memorabilia in Lyndhurst High Street and recruited unemployed punks from Southampton and Bourne-mouth. They had real money, business money behind them, no doubt about that with their Land-Rovers, boat on the Solent, paramilitary uniforms. Slaker money? Why not? Here's a scenario, Austen thought. I go home, find the Farm broken into, everything smashed, excreta everywhere, swastikas and so on, and I die of a heart attack.

The drab lift took him to a pedestrian precinct which was worse than drab. A monstrous junk 'sculpture' set in a dried-up pond where drifts of litter shifted in the breeze was surrounded by concrete and bricks shops whose windows were already 'decorated' for Christmas with tawdry gaudiness. A toddler in a space-walker's suit of padded nylon stumbled after a solitary pigeon, chased it into flight, then howled as his mother caught his hand and swung him into British Home Stores.

The punks appeared briefly across a terrace, between con-crete pillars, and a 7-Up bottle taken from a litter bin turned in the air and shattered on the concrete steps.

Silly to leave it to a heart attack; after all, I'm pretty robust. They'll be in ambush behind the curtains, they leap out and — what's the expression? — put the boot in. Carve my face with a broken 7-Up bottle, cut my throat. Austen touched the scar on his jawbone. That is, if Kitti hasn't got there first.

* * *

264

A jeweller's window caught his eye, the glitter of gold. They spray stuff on to make it shine, bevel the edges for extra glint, gilding refined gold. Sovereigns, St Christophers, lucky charms on chunky bracelets — horse-shoes, dice, cats, wishing-wells. And the prices! But it doesn't matter. Gold is incorruptible, can be used a million times. Every one of those tawdry trinkets, every bar of bullion in Fort Knox, will one day be made into wedding wreaths for maidens. Wedding rings. Clever of Kitti and Cargill to get my ring out of the coroner's office. Will I be able to get it back?

'Damn you, Kitti, for getting my ring.'

'But you gave it to Teddy. To pay the Ferryman.'

'And to Cargill too. But I expect both are across. Now *I* need it. Geoffrey is arranging for me to be kicked to death by neo-Nazi punks.'

'How stunning!'

This, thought Austen, will not do. Where *is* that bookshop? He left the, to him, entirely aptly named precinct and dropped into the Lanes. But the bookshop turned out to be an ambush too. In the window, next to *The Burning Matrix* was *Milton, a Man for Our Times* by Maud Lawson, DBE. There were even pictures of both of them. Christ, he thought, they've married us at last — what she wanted so badly. They're all on to me — Kitti, Geoffrey, and now poor, mad Maud.

With about as much free will as a pinball, he allowed the deflection to carry him safely into Wheeler's Oyster Bar. Six. No, a dozen, and a half-bot of your best Pouilly Fuissé. Pale, white gold, the wine. He sipped it, savoured its flintiness, and then as he placed the glass on the dark wood of the table a spot of light from the window glowed in it. Gold.

Like the sun itself, like the light on curling waves — it is incorruptible, malleable, can be melted without oxidisation, is very rare. First it was the source and sign of royalty and priest-hood — both (following Childe) the prerogatives of women. But revolutions followed — in modes of production first, which in turn shattered the matrices of the societies that had formed them. The mysteries of pastoral farming and then agriculture had to be better understood as the pressure of the ice forced

265

populations in upon each other; tribal and gentile systems which had for millennia provided the sort of cohesion that allows for migrations, cracked or withered; patriarchy superseded matriarchy and gold lost its magic, became symbolic merely — of power and prestige. The king whose gold crown had conferred royalty on him, who counted his wealth in bronze cauldrons, now set aside his crown except for ceremonial occasions, banished the cauldrons to the kitchens where they belonged, and counted his wealth in bullion, measured by weight. War ceased to be the ritual confrontation of bronze-glad champions, became instead...

A BIG DEAL FOR BRITAIN

With two oysters untipped and a half-glass of wine neglected in front of him, Austen realigned the newspaper on the bench beside him.

ANOTHER EXCLUSIVE FOR THE NEWS
FROM DESMOND SLEIGHT

'Excuse me. May I?'

His neighbour, awed perhaps by Austen's pallor, conceded his right to the paper he had just bought; the waiter arrived opportunely to con*sole* him *à la meunière.*

'Today I am able to reveal,' read Austen, 'that last night, in the offices of the Gold Museum, Bloomsbury, (the *bastards*!) a momentous agreement was thrashed out, and, after hours of brutally hard bargaining, initialled. Momentous? Yes. First, because it is the first time an entirely British computer firm has landed a large share in an international deal on this scale. Second, because the three major signatories are British, American — and Russian! The Cold War may be chillier than usual just now, or hotter if you prefer to look at it that way, but I can tell readers of the *News* exclusively that, where it really matters, it's business as usual.

'In an exclusive interview Lord Slaker admitted to me that at times he had thought an American firm was going to scoop the pool, but that at the end of the day the Russians had chosen British. "After all," he said, "the Russian tanks at Stalingrad were equipped with Slaker gyros, and those didn't let them down! Another factor of course could be that the present climate of opinion in America would be against selling computers, even ones with no military application, to Russia." He went on to say that the computers in question were almost identical, the same independent team of Japanese scientists lay behind both. "Make no mistake, the United Special Steels version is just as good as ours. Only ours," he added in a characteristically wry aside, "has a prettier face. I'm sure they'll get a fair share of the world market. There's going to be a great demand for these computers — every industrial state will want two or three, and, quite frankly, if they all come to us at once, we won't be able to handle the demand."

HELP FOR THE THIRD WORLD TOO

'Not the least important aspect of the deal is that several Slaker factories, notably in Malaysia and Sri Lanka, will now remain open, when, because of the world recession, it was quite on the cards that they would be progressively run down...'

Shit! thought Austen. And Newman builds his not in Jamestown, Pa., but in Manila and Taiwan. He pushed the paper back to its owner. But what had happened? Why had Newman capitulated when everything seemed to be going his way? Newman could have blown Austen and stopped the contract that way — on the other hand, Slaker should have backed down under Austen's threat to reveal how the Sidon Treasure had been made in Russia under his supervision, and how the two million pounds the Gold Museum had paid for it had ended up as credits for Palestinian arms buyers.

Of course, it's typical of Geoffrey that he's pulled some of his irons out of the fire in spite of everything — but how, at what cost? Has he just called Newman's bluff, hoping to ride the storm when I am exposed? Is he calling my bluff, or feels that after all I'm no sort of danger? Less than enthralled ... well certainly — and now what has it cost him, what will it cost to neutralise these threats? Austen shuddered. Clearly Slaker knows what he's doing. What Austen now realised was that it would be as well if he too knew what his ruthless cousin was up to.

Twenty minutes later he was back in his room at the Cosmopol, on the phone to the Grand Hotel, Russell Square.

'Roy Newman?'

'Who is this?'

'Austen. Richard.'

'Jesus. Sir Dick. Are you still alive?'

There was a long pause while Austen mastered the spasm of fear.

'Roy. I've just read the *News*.'

'Of course.'

'So. What I want to know, is... well, what happens now?'

'If you mean, do I now blow the whistle on you, the answer is no way.'

'Well, fine. But why not? I mean, what happened?'

'Come on, Sir Dick. You know I can't tell you that sort of thing. But listen. For old times' sake. Take a word of warning from the wise. *Duck*! If you don't know where else to go, use that shitty little shelter of yours. But keep off the instant stroganoff, it's yuk, yuk, yuk.'

'Why Roy? Why do you say all this?'

Again the silence.

Then: 'Listen, Dickie. You're not blown, but you've blown it. I don't know the details, but all I do know is that, just when I thought mission had been accomplished, the State Department aborted it. Slaker is to have his Russian contract after all. I don't know why. Maybe Thatcher owes him a favour and brought pressure, or perhaps someone else was pressuring in a way I don't know about.'

'But you keep your markets.'

'Right. Oh. You know about that side of it? Well, yes. We still had your past to bargain with, and the agreement is Slaker has Europe and the Warsaw Pact and we sell to the rest. But listen. As I said, I don't know the details, but you came into it somewhere. Something you said or did stirred it all up until everyone was pressurising everyone else. And I tell you, Dickie, if you did have a hand in it, well then no one loves you any more. None of the parties is going to shed a single tear if one of the others now decides you're more nuisance than you're worth. So, take a word from the wise, Dickie, and duck. Well, I've said more than I should. The car for the airport comes in twenty minutes and I'm still packing. *Ciao*, Dickie, *Sir* Dick.'

34

So much for my attempt to alter the course of history. A silly thing to do, and most un-Marxist. Behaving like a *petit bourgeois* turd, *doing it my way*. The Kremlin get their computers, Botha, Pinochet, Videla and all the other gangsters get theirs. Well, so be it. The struggle of the proletariat to win class hegemony doesn't, and never will, depend on the likes of me!

What happened? Geoffrey told my masters I was likely to bring down more than one house of cards if Newman blew me, so, thoroughly pragmatic people that they are, and wanting above everything to get their computers, they soon found ways of exerting pressure elsewhere. Who knows, the Dzerzhinsky Street photo album may have been deployed after all, and under pressure from everywhere the State Department, virtually leaderless between administrations, backed down.

And where does that leave me? Nobody loves you any more, Newman said. Well, good. Jolly, jolly good. School's out.

We've all wanted, needed, to come up into the daylight, and for almost all the need in the end becomes critical. It happens in different ways, and not always consciously. Did I know what I was up to when I wrote *The Burning Matrix*? I half wanted to put in so much that any fool would guess at what had been left out, and yet half wanted to make a puzzle of it, wrap it up and mystify it, give them a run for their money. Well, it wasn't any fool who unravelled it, but Cargill — one of God's fools. There have been other things: playing silly buggers with Olivia Shapiro; there was no need to push Newman into that absurd shelter and bolt for Briar Rose; no need to threaten Geoffrey with the Gold Museum. Above all, no need for that stupid messing about with Teddy's body. No need, except that critical if unconscious need for daylight and clean air.

I'm up now. And not in any vulgar way with TV interviews and articles in the Sunday papers, not in any humiliating way, unknighted, or bundled on to a Russian freighter, carried through Heathrow on a stretcher. But up because I've shown them all that I can betray any of them: I'm nobody's man now. I can do as I like.

He stood at the window, peered through the salt-splashed panes at the mink-coloured sea, flecked here and there with white, at the rust and cream piers beneath the opalescent sky. Let's get them open, he thought, let's feel the fresh air . . . But they were sealed, no catches even. The only air is conditioned, so let's get out, let's get out.

He put on his neat short coat again and the red muffler, ran his comb through his close-cut but thick and wiry hair. You'll do, Sir Richard. You'll do.

It was what his mother used to say when checking he was properly dressed to go back to school; what she had said, using the title, when he visited her before going to Buckingham Palace.

There were few people about on the beach. The trudge of his feet in the stones counterpointed the slower heave and rasp of the waves. In front, and then on his right as he turned to walk along the water's edge, the sea was empty and the line where it faded into the misty sky was indistinguishable. The weather was mild again, warm even.

Unburdened now, ideas flowed and mixed in his mind as they had not for months, years. The time came when kings ceased to be heroes, when war was no longer the ritual combat of bronze-clad champions, became instead the clash of massed phalanxes armed with iron — forged not cast, weapons that did not shatter with the heaviest blows. As arable and pastoral farming became better understood, as societies became geographically fixed (though far from stable), the late neolithic industrial revolutions demanded new modes of production: castes and classes ruling by virtue of their control of the means of production — land, herds, quarries, mines, labour itself institutionalised as slavery; and war ceased to be a relatively humane way of deciding which clan should migrate, or of widening the genetic pool, became instead the brutal means of appropriating fields, harbours, rivers, pastures and slaves.

All of which, and much, much more (this dapper, perky, but ageing little man, this mole up for air, thought as he passed between the rusty girders of the Palace Pier and headed on towards the distant marina beneath the cliffs) I have gone over again and again and the nicest thing my critics have said of me is that, as a theory of the development of primitive societies, it depends as much upon the intellectual proclivities of the theoriser as on any marshalled, cohesive, verifiable body of evidence — what would you expect from a Marxist other than historical materialism extended back to the dawn of time?

But use gold as the evidence, the framework, the changing uses of gold to reflect the changes in religion, commerce, society itself; collate the facts about every scrap of gold ever dug up and feed them into a computer (one with a lot less capacity than those sold by Slaker and Newman as instruments of oppression) and thus uncover the dialectical story of man's movement...

What's that? Up there. A light winking above the steep banks of tamarisk above Volk's Railway, winking like a heliograph in the sun, like a sovereign. He narrowed his eyes — always good, if now long-sighted — yes, a man was leaning on the parapet pointing something black with a lens.

Austen straightened. If it be now, 'tis not to come, but surely they're not going to gun me down in the middle of Brighton beach? He looked about him: behind, a hundred yards off, a tall man, dark hair, dark coat, like him out for a post-prandial stroll; then back to the lens on the high, distant parapet. It shifted, the light went out with the altered angle; he saw now what he should have guessed at in the first place: it was a camera with a telescopic lens. But why? To picture what? So, I'm to be spared for a time, let's get back to the History of Gold.

And at that moment his vision of what might have crowned the real achievement of his life was given a blessing — and it quite stunned him with its beauty, its propriety.

271

A woman and a man, hand in hand, lean, fit, with skin tanned to a healthy gold by sun and weather, rose from the empty beach (in fact, from a declivity shaped in the shingle by the tide) and walked through the raw grey air into the less raw water. Naked like Eve and Adam before the emergence of class society, they gasped as the small waves slapped on their thighs; laughter pealed, they embraced, then launched themselves into the tawny sea.

Austen beamed at them, scarcely attended the footstep in the pebbles behind him.

'Sir Richard.'

He half turned. 'Fosdike. My dear chap. What brings...'

The thick lips without generosity, the velvet collar, a gloved hand which momentarily gripped his upper arm. He felt a sharp prick, wondered what had happened. For three heart beats they remained thus, then bright pain exploded briefly in Austen's chest.

Fosdike let him fall, then called out across the waves to the bathers, 'I say, would you help? I think the old chap's had a heart attack.'

There was a notice, battered by weather and vandals, set in the shingle a yard from where Richard Austen lay. It read: BEYOND THIS POINT, CLOTHES NEED NOT BE WORN.